P9-EMR-646

Praise for *White Tombs*

Named Best Mystery of 2008 By Reader Views
Winner of the Garcia Award for Best Fiction

". . . Christopher Valen addresses a very wide range of extremely relevant social issues in White Tombs, and this book goes well beyond being just a detective story. The characters are fantastically well developed . . . the writing is solid an elegant without unnecessary detours. Any lover of solid writing should enjoy it greatly. White Tombs also screams out for a sequel — or better yet sequels."

—Reader Views

". . . Valen's debut police procedural provides enough plot twists to keep readers engrossed and paints a clear picture of the Hispanic community in St. Paul."

—Library Journal

"John Santana of the St. Paul Police Department is a man you will not forget. . . . The book is a great read, and Santana is destined to become one of my favorite detectives. Truly a five-star read from this author."

—Armchair Interviews

". . . Santana is an intriguing character. St. Paul readers will enjoy Valen's sense of place."

—St. Paul Pioneer Press

". . . In this page turner, Christopher Valen presents a clear picture of a modern, urban Hispanic community — plus the horrible Minnesota winter weather."

—The Poisoned Pen

". . . White Tombs is a well crafted who dun it I enjoyed immensely. It's action packed. On a scale of 1–5, I give it a 5."

—Futures Mystery Anthology Magazine

Praise for *The Black Minute*

Named Best Mystery of 2009 By Reader Views
Winner of the Lynda Goldman Award for Best Novel

"The second John Santana St. Paul police procedural is a terrific thriller. . . . Christopher Valen provides the audience with his second straight winning whodunit."

—Midwest Book Review

". . . Santana is an appealing series lead, strong and intelligent . . . Readers who enjoyed White Tombs will settle easily into this one; on the other hand, it works fine as a stand-alone, and fans of well-plotted mysteries with a regional flair . . . should be encouraged to give this one a look."

—Booklist

". . . The Black Minute grabbed me from the first page on, and pulled me into a complex world of evil, violence, deceit, bravery and search for justice . . . While the plot is complex and anything but predictable, his storyline stays comprehensible and easy to follow. The characters are well developed, very believable and constantly evolving. The setting of the story is vivid, detailed and engaging . . ."

—Reader Views

". . . There is not one reason why this book isn't a winner! Everything about it screams success. The book is masterfully written with a tightly-woven plot, visually detailed settings and well developed characters . . ."

—Rebecca's Reads

". . . Valen does a super job of keeping the suspense going as the action reaches a crescendo . . ."

—St. Paul Pioneer Press

To Chris

WHITE TOMBS

A John Santana Novel

Christopher Valen

Christopher Valen

Conquill Press

NOTE: If you purchased this book without a cover, you should be aware that this book is stolen property. It was reported as "unsold and destroyed" to the publisher, and neither the author nor the publisher has received any payment for this "stripped book."

This book is a work of fiction. Names, characters, places and incidents either are products of the author's imagination or are used fictitiously. Certain liberties have been taken in portraying St. Paul and its institutions. This is wholly intentional. Any resemblance to actual events, or to actual persons living or dead, is entirely coincidental. For information about special discounts for bulk purchases contact *conquillpress@comcast.net*.

WHITE TOMBS

Copyright © 2008 By Christopher Valen

All rights reserved. No part of this book may be reproduced in any form or by any electronic or mechanical means, including information storage and retrieval systems, without permission in writing from the publisher, except by a reviewer who may quote brief passages in a review.

Book design by 1106 Design

Library of Congress Control Number: 2007938630

Valen, Christopher.
White Tombs: a novel / by Christopher Valen – 1st edition

ISBN-13: 978-0-9800017-2-3
ISBN-10: 0-9800017-2-2

Conquill Press/March 2008

Printed in the United States of America

10 9 8 7 6 5 4 3 2 1

Dedication

For Martha
Te quiero mucho.

Acknowledgments

The author would like to thank Bill Kraus of the St. Paul Police Department, and the officers and staff of the Ramsey County Sheriff's Citizen's Academy.

Special thanks also to Abigail Davis, Linda Donaldson, Lorrie Holmgren, Archie Spencer and Peg Wangensteen for your help and support, and to Bart Baker for bringing us together. You are deeply missed. My deepest gratitude to my wife, Martha, whose love, encouragement and stories of Colombia inspired me to write this book.

This book would not exist in its present form without special contributions from Amy, Frank, Diane, Ronda and Michele at 1106 Design.

"Woe unto you, scribes and Pharisees, hypocrites! For ye are like unto whited sepulchers, which indeed appear beautiful outward, but are within full of dead men's bones and of all uncleanness."

— Matthew 23:27

Chapter 1

DAY ONE

JULIO PÉREZ SAT IN A SWIVEL CHAIR behind the mahogany desk in the study of his house on St. Paul's West Side. His eyes were closed and his left cheek was resting on the desktop. Were it not for the bullet hole in his head, one could have assumed that he had merely fallen asleep.

"What time did the call come in?" Detective John Santana asked.

He and his partner, Detective Rick Anderson, were talking with the first officer on the crime scene. The nameplate above her breast pocket identified her as Larkin.

"Just after five this afternoon," she said. Her uniform was pressed and starched and looked like it had just come out of a box.

"Who called it in?"

"Mrs. Pérez. She met me when I arrived. Told me she left her husband alone to do some shopping. When she returned, she found him like this." Larkin gestured toward Pérez's body without looking directly at it. "I called dispatch immediately."

"Shit," Anderson said. "The news media monitor police radio frequencies. No wonder they're streaming around this place like squad cars at a Krispy Kreme grand opening."

Larkin's face colored with embarrassment. "Sorry. I'll remember it next time."

"I know you will," Santana said. "Did Mrs. Pérez say anything else?"

"Only that she couldn't believe someone would do this to her husband."

Santana could hear sobs coming from another room. The warm, stuffy air in the house smelled like garlic, cumin, oregano and chili peppers.

Anderson said, "Anyone with Mrs. Pérez now?"

"Her daughter."

"Okay, Larkin. Keep your hands in your pockets so you don't touch anything on the way out. And be careful where you step."

Despite Anderson's warning, Santana knew it was impossible for anyone to enter a crime scene without changing it in some way. It was the reason he used gloves at a crime scene only if blood was present and AIDS was a concern, or if he needed to touch something. Gloves led to carelessness, which could destroy fingerprints.

"I don't see a gun," Anderson said. "But there's a shell casing on the floor near the desk."

He squatted near the shell casing. "Head stamp reads REM. Looks like the bullet came from a twenty-two caliber, Remington. Makes me wonder though."

"Why leave the shell casing?"

Anderson stood up. "Exactly. It can be traced to the gun."

Santana drew a rough sketch of the crime scene in his notebook showing the location of Pérez's body and the shell casing. Next to the drawing of the shell casing he wrote a question mark. Then he examined the gunshot wound in Julio Pérez's head.

Powder grains expelled from the muzzle of a gun had caused tattooing on one side of the angled wound indicating that it wasn't a contact shot. The reddish-brown color showed that Pérez was alive when he was shot. The tattooing would have been gray or yellow in appearance had he been dead beforehand.

Santana looked at Pérez's arms and legs without moving them, then at the hands and fingers. He detected no defensive wounds and nothing was visible under Pérez's fingernails. He saw no folds or rolls in the clothing that would suggest the body had been moved.

"No sign of a struggle, Rick. No fear in Pérez's face."

"I figure he knew the shooter," Anderson said, reading Santana's thoughts. "Maybe he was expecting company."

It was like that with a partner after awhile, at least a good partner. Santana imagined it was like being married for a long time.

"They come into the study together," Anderson said. "The shooter is behind him. Pérez sits down at his desk and gets capped in the head."

Santana noted that the powder tattooing was darker and denser behind the right ear, indicating the muzzle was near the ear when the gun was fired.

"I'll get some uniforms to help me canvas the neighborhood," Anderson said. "Find out if anyone saw or heard anything."

"Make sure you run the names of all the neighbors, Rick. See if anyone has a criminal record."

"Sorry about giving you the hard part, John, but you're better at dealing with the family."

Talking to relatives and friends of a murder victim was often the most unpleasant and difficult part of the job. But Santana knew at some point in the investigation he could tell those same relatives and friends that he had caught the perp who had caused them so much pain. It might be a small consolation for the victim's family, but he derived great satisfaction from knowing it was the murderer's turn to suffer.

He concentrated on the floor and the ground around the body next, looking for any stains or marks. He took a small flashlight out of his pocket and focused the light toward the ground at an oblique angle, checking for footprints or drag marks in the thin layer of dust on the oak floor. Then he let the beam play across the walls and ceiling as he searched for blood spatter.

When he was satisfied there was nothing of evidentiary value, he put away the flashlight, slipped on a pair of latex gloves and opened the folding door on a large closet that covered one wall. Inside it he found Pérez's summer clothes, a pair of leather sandals and a pair of Reebok walking shoes. The clothes smelled musty after months on hangers and yielded no clues. Mahogany bookcases lined a second wall to his right. The authors were mostly Latino writers. Gabriel García Márquez, Federico García Lorca and Pablo Neruda, one of Santana's favorites.

Framed photographs of Pérez with his wife and daughter hung on the wall behind the desk. Organized in clusters according to periods of time, they represented a visual record of a family's history. The daughter had black hair and looked to be in her early to mid twenties when the most recent photographs were taken. She had piercing ebony eyes and reminded Santana of the Mexican actress, Salma Hayek. Mrs. Pérez appeared to be in her late forties. Her dark hair had begun to gray, and she had put on a few pounds over the years. But she still retained the high cheekbones and luminous dark eyes that were clearly evident in the earlier snapshots of her. Santana wondered how her husband's death would change the peace and contentment he saw in her face.

Many of the photos of Julio Pérez were taken with local celebrities and politicians. In one he was receiving an award at a Chamber of Commerce dinner. In another he was throwing out the first pitch at a St. Paul Saint's game. Pérez had been a slender, good-looking man with silver hair, a neatly trimmed silver mustache and eyes the color of dark coffee. His chestnut skin looked firm and his complexion healthy.

A framed copy of *El Día*, one of the monthly Hispanic newspapers in St. Paul, hung next to the family pictures. A former mayor had signed it. Santana remembered reading the newspaper when he first came to Minnesota. *El Día* became his main source of information and events, his lifeline to the Hispanic community. Since he spoke and read very little English at the time and preferred solitude to groups, he would often reread the same stories while he anxiously waited for the next issue to appear in the newspaper racks along Grand Avenue.

He moved on to the desk. A humidor filled with cigars sat on one side. A half-smoked cigar rested on the edge of a ceramic ashtray beside a yellow pad of post-it notes and a Rolodex open to the card of a well-known local attorney, Rafael Mendoza. Santana wondered why Pérez had called a lawyer and if the phone call was related in any way to his murder.

He walked into the master bedroom off the study. A thin layer of frost filmed the lower panes of the windows that looked out on the lighted park behind the house. The January sun already lay far below the horizon and a starless darkness covered the landscape. It was nearly mid-winter, yet the hard ground was still brown and free of snow, making it difficult to find any impression evidence.

A small statue of the Virgin Mary stood on the nightstand beside the neatly made double bed. A large crucifix hung on the wall. On the wall opposite the windows was a Holy Card called *Estampa de la Santísima Trinidad*, the trinity, and one called *Estampa de Jesús*.

Santana took off his latex gloves and stuffed them in his coat pockets. Then he went into the living room where Mrs. Pérez and her daughter were huddled together on a tweed couch. He sat down in a matching chair across from them.

Serapes draped the backs of the couch and chair. Paintings of Native Americans on horseback hung on the walls. A picture window at one end of the room looked out onto the front porch.

A statue of the *Virgen de Guadalupe* stood on an end table beside a burning candle that gave off an aroma of cinnamon.

"I know this is a difficult time for you both," Santana said. "But I need to ask you a few questions."

"Por que alguien querría matar a mi esposo," Mrs. Pérez said, wiping her red, swollen eyes with a Kleenex.

"Mamíta," her daughter said, embarrassment evident in her voice. "Speak English, please."

"Forgive me, *señor,*" Mrs. Pérez said with a heavy accent. "When I am upset, I sometimes forget my English. I was asking why someone would kill my husband."

The words brought tears to her eyes again. She rubbed them with the palms of her hands like she had just awakened from a nightmare and was uncertain if what she had dreamt was actually true.

"It's okay," Santana said. *"Yo entiendo bien el Español, Señora Pérez."*

The two women looked at Santana as though he had just beamed down from the starship Enterprise.

"You are from Mexico?" the daughter said.

"Colombia. *Me llamo,* John Santana."

"You have only a slight accent, *señor.*

"It wasn't always that way."

Santana could tell by the way the daughter's body relaxed that she saw him differently, now that she knew he was not a *guero;* he was not the enemy.

"I am Gabriela," she said with very little accent as well. "This is my mother, Sandra."

"Mucho gusto."

"Te pareces a mi sobrino," Sandra Pérez said. She put a hand momentarily on her mouth to prevent the words from coming out. "I'm so sorry, Detective Santana. But you do look like my nephew. It is the dark, wavy hair and blue eyes. And you are both handsome young men."

"Muchas gracias, señora."

"You must be over six feet."

"Six feet one inch."

She confirmed the fact with a nod and cast her eyes downward for a moment, as though she were imagining a happier time, perhaps with her nephew.

Santana said, "You were home all day, *señora,* except for the two hours when you went shopping?"

"Yes."

"When was the last time you spoke to your husband?"

"When I left the house," she said. "He was working in his study."

"Do you recall what time you left?"

"It was just after three o'clock."

"Was your husband planning on going out later?"

"Why?" Gabriela asked.

"Your father was wearing a white shirt and tie."

"Julio was always a good dresser," Sandra Pérez said. "It did not matter whether it was a workday or whether we were going out or staying in. He was just that way." She dabbed her eyes with the Kleenex and sighed deeply.

Santana gave her a smile to reassure her that he understood. "Was your husband expecting anyone? A visitor, perhaps?"

"No. I do not think so."

"And you, Gabriela? When was the last time you saw your father?"

"Yesterday evening. I came over for dinner. I like to do that at least once a week."

Santana watched both of them carefully, their mannerisms, how they reacted to his questions. He had no reason to suspect them of committing the murder, but it would be unwise to rule either one of them out this early in the investigation.

"Your husband owned *El Día, señora.*"

"It was his life."

"Do you both work there as well?"

"No. Gabriela worked there before she went to college."

"And sometimes in the summer when I was home from school," Gabriela said.

"You're not in the newspaper business, then."

"I manage *Casa Blanca*, a restaurant in St. Paul."

Santana was familiar with the movie but not the restaurant. "Were you working when you got the call about your father?"

"Yes," she said hesitantly, as if he had implied she wasn't.

"Do either of you know a man named Rafael Mendoza?"

Both women shook their heads.

"Why?" Gabriela asked.

"Your father's Rolodex was open to Mendoza's name and number."

"My father never spoke of him," she said with a slight edge in her voice. "I do not know why he would call him."

Santana wondered if Gabriela Pérez had a reason for reacting angrily when Mendoza's name was mentioned or if she was just edgy by nature. Either way, he knew he would have to tread softly if he wanted her cooperation. He turned his attention to Sandra Pérez.

"Did your husband have any enemies, *señora*? Perhaps someone who worked for him at the newspaper?"

She shook her head vigorously. "Julio was a friend to many in this community."

"Did your husband own a gun?"

"No."

"Forgive me for asking, *señora*, but were you and your husband having any marital difficulties?"

"Difficulties? I do not understand?"

"My parents were very happy," Gabriela said. Her dark eyes burned right through Santana.

Asking personal questions, particularly to a grieving widow, always bothered him. Still, most murders weren't random acts of violence, but were committed by someone the victim knew. Santana considered explaining this fact to Gabriela Pérez before he concluded that she was not the least bit interested in hearing his reasoning behind the question.

"When you feel up to it, *señora*," he said, "I would like you to look carefully around your house to see if anything has been taken."

"You suspect robbery as a motive?" Gabriela said.

"We can't rule it out. *Señora*, we'll need to see your financial statements, bank accounts, credit cards."

"I do not know about these things," she said with a small shrug.

"I can help," Gabriela said.

"Would you mind if I borrowed a photograph of your husband, *señora*? I might need it during the course of the investigation."

"Gabriela will get one from the albums."

Gabriela put her arms around her mother and stroked the back of her head, as if she were consoling a child.

Santana took a card out of a pocket and placed it on the coffee table. "There's a name and number of a victim advocate, the medical examiner's number, and the Ramsey County Attorney's number on this card. Once we're finished here, your husband's body will be taken to the medical examiner's office at Regions' Hospital where an autopsy will be performed."

He stood and closed his notebook. Behind him he heard the front door opening and closing and the sound of footsteps in the hallway. The evidence techs and ME had arrived.

"If you think of anything else or have any questions, please call me." He gave them both a business card with his direct number at the station. "Is there someplace your mother could stay tonight?"

Gabriela looked at the card in her hand and then at Santana. "She will stay with me."

"That's a good idea."

He started to leave when Gabriela said, "My mother is right, Detective. No one who knew my father would want to kill him."

Her dark eyes had softened. An indication, perhaps, that she realized she would never see her father again.

"I'm very sorry for your loss," he said.

"Por favor," Sandra Pérez said with trembling lips. She pulled away from her daughter and stifled a sob. *"Encuentre al asesino de mi esposo."*

The desperation in her voice imploring him to find the person who murdered her husband triggered the sudden rush of adrenaline Santana always felt when he began a homicide investigation. He had no idea yet who had murdered Sandra Pérez's husband. But he had no problem promising her he would find out who did it.

"Si, se lo prometo, señora," he said and returned to the study.

Tony Novak, the crime scene investigator, and his usual contingent of forensic techs were measuring distances and collecting evidence. A police photographer used a Minolta 35-mm single-lens reflex camera to shoot black and white photos of the crime scene, the physical evidence and the body. Behind him, a sketch artist made detailed drawings. On the ground next to the .22 shell casing stood a small, yellow evidence marker with the number 1.

"Hey, John," Novak said. "I just got a couple of tickets for the Chandler fight on the twenty-seventh. This kid is the best lightweight I've seen in a long time. You interested?"

"I might be."

"I'll take that as a yes."

Santana smiled and said, "What do you have, Reiko?"

Reiko Tanabe, the medical examiner, leaned over the body. A strand of her dark hair fell across her face. She brushed it away with a latex gloved hand and touched the birthmark just below her right ear. The café au lait mark was small and light brown in color. Santana figured Tanabe wore her hair long so that it covered the mark when she was off the clock. At crime scenes she wore her hair in a ponytail and had a habit of unconsciously touching the blemish.

"Well, I'd say he's been shot dead." Tanabe looked up at Santana with a wry smile.

Santana had worked with her many times before and knew that she was as competent as they come, despite the lame humor. "What about the time of death?"

Tanabe felt Pérez's jaw and neck and then proceeded down the trunk to his legs and feet. "Rigor's just beginning in the lower jaw. Have to pop a thermometer in the liver and get the body temperature. But you know that can be unreliable."

She looked at the body now and not at Santana, as though talking to herself. "It's warm in the room. He's wearing clothes. Could keep the body temperature up. I'd say maybe between two-thirty and four-thirty p.m." She lifted Pérez's head off the desk. "Right side of the victim's face doesn't show any lividity."

Santana noted it was different on the left side of Pérez's face. It had turned the familiar maroon color of death. Postmortem lividity only formed on parts of the body exposed to pressure. More evidence that Julio Pérez's body had not been moved.

"Give me until tomorrow afternoon," she said. "I got a couple ahead of this one."

"Bobby," Santana said to one of the techs. "Hand me a pair of latex."

The evidence tech gave Santana a fresh pair of latex gloves and he put them on.

Santana hit the redial button on the phone on the desk. He picked up the receiver and held it close to his ear. A message machine answered after the fourth ring. The voice was unfamiliar, but he recognized the name. He hung up, took out his notebook and copied Rafael Mendoza's phone number and address from the card in Pérez's Rolodex. Then he began his search of the remainder of the house.

The bathroom towels were free of bloodstains and dampness indicating the perp had not bled at the scene and attempted to clean up. Santana found nothing hidden in or around the toilet tank and no illegal drugs in the medicine cabinet.

He left the bathroom and went to the small kitchen. A back-door opened into a chain-link fenced yard adjacent to a park and playground. The door was unlocked. Neither the bolt nor the doorjamb showed evidence of forced entry.

Three paper bags full of groceries sat on a kitchen counter. Santana found the sales receipt with a stamped time of 4:42 p.m. in one of the bags. If the ME's estimate of the time of death was accurate, then Sandra Pérez couldn't have shot her husband when she returned from the store. It was possible that she murdered him before she left, but Santana didn't read her as a cold-blooded killer.

He peeled off the latex gloves and pulled the used ones out of his coat pockets and tossed both pairs in a container brought to the scene by the techs.

Gabriela Pérez came up to him as he headed for the front door and gave him a picture of her father. Standing this close to her, Santana realized how petite she was. Even in this time of grief she exuded a sexual quality that clung to her like a tight-fitting dress.

The recent photograph of Julio Pérez looked posed and professionally done. He wore a red tie, blue shirt, and black pinstriped suit. He appeared fit and was smiling broadly.

"I'll return the photo to you," Santana said.

Her dark eyes held his for a time. Then her gaze shifted to the long, jagged scar on the back of his right hand and then to the picture of her father. "Make sure that you do."

She turned and walked back into the living room, her slim hips swaying like a rope in a gentle breeze.

The scene outside the house reminded Santana of Lautréamont's description of surrealism as the chance meeting on a dissecting table of a sewing machine and an umbrella. TV vans from the local NBC, CBS, and ABC news outlets were parked at the curb along with the mobile crime lab van, medical examiner's van and six white St. Paul squad cars with gold shields on the front doors. Flood lights illuminated reporters who waved microphones in front of anyone who wanted to speak and those who didn't. Yellow crime scene tape had been strung from oak to oak, cordoning off the house and yard. Neighbors had gathered behind the tape in the cold night air. A uniformed officer stood in the driveway recording the names of anyone who entered the house.

In his teens Santana had been fascinated by the paintings of Salvador Dali and the writings of André Breton. Now, he often filtered the dark and violent world of homicide through a surrealistic lens of both intention and chance. It was a world in which the real and the imaginary became one. A world in which bodies that could not speak were spoken for. Bodies beaten with bats and bricks and tire irons until their skulls looked more like smashed pumpkins than human heads; bodies and parts of bodies carved and sliced and sawed; bodies shot and suffocated and dragged bloated and blue from the Mississippi; bodies in bags and on gurneys and on cold slabs in the morgue with tags attached to their toes.

Only one would forever haunt him.

He gave a quick shake of his head to chase away that memory and focused on the current case. The most important hours in murder investigations were the first forty-eight hours after the discovery of the body. The longer the investigation went on, the less chance he had of finding the murderer.

Santana stood on the front walk and felt the cold, still air against his skin. The sudden absence of wind left him feeling as if the earth, like Julio Pérez, had quit breathing.

Rick Anderson walked across the brown grass toward Santana. "I gotta start hittin' the gym again," he said, rubbing his ample belly.

An unmarked car pulled up in front of the house and parked next to the ME's van. The driver's side door swung open and James Kehoe, special investigator from the mayor's office, stepped out. He appeared disoriented for a moment until he spotted Santana and Anderson and headed toward them.

Santana said, "What the hell is Asshoe doing here?"

He used the nickname given to Kehoe by certain detectives within the department.

Anderson leaned closer to Santana and said quietly, "Take it easy, John."

"Santana … Anderson," Kehoe said, acknowledging each of them with a nod.

Tanning beds had leathered Kehoe's once handsome face, and he wore his blond hair very short and an SPPD baseball cap to hide the fact that he was losing it.

"You got a homicide?" Kehoe said.

"Appears to be," Santana said, unwilling to give him anything to work with.

"I understand the vic is Julio Pérez?"

Santana said nothing.

Kehoe waited a moment for a response and then looked at Anderson. "How'd he die?"

"Gunshot to the head."

"Any idea who whacked him?"

"Nothing concrete."

Kehoe pulled on the brim of his cap and glanced behind him. "You talk to the inkslingers?"

"Not yet," Santana said. He could hear the reporters in the background yelling at them for a statement.

"What does the mayor's office have to do with this?" Anderson asked.

Kehoe shot him a look. "Julio Pérez was known and respected by a lot of people in this city. Including the mayor. Santana should know that since he's …"

"Hispanic?" Santana said.

"If the shoe fits. You a friend of Pérez's?"

"We don't all know each other."

"Forget the sarcasm, Santana, and concentrate on results."

"We will. Soon as you get out of the way and let us do our job."

"Look," Kehoe said, stepping close enough to Santana that he could smell the coffee on his breath. "If you want to play hardball, let's take it downtown."

"Come on, Jim," Anderson said, raising his hands in a calming gesture. "Give it a rest."

Kehoe's jaw muscles clenched. His eyes flicked back and forth before settling on Anderson. "You got any wits?"

"We're working on it."

"So what's the next step?"

"We start questioning the employees at *El Día*," Santana said.

"All right. But keep me in the loop. The mayor wants to know exactly how this investigation is proceeding."

"You'll be the first to know."

Kehoe stared at Santana for a long moment. Then he turned and headed for his car.

"Christ," Anderson said. "What's with him?"

"Se cree la vaca que mas caga. He thinks he's the cow that shits the most."

"Maybe. But you better not rub his nose in it, John. Especially if he's in the mayor's pocket."

"I'll keep that in mind. Let's talk with the reporters, and then we'll go see Rafael Mendoza."

"Who?"

"The last call Julio Pérez made on the phone in his study was to Rafael Mendoza."

"But that's not what you told Kehoe."

"I lied."

Santana could tell by Anderson's wary expression that he felt uncomfortable with the lie.

"You know anything about Mendoza?" Santana said, quickly changing the subject.

"No. You?"

"I met him a couple of times when I was in uniform and worked off-duty security at parties for the mayor."

"He a criminal attorney?"

"Immigration, mostly. Green Cards, visas."

"Think he's capable of murder?"

"I haven't met many who aren't."

Chapter 2

SANTANA CHECKED HIS REARVIEW MIRROR and saw Anderson cruising in the lane behind him as they drove over the Wabasha Bridge into downtown St. Paul. Mendoza lived in the Lowertown District, a block from the Farmer's Market in the Riverview Lofts, an eight-story Romanesque building overlooking the Mississippi River. Lofts were the latest marketing tool designed to lure upscale singles and couples into the city. They were being built as fast as developers could acquire enough capital and historic, abandoned buildings could be gutted.

Ice crystals pinged off his car as Santana parked the Crown Vic in a NO PARKING zone along Kellogg Boulevard across the street from the lofts. Anderson parked behind him. He got out of his Crown Vic and into the passenger side of Santana's car. Even in the dim light Santana could see his partner's pockmarked complexion.

The digital clock on the dashboard changed to 7:15 as Santana listened to the bursts of chatter from the police radio. The Crown Vic's heater was pushing out as much heat as a candle.

Cold weather had its advantages. Most gangbangers never ventured outside after dark when below zero wind chills could freeze bare flesh in minutes and hypothermia could mean a slow, silent death. Rape, robbery, burglary, arson, assault, theft and motor vehicle theft, seven of the eight crimes the SPPD classified as Part I crimes according to the FBI's Uniform Crime Reporting guidelines, all fell with frigid temperatures. Only homicide was unaffected.

"I'm freezing my ass off," Anderson said.

Santana detected a hint of alcohol in the tiny clouds of carbon dioxide vapor forming as Anderson exhaled.

"Get yourself some breath mints," he said.

Anderson looked quickly at Santana and then out the passenger side window.

Santana said, "Have you been going to your AA meetings?"

"Don't worry. I'm fine."

Santana hadn't detected any alcohol on Anderson's breath at Pérez's house. He considered pressing Anderson but decided now wasn't the time. Instead, he recounted his conversation with Sandra Pérez and her daughter, Gabriela.

"You think either of them are good for it?" Anderson said.

"Not the wife. We'll have to check out the *Casa Blanca* restaurant. Make sure the daughter was there all afternoon."

Anderson looked out the windshield at the city and the lights in the buildings that were burning like embers in the charcoal sky. "How long have we been together, John?"

"Nearly three years."

"How many murder investigations?"

"I'm not keeping count."

Anderson sat quietly, staring out the windshield.

"Something on your mind, partner?"

Anderson waited a couple of beats. Then he said, "Kehoe wasn't a bad guy when I partnered with him in the Narcotic's Division."

"He ever work homicide?"

"No. But we were pretty close once. I remember he took the great divide pretty hard."

"Maybe if he had spent more time pumping his wife rather than iron," Santana said, "he would still be married to her."

A large orange snowplow rumbled by with its plow up. The ground underneath the Crown Vic shook from the plow's weight as the spinning rotor attached to the rear end spread a special mixture of salt and sand over the ice that coated the street. A sign across the back of the cab read: STAY BACK, STAY ALIVE.

Santana checked his watch. It was 7:29. He turned off the car, got out and headed toward the Riverview Lofts. The cold night air smelled of diesel from a Metro Transit bus stopped at a corner. A slippery film underneath his feet slowed him down, made him feel like a child just learning to walk. Behind him, he could hear Anderson cursing the treacherous footing.

Santana had nearly reached the main entrance when he felt a sudden rush of air a moment before the body falling out of the dark January sky crunched like a bag of ice against the pavement.

Instinctively, he looked up. Saw a figure move in the dim light on a balcony above him — then it was gone.

The broken body lay face up. The impact had fractured the femur bone in one leg. Pushed it through the skin like a spike through paper.

"It's Rafael Mendoza," Santana yelled to his partner. "Call for back up and then watch the main entrance."

Santana ran into the building and up a set of stairs to the first floor where he waved his badge at a man in a security guard uniform.

"St. Paul P.D. What's Rafael Mendoza's number?"

The security guard pointed in the direction of the occupant names and numbers on the wall.

"Officers will be here soon," Santana said. "Don't let anyone leave."

As he rode the elevator to the eighth floor, Santana pulled his .40 caliber Glock out of the holster attached to his belt. A sound like wind rushing through an open door filled his ears, and his mouth felt as dry as sand. He removed his wool overcoat and dropped it on the floor. Inhaled a deep breath and let it out slowly.

When the elevator door slid open, he flicked on the emergency stop switch and peered out. Quiet. At the far end, the cement hallway turned ninety degrees to the left. He estimated Mendoza's loft would be halfway between the elevator and the angled turn.

He moved quickly across the hallway and flattened his back against the wall. Held the Glock at an upward angle and slid along the wall until he came to Mendoza's door. It was ajar. He pushed the door fully open with the gun barrel. Stepped inside.

The loft had brick walls and a high timbered ceiling. Light from a table lamp pooled on the hardwood floor. Drapes concealing the balcony and iron railing fluttered like angel's wings in the icy air blowing through an open sliding glass door.

Santana crossed the room in a crouch and went out the slider onto the balcony. He stood for a moment in the sleet that pinged off the railing and concrete. In the wind he heard the cry of distant sirens.

He went back inside and moved slowly down a narrow hallway until he came to a closed door on his left. He reached for the doorknob and then stopped, trusting his instincts. He waited.

Warm air poured through the heat vent on the floor. The sirens grew louder.

Then he heard someone running down the hallway outside the loft, the click of a crash bar.

He turned and sprinted out of the loft to the emergency exit door near the elevator and shoved it open. Fleeing footsteps reverberated off the concrete walls and metal handrails below him.

Santana raced down the stairs two at a time. When he reached the third level, he heard a heavy door slam shut beneath him.

"Rick!" he said, calling on his two-way. "I'm in pursuit of a possible suspect coming your way."

Santana wasn't certain what he would encounter when he pushed open the emergency exit door on the main floor, but he didn't hesitate. Still, the scene surprised him.

A crowd had gathered around a temporary stage in the center of a large atrium where an Irish band was preparing to play. A red and white St. Paul Winter Carnival banner hung from steel beams in the ceiling. Beyond the stage a boutique and gift shop flanked a market. Couples sat at tables behind a wrought iron railing of the Italian restaurant to his right.

Santana held his gun inside his sport coat pocket as he worked his way through knots of people. Their attention was focused on the stage and the upcoming performance, and they paid little attention to him.

At the edge of the crowd, he spotted a man in a brown bomber jacket. Their eyes met and the man suddenly turned and hurried away.

A moment later Anderson emerged from the throng and lumbered after him.

"POLICE!" he called.

The man froze for an instant. Then broke into a run.

Santana pulled his badge wallet out of his back pocket, held it open in front of him as he made his way through the crowd, urging people to move out of his way.

Anderson drew his weapon and yelled, "FREEZE!"

The man stopped and spun back toward the crowd, his face frozen with fear, his eyes skittering frantically.

Santana lost sight of him for an instant in a crush of people.

Anderson's Glock roared and a window imploded. Screams wailed through the atrium. All hell broke loose as people dropped to the ground and others scattered in panic.

Everything suddenly decelerated in front of Santana, as though he were watching a slow motion replay. He saw the man in the bomber jacket stumbling backward as glass rained down on him like ice cascading off a roof. Saw Anderson squeeze the trigger and the spent brass ejected from the Glock as it roared two more times.

The second round tore through the man's jacket. His chest erupted in a gush of red as he jerked backward and went down.

It was over in seconds.

Anderson remained in a combat stance, gripping the butt of the gun with both hands, rigidly pointing it where the man had fallen. The air smelled like exploding firecrackers.

Santana let out a long breath as he listened to the dying echo of the last gunshot bounce off the concrete walls, felt his heart beating once again. Then he moved cautiously forward.

Glass crunched under his shoes as he knelt down beside the man who lay sprawled on his back, his arms splayed over his head. His jacket was unzipped, revealing a .22 caliber Smith and Wesson semi-automatic tucked in his waistband.

Santana checked the carotid artery for a pulse. Holstered his Glock.

Anderson squatted down beside Santana and wiped his mouth with the back of a shaking hand. His complexion was the color of white-hot coals, his breathing quick and shallow.

"He dead?"

Santana gave a nod. He could smell the sour odor of fear mingling with Anderson's sweat.

"You okay?" he asked, keeping his eyes on his partner.

Anderson stared for a moment at the Smith and Wesson in the man's waistband before his eyes shifted to the Glock in his own hand and then to Santana. "He went for the gun, John."

Santana looked down at the dead man. His gaze never wavered as he peered intently into the dead man's eyes, eyes that were as empty as his own.

Chapter 3

THE CITY OF ST. PAUL AVERAGED TWENTY or so homicides a year, unlike LA or New York where they averaged that many in a week. Fewer homicides meant more media coverage and more pressure to solve them. And pressure was already being applied by the presence of James Kehoe, Rita Gamboni, commander of the Homicide Unit, and Assistant Deputy Chief of Operations, Carl Ashford. They had gathered around Santana in the living room of Rafael Mendoza's loft.

"Tell me what's going on, John," Ashford said, in a deep baritone voice.

Through the arched windows above the assistant chief's black, shaven head, Santana could see the muted glow of the streetlights near the riverbank, and the Mississippi flowing like a dark stream of blood in an open wound.

Santana told Ashford that Pérez had called Mendoza just prior to his death; how Mendoza's falling body had nearly hit him; and how he had gone to Mendoza's loft and then chased someone down the stairwell.

"You didn't tell me about the phone call to Mendoza," Kehoe said, giving Santana his best hardass expression. "You said you were going directly from Pérez's house to *El Día*."

"I changed my mind."

"Sure you did."

"I'll handle this," Ashford said with authority.

He was the kind of man who was used to giving orders, whether it was to men in green or blue uniforms, the kind of man who still carried his considerable width like an athlete rather than a couch potato. Santana figured it was a matter of time before Ashford became just the second African-American appointed chief.

"We got a name on the perp Anderson shot?"

"We've identified him as Rubén Córdova," Rita Gamboni said. "A reporter for *El Día*."

Santana and the others turned to look at her, which was always a pleasant thing to do.

Her white blond hair reminded Santana of the *monas de ojos claros* he used to see in Riosucio, Colombia. No one seemed to know where the families of the blue-eyed blondes had come from in that town in the Caldas region of the country, whether they were perhaps German or Basques from Northern Spain. Like most American women, Rita had worn her blond hair long until the age of thirty. Santana remembered that it had always smelled of strawberries.

"Who's the officer in charge?"

"Bill Kraus is the OIC. He's notified the chief and shift commander, IA, the union rep and the public information officer about the shooting. He'll make sure Anderson's name isn't released to the press."

"Good," Ashford said. "We don't want anything getting out to the media until IA and the county attorney conclude the preliminary investigation."

Santana had already completed a brief interview with Internal Affairs. They had also checked his Glock to make certain it had not been fired. Later, a private, more detailed tape recorded interview would be conducted. Santana felt the brief interview had gone poorly. He had been unable to corroborate Rick Anderson's account of the shooting because he had not seen what led Anderson to draw his weapon.

"We know anything about this Córdova?" Ashford asked.

"He was arrested for trespassing at a meat packing plant in Worthington," Gamboni said. "Apparently, he was investigating the company's hiring practices and the non-union wages they were paying illegals."

"Not exactly the profile of a stone cold killer," Santana said.

"You figure someone else killed Mendoza?"

"I think someone else was here besides Córdova. Someone in Mendoza's bedroom. And until I find out who it was, we can't close the book on this."

"What makes you think that?"

"Call it a feeling."

"That's real thin," Kehoe said.

Santana considered dragging Kehoe out the sliding glass door and throwing his sorry ass off the balcony. That might erase the permanent smirk on his face.

"If you'll shut the hell up, Kehoe," he said, "maybe I'll have some time to prove it."

"Detective," Ashford said. "We're all trying to make some sense out of this. Is that clear?"

Santana gave a reluctant nod.

"Good. We know the last phone call Pérez made was to Mendoza. And we know Córdova worked for Pérez's newspaper. Anyone have any theories?"

Kehoe said, "I'm guessing when ballistics runs tests on the .22 Smith and Wesson we found on Córdova, it'll match the bullet in Pérez's head. I'd say Córdova killed Pérez. Then he came here and threw Mendoza off his balcony. Maybe trying to make it look like a murder, suicide. He might've gotten away with it if Anderson hadn't sent him to the bone orchard."

Ashford looked at Santana and then Gamboni. When neither of them offered another theory he said, "So, it looks like we've got a double homicide and Córdova's our prime suspect."

Santana was thinking along the same lines. Still, he thought "looks like" was a good, if unintentional, choice of words.

He said, "We still need a motive."

"How many investigators can you spare, Rita?" Ashford asked.

"Well, with Anderson pulling desk duty until IA finishes its investigation, I suppose I could have Kacie Hawkins and Nick Baker work with Detective Santana. Their book is clear."

For a moment, Gamboni's eyes locked on Santana's.

He wondered if she ever thought of him in the way she once had.

"Then do it, Rita," Ashford said.

The forensic crew crowded the living room, so Santana slipped on a pair of latex gloves and walked into the master bedroom and looked around.

Mendoza's king-size bed was neatly made. A recent issue of *Twin Cities Magazine* headlined "Minnesota's Most Eligible Bachelors" rested on the nightstand next to an answering machine. Mendoza's picture was on the cover of the magazine. It came as no surprise then that Santana saw no photos of family in the room.

Santana checked the answering machine for messages. Then he went into a large walk-in closet. All the built-in drawers, shelves and clothes racks were carefully designed to maximize space. Mendoza's dry-cleaned shirts were arranged by color, light to dark, as were his Armani suits. Each drawer was slightly open. Santana could see that the underwear and T-shirts inside the top drawer were no longer arranged in tidy piles.

"Need a pair of these?"

Santana turned and saw Rita Gamboni leaning against the doorjamb holding up a pair of latex gloves. He considered telling her that it was always important to use latex in the bedroom but decided against it. Since becoming commander of the Homicide Unit, she had apparently lost her sense of humor. He understood. Some of the good-old-boy cops still resented taking orders from a woman.

Santana held up his hands. "Already protected."

"Find anything?"

"No. But this closet has been searched. You look around; you see Mendoza was a neat freak. Organized. But the drawers are all slightly open and the clothes messed up. Someone was looking for something."

"You thinking burglary?"

Santana shook his head. "A pro would start from the bottom, pull the drawer open and work his way up. No need to close each drawer. It's a waste of time. Plus, if robbery's the motive, why worry about covering your tracks?"

"Or if he wants to make it look like a robbery, he leaves a deliberate mess."

"Exactly."

"So, what do you think the perp was looking for?"

"Why don't you take this bedroom, and I'll check out the other? See if we can find out."

She slipped on the pair of latex. As he stepped past her, she touched his arm and he turned to look at her.

"There's a lot riding on this one, John."

She stood close enough to him that he caught the scent of strawberries.

"El color de la sangre siempre es el mismo. The color of blood is all the same, Rita."

"Meaning?"

"This investigation is no more and no less important than any other."

She let out a breath and peered down at her shiny black western boots with the squared toes.

Then she looked at him again. Given her height and two-inch heels, she was nearly as tall as him.

"You'll never change."

Santana knew that he, in fact, had changed. But it had happened in another time and in a place that was now just a distant memory, long before he met her.

"People should change only if it's for the better, Rita. But it doesn't always work out that way."

She frowned and he could tell that she had been stung by his comment, though he was speaking about himself rather than her.

"I haven't changed, John. I know there are other things, important things, that shouldn't have to be ..." she paused as if searching for the word.

"Sacrificed?" he said.

"Yes," she said after a time.

Santana knew that she wanted children. She had told him how she had tried with her ex-husband, Tom, for two years until they finally discovered that he was shooting blanks. It had driven a wedge between the two of them that could not be overcome. Once, after making love, when she had asked Santana to share his thoughts about having children, he had been clear. He would not bring a child into the darkness of this world.

"You all right?" he asked.

"The clock keeps ticking."

"On this investigation, too."

She gave him a thin smile. "Let me know if you find anything."

The second bedroom had a cherry wood desk, PC, printer, fax machine, four-drawer file, and built-in shelves filled with thick law books. Santana started with the files hanging on rods in the four-drawer cabinet. Each file had a neatly typed name inside a plastic tab attached to the top of the file. The files were arranged alphabetically by last name. All the names were Hispanic. The files contained a snapshot of each person and applications for visas. There were applications for the J1 and J2 visas, which restricted students to one year in the states, and the F1 and F2 student visas, those without restrictions.

Santana remembered how he had come on an F1 visa twenty years ago, how lost and alone he had felt. He wondered how many of these names in the files had come alone without their families, and how many were still here legally.

Some, he noted, had the B1 or B2 tourist visas, which prior to the 9/11 terrorist attack granted individuals a three-month stay but now were limited to one month; others had H1B, the temporary worker visas for professionals. But by Santana's count, there were nearly one hundred files of immigrants who had applied for the H2B visa for nonprofessional workers. The files contained labor certifications from the state and federal government. But as he looked more closely, he realized that many of the workers had applied for the same job at the same business within weeks of one another.

Santana jotted down ten random names and the places they worked in his notebook. He found nothing he deemed important when he searched the rest of the office. As he headed toward the hallway and the master bedroom room again, Rita Gamboni walked in.

"Anything?" she asked.

"An awful lot of applications for H2B worker visas. I'm going to check out a few of them. It's just a hunch, but I'm wondering if Mendoza was doing a little more than his share when it comes to diversifying the country."

"You think he was dealing in illegal documents?"

"We'll see." Santana pointed to the computer. "We should get one of the techs in here to take a look. We also need to check out Mendoza's office downtown."

"I'll give Nick Baker a heads up. Kacie Hawkins can take a look at Mendoza's financial and phone records."

"You find anything in the other room?"

"This." She handed Santana a 4 x 8 color print. "Found it taped to the wall behind the toilet tank in the master bath. A tech took a picture of it before I removed it. I wrote my initials and today's date on the back and logged it on the inventory."

Santana could see two naked men in the color photo. The man standing was photographed only from his chest down. The second man knelt before him. His face was partly covered by the other man's hand, but the photo left nothing to the imagination.

"The guy standing could be Mendoza," Gamboni said.

"If this gets out, female subscriptions for *Twin Cities Magazine* could plummet."

Gamboni tilted her head. Clearly, she had no idea what he was talking about.

"Mendoza was on a recent cover as one of Minnesota's most eligible bachelors."

"I didn't know you read the magazine, John."

"Every night just before bed with my milk and cookies."

"Think the guy on his knees is Córdova?"

"Maybe."

"You see any tats?"

Santana looked more closely at the photo. "No, but it looks like the guy standing has an appendix scar on his lower abdomen. Given the redness, I'd say the scar was recent. I'll have to check the autopsy report. See if Mendoza has a scar." Santana looked at the back of the photo. "It was taken in October of last year. You find any other sexually explicit photos?"

"Why?"

"Well, you figure if Mendoza was into this sort of thing, there would be more photos around."

"Spoken like a man who would know." Gamboni cracked a smile.

"Right. But ask yourself this, Rita. If Mendoza really didn't want this photo found, why wouldn't he put it where only he had access to it?"

"Well, if he wanted someone to find it, why not just leave it out in the open instead of behind the toilet tank?"

"Maybe for protection. It could be that someone didn't want this information to go public. People have murdered for less. If Mendoza gets killed, he knows someone doing a thorough search is going to find the photo."

"Like the police," she said.

"Exactly. But someone in a hurry might not."

"Like Córdova."

"Córdova or whoever else was going through the dresser drawers."

"You really thinking that someone killed Pérez and Mendoza and had Córdova take the fall?"

"Leaving the .22 shell casing at Pérez's house was real convenient."

"Could be Córdova was just careless."

"All I know is that we've got three dead Hispanics, two of them prominent community members. The mayor is going to want a quick resolution. Especially if the other dead Hispanic is the prime suspect."

"Come on, John. Give me some credit."

"It's not you I'm worried about, Rita. Just keep Kehoe and the mayor's office off my back until I've had time to look at all the evidence."

She thought about his request for a moment. "I'll do what I can."

It was midnight when Santana arrived home. Ice crystals had turned into large flakes of snow. The twenty-minute drive east on Interstate 94 from downtown to his house at the end of a narrow blacktop road in St. Croix Beach took him forty.

The renovated brick house he owned sat on two heavily wooded acres of birch and pine on a secluded bluff overlooking the St. Croix River, which formed a natural boundary between Minnesota and Wisconsin. The previous owner had been a well-known chef in town before an ugly paternity suit took most of his money and all of his house. Santana knew some members of the department wondered how he could afford the place on a detective's salary, but he couldn't care less.

He unlocked the front door and turned off the security system, tossed his wool overcoat and sport coat on the couch and unclipped his Kydex belt holster. He preferred the Kydex because it could be molded to fit the Glock 23 he carried and had a permanent memory of the gun's shape.

Santana lit the logs in the grate, undressed and took a long, hot shower. After he toweled off, he slipped on a robe and poured a couple of shots of aguardiente Cristal. Then he put an Armando Manzanero CD in the compact Bose system, turned the rheostat light switch down low, and sat down on the soft leather couch in front of the fieldstone fireplace. His body ached with exhaustion, but his mind still raced with the day's events.

Aguardiente helped him relax. Imported from the Caldas region of Colombia, the smooth mixture of sugar cane and anisette created a comfortable burn as it settled in his stomach. Only a few liquor stores around town stocked it.

He checked for messages on his answering machine. Then he picked up the phone and called Rick Anderson. He knew his partner and figured he would still be awake. Santana wanted to hear how Anderson's interview had gone. They had met separately at the station with IA after leaving the Riverview Lofts.

Anderson's phone rang six times before Santana broke off the connection. Anderson had probably unplugged his phone, something Santana had done on numerous occasions, and especially when he wanted to avoid the media. He considered calling Anderson's cell phone, but decided to let it go. He would talk to his partner in the morning.

Instead, he dialed a familiar number in Santa Fe, New Mexico. While he listened to the phone ringing on the other end of the line, he looked at the framed photograph on the mantle over the fireplace of the older couple. Phil O'Toole with his bulldog expression and the crewcut he had worn nearly all of his sixty-five years. And Dorothy with her sweet smile, untouched by deceit.

For a moment he saw his own mother, Elena. Her auburn hair the color of a maple leaf in autumn; her smooth, unmarked complexion deeply tanned and slightly freckled; her iridescent eyes that changed from blue to green depending on the color of clothes she wore and the ever-shifting light. He had called her *sancocho* because, like the stew, she was a beautiful mix of Spanish and English blood. The picture in his mind's eye still matched the photo of her in his wallet though it had been twenty years since her death. He thought she would have aged as gracefully as Dorothy.

"You still up, Phil?"

"Well, Dorothy and I were just talkin' about you this evening. Wondering why you haven't called in nearly two weeks."

"Sorry. Is she asleep?"

"Went to bed an hour ago. Sleeps like a baby. Wish I was so lucky."

"It's that old cop in you, Phil. Too many night shifts."

"Must be," he said. "You sleepin' much?"

"Enough."

"Then how come you're callin' after midnight?"

"New case."

"I figured as much."

He coughed and Santana could hear the rattle of fluid in his chest.

"How's the emphysema?" he asked.

"Horseshit. But I get by."

"You ever miss it, Phil?"

"Mostly at night after Dorothy's gone to bed. Darkness gets you thinkin'. You remember the one or two that didn't get solved. You play 'em over in your mind. Wonder what you could've done differently."

Phil had always been Santana's sounding board when it came to solving cases. He reviewed the current investigation with Phil and then said, "I'll send you some clippings on this one. You might find it interesting."

"That'd be great."

Santana could hear the excitement in his voice.

"When you comin' down here for a visit, John? Thought we might see you at Christmas."

"I couldn't get away."

"Don't you have some vacation time comin'?"

"This spring. I'll come down."

"Dorothy's going to be upset she missed your call. I could wake her."

"No, don't do that. I'll call again soon."

"You better if you know what's good for you. Have you been eatin' right?"

"Trying."

"I'll bet. Dorothy'll put some meat on those Colombian bones. Remember how thin you were when you first got off that plane?"

Santana laughed. "I remember. I remember how you two took care of me. Saved my life."

"Hell! We just fed you."

"You did more than that. And I'll never forget. If it weren't for you, I wouldn't be a detective."

"I'm proud of you, John. You've done all right for yourself."

"Is Emma still teaching in Peru?"

"Yes. She's comin' home this summer to finish her Ph.D. in languages."

"She sure gets around. When you talk to her let her know that I said hello."

"We will. You take care of yourself."

"Always."

Santana said goodbye and hung up the phone.

He drank another swallow of aguardiente and let his thoughts return to the current investigation and the 4 x 8 color photo Gamboni had found in Mendoza's loft. He wondered why Mendoza had the photo? Why he taped it to the back of the toilet tank in his bathroom? He would check with Tony Novak in the crime lab tomorrow. Perhaps enhancing the image would help identify the two men. He wanted to talk with some of the immigrants on the list he had made, specifically those who had applied for visas. Thinking of the immigrants reminded him of Sandra Pérez, which reminded him of her daughter, Gabriela.

He took a final pull on the aguardiente. He knew it would be a long time before he slept.

Chapter 4

DAY TWO

SANTANA AWOKE FROM A DREAM just before dawn to the howling of the wind; a lonely, plaintive sound like a wolf on a cold, barren landscape, howling at the moon.

He had been standing on a fog-shrouded bridge high above a river of fire. From somewhere in the darkness, a woman had cried out to him. He needed to find her. Needed to help her. But when he opened his mouth to call to her, to let her know that he heard her cry, there were no sounds, no words, only a numbness that rose like a tide within him, and a silence that hung in a breath of condensation in the cold night air.

He lay still for a moment, listening to the January gusts and the inner voice warning him it would be a mistake to discount or ignore the message in this dream. He had learned about the meaning and importance of dreams as a young boy from Ofir, the maid, who worked for his parents in the house that sat on a steep hill in the *Chipre* neighborhood overlooking the city of Manizales, Colombia, 7,000 feet high in the Andes, in the shadow of the *Nevado del Ruíz*.

He remembered listening to the old woman as he sat in the kitchen with the windows that faced the snow-covered volcano, the indoor air heavy with the smell of celery from the *apio* tea brewing on the stove. Ofir had warned him then that his two recurring dreams of falling from a high place and running from something that chased him would mean great misfortune and exile some day. She had been right on both counts.

He guessed this dream represented the doubts he still had about his sister, Natalia's, safety. He had wanted to bring her with him when he fled Colombia at sixteen. But she had no visa and waiting for her to get one would have put both their lives in jeopardy. He wished he could hear Ofir's voice again explaining the meaning of this dream. Yet, he only heard the wind pounding the frosty panes like a fist.

He got out of bed and went downstairs to the bedroom he used as a workout room. He did three sets of bench presses and curls. Jumped rope and hammered a speed bag against the rebound board with a rhythm that created its own music in his head until his arms ached and sweat soaked his T-shirt. He finished his workout with one hundred sit-ups, a hot shower and a close shave.

Once he would have described his face as soft and boyish. Now, at thirty-six, the complexion he saw in the mirror had grown harder and darker despite the close morning shaves, as though the darkness in his heart had suddenly appeared as a permanent shadow on his face.

For breakfast he ate two fried eggs, a slice of cheese and one of the *arepas* he had made two days ago. He washed it down with a cup of hot chocolate topped with cinnamon. The hot chocolate reminded him of the sugarless, dark chocolate made by the Luker Company in Manizales. He would often mix it with *Panela Del Valle* brown sugar. Sometimes in the mornings he would boil just the brown sugar in water and add cinnamon. He enjoyed the chocolate here, but nothing he found could match the taste he had once known.

Santana felt relaxed and focused as he drove west on Interstate 94, past the 3M building with its row upon row of windows looking blue in the reflected sunlight, then past the Sunray Shopping Center toward downtown St. Paul. The patches of snow that stitched the trees and bushes had changed the landscape overnight from dingy brown to gleaming white. A combination of heat from the bright morning sun, and sand, courtesy of the Minnesota Department of Transportation trucks, gave the surface of the freeway the texture of a snow cone.

Santana recalled his first winter in Minnesota as an unending nightmare of cold and ice and futile attempts to stay warm. He had come as a foreign exchange student and had stayed with the O'Tooles for nine months before returning home. He would not have picked Minnesota as a permanent place to live, but when he fled Colombia for good a year later he had no choice. He knew he could trust the O'Tooles, knew he had nowhere else to go. Over the years he had made peace with the weather and even found comfort in the isolation created by a snowstorm.

José López was the first name on the list of immigrants Santana had copied from the files in Rafael Mendoza's loft. Mendoza had filed four requests for labor certifications for short-order cooks over the last two years for the Bay Point Restaurant in downtown St. Paul. That seemed like a lot of requests for foreign cooks.

Santana parked the Crown Vic along the curb in front of the restaurant near Rice Park and the Ordway Theater. He badged the parking attendant on duty and walked to the entrance with the sign on the window stating that guns were banned on the premises.

The white signs with the large black letters were as commonplace as goose shit in spring ever since the legislature passed the conceal and carry law. Santana found it laughable that an average citizen armed with a permit, a handgun, and a three-week training course could deter a degenerate gangbanger who thought the only difference between taking a human life and stepping on a garden-variety insect was the weapon of choice. But what else could be expected from politicians who pandered to fear and the lowest common denominator in their zeal for votes, and whose limited vision stretched only as far as the next election.

The atmosphere inside the restaurant was nautical: nets and ship's wheels and aquariums. The aquariums were built into the rough-hewn walls and filled with brightly colored fish. Two waitresses in black slacks; white shirts, black vests and ties were arranging silverware and wine glasses on the tables, while another folded white linen napkins.

"Table for one, sir?"

The maitre d' was a short, bald man with a mustache.

Santana showed him his badge. "I'd like to see the manager."

The maitre d' examined it as if searching for the flaw in a factory second. When he was satisfied that Santana's badge had not come out of box of Cracker Jacks, he looked up and said, "Certainly, sir. One moment."

He scurried off and in a few minutes came back.

"It's through the kitchen," he said, pointing toward the back of the restaurant. He then turned his attention to two men waiting behind Santana, as if the detective no longer existed.

Santana skipped the customary thank you as he brushed past the maitre d' and went through a set of swinging doors where the air smelled of fried eggs and potatoes. Pots banged and a deep fryer sizzled. He walked along an aisle between the hot food table and two large ovens toward a second set of swinging doors on the opposite wall. Near the dishwasher and pre-rinse sink he came upon a Mexican kid wearing a wet, stained apron. He appeared to be about sixteen.

A fat man in a chef's hat standing in front of the kid said, "I don't want to hear any more goddamn Spanish, you understand? You want to work here, you speak English."

He jabbed the cleaver he held in his hand at the boy.

Santana recalled another scared kid who was once told by a boss to speak English if he wanted to keep his job.

"Is there a problem?" he asked.

The fat man gave him a menacing stare. "Who the hell are you?"

Santana showed him his badge. "This is who I am."

The fat man's beady eyes widened and he swallowed hard. "Hey, no problem, Detective."

His white face turned the same shade as the tomato on the counter. He lowered the cleaver and looked around for a place to put it.

Santana had an idea where it might fit. "You're sure?" he asked.

"You bet," the fat man said with a forced smile.

Santana turned to the Mexican kid. *"Hay algún problema aquí?"*

The kid glanced at the cook and then looked at Santana. *"No, señor. Gracias."*

Santana handed him a business card. *"Si algún día necesitas ayuda llámame."*

"Gracias, señor," he said.

Santana stepped close enough so that the fat man had to tilt his head back to meet his eyes. "I don't want to have to come back. *Comprende?"*

The fat man's chin went up and down like a bobblehead doll on the dashboard of a car.

Santana left the kitchen and went to the office where an Asian woman stood in front of a mahogany desk.

"I'm Kim Nguyen," she said. She had a small hand but a firm grip. She was slender, with short, jet-black hair whose ends were cut at a sharp angle. Santana made her for Vietnamese.

He handed her a business card.

"Please," she said and gestured toward an armchair in front of the desk.

The leather cushion let out a sigh as he sat down.

She went behind the desk and said, "What can I do for you, Detective Santana?"

"Your cook seems to have a problem with the help speaking Spanish."

"Really?"

"You might want to have a conversation with him."

"I most certainly will. Is that what you wanted to see me about?"

"I'm looking for a man who works for you as a short order cook. His name is José López."

"I don't recognize the name, but let me see what I can find."

She sat down and awakened the sleeping laptop on the corner of her desk with the deft touch of a finger. As she tapped the keys, she whispered "López," to herself, and looked intently at the screen.

Santana could tell by the manicured nails and the perfectly applied red polish that she took a great deal of pride in her appearance.

After a time she looked up, dark, thin eyebrows arched in surprise and said, "We don't have a José López working for us."

Santana looked at the list of names in his notebook from Mendoza's files. "Let me read three more names. See if they worked for you as cooks during the past year."

"All right."

He read off the names.

Kim Nguyen tapped expertly away on the keys, but each time she came up empty.

"Do you mind telling me what's going on, Detective?"

Santana wasn't completely sure, but he had a pretty good idea.

Santana drove into the parking lot at headquarters on 11th and Minnesota. The mayor had recently convinced the city council to move the police out of the Public Safety Building that had housed the department for seventy-three years. The plan to renovate the six-story, eighty-two year old Benz building northeast of the northern junction of Interstates 35E and 94, and relocate police headquarters there along with the new county jail under construction, was moving rapidly forward.

The current Ramsey County Adult Detention Center stood on the corner of Kellogg and Wabasha, just north of the bridge that linked downtown with the West Side. The ADC contained a small twenty-six space indoor parking area and one hundred thirty-four cells, each with its own aluminum toilet, washbasin and mirror. It sat on about an acre of prime real estate overlooking the Mississippi River and Harriet Island. Developers were salivating at the thought of turning the brick structure into office rental space, restaurants or condos.

The new jail in the renovated Benz building would have a capacity of over five hundred prisoners, housed in the most advanced concrete cells in the country. Another twenty-five holding cells would be installed for those awaiting arraignment.

Those in favor of the move argued that razing the old police station would free a large tract of downtown for redevelopment and provide more space for the state's new Department of Human Services building, despite reservations from the union and police administration. The current chief of police complained that the department might have even less space than they had now. But the SPPD feared that the ultimate goal of the move was a merger of the city police and county sheriff's department.

Last week, Santana had overheard a telephone conversation between Ashford and the chief. Ashford wanted to know just what the hell the department was supposed to do with the crime scene processing truck and the bomb truck, which were secured within the existing building, but would not fit at the new Law Enforcement Complex.

Santana understood that the whole issue would be solved as soon as the politicians figured out what decision brought in the most votes and campaign contributions. It reminded him of a saying he once heard. Integrity was a lot like oxygen. The higher you climbed up the chain of command, the less there was of it. Experience had convinced him that politicians were the same the world over. Although he had to admit that if you rejected the money and voted your conscience in Colombia, the risk was higher. Here, you just got voted out of office.

Santana used his card key to enter the building and took the elevator up to the Homicide Unit located on the third floor in the Crimes Against Persons Division. The long, narrow room contained small cubicles separated by sound partitions. The partitions flanked a corridor that divided the room in half.

Rick Anderson was the lone detective in the unit at this time of the day. He sat at his desk, typing out a report on a computer. A half-eaten jelly-filled donut and a can of Coke rested beside his computer and a stack of reports.

He said, "The background checks on Julio Pérez's neighbors turned up nothing unusual. And I called the *Casa Blanca* restaurant this morning. Gabriela Pérez's alibi is solid."

"I called you last night," Santana said.

"I figured I wouldn't get much sleep, so I stopped at O'Leary's." Anderson picked up the Coke and drank what remained in the can. His hand shook as he set it down on the desk again, as though he had just lifted a heavy weight.

"How did your interview with IA go?"

"They took my gun, John. Gave me a replacement."

"You know it's standard operating procedure."

"Yeah," he said, his eyes still fixed on the can. "As long as they agree the shooting was justified. But I've been thinking a lot about it and now I'm not so sure." Anderson's eyes locked on Santana's again. "Maybe Córdova didn't go for the gun. Maybe he didn't deserve to die."

It was evident by the look of anticipation on Anderson's face that he was waiting for Santana to disagree with him, to come to his defense. But Santana knew criminal charges were filed against police officers in only one of every five hundred shootings nationwide. Unless there was a witness who could contradict Anderson's account, in all likelihood, no charges would be filed once the Ramsey County Attorney's Office, Internal Affairs and the Citizens' Review Board completed their preliminary investigation, which generally took two weeks. But a breath test was required for any officer involved in a shooting. It would show that Anderson had been drinking. That would be a problem. Anderson had been sober for as long as they had been partners. Santana expected him to stay that way. He was unwilling to jeopardize his life and the lives of others by partnering with a cop who had a gun in one hand and a bottle in the other.

He said, "You going to be around awhile?"

Anderson did a poor job of hiding his disappointment at Santana's response. "What do you think?" he said, nodding at the stack of papers on his desk.

Kacie Hawkins and Nick Baker were already seated in chairs around Gamboni's desk when Santana walked in and closed the door behind him. Gamboni sat behind an oak desk in a dark leather chair, her hands folded and resting on the desktop. She glanced at her wristwatch as he approached.

"Sorry I'm late," he said.

A framed FBI certificate signifying a course she had completed in Behavioral Sciences at Quantico hung on the wall behind her along with a framed picture of her SPPD academy graduating class and one of her in uniform. To the left of the frames hung a large white board she frequently used to assign detectives and map out strategies for an investigation. She had a cluster of gold-framed photos of her two elementary age nieces on her desk along with a thick hardcover book entitled, *Conflicts of Integrity*.

Santana took a seat in a chair between Hawkins on his left and Baker on his right. He saw Baker fidgeting with the knot on his worn tie and shoving a stick of Nicorette gum into his mouth in a futile attempt to stave off the withdrawal symptoms that had no doubt begun the moment he stepped into Gamboni's office, an infamous non-smoking zone.

"Why don't you start, Nick," Gamboni said. "Tell us what you found in Mendoza's office downtown."

Baker pointed his chin at Hawkins. "She's got all the notes."

"All right, then," Gamboni said with a small sigh. Turning her attention to the black woman on Santana's left, she said, "Let's start with you, Kacie."

"In a nutshell, Lieutenant, we got jack shit," Hawkins said, flipping through her notepad.

"Could you be a bit more specific, Detective?"

Hawkins was concentrating so hard on her notes that she either had not heard Gamboni's sarcasm, or, more likely, Santana thought; she was smart enough to ignore it.

Hawkins was in her first year in Homicide after spending two years in Vice where it was rumored that she held the record for arresting the most johns in an eight-hour shift. When Kacie walked down the street, particularly in a skimpy outfit on a hot summer evening, men paid attention. Lots of them. She had long legs and what certain males in the department described as a 'designer ass'. Although Santana would not describe her as pretty, she was smart and tough for a twenty-eight year old. He figured she might be running the whole department someday.

"Well," Hawkins said, "we spent the morning going through Mendoza's office. We looked at his appointment calendar and files. His secretary gave us the password to his computer, so we printed some information, but we didn't see anything unusual in the folders. Looks to me like mostly case files."

"When you were looking through Mendoza's files or on the computer," Santana said, "did you see anything having to do with visa applications?"

Gamboni leaned forward and put her elbows on the desk. "That's the second time you've mentioned visa applications, John. What do you think is going on?"

"Mendoza had nearly a hundred files of immigrants who had applied for H2B visas in a file cabinet in his bedroom," Santana said. "The visa is for nonprofessional workers. Many of the workers in the files had applied for the same job at the same business within weeks of one another. I went to the Bay Point Restaurant this morning and then to three others. I think Mendoza was submitting phony visa applications for labor certifications from the Feds."

"I don't get it," Baker said. "What's the scam?"

"Mendoza sends an application to the Department of Labor certifying that an employer, say a restaurant, needs a foreign worker for a job because no U.S. citizens are available for the position. Once the Labor Department issues a certification, the worker can apply to Immigration and Customs Enforcement for permanent residency. It used to be INS, but it became ICE after 9/11."

"And Mendoza charges the worker for the residency," Gamboni said.

"Exactly. Mendoza filed four applications for cooks at the Bay Point according to the files in his loft. The restaurant didn't have a record of one."

"And none of the workers are gonna squawk 'cause they have their papers, which is what they paid for," Hawkins said.

"We're going to have to bring the Feds in on this, John," Gamboni said.

"Not yet, Rita. Let's see where this is going first."

Baker stopped fidgeting with the wrapper in his hands. He looked at Santana and then at Gamboni. "That makes sense. Once the Feds get involved, we might as well kiss the whole investigation good-bye. Besides, those idiots couldn't find their ass with both hands."

Santana watched Gamboni. He knew that she was considering all the options and weighing the consequences before making her decision.

"All right," she said at last. "I'll hold off for a while. But if Ashford gets wind of this before the investigation is completed, one of you is going to pay. So whatever you find out stays in this room."

Baker said, "Maybe Mendoza, Pérez and Córdova were all involved in the scam. Maybe Córdova wanted all the action and took out the other two."

"There should be a record of Mendoza's transactions somewhere, Nick," Gamboni said. "Keep looking. See if he deposited large sums of money in any accounts. Kacie you do the same for Pérez. Check their phone records. Look for a link between the two. And check out *El Día*, John; see what you can find out about Córdova. We need to connect the dots."

Baker was unconsciously tearing the nicotine wrapper in his hands into tiny strips. Beads of sweat dotted his forehead. Santana thought Baker looked ready to jump out of his wrinkled clothes.

"I want to ask Tony Novak about the photo you found in Mendoza's loft yesterday," Santana said to Gamboni. "See if he can enhance it. We might be able to find something that can help identify the guy with Mendoza."

"What photo is that?" Baker asked.

Santana explained.

"My, oh my," Kacie Hawkins said in her practiced street voice.

"Maybe this has something to do with why Mendoza was killed?" Baker said.

"Everyone loves a good mystery," Santana said.

Gamboni stood up, ignoring his comment. "Let's get moving."

Baker bolted out of his chair.

"The man has to kick that nasty habit before it kills him," Hawkins said, following Baker out the door.

Santana stood. "I need a warrant for Córdova's place, Rita."

"I'll take care of it."

He picked up the computer printouts on her desk from Mendoza's office. "Mind if I take a look at these?"

"Go ahead. If you're right about the visa scam, John, we might have a possible motive."

He looked at her for a moment without speaking.

"Something else on your mind, Detective?"

"You made the right decision about the Feds, Rita."

She started to smile, but then caught herself. "I still have my priorities straight."

"That's good to know," he said.

When he sat down at his desk, Santana heard the familiar whine of the north wind as it hurled itself against the building in ever increasing gusts, rattling the windowpanes with such force that he thought they might shatter. Wind seemed to be a constant in Minnesota. It steamed up from the Gulf of Mexico in the summer carrying hot, humid air that melted his flesh and sucked the energy right out of him. In winter it roared down out of Canada carrying icicles of frigid air that stabbed the nerve endings in his fingers and toes until they were numb.

He checked his voice mail.

"Hey, Santana. Kelly Quinn from the *Pioneer Press*. I'm still working the taco beat. I'd like to talk to you about the Pérez-Mendoza investigation and Rubén Córdova's death. Give me a call. Thanks."

He had shared information with Quinn in the past. She was a good reporter and he figured she would try connecting Córdova to Mendoza's death. Soon she would be asking if Córdova did Pérez as well. He elected not to return her call.

He booted up his computer, clicked on the file labeled reports and began typing a chronological record of his investigation. The information would become part of the murder book along with the autopsy protocols, witness statements, ballistic and crime scene reports and photos, printouts from Automated Fingerprint Identification System, and his notes.

SPPD crime statistics were collected in an automated Single Incident Tracking System known as SITS. They were coded and entered into a database that allowed queries by address, name and incident type. The city was divided into two hundred grids and advanced analysis could be conducted by grid and through combining grids by neighborhood. All SPPD officers had access to the department's informational systems.

"Excuse me. Detective Santana?"

Santana did a one-eighty in his swivel chair.

The pretty woman standing in front of him had long, thick, raven hair down to her waist. Her dark complexion suggested she had some Indian blood. For an instant he sensed that he had met her before, though he knew he never had.

"My name is Angelina Torres," she said with a smile that could melt ice. She gestured toward the priest standing next to her. "This is Father Hidalgo."

The lanky priest's long, thin hand felt damp and cold. He seemed timid and shy, like a groundhog afraid of its shadow.

"We've come to see you about Rubén Córdova's death," she said, and her honey-colored eyes suddenly filled with tears.

Santana rounded up two more chairs and sat down facing them.

"How do you know Córdova?"

Angelina Torres wiped her eyes with a Kleenex and said, "I met Rubén when we were in college in California. We had much in common. We were both from Mexico. Our parents worked together in the grape fields. After I came to Minnesota I took a job working for *Latinos in Minnesota* as a social worker. Rubén and I talked frequently. Eventually, he came here, too. And Mr. Pérez hired him as a reporter and editor. Rubén was a very good reporter."

"So you knew Córdova well."

"Well enough to know he would never attempt to shoot a police officer."

The way she said it suggested to Santana that she and Córdova were more than just friends.

"Why did he have a gun?"

She averted her eyes and looked down at her hands. "I don't know."

Santana sensed that she held something back. Had she been alone, he might have pressed her more.

He said, "Did Córdova have any family living here?"

"No. But Mr. and Mrs. Pérez were like family."

"Rubén belonged to my congregation," Hidalgo said softly. "The Church of the Guardian Angels. He was a fine young man. Incapable of killing anyone."

Santana had heard that said about many of the murderers he put behind bars. It ranked right up there with "I'm innocent" in the convicted felon's book of favorite phrases. Still, he was in no hurry to pin both the Pérez and Mendoza murders on Córdova, at least not until he had solid evidence and a clear motive.

"I'm afraid I'm going to need a little more than that, Miss Torres."

He could tell immediately by the disappointed look on her face that his reply had sounded sarcastic rather than encouraging. He tried a different angle to keep her talking.

"Do you know what Córdova was doing at the Riverview Lofts?"

"I know he was working on a story for the paper," she said, moving to the edge of her chair. "But Rubén never talked about what he was writing until it was nearly finished."

"Did Córdova know Mendoza?"

"Yes."

"Then it's possible Córdova went to the Riverview Lofts to see Mendoza."

"I suppose so."

"Did you know Rafael Mendoza, Miss Torres?"

"Yes. He represented many of the immigrants I work with. He helped them get their papers."

"Do you have any idea why anyone would want to harm Mendoza?"

She shook her head as if she could not conceive of it ever happening. "I don't understand Rubén's or Mr. Mendoza's death. But the last time I spoke with Rubén, he seemed afraid."

"Of what?"

"I don't know."

"When did you speak to him last?"

"About a week ago."

Santana paused before he asked Angelina Torres if she knew Julio Pérez. Her answer might help him establish a connection between Mendoza and Pérez. But it might also lead her to believe that there was a connection between the two murders. And Santana had no credible evidence to draw that conclusion. He had his suspicions, but all he knew for certain was that the last call Pérez made was to Mendoza. Still, he thought it was worth the risk, especially if it helped him solve one or both murders.

"How about Julio Pérez? Did you know him?"

"We went to the same church. I only knew Mr. Pérez through Rubén. He seemed to be a very humble, very private man."

Santana wrote down the information.

"It's quite a coincidence that Mendoza and Pérez's deaths occurred on the same evening?" Hidalgo said.

Santana looked up from his notebook. He had not considered what conclusions Hidalgo might draw from his questions.

"Do you think their deaths are connected, Detective Santana?"

There was a time when Santana would never have lied to a priest. That time had long since past.

"There's no indication of that," he said.

Hidalgo looked for a moment as though he wanted to pursue the possible murder connection in more detail, but then he nodded his head slowly in apparent agreement.

Rather than give the priest more time to think about it, Santana jumped in quickly with another question.

"Pérez and Córdova were members of your parish."

"That's right."

"How about Mendoza? Did you know him?"

Hidalgo set his jaw and tightened his lips. Had Santana not been watching the priest carefully, he would have certainly missed the nearly imperceptible movement. Maybe the whole ordeal surrounding Pérez's death provoked such a strong emotional reaction that Hidalgo chose to keep the full extent of his feelings private, particularly in front of Angelina Torres — or maybe he was actually hiding something.

"I didn't know him well," the priest said.

"Tell me, Father, does your church help immigrants?"

"Of course."

"Illegal immigrants?"

"If someone needs assistance, we provide it. It is not up to us to judge others, Detective. Only God has that power."

Santana got the distinct impression that the pointed statement was directed at him. Apparently felons were not the only ones who had a book of favorite phrases.

"So, Mendoza wasn't a member of your parish?"

"No, he wasn't."

Hidalgo got up suddenly, signaling the end of the conversation.

Angelina Torres hesitated and then stood up as well.

"Please let us know if there's anything we can do," Hidalgo said.

Santana pushed himself out of his chair and handed each of them a business card.

Angelina Torres looked as if she wanted to say something more. But she turned instead and followed Hidalgo out of the cubicle.

Chapter 5

SANTANA AND PETE CANFIELD, from the Ramsey County Attorney's Office, stood beside Reiko Tanabe in the morgue at the medical examiner's office, a one story building just off University Avenue next to Region's Hospital. They were dressed in green scrubs and booties. The ME wore large latex gloves and a disposable plastic apron over the scrubs. Stiff, white masks covered their mouths and noses. Santana and Canfield had rubbed wintergreen oil on the inside of their masks to cut the smell.

Tanabe had removed the black body bag and clean white sheet around Julio Pérez before fingerprinting and photographing his body with and without clothes. The tag that had been attached to his left big toe at the crime scene listed a case number, date, name and location of the body. Tanabe had attached a second tag to Pérez's right ankle when he arrived at the morgue. The tags maintained the chain of evidence and a record of who touched the body intact.

The perforated metal sheet underneath Pérez kept the stainless steel autopsy table in the center of the room clean by allowing running water and body fluids to seep through to a metal catch basin below and down into the drains in the tile floor. A scale used for weighing organs hung over the table. The scale looked like a larger and more precise version of those found at a supermarket. A dissecting block, scalpels, ruler, pruning clippers and an electric vibrating bone saw lay on a smaller steel table opposite the scale. A wide stainless steel refrigerator door covered most of one wall. Jars of preservative on the counter held tissue samples and excised body parts. The temperature hovered just above freezing, and the room reeked of astringent cleaner, tissue preservative and bodies on the verge of decomposition.

"Hey, Doc," Canfield said. "You know the difference between a surgeon, an internist and a pathologist?" He winked at Santana.

"I'm afraid to ask."

"A surgeon knows nothing but does everything. An internist knows everything, but does nothing. And a pathologist knows everything and does everything, but it's too late."

Canfield laughed uproariously at his own joke.

"Blow yourself," Tanabe said, but Santana could tell she was smiling behind her mask.

Santana knew that Canfield told jokes to relieve his uneasiness. Prosecutors, cops, medical examiners, anyone who had to watch a body being eviscerated, had coping mechanisms. Santana remembered how he had vomited the first time. Viewing another autopsy now elicited no more of a response than if he were at the market watching butchers prepare a good cut of steak. He had learned early on that it was important to remain as detached as possible. Each body told a story of how the victim lived and how he died. Emotions often impaired objectivity. Only the body of an innocent child lying on the cold metal table still lit a fire inside him. Whether it was the result of neglect, abuse or homicide, a child's death smoldered within him until the perp was either behind bars or dead.

Tanabe had nearly completed her external evaluation of Pérez's body. She had started with the neck and worked her way downward to the chest, abdomen, pelvis and genitalia, as she spoke into a microphone connected to a digital recorder. This sequence allowed the blood to drain from Pérez's head. Santana knew she would examine it last.

He went over to a second stainless steel table and looked at Rafael Mendoza's naked body. Santana could see immediately that Mendoza had no appendectomy scar. He was not one of the men in the photo Gamboni had found in the loft.

Rubén Córdova's naked body lay on a table next to Mendoza. Córdova had balloon-like paper bags around his hands and feet to entrap any trace evidence. The entry opening in his chest where Anderson's bullet had struck him had drawn together after the bullet passed through the skin. Santana could see the distinct contusion ring around the entrance caused by the bullet scraping off the external layer of epithelial cells. The contusion ring was round; indicating Anderson's bullet had struck Córdova squarely, though no smudge ring was evident because the bullet had first passed through clothing.

Santana walked to the counter and took Córdova's clothing out of the paper bags. Before undressing Córdova, Santana knew Tanabe had carefully examined his clothes for trace evidence. She had then placed his bloody clothing onto clean wrapping paper to let it air-dry before putting it into paper bags. Each item of clothing had been packaged separately and had not been cut. He could see the .40 caliber hole Anderson's bullet had made in Córdova's flannel shirt before it penetrated his body.

"John, can you help me out here?" Tanabe pointed at a clipboard on the counter.

Santana picked it up and returned to the autopsy table.

Having finished her external examination, she used a scalpel to make a U-shaped incision that began at Pérez's left shoulder and continued under his nipples over to the right shoulder. The cut opened Pérez's skin as if the ME were unzipping a coat. She then turned the U into a Y by cutting downward below the sternum to the abdomen. With no heart beating, there was no pressure and very little blood. She called out the weight and measurement of each organ to Santana who wrote them down on a sheet attached to the clipboard. She worked methodically, talking into the microphone as she removed each organ.

When she began work on Pérez's skull, Canfield looked at Santana and said, "You want a cup of coffee?"

"Hot chocolate if you can find some."

"Oh, that's right," he said. "You're the one Colombian in the world who doesn't like coffee. I'll see what I can do." He turned, slid his mask to the top of his head and hurried out of the room.

Tanabe made a deep incision starting just in front of one of Pérez's ear, over the top of his skull, to the other ear. This allowed her to pull the scalp down over the front of Pérez's face. Specks of white dust flew from the circular saw she then used to cut around Pérez's head.

Santana watched calmly as she put down the saw and used a twisting device that looked like a screwdriver to pop open Pérez's skull, as if she were removing a cap from a bottle of beer.

It took a while before she finally found the .22 caliber bullet. Often it was so misshapen that it could not be used for ballistic comparisons, but this time the wait was worth it.

Santana went back to the counter and discarded his mask. He placed the bullet in an evidence envelope and initialed it. The envelope had to be labeled with the initials of the individual collecting the evidence and each person who subsequently had custody of it, along with the date the item was collected and transferred, the case number, type of crime, victim or suspect's name, and a brief description of the item. If someone was ever brought to trial for Pérez's murder, Santana didn't want the evidence thrown out on a technicality.

When Canfield returned with a cup of coffee and no hot chocolate, Santana said, "Any idea when you'll complete the preliminary investigation on Rick Anderson?"

Canfield took a sip of coffee and wrinkled his nose in disgust. "You know I can't discuss the investigation with you, John. But I don't want it to drag on any longer than you do. If the shooting was justified, that's what the report will say."

"Okay. I'll let you know if ballistics matches the bullet Reiko took out of Pérez with the gun we found on Córdova."

"If Córdova is guilty of a double homicide, I sure as hell won't object."

"I won't cut corners, Pete."

Canfield's face darkened, and he stared at Santana with his clear, unwavering hazel eyes. "We've worked a number of cases together before, John. I consider us friends. So I know you'd never suggest that I would. I'm also aware that the mayor is looking for a new running mate and I'm first in line. So before you stick your foot in your mouth again and imply that I'm concerned about the direction the political winds are blowing in this town, I want to be clear that I'll file the same time you do."

Canfield was the Ramsey County Attorney. Minnesota didn't use the term district attorney. He had worked in the Prosecution Division of the Ramsey County Attorney's Office, and had eventually become assistant Ramsey County attorney before being elected to his present position. Attorneys in the Charging and Trial Section of the Prosecution Division handled most of the adult level prosecutions for child abuse, sexual assault, theft, robbery, burglary and murder.

Canfield had been asked several times to run for higher office. He had all the necessary qualifications. He dressed well, wore his dark brown hair just long enough to be fashionable, and could give a terrific speech without offending anyone or saying anything of substance. But he had never expressed a desire to run for higher office. Santana admired him for it.

"I appreciate your candor, Pete. But I'm getting a lot of heat."

"Since when did that start bothering you?"

Santana held up the evidence envelope. "The lab will match this bullet with Córdova's gun."

"If you've got a problem with that and want me to run interference for you, just so say. I'm not going to pin the murders on Córdova unless you can prove he's guilty." Canfield took another sip of coffee. "God, this is awful." He headed toward one of the sinks on the counter. "I hate to admit it, but I may have to switch to hot chocolate."

Large flakes of snow fell as Santana drove back to headquarters. He took the elevator up to the evidence room on the second floor where he filled out a property-booking sheet on the .22 caliber bullet removed from Pérez's brain. He placed the envelope with the bullet in a temporary storage locker where all evidence was stored until the property clerk could log it into the evidence room. The lockers had a self-locking system that could not be reopened from the outside once the door was closed. Each locker had a second door on the property room side that the property officer could open to remove the evidence. The officer could then reach through and release the door latch so the locker could be used again.

Santana asked to see the sexually explicit photo Gamboni had found in Mendoza's loft and the items found on Córdova the night he was shot. The property officer brought him the photo and Córdova's wallet, notebook, and keys. Santana found Córdova's address in the wallet. Then he signed a release for the notebook and the photo and went over to the crime lab adjacent to the evidence room. He pressed the speakerphone button on the wall outside the lab and identified himself.

When the door buzzed open, he entered and found Tony Novak sitting on a metal stool under a bank of fluorescent lights near a large L-shaped metal desk and a couple of four drawer metal filing cabinets. The room smelled of chemicals and looked like a chemistry classroom minus the student desks.

The gray laminate counters were cluttered with microscopes, beakers, volumetric and Erlenmeyer flasks for mixing and boiling substances, graduated cylinders, test tubes, small, concave dishes called watch glasses for dissolving powders and viewing materials under a microscope, a vacuum kit for picking up trace evidence, a television monitor and two VCRs, and a large gas chromatograph linked to a mass spectrometer, often called a GC-mass-spec, for separating and identifying organic substances.

Santana had worked with Novak before and respected his intelligence. A former Golden Glove champion in the late 1970s and early '80s, Novak's once chiseled frame had softened and expanded. He had a computer and printer on the desk along with a framed photograph of his wife and two teenage sons and two books held up with metal bookends. One was entitled the *Manual of Fingerprint Development Techniques* and the other *Scene of Crime Handbook of Fingerprint Development Techniques.* On the wall above the desk was a framed certificate from the International Association for Identification and a framed black and white photo of a handsome young Novak as a middleweight, before he had gotten his nose broken a few times and put on the extra pounds.

"Hey, John," Novak called when he saw Santana.

I SEE DUMB PEOPLE was stitched in large white letters across the front of a black T-shirt Novak wore underneath his open, white lab coat. He got off his stool and came toward Santana, moving lightly on his feet, as though he were still bouncing around the ring.

"I'd like you to take a look at the photo Gamboni found in Mendoza's loft, Tony."

Santana took the photo out of the evidence envelope and showed it to Novak. "I want to know if there is anything we can use to identify the guy on his knees."

"What about the guy standing?"

"Look closely. He's got what appears to be an appendectomy scar."

Novak's mustache and short curly hair were both gray, and as he tilted his head forward to look down at the photo, Santana could see the small, round bald spot on the crown of his head.

"That's what it looks like to me. Fairly recent, I'd say. Although this isn't a real clear photo," Novak said, pushing his heavy black frame glasses back up to the bridge of his wide nose. "Let me guess. You need to know soon."

"Very. Along with the results of the ballistics test on the .22 Córdova had on him the night he was killed. I just put the bullet Tanabe removed from Julio Pérez in a temporary locker."

"You think they'll match?"

"I'd bet on it."

"We still on for the Chandler fight on the twenty-seventh?"

"Maybe."

"Well," Novak said with a shrug, "I don't know when I'll be able to get to this, John. I'm really backed up here."

"So you're not going to help me out if I don't go to the fight with you?"

"Did I say that?"

Santana let out a sigh. "Okay. You're on."

"Great," Novak said with a big grin. He headed back to the microscope he had been looking through when Santana entered the lab. "We'll stop at Mancini's for dinner first. You can buy."

"Eat a big lunch," Santana said.

He found another stool at the counter. He spent the next twenty minutes paging through the spiral notebook Córdova used for his interviews until he reached the last page dated two days ago. If Córdova had talked with Mendoza, he had not taken any notes.

Snow was still falling. The flakes were smaller than before, but more numerous. Santana brushed off the windows of his Crown Vic before driving to the offices of *El Día,* which were located in a small, one level brick building on the West Side of St. Paul. The chairs in the reception area were vinyl-padded and had aluminum legs, as did the Formica topped coffee table. On the table were two copies of the latest edition of the paper and on the walls were framed certificates recognizing it as a member of the National Federation of Hispanic Newspapers and the Minnesota Newspaper Association.

Santana spent two hours interviewing the staff that consisted of a receptionist, a marketing and sales manager, an art director, a photographer and two contributing writers. Everyone appeared upset by Julio Pérez's murder and seemed to have concrete alibis for the day and approximate time of his death. Santana made a note to check out each alibi. Then he moved on to Pérez's office where he went through the dead man's desk, date book and papers. Nothing he looked at seemed important or offered clues to Pérez's murder, so he walked down the hall to Rubén Córdova's office.

In a desk drawer, Santana came across Córdova's calendar and appointment book. He flipped the pages until he found yesterday's date. Córdova's handwriting was nearly illegible, but he had no appointment scheduled with Julio Pérez. He had, however, scribbled Mendoza's name on the line next to 7:30 p.m., which placed him at the crime scene at the time Mendoza died. In a space below the line, Córdova had scrawled what looked like the words: *learn more about scandal.*

Experience had taught Santana that most criminals were as bright as a dimly lit bulb, despite how they were portrayed on television crime shows and in movies. Córdova appeared to be even dimmer than most. Along with his appointment book, he had conveniently left a .22 caliber cartridge in Julio Pérez's study that could be matched to the weapon used in the killing. The evidence clearly suggested that Córdova murdered Pérez and then Mendoza. Then why, Santana thought, did he still have doubts?

Chapter 6

Rubén Córdova lived in Frogtown, one of St. Paul's most diverse neighborhoods. A mile and a half square area bounded by University and Lexington Avenues, Rice Street and Pierce-Butler Route, Frogtown was a working class neighborhood, settled by Germans, Poles, Swedes and Hungarians in the 1880s, immigrants who wanted to be close to their jobs in the railroad yards and those who worked in the industries that developed as a result of the railroads. Asians were the majority now, with whites and blacks in the minority. The area had the highest crime rate in the city until the SPPD instituted a weed and seed program that targeted drug dealers. Called Operation Sunrise, the weed part of the program managed to lower crime by pushing the dealers and prostitutes into other neighborhoods, but economic development had stalled due to a lack of funds.

Legend had it that Frogtown got its name from the French who first settled the area, or from the late Archbishop, John Ireland, who named the area Frogtown after he heard frogs croaking in the wetlands near Calvary Cemetery.

The houses along Charles Street were built in the 1930s and '40s and their dark windows looked out onto the street like eyes blinded by cataracts. Córdova lived in small, white, two-storied clapboard with a peaked roof and an enclosed porch that looked as though it had been added as an afterthought. Two porch windows were covered with plastic instead of glass and the paint was chipped and peeling. A satellite dish attached to the flat porch roof looked as out of place as a sailboat in the desert.

A dog began barking in the yard behind the house as Santana walked up the sidewalk that was now covered with three inches of snow. The flakes came down fast and were accumulating at an inch every hour.

Santana opened the screen door and entered the porch. Gamboni was working on a search warrant, but the doorjamb looked worn and weak. Inserting a pry bar horizontally across the doorframe, he pushed until the bolt popped free from the striker plate and he could easily open the front door. He leaned the pry bar against the siding and took a moment to examine the bolt. A series of fresh scratches ran lengthwise along it indicating someone had used a sharp instrument to force it back. He jotted the information down in his notebook and then went into the house.

The stained and worn beige carpet in the living room had a heavy odor of dog. Each piece of furniture looked second hand. On the wall above the bureau in a glass frame was a red flag with a white circle in the middle. Inside the circle was a black Aztec eagle. FARMWORKERS was stenciled in black letters above the eagle and AFL-CIO was below it.

Santana always felt like a thief as he walked through each room in a stranger's house, looking for clues or evidence that could help solve their murder. While he entered their property and searched their most intimate papers and belongings, the ME carved up their naked bodies and examined each of their organs. No privacy existed for the victim of a homicide.

Santana went into the kitchen. Dirty dishes littered the sink and counter. No messages were recorded on Córdova's answering machine. He looked through the drawers and cupboards and then opened the door leading to the backyard. A Golden Retriever stopped barking and looked at him with sad, curious eyes.

Santana went back inside and got a can of Alpo dog food from the cupboard. He opened it and used a tablespoon to scoop the food into one of two plastic bowls on the floor next to the refrigerator. He filled the second bowl with fresh water, left the back door open and walked down the hall and checked out the bathroom.

The tub and sink had a permanent rust ring. Santana scanned the medicine cabinet for drugs and then went into the bedroom where he searched the dresser drawers and walk-in closet, saving Córdova's desk for last.

He found no ammunition and no permit for the .22 caliber gun Córdova had supposedly used to murder Julio Pérez. But he did find two 4 x 6 framed photos on the dresser. One was a photo of Rubén Córdova with Angelina Torres. Córdova had an arm around her waist and a youthful, exuberant smile obviously fueled by love. The other photo was of Julio Pérez and his wife, Sandra, their daughter, Gabriela, Rubén Córdova and Angelina Torres. It had apparently been taken outside the Church of the Guardian Angels. Santana put the family photo in the pocket of his overcoat, the frame under a pile of underwear in the dresser.

He sat on the chair in front of the desk in the corner where he opened the Apple laptop and turned on the computer. In a moment it booted up in a bright blue color and several icons appeared on the screen. Córdova had obviously assumed he would be the only one ever using his computer and, therefore, needed no password.

Santana moved the arrow using the touch pad and touch pad button in front of the keypad and clicked on a folder entitled *El Día*. In a moment the folder opened and a list of individual files appeared, organized by names and dates. He quickly realized that the files were stories Córdova had completed or was currently working on. He scanned the list and clicked on one labeled Mendoza.

When the file opened, he saw that it contained a series of notes Córdova had compiled. He felt a surge of adrenaline as he read them. Córdova was writing a story about Mexicans obtaining illegal worker visas. Córdova had suspected Mendoza was somehow involved and had previously interviewed him. The last line of the final paragraph written in capital letters read: THIS MAY BE ONLY PART OF THE STORY.

Santana sat back and remembered what Gamboni had told him. Connect the dots. Córdova worked for Pérez at *El Día* and had scheduled an interview with Mendoza for a story he was writing. Clearly there was a connection. Santana made a note to check Córdova's phone records. But if Córdova was responsible for two murders, then what was his motive? What did he have to gain by murdering Mendoza and Pérez? According to Angelina Torres, Pérez and his family had reached out to Córdova. Why then would Córdova turn around and murder Pérez?

Santana closed the Mendoza file and clicked on a few others. All the stories were well written but contained nothing relating to the case. He closed out the folder and opened the Quicken icon containing Córdova's financial records. As sloppy as Córdova was about his house, he was just the opposite when it came to his finances. He had kept precise records of his transactions including his gas and grocery bills, his monthly payment on a thirty-year mortgage, his car payment and MasterCard bill. He had a little over a thousand dollars in a TCF bank saving's account and fifty-six in his checking account as of the end of December. Córdova, like most Americans, lived paycheck to paycheck. If he made any money in the visa scam, he wasn't living like it.

Santana shut down the computer and opened a lower desk drawer on his right. Inside a manila folder, he found Córdova's phone records. Santana took out his notebook, located the page where he had written Mendoza's phone number, and checked Córdova's December wireless bill until he found a match. Córdova had called Mendoza three times from his cell prior to his death. Córdova made the third and last call to Mendoza on the same day Mendoza died.

A sudden noise startled Santana and instinctively he reached for his Glock, but hesitated when he saw the retriever standing in the bedroom doorway. The dog took a couple of hesitant steps toward him, its head lowered in submission.

Santana called and the dog came immediately. The name on the dog collar was *Gitana* or Gypsy. Her tail thumped against the desk as Santana pet her coat, still wet from the falling snow. He thought the name fit. She had lost her owner and was alone.

Santana swung by Mickey's Diner on West Seventh Street. Listed on the National Register of Historic Places, the art deco red-cream dining car had appeared in a number of Hollywood movies. The food was cheap and the clientele eclectic. Posted signs warned of a two-person minimum per booth and a three-dollar minimum per person.

He sat on an open stool at the counter and ordered a hot roast beef sandwich with mashed potatoes and gravy. Having dropped the dog at an animal shelter, he could not forget the look she had given him when he left her there.

He took the computer printouts Baker and Hawkins had collected from Mendoza's law office out of his briefcase and placed them on the counter. He spent little time on each page since it appeared that most of what he had in front of him were memos from cases Mendoza had worked on, but it took him a long time to shorten the stack simply because there were so many pages. Three-fourths of the way through the stack, he wondered if he was wasting his time. Then he came across a page entitled VISA REQUESTS. The names were similar to those in the files at Mendoza's loft in that they were Hispanic, and all of them were supposedly working at restaurants around the Twin Cities. He recognized many of the restaurants, but one stood out more than the rest. The *Casa Blanca*; the restaurant managed by Gabriela Pérez.

Chapter 7

HEAVY SNOWFALL SNARLED downtown traffic. Like judges gone berserk, beleaguered forecasters who earlier had predicted a moderate one to two inch snowfall kept raising the sentence by four to six inches.

Santana drove the Crown Vic to the station and took his four-wheel drive Explorer out of the lot. It took twenty-five minutes to reach Interstate 94 where cars continued moving tentatively along escorted by MnDOT plows.

He called dispatch for Gabriela Pérez's address. She lived in a small, gray, two-story townhouse in Woodbury that overlooked a pond and woods about a half-mile from an outlet mall and a Holiday Inn. A light wind blew the snow into drifts that were nearly up to his knees. He stomped it off his pants legs and boots as he stood under an eave on her lighted front stoop and pushed the bell. She opened the door on the second ring.

"Remember me? Detective Santana. St. Paul Police Department." He held up his badge wallet.

Her dark eyes stared at him for a long moment before she finally said, "I remember."

"Something has come up regarding the investigation. I wonder if I could come in?" He kept his tone neutral and nonthreatening, like he was merely asking for directions.

She had one hand on the doorknob and the other fisted on her hip. She wore a bulky pullover with Victoria's Secret stitched across the front, black tights and no shoes. Her tousled, shoulder-length hair and faded makeup and lipstick gave him the impression that she had recently arrived home and decided to change into something comfortable.

"There's a storm coming," she said.

Santana gestured toward the heavens and smiled. "It's already here."

"Then you shouldn't stay too long," she said, stepping back and allowing him to enter.

He walked into the foyer, left his boots on a rug on the tile floor and handed her his wool overcoat, which she tossed over a wicker chair in the kitchen. She led him down a short hallway, past the stairs to the second level, and into the small living room where she directed him to a cushioned leather chair.

She drew the drapes over a sliding glass door along one wall, turned off the television and sat down on the couch across from him with her legs tucked under her. A half-empty wine glass and open bottle of Kendall-Jackson rested on the bleached oak coffee table in front of her, beside the latest *Vanidades* and *People* magazines. A fire burned in the glass-door fireplace next to him.

"Have you caught the person who murdered my father, Detective? Is that what was so important that you had to drive out here in a snow storm?"

He could have told her that he had a suspect, but his doubts about Córdova were growing faster than the drifts of snow.

"Not yet."

"Then what was so urgent that you had to talk to me tonight?"

He retrieved the notebook from an inner pocket of his sport coat. "I needed to ask you if you recognized some names."

"Couldn't you have phoned?"

"Perhaps. But your house is on my way home."

"Maybe you just wanted to see how I would react to your questions?"

She was right, though he would never admit it to her.

"Maybe you suspect me of murdering my own father?" she said, giving him a hard stare.

"No, Miss Pérez. I don't suspect you of anything." *At least not yet,* he thought.

Her hard look lasted a moment longer. Then her gaze softened and she reached for the glass of wine on the coffee table and took a sip.

"I'm sorry if I offended you, Detective. But I hope you understand. I want to know who killed my father and why." Raising her glass, she said, "Would you like something to drink?"

"No. Thank you."

She held the wine glass close to her lips and watched him. "Tell me something, Detective Santana. Are you a man who always follows the rules?"

"Always would be pushing it. Why do you ask?"

"I remember that it often seemed like there were no rules in Mexico."

"Not much different in Colombia," he said.

She smiled grudgingly.

"You weren't born here, Miss Pérez."

"No, in Mexico City. My father was a journalist. He did a series of reports on the drug cartels. When he began receiving death threats, he moved us here. I was seventeen at the time."

"Could that be a reason why your father was killed?"

"That was many years ago, *señor.*"

"The drug cartels have very long memories."

"So I have heard."

"Was your father doing any investigative work here?"

"He'd had enough of it in Mexico. The corruption. The killing. The drug lords were gaining more power every day. *El Día* is different. Its focus is on community issues. My father wanted to bring people together here. Not tear them apart."

She poured more wine.

"Who will run the paper now?"

"I believe my father wanted Rubén Córdova to take over once he retired. Now, I don't know. My mother has no interest. And I enjoy managing the restaurant."

"Tell me what you know about Córdova."

She peered at the glass of wine in her hand and considered the question before responding.

"He was young and enthusiastic. My father gave him a job as a reporter when he came here from California. I believe he had won an award for some stories he had written involving the *braceros* and pesticides. My father eventually made him editor. I did not know Rubén well, though I am surprised the papers are saying he is a suspect in Rafael Mendoza's murder."

"So you didn't know Mendoza."

She shook her head.

"But Córdova was a member of the Church of the Guardian Angels. The same as your family."

"I must confess I have not been to church in quite some time."

That makes two of us, Santana thought.

"You said at the door that something's come up regarding the investigation, Detective Santana."

"Yes, I did. How long have you worked at the *Casa Blanca* restaurant?"

"Nearly three years."

"Then you would remember the names of the cooks that worked at the restaurant during that time."

"Some of them, I suppose."

Santana reached into a pocket and took out the paper with the list of illegals Nick Baker and Kacie Hawkins had retrieved from Rafael Mendoza's office computer.

A slim black cat ambled into the living room and peered at Santana as if he were a large rodent.

The cat came over to him and arched its back and rubbed it along one pants leg and then the other.

"She likes you, Detective."

Santana rubbed his suddenly itchy eyes. "For some reason, they always do."

He read from a list of names generated from Mendoza's office computer.

"I don't recognize any of them," she said.

Next he read from the list he had created from the files in Mendoza's loft, starting with José López.

"Why are you asking me this, Detective Santana?" She placed her feet on the floor and leaned forward as the cat jumped up on the couch and curled up next to her. "These names are all Hispanic. Do you think I am bringing illegal workers into the country?"

"It would help if you thought about a possible connection between your father and Rafael Mendoza."

"Well," she said suddenly angry, "the connection is not that my father was helping him run illegals into the country."

"Then what was the connection?"

"I have no idea. I told you before that my father never knew …" she stopped speaking. Her lower jaw dropped and her eyes widened. "My God! You think Rubén Córdova killed Mendoza and my father."

She sat back on the couch and stared straight at him. But he could tell by her glazed look that she was not seeing anything.

"I have no evidence to support that."

She sat stiffly on the couch for a time before her eyes finally blinked and seemed to focus again.

"Please don't be evasive, *señor*. Why else would you be asking me these questions about my father, Mendoza and Córdova?"

"There's no sense in speculating, Miss Pérez. I'm still gathering evidence."

"Why?" she asked. "Why would Córdova do this?" She took another drink of wine and ran a hand through her hair.

"Miss Pérez. It's very important that you think about this carefully. How long had your father known Mendoza?"

"My father did not know him."

"Mendoza's card was in your father's Rolodex."

"I was close to my father. I knew all his friends."

"What about your mother? Would she remember?"

"She already told you what I have told you." The frustration was evident in her voice. "Besides, my mother is in no condition to answer more questions, Detective. My father's funeral is in two days."

"Could your father have known Mendoza in Mexico before he came here?"

"I do not know. It is possible, I suppose."

"Where was your father born?"

"In Valladolid. But even if my father had known Mendoza years ago in Mexico, what could he have done that got him killed now? And what does any of this have to do with Rubén Córdova?"

Santana didn't respond. But he intended to find out.

Chapter 8

WET SNOW AND FREEZING MOISTURE from car exhaust coated Interstate 94 with black ice, and cars moved slowly along like novice skaters on a recently flooded rink. A large snowplow loomed in Santana's rearview mirror. He could tell by its size that it was one of the new 30-ton Superplows that MnDOT had purchased. The trucks were loaded with sand and had onboard computers, guidance systems and video cameras. He considered pulling over and letting it pass, but he knew that once he got behind it his Explorer would be pelted with sand and salt, damaging the finish and possibly the windshield. He decided to take his chances on the slippery freeway. He accelerated, putting some distance between the snowplow and the SUV.

He found it difficult to focus on driving instead of his conversation with Gabriela Pérez. From the beginning of the investigation, he had believed there was a connection between Julio Pérez and Rafael Mendoza. Perhaps Pérez and Mendoza had known each other in Mexico, and that association had somehow started a chain of events that inevitably led to their murders. He needed to find out more about Mendoza's background and how Rubén Córdova fit into all of it.

Santana took the County Road 18 exit south and followed the tire tracks made by previous cars for about a quarter mile. He turned left onto Fourth Street, drove down four blocks and turned onto a narrow road, which ran parallel to the river. More snow had accumulated here than on the well-traveled freeway. The Explorer muscled its way in four-wheel drive through ever deepening drifts before the road dipped slightly and the sheer weight and depth of the snow forced him to stop fifty feet from his driveway. He shifted into reverse, but the rear tires spun helplessly on the ice. When he tried opening the driver's side door, it refused to budge. He envisioned the headlines in tomorrow's *Pioneer Press*: DETECTIVE TRAPPED IN CAR FREEZES TO DEATH.

He turned off the engine and headlights. Sat in the darkness thinking. Noted that something or someone had shattered the bulb in the nearest streetlight. Finally, he decided to crawl through the cargo area and out the tailgate. He unbuckled his seatbelt, slipped out of his overcoat and sport coat and unclipped his holster. As he adjusted the seat to give himself more room to move, he heard the rattle of chains and the scraping of metal against blacktop. In the rearview mirror he could see a MnDOT plow turning into the street behind him, sweeping snow aside like a gigantic steel broom. It seemed odd that this narrow stretch of road would be plowed so soon. Usually it was one of the last roads to be plowed, which was why he had bought the Explorer, but he wasn't complaining. All he had to do was wait and the blacktop would be clear enough for him to back up.

Snow arched like a geyser off the plow as the truck picked up speed, coming toward him, pushing a white wave ahead of it. Headlights bore down on him. Santana suddenly felt a prickling sensation on his skin and a rush of adrenaline. The truck wasn't slowing down.

He slammed his shoulder against the driver's side door, tried to force it open as a wall of snow thundered down on the roof. The plow caught the Explorer's right rear bumper in one grinding crunch, lifted the SUV off the ground and momentarily out of the snow. In that split second, Santana got the driver's side door open enough to hurl himself free amid chunks of ice that clubbed him across the head and shoulders. Dazed, lost in an avalanche of snow, he barely avoided a truck tire by rolling away from it at the last second.

The ground trembled as the plow pushed the Explorer forward and hammered it like a nail against a thick oak tree on the side of the road. The collision triggered the airbags and collapsed the Explorer's front end. Steam hissed into the air, leaving an acrid odor, as fluid from the shattered radiator drained over the hot engine. A loud, repetitive beeping began as the truck shifted gears, backed up and stopped.

Santana rose to his hands and knees and then into a crouch. He knew from the moment the snowplow hit the Explorer that it was no accident, that it had been following him on the freeway. Once the driver discovered Santana had gotten out of the SUV alive, he would come looking. Instinctively, Santana reached for his Glock. Then he remembered he had left it on the front seat in the Explorer.

The snowplow was at a forty-five degree angle with its front tires on the shoulder of the road, directly behind the back end of the crumpled Explorer. Light from the truck's headlights reflecting off the SUV painted the scene in an eerie glow and cast long shadows along the roadway, as if dark spirits were crawling out from graves.

Santana brushed away the snow clinging to him and cleared his head with a deep breath. The plow had swept away most of the fresh snow. What remained on the road was icy and compacted. He moved fast behind a huge rear tire on the passenger side of the truck. The metal rotor was still turning, spitting bits of sand on the pavement. Clouds blanketed the moon. The truck's headlights and the red glow from its taillights was all that illuminated the darkness along this stretch of road.

A pair of heavy boots hit the ground as the driver jumped down from the cab. He checked the action on an automatic and walked to the Explorer.

Santana moved past the spinning rotor again and crouched near the left rear taillight. Peering around the corner, he saw the driver up ahead in the headlights.

He wore a red ski jacket and knit stocking cap and carried a gun in his right hand. He wrenched open the Explorer's driver side door with his left hand, pulled back and whirled around. He looked in the direction of the side of the road and the stone wall in front of Santana's house. Then he crept away from the SUV, knees bent, holding the gun steady with both hands, as only a professional would.

Santana had no weapon. But he had his wits, the cover of darkness and the element of surprise. The situation reminded him of the moment he began living in the shadow of death. The moment he realized that he had to accept death in order to control his fear of it. Fear often led to mistakes; mistakes that could cost him his life. And though he had long ago accepted the inevitability of an early death, he had vowed never to go quietly.

The driver moved cautiously toward the truck again, climbed up into the cab. The bed rumbled.

He thinks I'm hiding up in the truck bed.

The huge bed whined and rose slowly like some mechanical monster rising out of the earth. Sand poured out the tailgate. Santana turned and ran counterclockwise around the rapidly growing sand pile and along the passenger side. He stopped near the front tire and looked underneath the truck. The gunman climbed down from the cab and headed toward the sand pile. Looking for Santana to slide out the tailgate. Waiting to put a bullet in Santana's brain.

Santana rolled under the truck and out the other side behind the gunman and got to his feet. He could tell that the dark silhouette just ahead of him was about three inches shorter, more wide than lean. Santana came in low, hard and fast. He drove his right shoulder just below the back of the knees. Hooked both arms around the gunman's legs and took him down like a free safety tackling a squat, powerful, running back. Then Santana was on his feet again.

The man rolled onto his back and raised the gun and aimed it in Santana's direction. Santana kicked it. The muzzle flashed and the gun flew out of the man's hand. Santana felt a bullet whiz past his left ear a split second before he heard the explosion of gunfire and a round slap into the metal siding of the truck.

Santana bent down and gripped the gunman's ski jacket with both hands, jerked him off the ground. He blocked a looping punch with his left arm; drove his right fist into the man's solar plexus, heard the wind rush out of him, as if he were a balloon losing air. Then he threw a right cross that caught the man solidly on the jaw and sent him stumbling backward. Santana stepped forward quickly, grabbed the gunman's right wrist and spun him one hundred eighty degrees and threw him into the sand pile. The man cried out.

Santana wasn't sure what had happened until he saw the dark stream squirting out of the man's neck. Then he realized that the sharp metal rotor at the back of the truck had cut easily through the thin layer of exposed skin, sliced open the carotid artery.

"Hijueputa malparido," the gunman said in a raspy voice.

Santana recognized the Colombian accent.

The man struggled to his knees. Tore off his stocking cap. He pressed it against the wound, trying to stop the bleeding. It took two minutes before he went into hemorrhagic shock and three more before he bled out, toppled forward and lost consciousness.

Santana dragged him off the sand pile and rolled him over. He unzipped the ski jacket, searched the pockets for an ID he knew he would not find.

The metal rotor continued spinning, flinging bits of sand, flesh, and blood into the air.

Breathing hard, shivering from the cold now, his face and bare hands burning from the wet snow, his ears ringing from the gunshot, Santana looked upward at the unending darkness. They had come for him again. And he knew they wouldn't quit until he was dead.

Chapter 9

DAY 3

FLASHING RED LIGHTS FROM THE ROW of squad cars parked along the blacktop road in front of Santana's house pulsed like hearts pumping blood across a bruised sky. Heavy snow had turned to flurries, and a gusty, northwest wind created miniature tornados that whirled out of the snow.

The oak and birch logs burning in the fireplace and a glass of aguardiente had warmed Santana's chilled bones. The ice bag he held over his right hand had reduced the swelling and numbed the throbbing pain in his knuckles.

"Why don't we go through it one more time, John, just to make sure I've got everything."

He turned and looked at Rita Gamboni in her burgundy ribbed turtleneck and stonewashed jeans, sitting on the leather couch and holding a notebook and pen in her hands. Then he walked away from the window and sat down in a leather chair across from her.

"All right. I got stuck in the road near my driveway. A plow deliberately rammed the Explorer and pushed it into a tree in front of my house."

"Okay. Go on."

"The driver got out carrying a 9 mm Beretta." Santana pointed to the gun in an evidence envelope on the coffee table. "If he didn't intend to kill me, Rita, then what's the Beretta for?"

"And your weapon was still in the Explorer?"

"I left it in the SUV when I exited rather quickly."

She paused for a moment, taking it all in, before she continued. "There was a struggle. The metal rotor that spreads sand and salt on the road sliced open his carotid artery and he bled to death. Is that right?" Her tone was incredulous.

When Santana didn't respond, she let out a long, slow breath. "So who the hell was this guy, John?"

"He had no ID."

"You think it has something to do with the Pérez-Mendoza murders?"

"I don't know."

She stared at him without speaking. Finally, she said, "Why is it that I think you're not telling me everything?"

"Cops get that way after a few years, Rita. They don't trust anyone. Apparently, not even their ex-partners."

Her expression hardened. "Don't hand me that bullshit, John. You want me to trust you, yet you won't trust me with the truth."

"Just do me a favor and write this one off as a nut case, Rita. MnDOT driver goes berserk."

"It's not that simple. The actual MnDOT driver was found unconscious in the cab of the truck. He was hit in the head. Sustained a mild concussion, but he'll recover. No, John," she said, shaking her head in denial. "This guy didn't just suddenly go berserk. He took out the driver and went after you. If this doesn't have anything to do with the Pérez-Mendoza case, then I want to know why you're a target."

She tossed her notebook and pen on the coffee table in front of her and got up off the couch. She walked in front of the fire where she stood in profile with her arms crossed.

The fire crackled as flames stripped the bark off the birch logs. She had been at him for over an hour now. The hot shower, aguardiente and fire, along with her persistence, had just about drained the last of the adrenaline out of him.

"It was a long time ago, Rita. I made some enemies in Colombia. They don't forget. Ever. That's all I can tell you for now."

She picked up a small plaque that was on the mantel and quietly read the inscription.

Santana knew she had read it before because she had joked with him about it over breakfast one morning. The inscription read:

> *Life is nothing but a competition to be the criminal rather than the victim.*
>
> Bertrand Russell

She turned and looked at him. "You ever think Russell was wrong about this?"

"No."

"What makes you so damn sure? The job?"

"Among other things."

She set the plaque down gently on the mantel and looked at him again. "This isn't the first time they've come after you, is it?"

He said nothing.

"And you're not afraid?"

He hadn't had time to be afraid. It had all been reaction. Fight and live. Or panic and die.

"Fear leads to panic and panic is the enemy of survival," he said. "I may be a target, Rita, but I refuse to be a victim."

She gave a slow shake of her head. "You're dangerous, John. To yourself and to others."

"You going to put this in my jacket?"

"I could. And I could suspend you. Until we complete an investigation."

He had worked with her long enough to know that she was bluffing. Still, he knew he would have to tell her more soon. He was running out of favors.

"I just gave you more information than any investigation will ever turn up, Rita. This guy, whoever he is, doesn't exist in any data bank. Believe me. The people we're dealing with made sure of that."

"Then what am I supposed to do?"

"Write it off as an accident."

"Just like that," she said, as if she could not imagine how this whole investigation would end.

"He'll be another John Doe down at the morgue. No one will come looking for him. Let me get back to the case." He let her think about it before he continued. "Ask yourself this, Rita. If our roles were reversed, what would I do?"

"Dammit, John, if I let this go for now, I want to know everything when the murder book is closed on Pérez and Mendoza. No more secrets between us."

"All right."

She went back to the couch and sat down with a heavy sigh.

His eyes met hers and he knew immediately there was something she was holding back.

"What is it?" he asked.

She waited.

"What?" he asked again.

She looked at him for a moment longer. Then she said, "The lab found more than one set of prints on the .22 we found on Córdova."

A fresh rush of adrenaline shot through Santana. He sat up in the leather chair.

"We also got a palm print we couldn't run through the AFIS data base," she said.

Santana knew that the Automated Fingerprint Identification Systems could not be searched for palm prints.

"One set of prints matches Córdova. But we got another match with a fingerprint out of San Diego." She smiled.

"And?" Santana said.

Gamboni held the smile and her secret.

"Come on, Rita."

"How does it feel?" she asked, obviously enjoying his frustration.

"Like hell. Now tell me."

"You know when you apply for citizenship, you have to be fingerprinted."

"The name," he said with a nod.

"A woman named Torres," she said. "Angelina Torres."

The next morning as Santana rode into downtown with a patrol officer, the sun's red rays seeped through a thin bank of clouds like blood through gauze. The Crown Vic he signed out of the 11th Street lot was nothing more than a stripped down version of a squad car with the cage removed. He was certain his insurance company would write off the Explorer as a total loss, and he was thankful that he had the use of the Crown Vic. He had no time to look for a new SUV.

A northwest wind had sent the temperature plummeting faster than a skydiver without a chute. It pushed the big car to the left as he drove across the Wabasha Bridge over the Mississippi River. Small American flags atop each of the bridge supports flapped in the wind. Along the riverbank to the west, Santana could see the empty marina on Raspberry Island where the Minnesota Boat Club docked its boats in summer. At a traffic light at Plato and Wabasha he watched as an elderly black man with his right leg in a walking cast limped across the street and headed for the HealthPartner's clinic on the corner. Buffeted by a sudden gust, the old man swayed like a drunk as he moved tentatively along the sidewalk. Santana wondered if the man had broken his leg falling on an icy sidewalk, as so many senior citizens were prone to do.

Just south of the light, Del Sol pennants began appearing on lampposts. Mexican families had first immigrated to the West Side of St. Paul as early as 1900 after the original Wabasha, Robert and High bridges were completed across the Mississippi. Crop failures in the state's sugar beet fields after World War I forced poor migrant workers to seek employment in the city. Many became permanent residents. Since the 1900s, the Mexican population had swelled in St. Paul to more than sixteen thousand.

Santana drove past the Torres de San Miguel housing project and the Boca Chica restaurant. He merged onto Cesar Chávez Avenue and then onto State Street in the Latino commercial district.

Before Gamboni had left his house last night, Santana told her that Angelina Torres and Father Thomas Hidalgo had come to see him yesterday at the station. He went over his notes with her, reviewing the conversation he'd had with Gabriela Pérez about her father and a possible Mexican connection with Rafael Mendoza.

When he finished recounting the conversation, Gamboni explained that the gun found on Córdova was reported stolen in California. He had asked her to update Baker and Hawkins and requested that they interview a short list of *El Día* employees to make sure their alibis were solid. The give and take discussion reminded Santana of how it used to be with Rita when they were partners and lovers.

The office where Angelina Torres worked was located in a converted, two-story apartment building. Santana parked in the lot out front and walked under a green canopy and in the main entrance.

A receptionist sitting behind a counter directed him to a hallway and to Angelina Torres' small, windowless office.

"Detective Santana," she said, standing to shake his hand.

She wore a black skirt, turquoise blouse, a thin gold necklace with a heart, and small gold earrings.

"Tome asiento, por favor," she said, closing the door and pointing to a chair.

Santana sat down on a steel-legged chair with black vinyl pads opposite her desk. The walls of her office were bare except for a framed diploma from the University of Southern California. Next to him was a glass table with today's edition of the *Pioneer Press*. One of the stories on the front page was about an unidentified illegal immigrant who stole a MnDOT truck after rendering the driver unconscious. The story went on to say that:

> The man apparently lost control of the vehicle near the town of St. Croix Beach where he died in a collision with an Explorer driven by John Santana, a St. Paul homicide detective. The detective escaped serious injury.

A separate story further down the page described the deaths of nine illegal immigrants who were crammed into a pickup that crossed the median on Interstate 80 in Iowa at 2:40 a.m. and collided with a tractor-trailer. All of the victims were Hispanic men and women.

"I've been reading about you, Detective. Are you all right?"

The soreness in Santana's right hand stilled throbbed with each beat of his heart. "Fine."

"Have you found out something that might clear Rubén?"

"Not yet. I'd just like to ask you a few more questions."

"If it will help," she said, and sat down in a chair facing him.

He had considered bringing a tape recorder along, but figured it might intimidate Angelina Torres. He didn't want her to know yet that she was a suspect in Rafael Mendoza's death and possibly in Julio Pérez's death as well. Once she was Mirandized and placed under arrest, she could get a lawyer who could derail the whole investigation.

He took out his notebook and a pen. Rather than interrogating her, Santana preferred a low-key interview so he could watch how she reacted to the questions he had mentally prepared. This would give him a chance to find out more about her background and to build rapport. He would have to rely on his intuitive skills and the training he'd had in college.

While majoring in criminology with a minor in criminal psychology, he had studied the Facial Action Coding System or FACS, based on the work of Paul Ekman and Wallace Friesen. Through years of research, the two psychologists had created a taxonomy of about three thousand facial expressions. Santana had been trained to look for discrepancies between what someone said and what was signaled through facial expressions. It wasn't a perfect science, but it gave Santana an edge.

"How long have you been in the states, Miss Torres?"

"For ten years."

"Are your parents still living in California?"

He could tell by the way the corner of her lips drew down that they were not living in California or anywhere else.

Finally she said, "Like many of the *braceros,* they died of cancer."

"Lo siento," Santana said.

"You know Spanish, Detective, but you are not Mexican."

"Colombian."

A smile flickered across her face. "Do Colombians know anything about what happened to the *braceros* working in the fields?"

"I know a little something about Cesar Chávez."

"Then you know how he organized the workers before he died. But the pesticides are still being used in California.

Toxins like meta-sodium and chlorpyrifos. Workers are still not being told that a field is restricted. Employers do not provide translators when there is a complaint. When the government comes to investigate illnesses, the employer is there during the interview. The workers won't speak up in front of them because they are afraid."

She was remembering it all now, and the tone of her voice grew angrier.

"It is illegal not to give farm workers, even undocumented ones, breaks, toilets or drinking water. It is illegal to pay them for less than four hours of work per day and not to pay overtime. It is illegal to charge them for rides or tools. But these abuses happen all the time. If the workers complain, they are fired. They have no legal recourse. Even if they did, the companies could hire very expensive attorneys to shield them from litigation."

Santana recalled the AFL-CIO farm worker's flag he had seen in Córdova's house. "So you have sympathy for the illegals."

"Who keeps the service economy of this country running? You think the whites want to mop floors, clean toilets and flip burgers? Illegals are doing the jobs no one else wants. Businesses hire them cheap because they are afraid to join unions. Once in awhile ICE closes some small business for hiring illegals. That way they can claim they are doing something. But everyone knows what's going on. The schools, the businesses. So, yes, I have sympathy for illegals. Don't you?"

"There are legal means of entering the country."

She grimaced. "If you were desperate, and there was nothing for you in your own country, then you might think differently."

"I might."

She nodded as if to say, "I told you so."

"What about you, Miss Torres? Are you illegal?"

She remained silent for a time before responding. "Once," she said. "But now I have my papers and my citizenship."

"You ever help get any illegals into the country?"

"No. I only want illegals to be treated fairly when they are here." Her tone was calmer now, but he could hear the frustration in her voice. "Many of the young people I see in my office have tried working, but they have no rights. They see no future. Some give up and turn to crime."

Santana remembered the Hispanic kid in the Bay Point Restaurant and the kids he had seen hanging around street corners in their baggy pants and do-rags. He wondered what he would have eventually chosen if he had not had Philip and Dorothy O'Toole to help him.

"Lot of crime out there, that's for sure," he said. "Citizens feel they need to protect themselves. Some of them buy guns. How about you Miss Torres? Do you own a gun?"

"No, I don't."

He watched Angelina Torres closely looking for any signs of deception. Because it was easier, most people lied with words rather than with their faces or body movements. Words were voluntary and could be managed, manipulated, rehearsed. Facial expressions, however, were involuntary and harder to control unless you were a con artist, actor — or politician. A suspect's face was usually a roadmap of uncontrolled emotions. Santana knew the better a detective was at reading those emotions, the better he would be at locating the truth.

"You know," he said, "Córdova had a gun on him when he was killed. The gun had your fingerprint on it. How do you suppose it got there?"

She let out a long breath. Let a few seconds pass. "I'm sorry I didn't say anything the day Father Hidalgo and I came to see you. But Rubén gave me a gun when I left California for Minnesota. I was driving alone and he wanted me to have it for protection. I really didn't want to take it, but he insisted."

"A .22 caliber?"

She looked down at her hands. "I don't know much about guns."

Suspects being interviewed or interrogated often manipulated their brow or forehead, so Santana looked for any signs that Angelina Torres was lying or trying to control what she said by focusing his attention on her lower jaw and mouth where it was more difficult to disguise an emotion. But she made it more difficult for him when she consciously or unconsciously looked down at her hands.

"How long ago did you give the gun to Córdova?"

She thought for a moment before she answered. "Two weeks."

Santana looked back at the notes he had taken the first time they met in his office. "You told me before that Córdova was afraid, but he wouldn't tell you why."

"That's right," she said, looking at him again.

"What was your relationship with him?"

"We were … friends."

"Nothing more?"

"Once," she said with a trace of regret.

"Do you know any reason why Córdova might want to kill Rafael Mendoza?"

"Rubén did not kill Mendoza."

He had expected her to say that, so he let it go and moved on. "Where were you the night Córdova was killed?"

"I worked late that day. I heard about the deaths on the radio."

"Anyone verify that?"

"Everyone went home at five. I locked up the office."

"Do you know where Córdova was when Julio Pérez was killed?"

"Are you suggesting Rubén had something to do with Mr. Pérez's murder?"

Santana remained quiet, hoping that she would answer her own question.

Someone pounded on the office door and Angelina Torres nearly jumped out of her shoes.

"Police!" a voice shouted. "Open up!"

She looked uneasily at Santana. "What's going on?"

Santana got to his feet and went to the door and opened it.

James Kehoe stood in the doorway flanked by two uniformed officers.

"What the hell are you doing here, Kehoe?"

"Your job. I got a warrant here for Angelina Torres." He held it up like it was a badge of honor.

Santana wondered who had leaked the information about her fingerprint, and what he was going to do about it once he found out.

"You're going to fuck up this whole investigation, Kehoe."

"Yeah, right. What are you doin' in there anyway? Tryin' to get your Hispanic friend off?"

He gave a contemptuous laugh and looked at the uniforms on either side of him to see if they had caught the dual meaning in his sick joke. If they had, they were not showing it.

"Listen," Santana said. "I don't care if you're the mayor's chief ass kisser or not. Stay out of my way."

Kehoe said, "Enough of this dickin' around, Santana. I got the murder weapon and her print is on it. That's all I need."

"What about a motive?"

That point seemed to confuse him. He took a moment to compose himself before he held up the warrant again, as if Santana had not seen it the first time.

"But I got this."

"You got shit," Santana said.

"Outta my way," Kehoe said with dismissive wave. He took one short step forward, but when Santana stood his ground, he stopped.

Kehoe looked at the two officers on either side of him for support. One was staring at his shoes, the other at an apparent stain on his uniform.

"Remember that I warned you, Kehoe," Santana said, finally stepping aside to let him pass.

Kehoe barged into the room.

As he Mirandized Angelina Torres, she said, *"Yo no lo hice."* I did not do it.

Her eyes had a look of desperate hopefulness, as though Santana held the last extra lifejacket on a sinking ship.

Chapter 10

"I THOUGHT YOU WERE GOING TO KEEP Kehoe off my back, Rita."

Santana was seated in one of the uncomfortable hard backed chairs in Gamboni's office at the 10th Street station, trying to throttle the anger that raced inside him.

Gamboni sat behind her desk, biting her bottom lip. The expression on her face was a mixture of turmoil and dread, as if she had just witnessed a murder and knew the killer was coming for her next.

"Am I the chief detective on this case, Rita, or is it Asshoe?"

She appeared to be contemplating his question. Santana was about to protest when she said with a slight smile, "Is that what Kehoe's known as?"

"Among other things."

"And what do they call me, John?"

He was reluctant to tell her that she was affectionately known as "Bony" among the males in the Homicide Unit. The nickname had absolutely nothing to do with her figure, but rather the reaction it inspired.

"Commander," he replied.

Her blue eyes were dubious. "I'll bet."

She had a knack for steering the conversation in the direction that she wanted it to go, both as his partner and his lover. Santana compared it to daydreaming while driving a car. Before you realized what had happened, you had drifted over the centerline, lost control. She was doing the same thing to him now and he needed to refocus.

"Who the hell leaked the information about Torres … Commander?"

Gamboni smiled a little more and reached for a cinnamon Altoid in the metal container on her desk. "I can tell you it didn't come from this office." She placed the Altoid delicately in her mouth and offered him one from the box.

He declined.

Unlike many of the pretty women with good figures Santana had known, Rita Gamboni was smart. He admired that trait, just as he had admired it in his mother. She, too, had been pretty and smart; a doctor in Colombia at a time when women's rights meant you could have five kids instead of ten. Thanks to his mother's influence, coming to the U.S. was less of a cultural shock for Santana than it could have been. Most of the Latino males he had met here over the years complained that American women were too assertive, too pushy. In his mind's eye, Santana could see the Latino men walking around with stunned looks on their faces, like aliens on Pluto rather than in the U.S.

"Where are Baker and Hawkins?" he asked.

"Doing background checks on Mendoza and Pérez. Like they're supposed to do."

"Well, Kehoe got the information about Torres' print from someone, Rita. And it sure as hell wasn't me."

She gave him a sharp look. Leaned forward and placed her palms flat on the desktop.

"Instead of worrying so much about a leak in the department, Detective, maybe you should concentrate your efforts on finding out who really murdered Pérez and Mendoza. If you still believe Córdova and Torres weren't involved."

He knew she was upset when she called him "detective" instead of using his surname, that and the fact that her light complexion had become as red as a drop of blood.

Her office door suddenly swung open and Assistant Deputy Chief Carl Ashford strode in. He nodded at Gamboni and acknowledged Santana with a curt, "Detective." Hiking up his trousers around his wide waistline he said, "I heard about your accident. You all right?"

"Fine."

Ashford gave a quick nod indicating that he wasn't interested in the details. "I don't have a lot of time so I'll skip the customary banter. We've got Hispanic groups picketing the mayor's office. The press is suggesting that the Pérez-Mendoza murders may be a hate crime. Needless to say, we don't need that. John, you and your team will continue working the case, but I'd like Detective Kehoe to head up the investigation from now on. It appears that Córdova murdered Pérez and Mendoza and the Torres' woman was his accomplice."

Santana looked at Gamboni for support, but he could tell by her blank expression that she had no intention of challenging Ashford's decision. He was on his own.

"I guess that makes it easier, Chief," he said.

"What's that supposed to mean?"

Ashford's accusatory tone was clearly a warning to Santana that he should just let it go. After all, he could work around Kehoe. Let Asshoe think he was actually in charge.

"Well?" Ashford said.

"I was just thinking …" Santana began.

"John," Gamboni said.

Santana could hear the caution in Gamboni's voice. He considered keeping quiet. Then continued despite her misgivings.

"If the department can pin the murders on Córdova and Torres, it makes it much easier. I mean the city expects Hispanics to be killing Hispanics. Better for everyone concerned if the murderer isn't white."

Ashford clenched his large fists and glared at Santana.

Santana could imagine the same look on Ashford's face as he stormed into an opponent's backfield as a Minnesota Gopher linebacker and put a vicious hit on the quarterback.

"That's bullshit, Santana! You're talking to a man who's dealt with race issues all his life. This murder investigation has got nothin' to do with race. And if you think differently, then perhaps you need to be pulled entirely off the case."

"Carl," Gamboni said evenly, "I believe Detective Santana is just upset that he's no longer heading up the investigation. I'm sure he wants to continue working with the team. Isn't that right, John?"

She gave him a look that passed through him like a bullet.

Given the political flack that the Pérez-Mendoza case had generated, it was no surprise that Ashford was looking for cover anywhere he could find it, Santana thought. He had little sympathy for Ashford, but he had less for the mayor. He was tired of compromises and empty promises from bureaucrats and politicians. He wished sometimes that Minnesota were more like Colombia where a well-placed phone call and a substantial contribution could make a certain problem disappear forever.

"All right," he said. He wanted to add 'for now' but he resisted the urge.

Ashford gave a nod. "Fine. But I don't want to hear any more of this racist bullshit, Detective Santana. And I want you reporting directly to Detective Kehoe from now on. Is that clear?"

Ashford's deep baritone was loud enough that Santana figured it could be heard in the squad room outside Gamboni's office. Ashford had bitched him out before and probably would again. Still, he hated to be reprimanded like a student in front of the principal.

"It's clear."

"Good. Then let's get to it." Ashford gave him a tight smile and clapped his hands together, as if he were concluding a pep talk before a big game.

He left the office. Slammed the door behind him.

Gamboni exhaled deeply. Released her tension in a cinnamon sweetened breath. She pointed a finger at Santana and said, "You're damn lucky that Ashford didn't pull your ass off this case."

Santana shrugged, but he knew she was right.

"Why can't you learn to keep your mouth shut?"

"It's my nature."

"Oh, fuck your nature, John. You know as well as I do if Kehoe gets Torres to confess, the case is closed."

"If Kehoe brings this to Canfield, Rita, he's not going to the grand jury with it."

"You don't know what Canfield is going to do."

"What the hell is Torres' motive?"

Gamboni threw up her hands. "Maybe Pérez and Mendoza were involved in the visa scam with Córdova and Torres. Maybe Córdova and Torres decided they wanted the money for themselves."

Santana shook his head. "I think these murders are about more than the visa scam, Rita."

"Then go out and prove it, Detective."

Santana stood in a small office outside an interview room next to James Kehoe. Santana was holding a briefcase and looking through a two-way mirror where he could see Angelina Torres sitting stiffly in a chair in a corner next to a small white table bolted to the floor. She was staring at the glass as if she could not believe the face she saw was actually her own.

After leaving Gamboni's office, Santana had gone back to his desk and copied the pages and notes from the Pérez-Mendoza murder book. He had placed the copies in a desk drawer and left the originals in the murder book on his desk.

"Torres lawyer up yet?" Kehoe said.

"Says she's innocent. Doesn't need one. Maybe she's telling the truth."

Kehoe took a sip of coffee from a Styrofoam cup and shook his head doubtfully.

"Look, I know you like to yank my chain, Santana, and you're pissed off that I'm in charge of the investigation and you didn't get the collar. Frankly, I don't give a rat's ass. What I want is the perp who committed the murders. We got the murder weapon and it belongs to Torres. I'd say that makes her an accomplice."

"Just because she's waived her rights to have an attorney present, doesn't mean she has to tell us anything."

Kehoe pointed the coffee cup at Santana. "That's why you're still on the case, hotshot. We're going in there in a minute and you're going to use your expertise to get her to confess."

"I questioned her already. I don't like her for the murders, Kehoe. You're making a mistake."

"No, you're the one making the mistake thinking she didn't do it. Besides, you can always walk now if you want to. You got that expensive house out on the river, probably a lot of money in the bank. You could walk away from the job and never miss a beat."

Kehoe gave him that practiced smirk he was so accustomed to using, the same one he had used since he was in elementary school bullying the smaller kids out of their lunch money.

"I wouldn't hold your breath," Santana said, starting for the door.

"Wait a minute," Kehoe said. "The CCTV system turned on?"

"I like to leave it off until we're certain we're going to get a confession."

"Turn it on now."

Santana made sure that the Closed Circuit Television system was running.

"One other thing, Santana. Now that I'm in charge of the investigation, I want the murder book."

"It's on my desk. You can pick it up on your way out."

"Everything better be in it. Including your notes."

"Don't worry," Santana said.

He opened the door to the interview room and walked in.

Angelina Torres seemed relieved to see him. But as she peered over his shoulder and saw Kehoe enter the room, her confidence appeared to melt as quickly as an ice cube on a hot stove.

Santana placed the briefcase on the table and sat down across from her in a chair the same size as hers. He left a higher chair at the far end of the table, the one he used when he wanted to establish a psychological advantage over a suspect.

He began by identifying the three occupants of the interview room and then placed a right's waiver form on the table. "I know you've been advised of your rights, but I want to re-advise you, make sure you understand."

Kehoe, standing in the far corner, coffee cup still in his hand, coughed loudly.

Santana ignored him and read Angelina Torres her rights again. When he finished, he asked her once more if she understood.

"Yes."

He asked her to sign the waiver form. Then he asked her to state her name and address, place of birth, nationality and occupation, trying to make it casual, as though they were sitting down to have a chat.

"Ever been arrested or in trouble with the police?"

"No. Never."

Santana could tell that she had placed her trust in his hands, and that she was willing to talk openly about the case, despite what was at stake.

"Let's get on with it, Detective," Kehoe said, a slight edge in his voice.

Santana opened the briefcase and took out a .22 caliber Smith and Wesson, single action, semi-automatic with a ten shot clip. "Is this the gun Córdova gave you?"

He could hear Angelina Torres' breathing accelerate and sense her tension rise.

"It looks like it."

"You brought the gun with you from California."

"I was driving to Minnesota alone. Rubén wanted me to have protection. Everything I owned was in my car."

"Ever fire it before?"

"Never."

He put the gun back in his briefcase. "You thirsty, Miss Torres? Need something to drink?"

"I could use some water."

"In a minute," Kehoe said. "Come on, Detective. Unless you want me to take a run at her."

Santana said, "Tell me again where you were when Mendoza was murdered."

She peered tentatively over Santana's shoulder at Kehoe.

"It's all right, Miss Torres. Just tell me what you told me before."

She went through it again; how she worked late; how she heard about Pérez and Mendoza's deaths on the radio; how Rubén had been afraid.

Kehoe blew out a breath. "Maybe you left your office, Miss Torres. Easy to do when you're all alone."

"No," she said with a firm shake of her head. "I did not leave."

"Ballistics confirmed that the shell casing found at Pérez's house and the bullet the ME pulled out of Pérez are a match."

Santana tried to keep his emotions in check. Kehoe had blindsided him with the ballistics report. As lead investigator on the case, Kehoe was getting regular updates from the crime lab.

Kehoe came forward, set his coffee cup down and rested his hands, palms down, on the table. "The gun had your fingerprint on it, Miss Torres. Someone attempted to file off the serial numbers, but the lab was able to restore them. The gun was reported stolen in California."

Santana felt the investigation was getting away from him. It was like chasing an accelerating car. The faster he ran to keep up, the more the distance increased.

"You want to know what I think, Miss Torres?" Kehoe said. "I think you and your boyfriend planned the murders. I think you're as guilty as he was."

"I did not murder anyone. And neither did Rubén."

Though her voice quivered slightly, there was firm conviction in her eyes.

"If you or your boyfriend didn't kill Pérez, you have any idea who might have?"

She looked at Santana like she was wondering who was in charge here, like maybe she had made a huge mistake in trusting the Hispanic detective.

Despite his sense that Angelina Torres did not murder Julio Pérez or Rafael Mendoza, Santana could not shake the feeling that he was missing something, that she knew more than she was telling him. He was thinking that his dislike of Kehoe might be clouding his judgment when the interview room door swung open and banged against the doorstop. Alvarado Vega, a Hispanic attorney with a big reputation and an ego to match strutted in.

"That's enough, gentleman. My client has nothing more to say."

Kehoe said, "Shit, Vega, who called you?"

"Miss Torres' co-workers. They were a little concerned when you hauled her out in handcuffs."

Vega reminded Santana of Geraldo Rivera. He had the same facial features: glasses, dark mustache and thick, wavy hair, worn long enough to suggest he was still a rebel fighting the establishment. He had built a reputation defending clients accused of murder and drawn the ire of the police department in the process. Vega was good, but he had an inflated ego. In Santana's mind, Vega was like a Diet Coke. It might satisfy you for the moment, but it left an awfully bad taste in your mouth.

"You charging my client?" Vega said.

"We got her print on the gun that killed Pérez," Kehoe said. "Ballistics confirms it was the gun used to kill him. And she's admitted she brought the gun with her from California."

"But I didn't kill anyone," she said.

Vega glanced at Angelina Torres and raised his hand in a stopping gesture. "You running this investigation, Kehoe?"

"That's right."

Vega looked at Santana for confirmation.

Santana hiked his shoulders and nodded.

Vega said, "You two got anything else you want to ask my client?"

Kehoe walked over and held the door open wide. "Officer'll take her over to the Ramsey County Jail."

"That all you got?" Vega said sarcastically.

"That's all we need for now," Kehoe said.

"Hell," Vega said. "This is going to be easier than I thought. I'll have her released on insufficient evidence to prosecute in twenty-four hours."

"Good luck getting a RIEP," Kehoe said, jerking a thumb toward the door. "Let's go."

Angelina Torres' expression turned from hope to despair. Suddenly, she looked resigned to her fate.

Seeing the vulnerability and desperation in her eyes as they darted from side to side, seemingly searching for a way out of all of this, Santana said to Vega, *"Déme tiempo. Yo encontrare la persona responsable del asesinato."* Give me some time. I'll find the person responsible for the murders.

"Si usted piensa que mi cliente es inocente, entonces que hace el aquí?" Vega said. If you think my client's innocent, then what's she doing here?

Santana pointed his chin at Kehoe.

"Hey!" Kehoe said. "This isn't fuckin' Mexico. Speak English."

"Never mind," Vega said. He led Angelina Torres out of the interview room.

Santana closed his briefcase and stood up. "That went well."

"Shit," Kehoe said, blowing out a breath. "I thought you're supposed to be good at this, Santana. You with the big reputation. Cases all cleared. Mr. Hardass and all that. Hell, you give the woman any more time before you hardball her, I could retire."

"Not a bad idea."

"Fuck you."

"Oh, that's brilliant, Sherlock. You arrest her; haul her in here with nothing but a fingerprint as evidence, and then act surprised when her attorney arrives and it all turns to shit. What did you expect?"

"I expect you to get me more evidence. And quick if you want to stay on this case and in this department."

Kehoe turned and stomped out of the room like a spoiled kid who had not gotten his way.

When Santana returned to his desk, Rick Anderson came over and said, "Hey, partner. I heard about the accident with the snowplow. You all right?"

"A little sore is all."

"You're damn lucky to be alive. So how's the case goin'?"

"Shitty, you want to know the truth."

"What could be wrong? I heard you arrested an accomplice in the Pérez-Mendoza murders."

"I didn't arrest her and I don't think she's responsible. There's something else going on here, Rick. I just can't see it. Not yet."

"But I thought you had her print on the weapon."

Santana, who had been looking blankly at his desk, turned his head quickly and stared hard at Anderson. "How did you know that?"

"Hey, easy, John. It's all over the department. You know this place is a fuckin' gossip mill."

"But who specifically told you?"

"It was Kehoe."

"What are you doing talking to Kehoe?"

Anderson held up his hands, as if surrendering. "What the hell's the matter with you, John? Kehoe was bragging he'd nailed Córdova and Torres for the two murders. I wasn't the only one who heard him."

"Sorry, Rick. I'm a little edgy. Ashford's put him in charge of the investigation."

"Jesus. No wonder he took the murder book on your desk. What the hell's Ashford usin' for brains?"

"His balls. And the mayor's holding both of them and squeezing hard."

"So, I guess you don't figure Córdova and Torres for the murders."

"No."

"Then, who?"

"Well, if it isn't Córdova and Torres, and it isn't you or me, I've eliminated at least four people."

The phone on Santana's desk rang and he picked it up after the second ring. "Homicide. Santana."

"John. It's Nick. Been checkin' out Mendoza's background and friends."

"Where are you now?" Santana could hear loud music in the background.

Baker was silent.

"Nick?

"Yeah."

"Where are you?"

"Club Apollo."

Santana couldn't help but chuckle. "How is it?"

"Gay as pink ink. Know what I mean?"

"Not really. But you can explain it to me if you want."

"Some other time. Maybe you wanna hear what I found out."

"It better be good. I'm standing in quicksand and sinking fast."

"Better than where I'm standin'. Hold on. I think you're gonna like this."

Santana could hear Baker turning pages in his notebook.

"The people I talked to who knew Mendoza say he wasn't involved in any kinky shit," Baker said. "But get this, John. He was from Valladolid, Mexico."

"Valladolid. That's where Julio Pérez was from."

"That's what Gamboni told me."

"You know, if you weren't so ugly, Nick, I'd give you a big kiss."

"Thanks. But I've seen more than enough of that today," Baker said and hung up the phone.

Santana knew the adrenaline rush he had just gotten from Baker's phone call was temporary. He knew, too, that he was at a crossroads in the investigation. It was like that with most of the homicide cases he had worked over the years. There always seemed to be a point where he needed to slow down and figure out what direction to take. He hadn't slept much last night. Haste and exhaustion could lead to carelessness. He needed a good meal and a good night's sleep; time to let his subconscious do some of the legwork. In the morning he would begin again, fresh and alert; emboldened by his intuition and the knowledge that he was getting close. He could feel it. Somewhere out there in the cold darkness a murderer was waiting, and Santana was coming for him.

Chapter 11

DAY 4

IT WASN'T A GOOD DAY for a funeral. Then again, Santana thought, what day was?

He stood with a crowd of people gathered near the white mausoleum where Julio Pérez would be laid to rest. The mausoleum was located off a narrow roadway that zigzagged through Calvary Cemetery, the oldest of the Catholic Cemeteries in St. Paul, and the resting place of Archbishop John Ireland and more than one hundred thousand believers. A motorcycle cop smoked a cigarette as he leaned against the hood of a black hearse parked on the road, its back door still open like a raven's wing. Between the bare branches of the oak trees, Santana could see the low, gray sky and the Cathedral dome in the distance, the afternoon sun seemingly frozen above it like a gold coin lying beneath a sheet of thin ice.

All the crying he had just witnessed reminded him of the women called *Plañideras* who were hired to cry at his uncle Fernando's funeral in Cartagena years ago. He remembered his father explaining that hiring the women was an old African tradition that was common along the Atlantic coast of Colombia. After the funeral, the crying had ended and everyone partied. But St. Paul wasn't Cartagena, and the cries Santana had heard were not from *Plañideras*.

There would be no partying today.

Father Thomas Hidalgo had led the Latin prayers for Julio Pérez with an assist from Father Richard Scanlon. Because Scanlon had recently been named to replace the retiring archbishop, there were several reporters from the local news media waiting like vultures at the entrance to the cemetery on Front Street, hoping, no doubt, that they might scavenge a few quotes from the bereaved family and from the archbishop.

Santana had come to the cemetery to pay his respects and to observe the faces of the mourners. It was a long shot, but someone attending the service could be the murderer.

As his eyes swept the crowd, watching for a nervous smile, a false expression of sadness, he made eye contact with Gabriela Pérez. She stood next to her mother near the mausoleum. As she strode toward Santana across a section of ground that had been cleared of snow, it became apparent that she had shed no tears and had no intention of succumbing to the temptation. No doubt she would do her crying alone. Santana admired her resolve. He wished she were as resolute when it came to controlling her temper.

"Thank you for coming, Detective," she said. "And thank you for finding the people responsible for my father's murder."

"You've been reading the paper."

She glanced at the casket on the floor of the mausoleum. "My father treated Rubén like a son. I don't know how Rubén and Angelina Torres could have done this."

It was more of a statement than a question and it was steeped in anger and frustration. Rather than arguing about whether or not Córdova and Torres were responsible for the murders, Santana wanted to know more about her father's past. Still, he had to be careful. Questioning her about her father now was like asking a murder suspect if she would like to borrow your gun.

"You told me that your father was born in Valladolid, Mexico." He made it sound like he was just making polite conversation.

"Yes. On the Yucatán Peninsula. Near Cancún."

Santana smiled. "Big tourist spot."

"Now, yes. Years ago, no. Do you have family here, Detective?"

"No … no, I don't."

"Do you visit Colombia often?"

"Not often." *Not ever,* he thought.

"You should. Life is fleeting. Go before it's too late."

Santana felt uncomfortable talking about his family and wanted the conversation to focus on hers.

"Ever been to Valladolid?" he asked.

She seemed to think a long time before she spoke, and he wondered if she was picturing the city in her mind.

"Yes. I have many relatives in the area."

"When were you there last?"

"Two years ago."

"So you know the city pretty well."

"Well enough. Why?"

"I was wondering where in the city your father was born?"

Her face clouded and she gave him a hard stare. "Why do you want to know, Detective Santana?"

The throng of mourners in black, heavy coats parted and Father Scanlon and Father Hidalgo suddenly appeared.

"Ah, Gabriela." Hidalgo came to her and nodded at Santana. "Detective. It's good of you to come."

Santana looked over Hidalgo's shoulder at the other priest.

"Have you met the archbishop?" Hidalgo asked, following Santana's gaze.

"No, I haven't."

Hidalgo motioned toward Scanlon who was standing a few feet away. The archbishop excused himself from Sandra Pérez and a group of mourners and walked up to Santana. He moved deliberately with the practiced grace of an unskilled dancer who had learned only one set of steps.

"This is Detective Santana," Hidalgo said, touching Scanlon gently on the shoulder. "He's conducting the investigation into Julio Pérez's murder."

Scanlon had a firm grip in a thick hand that felt more like a construction worker's than a priest's. His gunmetal-gray hair was cut short, and his nose had a reddish hue Santana figured was caused by something other than the cold.

"I'm sorry I never met your father," Scanlon said to Gabriela Pérez. "I understand he was greatly admired." He made a sweeping gesture toward the mausoleum and the crowd. "It's no wonder we had to hold the service at the Cathedral."

"My father had many friends."

And at least one enemy, Santana thought.

Hidalgo said, "Detective Santana, have you found out anything that might free Angelina Torres and clear Rubén Córdova's name?"

Santana suddenly felt as if he was in an elevator free falling from the top floor of a skyscraper.

Gabriela Pérez looked at Hidalgo and then at Santana, her eyes suddenly burning like candles. "What do you mean?"

"Gabriela," Hidalgo said quietly. "We cannot condemn innocent people. Certainly you understand."

"Innocent? How do you know they are innocent?"

Hidalgo seemed at a loss for words. He shifted his gaze to Scanlon, who remained silent as falling snow. Finally, Hidalgo said, "I don't believe Rubén or Angelina could have done such a thing to your father."

Gabriela Pérez's expression, which a moment ago had been softened by the tender hands of tragedy, hardened in an instant. "You are in no position to judge him."

"But I am," Santana said.

She glared at him for a long moment before she said, "I understand now, Detective Santana. I understand perfectly." Her tone was as cold as the chill in the air. "You did not come to my father's funeral to pay your respects. You came here to question me."

Santana started to protest but she cut him off.

"You are a man without feelings!" she said loudly.

Heads turned. Eyes stared.

"Leave!" she said, backing away from Santana as if he had a communicable disease.

"If you'll let me explain —"

"Now!"

Santana made his way through the dwindling crowd and got into his car.

"You are a man without feelings."

He told himself it was untrue. But as he drove away, Gabriela Pérez's words reverberated inside his head, as though she were in a pulpit speaking into a microphone.

The air inside O'Leary's bar was thick with a blue haze that hung like smog over the tables in the center of the room and the booths, which formed an L along two walls. It was 3:05 p.m. according to the clock behind the bar. It would be another two hours before cops getting off Tour II would pack O'Leary's, as if it were the Metrodome before the seventh game of the World Series.

The 10:00 p.m. to 8:00 a.m. shift was known as Tour I. Tour II had two shifts. The first ran from 7:00 a.m. until 5:00 p.m. A second began at 9:00 a.m. and ended at 7:00 p.m. Tour III also had two shifts. One ran from 4:30 p.m. to 2:30 a.m. Another started at 6:30 p.m. and ended at 4:30 a.m. Shifts overlapped so that squads were always on the streets.

As Santana stood near the doorway, surveying the room, he saw a familiar figure coming out of the men's room. "Rick," he called.

Rick Anderson's eyes slid away from Santana.

"Rick!" Santana called again.

Anderson acknowledged Santana with a nod and came hesitantly toward him.

"Don't see you in here often, John," Anderson said with a little laugh.

"I shouldn't see you in here at all."

Anderson looked as if he had just been told his dick was hanging out. "I only had one drink."

Santana was sure Anderson was lying, but he said nothing.

"What brings you here, John?"

"I'm meeting Kacie and Nick."

"Well, I'd love to hang around," Anderson said, not all together convincingly. "But I'm meeting my ex for dinner at Ferns."

"Lisa or Cheryl?"

"Lisa."

"You two back together?"

"It's her birthday. Hey, gotta run. Keep me informed." He waved and headed for the door.

Santana was looking for Baker and Hawkins when he spotted James Kehoe sitting on a barstool. Kehoe was holding a mug of beer in one hand, a thick cigar in the other. The stool next to him was unoccupied, but there were a couple of empty mugs on the bar in front of it.

Santana found Kacie Hawkins and Nick Baker in a booth near the back. He slid into the space next to Hawkins.

Baker pushed a full mug of beer across the table to Santana. Some of the thick foam spilled over the side of the glass.

"To winters without snowplows," he said, raising a frosty mug of his own. His eyes were bloodshot and a cigarette dangled from his lips.

Santana joined Baker and Hawkins in the toast. The cold tap beer slid easily down his throat.

"Good to see you're okay, John," Hawkins said.

Baker pointed a cigarette stained finger at her. "I got less than a year left before retirement. I'm gonna make sure I go someplace where they don't have snow in winter and they don't need snowplows. What's Colombia like, John? Have much snow there?"

"Only near the top of the Andes."

"Don't plan on goin' that high up." Baker finished off the beer in one swallow and set the empty mug on the table with a thud. Stabbing the cigarette in Santana's direction, he said, "You could've been killed by the plow. Or Córdova could've punched your ticket."

"If he had drawn his gun," Hawkins said.

Santana gave her a look.

"You know the department is like a small town, John," she said. "Everybody knows everybody else's business."

"If Anderson says the punk was going for his gun, that's all I need," Baker said.

"He better hope it's all IA and Canfield need," Hawkins said.

"I don't think Córdova or Torres are guilty of murder," Santana said.

Hawkins said, "You mind telling us why?"

Santana shared what Angelina Torres had told him when she came to his office with Father Hidalgo, and when he spoke to her in her office before Kehoe arrived with a warrant. Then he explained what he had found in Córdova's appointment book and on his computer.

"Does Torres have an alibi for the day Pérez and Mendoza were murdered?" Hawkins asked.

"She worked late that day. Said she heard about the deaths on the radio. Not real easy to verify. But Córdova's cell phone records show that he called Mendoza three times prior to his death. I'm guessing to set up appointments."

"I checked Mendoza's phone records," Baker said. "He called Córdova once as well. The day before they both died."

Hawkins said, "Maybe Córdova was on to the visa scam, John."

"That would be my guess. After Mendoza's name in his appointment book, Córdova wrote the words, *learn more about the scandal.*"

Baker motioned to the waitress and held up three fingers. "I'm guessing we're having another round, John."

"What gives you that idea?"

"My mug's empty and we've got a whole lot to talk about."

"You've got this whole detecting thing down to a real science, Nick," Hawkins said.

He smiled and picked up a pretzel from the bowl on the table. "Stick around, kid, you might learn something."

"What do your detecting skills tell you about Kehoe?" Santana asked.

Baker chewed on a pretzel and gave a derisive laugh. "If the Feds are bad, this guy's worse. And he's a real prick to boot."

"Someone told Kehoe about Torres' fingerprint."

"Maybe it was Novak."

"Tony wouldn't do that unless he was ordered to. He knows I'm lead investigator. At least I was."

"Hell," Baker said, waving the fact away. "Putting Kehoe in charge of the investigation is nuts."

"Well," Hawkins said, looking across the table at Baker, "If neither Gamboni or Novak leaked the information to Kehoe, that means John thinks it's one of us."

"What the hell are you talking about, Kacie?" Baker asked. He leaned across the table, one hand clutching the handle of the mug, as if for support.

"Take it easy," Santana said. "The department *is* like a small town. Everybody *does* know everybody else's business. I'm not suggesting either of you leaked the information. But keep your ears open. Let me know if you hear anything. What I need to know right now, Nick, is what you found out about Mendoza. Besides the fact that he was born in the same city in Mexico as Pérez."

Baker raised a bushy eyebrow. "You planning on running all of this by Gamboni at some point?"

"At some point."

Baker wiped his mouth with a cocktail napkin, lit a fresh cigarette with a match, and retrieved a small notebook from an inside pocket of his sport coat. Flipping open the cover, he said, "From what I could piece together after talking with his friends, Mendoza came to St. Paul when he was nine years old. His mother raised him. She worked as a cleaning lady. Mendoza was the only child. Apparently, she couldn't have any more kids. Might explain why the father went back to Mexico when the kid was ten and never came back. Mendoza went to Harding High School. Good student. Got a scholarship to the University of Minnesota. Went on to law school. Mother died of cervical cancer just after he graduated. Seems Mendoza took it pretty hard. Guess he never got the chance to make her life a little easier."

Santana remembered his own mother; how she had hoped to see him become a doctor; how she never got the chance.

Baker turned a couple of pages in the notebook. "Mendoza went to work for Spencer and Wangensteen, a large law firm in the IDS building in Minneapolis that represented major corporations. Apparently Mendoza discovered his roots a few years later and left to start his own firm in St. Paul primarily representing spics." Baker stopped abruptly and looked up from his notebook. "Sorry, John. I meant Hispanics."

Hawkins rolled her eyes.

Baker smiled tightly, took a drag on his cigarette, let the smoke out through his nostrils. "Hard to teach an old dog new tricks. No offense."

"None taken."

Baker crossed something out in his notebook and continued.

"The move paid off. Immigration law grew and he moved into the World Trade Center in St. Paul. Became a big contributor to AIDS foundations. No dirty laundry that I could find."

"But he must've pissed off somebody," Hawkins said. "What about boyfriends?"

"I ran into pretty much of a dead-end there. Mendoza wasn't into cruising. He was seeing someone, but nobody's willing to talk about it."

He took another swallow of beer and fell silent for a moment before he appeared to remember something else.

"Hey, John, what about that photo Gamboni found in Mendoza's loft? You know, the one with the two mystery men? Any leads?"

"Tony Novak is supposed to get back to me. Anything unusual in Mendoza's phone records or credit card statements?"

"Nothing I could see."

"What about his financial records?"

"Mendoza made a good living as a corporate attorney in the nineties. Appears most of his money went into the stock market. When it tanked, he lost a bundle. Then, a few years ago, when he began representing immigrants, he started investing large sums of money in real estate. He had rental property in Lake Tahoe and Mazatlan, as well as his condo in St. Paul. Hard to see how representing poor immigrants paid as well as it did."

"Unless a good share of his money was obtained illegally," Santana said.

"I always thought real estate was a good investment," Baker said, behind the stream of smoke from his cigarette. "Ever listen to one of those real estate infomercials that are always on Saturday mornings and late night TV? You know, the ones where you buy property with no money down?"

"Yeah, right," Hawkins said. "The only reason those hucksters are millionaires is because idiots buy their stupid programs."

"Maybe. But it'd be a cheap way of investing in rental property after I retire. Be a good source of income to supplement the pension. Problem is, I can't fix shit."

"Neither can most slum lords," Hawkins said. "We don't need any more white men investing in rental property so they can get rich by ripping off the poor."

"What's got you all wound up today?" Baker asked, draining the last of his beer. "Boyfriend troubles again?"

Santana saw the anger flare in Hawkins dark eyes. He said, "Let's stay focused on the case. What else you got, Nick?"

Baker set the glass down and picked up an 8 x 11 manila envelope on the seat beside him. Inside were copies of monthly bank statements.

"Take a look at these."

There were five columns of single-spaced numbers on each bank statement, dates to the far left, transactions to the right, followed by columns of debits, credits and balances.

"I don't believe it," Hawkins said, running a long index finger down the column marked credits. "Mendoza had to be raking in thousands. Where the hell was ICE?"

"The Labor Department monitors visa requests," Santana said. "Not ICE. Applications from immigrants for labor certification are sent to the state employment agency. They check to see if U.S. workers are available. If not, the state agency sends the application to the Labor Department and they decide whether to issue a certificate. An immigrant can then take the certification to ICE. My guess is Mendoza made sure the applications for foreign workers were coming from a variety of restaurants so ICE wouldn't become suspicious."

"Sounds like the state fucked up, too," Hawkins said.

"It wouldn't be the first time."

"So we can probably tie Mendoza to the visa scam," Baker said.

"If someone other than Mendoza had access to his accounts," Hawkins said, "then he could've been killed for the money."

"Except most of the money is still in Mendoza's accounts," Baker said. "Other than what he invested in real estate. But you can see that he took cash out twice each month."

"The withdrawal on the fifteenth is about half the one on the thirtieth," Hawkins said.

"Could be pay outs," Santana said. "One, maybe two people."

"Someone who wanted all the action," Hawkins said.

Baker closed the notebook, slipped it back into an inside pocket.

"So what's the next move? Besides another round?"

"What about you Kacie?" Santana asked. "Find anything in Pérez's financial records that connects him to the visa scam?"

Hawkins lifted a purse the size of a suitcase off the cushion beside her and placed it on the table.

"I got copies of everything Gamboni asked for here. Nothing I see in his financial statements connects Pérez with Mendoza and the visa scam. Pérez made a decent living running the newspaper, but nothing out of the ordinary. But," she said, digging into the purse, "I did find something interesting in his phone records."

The paper she pulled out of her purse and set on the table in front of Santana was a copy of the phone calls Julio Pérez made from his home phone in the month of December through mid-January.

"Not only did Pérez call Mendoza the day he was murdered," she said, "but he called him three previous times. Once on January seven, and twice the last week in December."

She had circled the dates in red.

"You check the previous months?" Santana asked.

"I checked back through last year. No calls to Mendoza either from home or his newspaper office. And Pérez didn't have a cell."

"What about Mendoza?" Santana said to Baker.

He shook his head. "No record of him calling Pérez from his home phone or his cell over the last year."

"So why does Pérez suddenly decide to contact Mendoza?" Hawkins said.

"Something must have triggered it," Santana said.

Hawkins spread her hands. "But what?"

"We know they were both born in Valladolid, Mexico. That's the only connection we have."

"What about Mrs. Pérez or the daughter? Maybe they can help?"

"I spoke with Gabriela Pérez right before the incident with the snowplow. She insisted that her father didn't know Mendoza. She didn't want me talking with her mother before the funeral, but now that it's over, I'll give her a call, see what I can find out."

"I don't know anything about Valladolid," Baker said, "but if it's a good sized city, then maybe Pérez and Mendoza didn't know each other as children."

"Only one way to find out," Santana said.

"If you think Gamboni's going to approve a trip to Mexico, you're dumber than Kehoe," Baker said.

"I can take a couple of vacation days. See what I can dig up."

Hawkins said, "Know anyone down there, John?"

"Not in Mexico. But remember a couple of years ago when I had to fly down to Houston to bring back Joey Moore?"

"The sick little fuck who murdered his wealthy parents?"

"That's the one. Took his parent's credit cards and was on his way to Mexico when the Houston P.D. caught up with him. Anyway, a detective I met in Houston, Ricardo Vasquez, used to be a cop in Mexico. Thought I'd give him a call, see if he can put me in touch with someone in Cancún or Valladolid."

Baker said, "What the hell are you looking for, John?"

"I don't know for sure. But Pérez and Mendoza were born in the same city. They both ended up here in St. Paul. And the last call Pérez made on the day he was murdered was to Mendoza."

"And Mendoza took a swan dive off his balcony the same day," Hawkins said.

"Lot of coincidences," Baker said.

"Too many to ignore."

"What if Vasquez can't help you?"

"I'll go it alone, Nick. After all, I do have one advantage."

"What's that?"

"I'm a spic," Santana said with a smile.

Chapter 12

SANTANA HAD ONE MORE ROUND OF DRINKS at O'Leary's. Then he decided to see if Angelina Torres could tell him anything more about Rubén Córdova — or anything else. He knew that she could be held no more than forty-eight hours without being charged or released. The Adult Detention Center was near O'Leary's, but rather than park in the underground garage at the ADC and take the elevator up to the jail's sixth floor visitor's center, he called ahead, knowing even a cop needed to get her permission to see her. A Ramsey County deputy answered the phone and told him that Canfield had declined to prosecute her at this time. Santana decided to try Angelina Torres at home instead.

He took Kellogg to West Seventh and then drove up Grand Hill past the University Club and west along Summit Avenue, past the turn of the century Victorian, Romanesque and Tudor stone mansions once owned by prominent lumber and railroad barons like John Irvine, Lyman Dayton and James J. Hill.

As residents moved to the suburbs in the 1950s and '60s, some of the large homes had been designated as historical sites; others had been broken up into rental units for college students going to the University of St. Thomas and law students enrolled at William Mitchell. Hmong families migrated to the area after the Vietnam War, and the black community that had been living along Selby and Dale retreated north across University Avenue. Yuppie white families began purchasing the old homes again in the eighties and nineties and restoring them. Restaurants and businesses that catered to their trendy tastes soon sprang up along Selby and Grand Avenues.

Santana drove by the home where F. Scott Fitzgerald wrote *Tender Is The Night*, turned south on Dale and then west again on Grand.

It was 4:52 p.m. when he parked the Crown Vic on the street in front of Angelina Torres' apartment near Victoria Crossing in the Ramsey Hill neighborhood.

Dusk was fading swiftly into darkness as he walked up the sidewalk to the three-story brick building, like lights in a movie theater just before the feature presentation. A maple tree to the right of the steps that led up to the doorway was still lit with a couple of strings of Christmas lights. Someone's attempt to give the bare branches some color.

Inside the visitor's foyer were banks of mailboxes with nameplates to the left and right. Santana used a phone to dial the three-digit number that was listed under Angelina Torres' name on her mailbox.

"Yes?"

"It's Detective Santana, Miss Torres. Sorry to bother you, but I wonder if I could come up and ask you a few questions?"

There was a long pause.

"Miss Torres?"

"I am on the second floor, Detective," she replied, and the door buzzed.

Santana opened it and walked up two flights of stairs to a hallway with a carpet runner down the center. The air was filled with the heavy smells of people cooking dinner, and it reminded him that pretzels and beer were all he had eaten since breakfast.

As he walked down the hallway toward the back of the building, he heard muffled voices and the sound of canned laughter from television sitcoms behind the doors.

He knocked on Angelina Torres' door. A moment later he heard a safety chain removed and a lock turned before the door swung open.

"*Buenas noches,*" she said with a genuine smile.

"*Buenas noches.*"

She invited him in and closed the door behind him.

There was nothing remarkable about her place — it appeared to be a standard one-bedroom apartment with a bathroom, kitchen, small dining room with a table and two chairs, and a living room with a couch and television — except that it had the makings of an arboretum. There were plants in pots on small tables, hanging from brackets around the windows that overlooked an alley behind the building, and in larger pots on the floor.

The scent of freshly cut eucalyptus in a vase on the dining room table carried Santana back in time to *Los Termales del Ruíz,* the little hotel in the Andes near the *El Nevado del Ruíz* volcano where his parents would take him and his sister every year. During the day they swam in the pool filled with the warm sulfur waters from the volcano, and at night they burned eucalyptus leaves in a bonfire close to the pool to stay warm. He saw it all so clearly in his mind's eye now. Felt the warm water rippling against his skin.

"Could I get you some coffee, Detective Santana?"

"Huh?"

"Coffee?"

"Oh, no thank you."

He stood in front of the couch, gazing into her honey-colored eyes, trying to release the cord that had held him momentarily in the past.

"You wouldn't happen to have some hot chocolate?" he asked.

"I don't. But I am making *mole con pollo.* Would you join me?"

He was about to decline the offer when the thought of a hot meal of chicken with chocolate sauce caused his stomach to emit a loud growl.

Angelina Torres smiled. "I will take that as a yes."

"Really. I shouldn't."

"Why not?"

"I normally don't have dinner with a …"

"Suspect?"

Santana doubted that Angelina Torres had committed one or both murders. He thought she had been swept along in the wave of the investigation simply because of her connection with Córdova. Yet, he never drew his final conclusions until he had all the evidence. He didn't want her drawing any conclusions either.

He was still searching for an appropriate response when she said, "You have to eat."

He hesitated.

"You can still ask me questions later, Detective Santana. But only if you say you like my dinner."

"Okay," he said. "It's a deal."

Angelina Torres poured Santana a glass of Sauvignon Blanc as he sat down at the kitchen table. She had taken the wine bottle from the refrigerator and then searched a long time for a wine opener, which he used to remove the cork. Given the rather modest furnishings in the apartment, he figured she could not afford to spend her salary on expensive wine. He wondered if this was the only bottle she had and if she had saved it for a special occasion. Then again, it would not be the first time he had engaged in wishful thinking when it came to an attractive woman.

"So tell me," she said, sitting down in a chair at the other end of the small, rectangular table, "do you live in the area?"

He shook his head. "Along the river in St. Croix Beach."

"It sounds like a nice setting."

"A chef in St. Paul who had to sell the house after a divorce once owned it. It has a lot of amenities, which I like. I'm not much of a cook, but it's secluded and private."

"How long have you been a homicide detective?"

"Five years."

"And before that?"

He put a forkful of chicken smothered with chocolate in his mouth. The chicken had been boiled for a long time, and it was so tender and tasty that it nearly dissolved in his mouth before he chewed it.

"I worked Narcotics for two years."

"Why Narcotics?"

"I wanted Homicide. And before you can work Homicide, the department wants you to have experience writing search warrants and investigating long-term cases. You get that experience with either the Sex and Domestic Crime Unit or Narcotics."

"How long were you a police officer before you became a detective?"

"Seven years. I worked out of the west side station on University and Dale."

"Did you always want to be a police officer?"

He preferred to concentrate on the meal instead of the conversation, but when he realized that he was devouring the chicken breast like a ravenous dog while she had barely started, he decided conversation might slow him down some.

"I wanted to be a doctor once."

"What changed your mind?"

Santana took one more bite of chicken. Washed it down with a swallow of wine. "My mother died. Soon after that, I left Colombia."

Her eyes told him that she knew there was more to it. That telling her now about what had happened to his mother would be like tearing a bandage off a wound that still had not healed.

"What about your father?"

"We have a saying in Colombia. *Dios cuida de sus borrachos."*

"God takes care of the drunks? Was your father a drunk?"

"He was killed by one. Car accident. The drunk lived."

"I am sorry. Were they your only family?

"I have a sister in Colombia somewhere."

"You do not know where?"

He gave her a practiced look that warned her she was getting a little too close.

"Well," she said, "whether you are a doctor or a police officer, you save lives."

"I look at it more like preventing death. When I get involved in a case, someone has already died. If I can find out who committed the murder, maybe I can prevent another death."

"So you believe in justice."

"Justice is a fine idea. But good lawyers get guilty people off all the time."

"Then why do it?"

Santana knew the simple answer to her question. It was all about the demon that had nearly eaten him alive twenty years ago. Each case that he solved satisfied its insatiable cravings for a while, kept it at bay. The demon was what got his juices flowing in the morning, was his reason for living. It haunted his dreams and often kept him awake at night wondering what would happen to him if he quit. "I do it for revenge," he wanted to say. Revenge was his demon. Plain and simple.

But instead he said, "I'm good at my job. It gives me a purpose in life. A mission."

It sounded noble as hell. And maybe there was actually some truth to it.

After they finished dinner and the dishes were cleared away, Santana took a glass of wine into the living room and sat down on a couch that was as stiff as his back. Probably a hide-a-bed. On a bookshelf there was a collection of coffee cups from different places that maybe she had visited, as well as framed photos of her family. Like all good Latinas, she treasured her family photos.

A statue of St. Anthony, the saint of lost things, stood on an end table. Santana wondered if she had always had the statue in her apartment, or if she had purchased it after her breakup with Córdova. Maybe hoping for some divine intervention to salvage the relationship.

A beaded rosary was draped over the statue. The strong scent of rose petals crushed and formed into beads carried him back to when he was twelve years old and had seen a similar Spanish Rosary entwined in his father's lifeless hands.

Santana had gone with his mother and younger sister, Natalia, to a private room at Aparicio's Funeral Home, the most elegant in Manizales, Colombia. There, his mother had opened the window of the casket to say her final, tearful goodbye to her husband. Time had dulled the sharp pain of that moment but not the memory of it. Ever since that day in the mortuary Santana had never appreciated the beauty of a rose, for he always associated its fragrance with sadness and death.

The wine and the meal had relaxed him, and the tension of the day began melting away. He took out his notebook and a pen, figuring that taking notes would give him something to do besides fall asleep.

Angelina Torres came into the living room carrying her wine glass and the half-empty bottle of Sauvignon Blanc. She struck a match and lit a thick white candle resting in a three-legged metal stand on the coffee table in front of the couch. A burst of phosphorus filled Santana's nostrils followed shortly by the pleasant scent of vanilla.

As she sat down in an armchair across from him, he said, "I'd like to talk to you further about your relationship with Córdova."

She looked at him for a time, as if deciding something, before she said, "You can call me Angelina. *Por favor.*"

She said it softly but with feeling. He could have sworn there was something more in her request.

Santana knew that getting too close to a suspect could cloud his judgment, but again a feeling of déja vu came over him, that he had known her before. This time the feeling was stronger, floating closer to the surface of his memory like a familiar name he could not quite recall.

"All right … Angelina."

Her eyes remained fixed on his.

Then she said, "I knew Rubén for a long time. We were … close once. I can assure you that he did not kill anyone."

"If that's true, then I still have to prove someone else did. You could help by answering a few more questions."

Santana assumed the dinner and wine and lack of sleep would have dulled his senses rather than heightening them, yet the short distance between the two of them suddenly felt as charged as the air before a thunderstorm.

She brushed a strand of her thick hair away from her face and gave him a hesitant smile. He knew then that she felt something, too.

"So tell me," he said, clearing his throat, "how did you end up in Minnesota?"

He detected a split second of disappointment as her eyes held his gaze for a moment longer before it was replaced by confusion.

"I thought you wanted to know more about Rubén?"

"I think knowing more about you will help me learn more about him."

"I see. How much do you want to know about me, Detective Santana?"

"Anything that will help me better understand this case. What happened in the past might have contributed to Córdova's death."

Santana knew from his own experiences that revisiting memories, particularly if they were traumatic, was like asking her to strip naked in front of strangers. Still, he could never erase the past any more than she could. A part of him would always be the tall, skinny Colombian kid who was born Juan Carlos Gutiérrez Arángo. The sixteen-year old who had changed his name because he naïvely believed it would protect him.

His adoptive parents were the only people he had trusted enough to reveal the dark secrets of his past. Both of the O'Tooles had provided a safe, loving environment. But it was Phil who had charted a clear course for him and given him a renewed sense of purpose.

Phil had taken him to headquarters on many occasions, introduced him to his fellow detectives and convinced him to become a homicide detective. Every murderer Santana put behind bars — or happened to kill in the line of duty — would be one less scumbag terrorizing society. It wasn't much, but it was enough.

"Talking about the past is difficult," she said. "But I will tell you if it will help."

Chapter 13

WHEN SHE BEGAN SPEAKING, Angelina Torres' eyes searched Santana's face, as though looking for some kind of map that might make her journey back in time less difficult. He hoped that the trust and understanding he tried to project would assure her that she was not traveling this difficult road alone.

"I was with my mother, Maria, and younger sister, Margarita. We rode a bus from our small village of Santa Rosa to Agua Prieta on the Arizona border. The bus had a sign on its side that read *Bienvenidos a su Futuro.* I remember thinking as I stood behind the bus terminal with only my jeans, T-shirt and the denim jacket on my back, that our future was very much in doubt. My mother had arranged to meet a man named Ramón who would help the three of us cross."

Thick smog from the *maquiladoras* made Angelina cough as Ramón led the three of them along a dusty street past the factories, whitewashed adobe homes and churches, and the concrete shells of buildings under construction. Ramón was tall and light skinned like many Mexicans along the border. He had helped her father cross safely three years before. He promised to do the same for the rest of the family for three thousand American dollars, one thousand dollars apiece.

Angelina used a hand to shield her eyes from the dry, warm wind that whirled around her while hustlers trailed along beside them like rats looking for food.

The air smelled of dust, garbage and meat roasting at the stands. Men with new clothes and gold jewelry stood at street corners beside expensive cars with booming stereos calling, *"Hay muchas rocas aquí."*

She wondered why anyone would want to buy a rock of anything, yet some of the filthy, gaunt men who were clustered around the plaza and park benches walked over to the cars and gave the men money.

"They were buying crack," Santana said.

"I know that now. But at the time I was so naïve. I remember seeing pictures of white crosses, shoes and clothes hanging on the metal wall in Tijuana. I did not know until my mother told me that each cross stood for someone who had died in the desert. I prayed to *La virgen de Guadalupe* that we would not end our lives that way. That night we stayed in a safe house."

It was a dilapidated clapboard *taqueria* with bunk beds in small rooms and *cucarachas* that skittered across the floor when candles were lit. Patches of cement hung like loose skin peeled away from bone, revealing the skeleton of pine beams that held up the fragile frame.

"We will cross at eleven tonight when the border patrol changes shifts," Ramón said. "It has been done many times before. Do not worry. This is how your father, Juan Miguel, crossed safely."

Ramón's smile seemed to be genuine, though it revealed one missing front tooth and gaps between many of the others.

"There is a full moon tonight," he said. "But we must avoid the *judiciales*. The Mexican police will want us to pay the *la mordida* to let us cross."

The house had no heat, and as the shadows along the horizon extinguished the last rays of sunlight, Angelina wrapped herself in a *serape* and sat on an old mattress on a small bunk in the room and slowly ate a cold *tortilla.* Through the thin door she could hear whispered voices and occasional footsteps in the hallway.

She thought of her father and how much she missed him. He had not written because he did not know how, but he always sent a picture with the money he had earned. In the last picture he had sent he looked very thin and very pale. She worried that the work in the grape fields in California with the *braceros* had not been good for him. If he was sending all his money to them, what was he living on she wondered? When they were all together again, she would help him get strong once more. As the oldest child in the family, she had a responsibility to help. She had to be strong for all of them.

"Drink plenty of water," her mother advised them. "The night will be long."

Angelina Torres paused for a moment in the story and sipped her wine. The candles burning on the coffee table had filled her apartment with a rich, vanilla scent.

Santana held her gaze for a time, but then her eyes drifted away from him and focused on some distant point beyond the room.

"It was ten thirty when Ramón drove us along Pan American Avenue and past the searchlights to the outskirts of town," she continued.

The wall had not been completed between Agua Prieto and Douglas, Arizona, and barbed wire was still the only barrier along the border. Another coyote had joined them. Ramón called him Jesse. He sat up front in the Ford Bronco with his back against the passenger door, half-turned, an arm resting on the back of the seat.

"Buenas noches, pollitos," he said with a hard laugh.

Angelina did not know why Jesse called them chickens and she did not ask. *El cara cortada,* as she would remember him, had a long scar on the left side of his face. A wiry, dark Zapoteca Indian from Huaxaca, she thought he was about thirty-two, the same age as her father.

Ramón parked the Ford Bronco in a restaurant lot and got out. Angelina saw other trucks and vans unloading groups of people.

"Ándale!" Ramón said.

She took one of Margarita's hands and her mother took the other as Ramón hurried them across the highway and down a steep embankment toward the border road. Her heart pounded as she ran, and she tried to calm the fear that rushed like blood through her body. In the light of the full moon she could see that the desert floor was littered with empty water jugs and discarded clothing as she fell in line behind her mother and sister. Others had joined them now, and she counted ten shadows in the group.

When they approached the border road, Ramón stopped suddenly and said, *"Agáchate!"*

Angelina crouched in the darkness in a ditch and watched as a border patrol car passed by, dragging a tire along the soft dirt road, smoothing it out. Her mother and sister were on either side of her and she grabbed each of their hands and held them tight.

"They will come back every half hour looking for footprints," Ramón said when the car had passed. "Tie these around your shoes."

Out of a burlap bag, he took pieces of carpet and rope.

Angelina helped her mother and sister before tying the carpet around her own shoes.

"We must cross through the barbed wire now," Ramón said. "Be careful of the camera."

He pointed to his right. "It moves like magic and has the eyes of an owl."

About a hundred yards away, Angelina could see the tall pole where a camera was mounted.

"When it is time," she whispered to her sister, "stay low."

"Vamos," Ramón said in a hard whisper.

Bent double at the waist, she led her family to the barbed wire fence. The one called Jesse put his foot on the lower strand of barbed wire and lifted the upper strand with a hand.

"Cuidado, señorita," he said to her.

She smelled the tequila in the open bottle he held in one hand as she passed carefully under the wire and stepped into the United States. Jesse cut the rope holding the carpet on her shoes with a large knife while she waited for her sister and mother to cross.

Then Ramón said, *"Ándale, ándale.* We have many miles to go."

Stumbling along, trying to find the ground that seemed to drop away from her with every step, Angelina occasionally heard the low whirring noise of a helicopter in the distance.

"Remember," Ramón warned, "lie down in the bushes and do not look up at the helicopter if it comes. Your eyes will reflect in the searchlight, and they will know we are here."

Thorns from the *mesquite* and *creosote* bushes snagged her jeans. A branch of lightening lit the belly of dark clouds that crested the mountains to the northeast. Finally, at the top of a hill, she saw the lights of a city in the distance.

"Are we in California?" Margarita asked loudly enough that others in the group heard her and broke out in laughter.

"That is only the town of Douglas, Arizona," Ramón said. "We have come only three miles. There is a van waiting for us, but it is another eighteen miles. You will see. We must circle the city first to avoid the vigilante patrols. We will rest later."

Angelina's legs began to ache as they continued walking for hours through riverbeds and barbed wire fences and up and down sloping foothills, though she refused to complain.

"I am tired," Margarita said.

"Are you planning to have us walk all the way to Phoenix, *señor?"* Maria asked.

"No, no, *señora*. We can rest here for a short time."

The desert sand felt cool to the touch as Angelina sat down beside her mother and sister. Though it was May, her breath floated like smoke around her, and the three of them huddled together trying to protect themselves from the night air that was as cold as ice water against the skin.

"It was my fifteenth birthday," Angelina Torres said to Santana. "My mother promised me that when we reached California and were reunited with my father, we would celebrate my *quinceañera*."

Santana knew that fifteen was the most important age in a Mexican girl's life. But instead of a beautiful dress and a big party with very special gifts, her mother had bought a one-way ticket to hell.

"I remember we were sitting in the moonlight near a tall saguaro cactus filled with white flowers," she went on. "The flowers had blossomed in the darkness. It was so beautiful and so strange. I learned later that the flowers bloomed only for a single night before they withered and died the next afternoon."

The one that was called Jesse was drinking from the bottle of tequila. Angelina watched as the beam of light from the flashlight he carried swayed back and forth like a scythe with each step that he took. He came up to her and squatted down beside her.

Momentarily blinded by a bright flash, she heard Ramón say, *"Idiota. Apaga esa linterna."*

Jesse flicked off the flashlight. "Would you like a drink, *señorita?* It will keep you warm."

He smelled as if he had not bathed in a week.

"Estas borracho," her mother said.

"Maybe I am drunk, *señora*. But I could keep you warm. And your daughter, too."

"Vamos! Deja a mi hija sola."

Jesse laughed as he stood up and stumbled off into the darkness calling, *"Señorrrritas!"*

"I do not like that man," Margarita said.

"Stay close to me," Maria said. "He cannot be trusted."

Ramón came around and gave them a drink from a jug. *"Es tiempo de irnos."*

Angelina was happy that it was time to go. The water had refreshed her. She was ready to walk again, ready to walk forever if it would bring her to her father. She led her sister and mother to the cactus where they rejoined the others. Somewhere in the darkness, she heard the plaintive whistle of a train.

They walked through the night until the rising sun lit the clouds on the eastern horizon and heat began rising in waves off the desert floor. As they neared a sign that read U.S. 80, Angelina glimpsed a maroon and gray van parked in the tall grass near a set of railroad tracks that ran parallel to the highway.

"Get in and stay down," Ramón said as he slid open the side doors and the group clambered into the back of the van whose rear seats had been removed.

Hot bodies pressed against Angelina as she lay down on her stomach under a blanket. The unwashed odor of fear and sweat was a living presence in the van. She grabbed Margarita's hand and gave it a squeeze, letting her know that as long as they were together, her little sister would be safe.

"It took us four hours to get to the safe house in Phoenix," Angelina said to Santana. "We had to stay off the highway to avoid the checkpoints."

She drank the last of the wine in her glass. Filled it half full again.

Santana noted that her words were slightly slurred now. He didn't mind. Maybe she needed the alcohol to continue her story, to deaden the pain.

"It was late when I awoke to the sound of loud voices coming from the blackness surrounding me," she continued. "At first I thought I was in the bedroom that I shared with Margarita in Santa Rosa. But then I remembered I was in a safe house somewhere in Phoenix."

She could not hear exactly what was being said, but it was clear that Ramón was arguing with the one called Jesse. She listened for a time, straining to hear, when suddenly the voices grew quiet and she knew that the two men were coming.

Her mother awoke now, too, though Margarita continued to sleep soundly beside them in the large bed. The bedroom door swung open and the lamp on the nightstand next to the bed lit up.

"What do you want?" her mother asked.

"Señora," Ramón began with a nervous laugh, "there has been … a slight change in plans."

"What do you mean? We paid you the money."

"Si, señora. But you know there is much danger, much risk in what we do. The money you paid, it, ah, will not be enough to get all of you tickets at the airport."

"We have no more money, *señor.* We have nothing."

"Señora," Jesse said. "You do have something of value."

"No, you are mistaken, *señor.* We have nothing. We …" her mother's voice trailed off. Then with a determination that Angelina had never heard before her mother said, "No! This is something you will never have, *señor.* Never!"

Margarita awoke with a start. "What is it?" she asked, her voice heavy with sleep. "What's wrong?"

"Shh, *chiquita,"* Angelina said, wrapping her sister in her arms. "We are fine."

"Señora," Jesse said, in a voice that was a hoarse whisper. "I know you and your daughters want to get to California so you can see your husband again."

"Give us our money and we will find a way," Maria said defiantly.

"I'm afraid that is not possible, *señora."*

Maria glared at Ramón. "You!" she said with venom in her voice. *"Hijo de la chingada tienes dos caras."*

Jesse gave a small laugh. "So, now you are a fucking two-face, Ramón."

Angelina had never heard her mother use this language before and she told herself to stay calm. She did not know what Jesse wanted and fear began to crawl like a scorpion up her spine.

"Take me, *señor,*" Maria said. "But not Angelina, *por favor.* I will do whatever you want."

"*Señora,* please," Ramón said. "You must do what he wants. Let your daughter go with him. She is old enough and it will not take long and in the morning we will take you to the airport and you will soon be with your husband."

"No!"

"I could always take the little one?" Jesse said.

Ramón gave him a hard look. "You will not do that, *amigo.*"

Jesse shrugged his shoulders.

"I will go with him, *mamíta,*" Angelina said.

"No! You will not!"

"It will be okay."

"No, Angel," her mother said with tears in her voice. "You do not understand what will happen."

"But if we want to see father again."

Angelina got out of bed and stood up, but her mother grabbed her by the wrist.

"No, *por favor.*"

Angelina suppressed the fear in her voice. "It is what I must do," she said.

Ramón stepped between them. "*Señora,* please."

He pried her mother's fingers off Angelina's wrist.

"What is wrong?" Margarita asked, beginning to cry. "Angel, what is wrong?"

With a scream, Maria sprang from the bed and threw herself at Ramón. Tried to rake his face with her fingernails.

Angelina instinctively moved toward her mother to help, but Jesse came up behind her quickly and locked her in a chokehold. The pressure of his forearm against her throat kept her from moving or speaking.

"Stop, *señora*," Jesse yelled, "or I will break your daughter's neck!"

Ramón had her mother's wrists and back pinned against the wall. He kept a hip pressed against her legs, so that she could not kick him. Margarita was sitting on her knees in the bed, crying loudly as she watched what was happening to her mother and sister. Maria made one last attempt to free herself, but Ramón was too strong. She let out another scream, but this one was a scream of anguish.

Angelina saw the tears running down her mother's cheeks. She knew that in order to protect her mother and younger sister, she had to do what the men wanted. As Jesse led her out into the hallway, she could hear her mother weeping and her sister's cries of "Angel, where are you going?"

Under the glare of the ceiling light in another bedroom, Angelina stood facing the one called Jesse. She watched as his eyes fondled her body and a half-grin of expectation played across his wet, thin lips. There was a musty, feathered mattress with yellow stains on the bed, and as he pushed her down upon it, she had a feeling that what was about to happen to her had happened here before, that this was not the first time a family crossing the border with him had suddenly been short of money.

He was breathing heavily as he pulled off her jeans. Yanked her white T-shirt up over her head. His breath smelled as though something had died and was rotting inside him.

"I will never forget the smell of his awful breath," she said, looking at Santana.

Angelina Torres had spoken dispassionately about all of it, as if it were a bad dream she had once had. But Santana could see the lingering pain in her eyes.

She said, "Ramón took us to the airport in the morning."

"And the one called Jesse?"

She gave a weak, little shrug.

"He didn't go to the airport with you?"

She shook her head slowly.

Santana studied her eyes. Tried to read them to see if she was lying.

"Tell me what happened," Santana said.

The color drained from her complexion. Angelina Torres looked down at her hands and then at the darkness outside the window. When she looked at him again, tears glistened in her eyes.

"You are a very perceptive man, Detective Santana. I am sure this skill helps you in your job."

"Sometimes it helps," he said.

"Do you think I killed the coyote after he raped me?"

"Why don't you tell me about it?"

She reached for a Kleenex in a box on the coffee table and wiped away the tears that ran down her cheeks. Then she fixed her eyes on his before she spoke again.

"When I came back to the room after I had been with the coyote, my mother saw my blood. I thought I could do anything to see my father again, to make sure we all arrived safely. I did not realize at the time what I had lost. But my mother did. I saw darkness in her that night I had never seen before."

She drew in a shaky breath and let it out before she continued. "The next morning when Ramón took us to the airport and *el cara cortada* was not with us, I suspected something had happened to him."

Santana waited for her to continue.

"Are you going to contact the Phoenix police?"

Santana thought about his own mother's death. He wondered what he would do if someone came out of the shadows and wanted to look into his past, wondered about right and wrong and truth and lies and justice.

He said, "What happened after you left the safe house?"

Her eyes lingered on his, as though trying to read his thoughts. Finally, she said, "We were in California that afternoon with my father. For a long time I could only write of my experiences in my journal. A teacher in my high school read what I had written. She had my journal published as a book. I won an award. Some important people in California got me my citizenship and a scholarship to the University of Southern California."

"That's where you met Rubén?"

"He was a journalism student. He was already writing stories about the *braceros* and the pesticides that were killing them. My mother and father were both sick by then. My mother never spoke of the incident in Phoenix until the day she died. Her last words to me were *'Lo siento'*. But I never blamed her for what happened. She was only trying to better our lives. This is why I help the illegals whenever I can."

"Help them how?"

"Through the Church of the Guardian Angels. We get them clothes, food, housing."

"Father Hidalgo helped as well?"

"Of course."

"What about jobs? You ever get illegals jobs or papers?"

"Jobs if I can, yes. Papers, no. Many of the fast food places hire them without papers."

"Did Córdova help the illegals, too, before he died?"

"Sometimes, yes."

"Did he ever get them papers?"

"No."

"You're sure?"

"Yes, I am sure."

"How about Rafael Mendoza?"

"Mr. Mendoza helped many of the immigrants get jobs and citizenship. He helped Father Hidalgo, too."

"Córdova had an appointment with Mendoza at the time that Mendoza died."

She stared at him for a time, apparently trying to get her mind around the idea. "If I had not given Rubén the gun," she said with regret. "He would never have been a murder suspect. He would not be dead."

Santana could not argue with her logic, so he changed the subject.

"What happened to your younger sister, Margarita?"

"She is studying to be a doctor in California. We talk often."

Santana could hear the pride in her voice.

Angelina Torres went quiet for a time, seemingly lost in the fog of a distant memory. Then she said, "We have never spoken about *el cara cortada*."

Santana noted how she lowered her head and let her shoulders slump. He knew from victim reports that the psychological damage of rape was often worse than the physical injury. Victims usually felt shame, especially in a machismo culture where Hispanic women often paid a high price for losing their virginity before marriage.

"You need to understand," she said, looking at him again. "The coyote, Jesse, used my body, but he never touched my soul."

"Aren't they one and the same?"

"You did not always believe that." She said it softly and without any recrimination.

"You seem awfully certain."

She hesitated a moment before answering, as if embarrassed by what she was about to say. "I'm afraid there is much anger in you, Detective Santana. Though some might mistake the anger for emptiness."

"But you don't?"

"No. What they see is not really who you are. Or who you once were. You have a soul", she said with a firm nod. "A very good soul."

"Not everyone would agree with you."

"They would be the same people who saw only anger or emptiness in you. Perhaps it is only what you see in yourself."

Dark clouds shadowed the moon, and the night sky was as black and empty as a tomb when Santana pulled the Crown Vic into his garage and made his way along the narrow, shoveled path to his front door. He punched in the code that deactivated the security system, went inside and hung up his coat. He'd had trouble shaking the feeling of melancholy that had enveloped him as he drove home. Maybe it was the cold winter darkness that always seemed to chip away at the fortress he had constructed around himself, or maybe it was something else.

In the kitchen he set his holster on the counter and poured himself a shot from a bottle of aguardiente. The smooth, licorice scented liqueur was like a thin lifeline to home, and it drew him to the mantel over the fireplace where he kept his father's favorite meerschaum pipe, one of the few mementos that he had managed to take with him when he fled Colombia.

Holding the pipe carefully in his hands, he lifted the bowl to his nose and inhaled the aroma of the cherry blend tobacco embedded in the wood. The sweet scent triggered his olfactory senses and in a heartbeat he was lying in his bed in his boyhood home in Manizales. It was late at night and his father was in the living room listening to a Julio Jaramillo record and lighting a pipe from his collection, the smoke and romantic guitar music wafting gently throughout the house. The pipe his father was smoking could have been a Hardcastle with the dark wood and silver band, or a Sherlock Holmes with the curved mouthpiece; perhaps it was a briar or more likely the meerschaum.

Santana remembered how his father would put a clean white cloth into a wide-mouthed glass jar. Place the meerschaum on the cloth. Blow smoke into the jar and seal the lid. Each day his father would patiently change the cloth and rotate the bowl of the pipe until it had changed from its distinctive white into a golden-brown color like an evenly roasted marshmallow. A process that usually took thirty years was complete in weeks.

The memory lingered for a moment longer; then, like a wisp of smoke, it was gone.

Santana placed the pipe gently back on the mantle and walked over to the end table next to the leather couch and looked at the answering machine and the blinking light. He pushed the play button and waited while Tony Novak's voice informed him that he had great seats for the Chandler fight and that Santana "had damn well better be ready to go."

Santana thought it was strange that Novak had not mentioned anything about the photo he was supposed to be examining at the lab. It was only 9:00 p.m., so he looked up Novak's home phone number in his address book in the end table drawer and dialed the number. The phone rang five times before one of Novak's three teenage daughters answered.

"Is Tony home?"

"Yeah."

There was a pause. Santana could hear her working on a wad of gum.

"Could I speak to him please? Tell him its John Santana."

"Hi, John," the teenager said with a giggle. "It's Kim." She was Novak's middle daughter.

"Hi, Kim."

"How come you haven't been over for a while? I've missed you."

Fourteen and flirting with him like she was thirty. All three of the girls had a crush on him according to Novak. Kim's was the most obvious.

"I've been a little busy."

"Have you been, like, working on a case?"

It was Santana's turn to be silent.

"Okay. Like I need to know. Hold on."

She clicked off and Santana could tell that she was on the other line. After an interminable pause she said, "Dad's coming. See you soon?"

Before Santana could respond, he could hear Tony wrestling the phone away from her. "Oh, Dad," Santana heard her say.

Tony cupped his hand over the phone, but Santana heard his muffled voice. "Don't you have homework to do?"

The hand came off the receiver and Novak said, "You still there, John?"

"Barely."

"Listen, living with three teenage daughters is tougher than going fifteen with Ali."

"You have my sympathies."

"I heard about the accident with the snowplow. You're lucky to be alive."

If you only knew, Santana thought. "I'm okay, Tony."

"You set for the Chandler fight and dinner at Mancini's?"

"Looking forward to it. Say, Tony, I was wondering if you'd come up with anything on that photo I dropped off?"

"Well, there was nothing I could find to help you identify the guy on his knees. I did a TMDT test on Córdova. There was no GSR on his hands, but that's unreliable, John. He could've washed his hands or put 'em in his pocket."

The trace metal detection test was commonly used to test if a suspect had recently held a metal object, such as a gun. Under ultraviolet light it was sometimes possible to see the location of the trigger on the index finger and the location of the metal frame that touched the palm. But Santana knew people came in contact with metal objects every day, so there would always be some trace metal present on a subject's hands. The amount of perspiration on the hands could also alter the results of the test. And Córdova could have washed any gun shot residue off his hands.

"I also detected backspatter on the gun, John, but not on Córdova's clothes."

Santana found this information troubling. If Córdova had held the gun close to Pérez's head when he fired, there should have been evidence of blood spray on Córdova's sleeve.

"I left a message with your partner at the station," Novak said. "Told him I found Torres' fingerprint on the murder weapon and that the ballistics tests matched."

Santana had a sharp feeling deep in his chest, as though a scalpel had been plunged into it.

"How come Anderson didn't tell you, John?"

Santana didn't want to believe what he was hearing, but suddenly things made a lot more sense.

Chapter 14

DAY 5

RUSH HOUR TRAFFIC MOVING WEST toward downtown St. Paul slowed to a crawl as Santana neared the 3M complexes. A haze of exhaust fumes swirled around the cars and trucks sitting at a standstill and drifted off the concrete and into the air like phantoms rising from tombstones.

Trying to quiet his mind last night so that he could get some sleep had been impossible. The moment he drifted off, he would think of Rick Anderson again, and his mind would take off in a different direction, searching for some legitimate reason why his partner had not told him about Tony Novak's phone call. But no matter how many excuses Santana came up with for his partner's behavior, the end result was the same. Anderson had withheld key information. Or worse yet, he was feeding that information to James Kehoe. Santana was going to find out what the hell was going on with Anderson if he had to beat it out of him.

He parked the Crown Vic along the curb on 10th Street and walked past the department smokers standing on the sidewalk in the cold, getting one last nicotine fix before they went inside. The frigid air felt like shards of glass entering his lungs. He used his key card to open the security door and walked down the narrow corridor to the elevator near the report writing room and the watch commander's office. The watch commander only worked afternoons and weekends, so the office was dark. Santana took the elevator up to the third floor. It was 7:56, and he was hoping that Anderson, a notoriously early riser, would be there.

He walked down the corridor until he came to Anderson's workstation. The computer was on, a wool topcoat hung over the back of his chair. A pair of leather gloves lay on the seat. On the wall above Anderson's station was a whiteboard listing which homicide investigators were working during the weekend. Santana's name was absent from the list, but as long as the Pérez-Mendoza case was still open, he would be working.

Santana reversed his direction, left his overcoat and gloves in his own cubicle, and went back out into the hallway where he nearly ran into Tom Gamboni from the Sex Crimes unit. Tom Gamboni was Rita's ex-husband, and he was the last guy Santana wanted to see this morning.

Gamboni wore street clothes: blue jeans, faded denim shirt and a pair of cowboy boots. He was heavy-set with dark, curly hair and a complexion that matched. A gold shield hung from the black nylon cord around a paunchy neck that spilled over his shirt collar.

"Well, well, John Santana."

His tone was no doubt the same one he used on a pedophile busted with a video of child porn.

Santana said, "Have you seen Rick Anderson around?"

Gamboni gave him a hard stare and took a sip from the mug of coffee he was carrying.

Santana waited.

The saying written in small letters on the side of the mug read:

LOOKING AT SOMEONE'S HIND END

DOESN'T REQUIRE ALL THAT MUCH VISION

"I guess you haven't seen Anderson," Santana said at last, and started down the hall again.

"I saw him," Gamboni said.

Santana stopped, turned, and waited some more. "You going to tell me where or are we playing twenty questions?"

Gamboni jerked a thumb in the direction of 10th Street. "Anderson was headed over to the range this morning. Guess he's gotta stay in practice in case he has to save your ass again."

The sardonic smile that slashed across his face showed off his coffee-stained teeth.

Santana shook his head. He had no intention of wasting his anger on Gamboni, especially since he and Rita were no longer dating.

"Get over it," he said, and headed toward the elevator.

"Get over what?" Gamboni called after him. "There's nothin' to get over. You hear me, Santana?"

Santana ignored him.

The target range was located in a building on the south side of 10th Street. Santana took the elevator down to the second floor and walked past the evidence room and the police museum where there were glass cases filled with memorabilia from as far back as the thirties. The wall opposite the glass cases was lined with plaques commemorating actions of valor and merit and plaques honoring officers who had been killed in the line of duty over the years. Santana had once counted the twenty-nine names of officers who had been killed.

He went across a skyway with glass windows that linked the two buildings, past the gym, to the target range where he opened a door that led into a dimly lit corridor. The range was to his left through a second door, though this one was soundproofed. Up ahead, the corridor led to a storage area where weapons were housed and to a cleaning room where the Glocks were field stripped once a year in February and March as required by the department.

Santana grabbed a set of ear covers and went in the soundproofed door to the firing range. There were six side-by-side stalls from which officers shot at targets that were sent downrange using electric pulleys activated by a push-button code on a metal box in the stall. The floor was littered with .40 caliber shell casings. A sign on the wall read:

SPEED IS FINE

BUT ACCURACY IS FINAL

The range was usually well lighted, but now the lights had been lowered so that only the targets were brightly lit. Night shooting.

The picture on one side of the target that hung in the stalls was of an old man with glasses holding an umbrella. On the other side of the target was a picture of the same old man only this time he was holding a gun. Either side could come up when an officer was being tested monthly on the range. Santana had a good idea of which side you wanted to shoot, night or day.

Rick Anderson stood to Santana's left. He was facing down range, holding a Glock against his right leg. Standing perfectly still. Staring at a fixed target ahead of him. He would stare at the target for a time and then look down at the Glock in his hand, trying to answer the question every cop who killed someone in the line of duty had to answer. Would he pull the trigger again if he had to? If there were lingering doubts, any hesitation, word got around the department and suddenly the cop had trouble finding a partner. That usually meant a desk job — or no job at all.

Santana watched Anderson look twice more at the target and at the gun he held in his right hand. Then he walked over and yanked the Glock out of Anderson's hand.

Anderson jumped as if hit with a jolt of electricity. He took off his ear covers and hung them around his neck. Santana did the same.

"Hey, John!"

Santana said, "Having a little trouble pulling the trigger?"

Anderson shook his head. "Hell, no."

"You sure?"

"Positive. If I have to, I will."

"Maybe you won't get the chance."

Anderson's eyes narrowed. "What do you mean? You think I can't watch your back if things get tight?"

"You haven't been watching my back for a while now, Rick. You've been going behind it."

"What're you talking about, partner?"

"Don't give me that partner bullshit," Santana said, anger burning like a wound in his stomach. "You sold me out."

Anderson glanced down at the Glock in Santana's hand. Then he looked up quickly, as if he was afraid Santana might have noticed.

"No, John," he said, forcing a smile. "That's not true."

Santana took a step forward. "Not true, huh? Then how did Kehoe know that Torres' fingerprint was on the gun? And how come you never told me Tony Novak called with information on the photo found in Mendoza's loft, and that there wasn't any GSR on Córdova's hands or backspatter on his shirt. Or were you too busy telling Kehoe about it at O'Leary's last night."

Santana could see the fear in Anderson's eyes now.

"You don't understand, John. I can explain."

"You're right. I don't understand. I don't understand how my partner could fuck me over like you did."

"It wasn't like that."

"It wasn't, huh?" Santana poked him in the chest with an index finger. "What else did you tell Kehoe?"

"Nothing. Really. You gotta believe me."

"What? Now you're asking me to trust you?"

"Listen," Anderson said, spreading his hands. "Kehoe told me if I helped him out with some information involving the case, he'd have the mayor put some pressure on IA to speed up their investigation. Clear me of the Córdova shooting. So I could get back on the case. Help you out."

"Oh, you helped out all right."

"Look, John. I'm sorry. I made a mistake."

"So did I. *No debés confiar ni en tú propia sombra.*"

Anderson shook his head, indicating he didn't understand.

"It's a Colombian saying. Don't trust even your own shadow. I made a mistake trusting you, Rick."

"There was no mistake, John. You can trust me. We're partners."

"I don't think so."

Anderson's face went white. "What're you saying?"

"I'm saying I should go to Rita. Ask for a new partner."

"Don't do that, John. It'll never happen again."

Anderson's eyes were wide and filled with regret, as though he had just bet his career on a throw of the dice and lost.

Santana said, "You worried about me telling Rita?"

"I don't give a shit about that."

"What is it you give a shit about?"

"I don't want to lose you as a partner. As a friend."

Santana let him squirm awhile. "I have to think about it."

"That's fine. Take all the time you need. You want me to do anything, just ask. I'm through with Kehoe."

Santana shook his head. "You're not through with Kehoe."

"I am." His voice was strained. "I swear." He raised his right hand tentatively like he was taking an oath.

"I still may want you to meet with him."

Anderson blinked hard. "Why?"

"Because I'm going to tell you what I want you to say to him."

"You want me to lie to him?"

"You have a problem with that?"

"No, John. Whatever you want. Name it."

"Good. I'll let you know."

"What about us? We still partners?"

Santana fixed his eyes on Anderson. The cavernous range was as quiet as a crypt.

Santana ratcheted a bullet into the Glock's chamber and put on the ear covers.

Anderson took a step back.

Santana smiled. Punched in the code on the metal box in the stall.

Tiny beads of sweat appeared on Anderson's brow.

Santana motioned with the Glock for Anderson to put on his ear covers.

Anderson hesitated, unsure.

Santana motioned again.

Anderson's hands shook as he put on the ear covers.

Suddenly the target spun and Santana half turned. Raised his right arm and fired the shell in the Glock's chamber. Then he walked over and handed the magazine and the empty Glock to the ashen-faced Anderson and headed for the door.

Santana had no desire to confirm whether the old man pictured on the target was holding an umbrella or a gun, or where the bullet had landed. He knew.

It was 8:42 when Santana returned to the Crimes Against Persons Division, poured himself a cup of hot chocolate from his thermos and sat down in his chair. The muscles in his neck and deltoids were ropes strung tight with tension. His right hand was still sore from the fight with the Colombian assassin. He was frustrated with Anderson, frustrated with Kehoe, frustrated with the whole damn investigation.

He ran through the tape of the case once more in his mind, looking for something that he had missed, a reason to change his mind, but no matter which way he played it, the ending always came out the same. Whoever had killed Pérez, had killed

Mendoza. The two men had known each other despite what Pérez's daughter had told him. Pérez had called Mendoza from his home on the day he was murdered. But what was the connection? Both men were the same age and were born in Valladolid, Mexico. It was a large city, but it was certainly possible that the two men had known each other as children. Mendoza was bringing illegals into the country on phony worker's visas and making a lot of money, but if Pérez was involved in the scam, where was his cut of the money? And if the double murder wasn't about money, then what was it about?

Mendoza was gay and had an explicit photo of two anonymous men engaging in oral sex in his loft, but was that reason enough for someone to kill him? It might be if that someone wanted the photo kept secret. But if Mendoza were threatening to use the photo to blackmail someone, then he would have to out himself. And why kill Pérez? There was no evidence that he was gay. Whoever killed Pérez and Mendoza had used Rubén Córdova's gun to do it and had tried to set up Córdova to take the fall. Córdova had been at the wrong place at the wrong time. So who or what was the connection between Pérez and Mendoza? And who benefited the most from their deaths?

Santana set his cup on the desk, pushed himself out of the chair and went over to Internal Affairs. He paused in the open doorway and looked at the office, wondering if he had time to walk in and search for the file on the Córdova shooting before anyone arrived. He was about to enter when he spotted Trina Martelli, one of the investigators assigned to IA, coming down the hallway, briefcase in one hand, a brown paper bag in the other.

She acknowledged Santana with a nod. "Looking for me, John?"

"Something you have."

"Yeah?"

"The report on the Córdova shooting."

"No can do," she said, squeezing past him in the doorway.

"This isn't about Anderson."

"Sure."

He followed along beside her. "What's with the uniform?"

"Rumor has it the chief's planning to issue an order about wearing our uniforms whenever the country's on orange alert."

"You're kidding?"

"The hell I am. Chief figures it gives us more of a presence around the city. Keeps the citizens calm. I agree. Thought I'd get a head start."

"Not real good for clandestine investigative work."

She set the leather briefcase on her desk next to a copy of a Weight Watcher's recipe book. "I haven't done much of that lately."

"But you're part of the preliminary investigation on Anderson."

"That's pretty much wrapped up from what I understand. The mayor's office took it over. Cut us out."

"Kehoe?"

"Oh, yeah." She kept nodding as she spoke. "Came in here like he owned the place. Wanted all the information on the shooting. Like we were working for him. Sorry if he's a friend, John, but the guy's a first class prick."

"He's no friend of mine."

"Well, at least we agree on that."

"You keep copies of everything?"

She gave him a look that said I'm not an idiot. "Of course I kept copies."

"Look, Trina, there's a woman suspected as an accomplice in two murders. And there's a dead guy who everyone seems to think was a killer. How about helping me out here?"

"You don't think Córdova's guilty?"

"I don't. But Kehoe does."

"Jeez," she said with a shake of her head. "I'd really like to help you, John. But Anderson's your partner. If word got out I gave you access to the report before the investigation was complete, I might as well kiss my career goodbye."

She opened the paper bag and took out a naval orange the size of a grapefruit.

"I understand if you're worried about pissing off Asshoe."

She laughed. "That what you call Kehoe in Homicide?"

"Fits, doesn't it?"

She laughed again. "That's for sure."

"I just want to look at the wit's statements on the shooting, Trina. That's all. You'd really be doing me a favor. And if I can prove Córdova was innocent, you'll be shafting Kehoe at the same time."

She clicked the locks on her briefcase and opened it. Inside were a manila folder, a copy of the *Pioneer Press*, and two black pens.

"I tell you what," she said. "I'm going to make a fresh pot of coffee and use the restroom." She looked at Santana. "No copies. And when I get back, you're gone?"

"Hey, I was never here."

"Remember," she said, walking away. "You owe me."

"If I forget, I'm sure you'll remind me."

"You got that right."

Inside the manila folder were witness statements along with photographs of Rubén Córdova lying in the broken glass from the store window on the ground level of the Riverview Lofts. Each statement was about one typed page with a signature at the bottom and an information box at the top. The first uniforms on the scene, Roy Davis, Joe Donaldson and Keith Holmgren, took the statements.

Santana scanned each of the statements. None of the witness statements contradicted Rick Anderson's contention that Córdova had gone for his gun because no one had actually seen the shooting, which was good news for Anderson. But there was nothing that stood out in any of the names or the statements, which was bad news for Santana.

He put the manila folder back in Trina Martelli's briefcase and returned to his desk. He took Rubén Córdova's notebook out of his briefcase and began looking carefully at each page. Halfway through it he came across a name he recognized from Rafael Mendoza's files. José López. Prior to his death, Córdova had been arrested for unlawful assembly in both Worthington and Minneapolis while protesting the unfair treatment of illegals. He had written articles about their plight and obviously sympathized with their cause. Someone had given Córdova a tip about Mendoza's visa scam. Santana had a hunch it was López.

José López lived in a cluster of low-income town homes on Maryland Avenue not far from the Bureau of Criminal Apprehension field office. The young woman with the dark, wary eyes who answered the door was reluctant to speak to Santana in Spanish, even after he showed her his badge and after he assured her that José wasn't in any trouble. She finally told him that her brother was working at *El Burrito's*. Santana thanked her and left.

Almost half as big as a large chain store, *El Burrito* was the most popular Hispanic grocery on St. Paul's West Side. It was advertised as offering a unique *Mercado* experience and sold everything from hard to find spices and fresh peppers to homemade tamales and salsa. The grocery also contained a specialty meat department, imported gift items, a few pieces of furniture, a deli, fresh *pan dulce* and the authentic *El Cafe* restaurant.

Santana parked in the small lot behind the yellow and blue building and entered through the rear doors. He walked past the racks that held Hispanic newspapers like *El Día*, *Gente* and *La Prensa* and went up to one of the two registers. From where he stood, he could see the restaurant at one end of the store that featured *tortillas, burritos, enchiladas* and *carnitas.*

"Estoy buscanto a José López."

The Mexican teen in a blue smock behind the counter pointed two aisles over.

Santana thanked him and went up a narrow aisle, past a heavy-set Mexican woman pushing a cart filled with groceries and a baby strapped in a car seat, toward the front of the store. Purple, orange and green *piñatas* in the shape of animals and stars hung from the pipes that veined the ceiling tiles, as speakers pumped *Rancheras* music throughout the store. Santana found López lifting cans of *frioles* out of cardboard boxes and stacking them on shelves.

"Hablas Inglés?"

"Si."

Santana showed López his badge. "My name's John Santana. St. Paul P.D."

López only glanced at the badge as he continued stacking cans, but Santana saw immediately that López's left eye was black and blue and swollen to the size of a small egg, which suggested the injury was recent.

"I want to ask you some questions."

"Sobre qué?"

"It's not about your status or your papers, José — but it could be."

López stopped stacking the cans and straightened up. He was short and slightly pudgy and his black hair was combed forward so it formed bangs.

Santana made him for no more than nineteen.

"I no in trouble?" López spoke quietly and with a heavy Mexican accent.

"Not as long as you answer my questions truthfully."

He gave a hesitant nod. "Okay."

Santana followed him to the cafeteria where they sat down in a pair of wooden chairs across a square table from one another. "You want some coffee or a Coke, Jóse?"

López shook his head.

Santana took out a pen and his notebook and opened it. "How long have you been in the country?"

"Two years."

"You come to the states alone?"

"With my sister."

"Is she working?"

"Not now. She work in a packing company. But the manager, he say she must sleep with him or lose her job. She say she will do it so she can keep working and make money. Then we can bring our parents here. But I tell her she has to quit before I kill the pig."

Santana remembered his younger sister, Natalia. Imagined what he would do to the man who tried to force her into sleeping with him.

"Looks to me like you already had a discussion with the manager, José. Maybe his eye looks worse than yours?"

"No. The pig is a weak man. He can only hurt women."

"You and your sister live alone?"

"There are six in the house."

"All around your age?"

"*Sí.*"

"Any of you go to school?"

"We must work to live."

"You ever work as a cook?"

"No," he said with a little smile. "I no cook so good. My sister, Rosa, she cook real good."

"Did Rafael Mendoza get you a visa?"

López hesitated.

Outside the windows facing the street, Hispanic men and women wearing clothes more suited to a southern climate, walked resolutely along the sidewalk in the cold. Like López they came across the southern border, chasing a dream most would never achieve.

"Si," López said at last. "Mr. Mendoza. He get me a visa."

"You always work here at *El Burrito*?"

"No. I work at a hotel in Minneapolis in the laundry. But I lose my job when we strike."

"You were asking for more pay?"

"Not more. Just the same as the *gueros*."

"Is that when you met Rubén Córdova? During the strike?"

"Si,"

Santana leaned in. "This is important, José. Did you tell Córdova that Rafael Mendoza was bringing Mexicans into the country illegally?"

López worked his jaw, as if chewing the answer. "Rubén was my friend. He get me this job." His eyes teared and he looked down at his hands that were clasped in front of him.

"So you did tell him."

"*Si*. Rubén no like it when he find out what Mendoza was doing." López rubbed his uninjured eye with the heel of his hand, like he was only tired and not really crying.

"I'm going to get something to drink," Santana said. "You sure you don't want anything?"

"Coca Cola," he said.

Santana went to the counter and ordered a Coke and a hot chocolate.

When he brought the drinks back to the table and sat down again, López stared at the open can in front of him, as though peering into a deep well.

"I wish I did not tell Rubén. Maybe he will still be alive if I did not tell him about Mendoza."

"You did the right thing."

As López picked up the can with both hands, his shoulders seemed to sag from the weight of it. His eyes drifted from the Coke until he was looking directly at Santana. "I say this to myself every day. But, you know, I no feel any better."

"I imagine you don't feel good about your eye, either, José. Who did this to you?"

"No one of importance," he said. But the momentary panic that flashed across his good eye indicated the opposite.

Santana said, "I need to know."

López looked at the can again. He rubbed his chin with his right hand and considered his options, which were basically slim and none. Finally he said, "You will keep my name out of it?"

"If I can."

"His name is Luis Garcia. He worked for Mr. Mendoza."

"What exactly did he do for Mendoza?"

López pointed to his eye. "He make sure no one talks about Mr. Mendoza's business."

"You know where Luis Garcia lives?"

"No," López said with a shake of his head. "And I don't want to know."

Chapter 15

HEAT FROM THE SUN'S RAYS radiated throughout the Crown Vic as Santana took the White Bear Avenue exit off Interstate 94 and turned north. A quick-moving warm front had blown in late in the morning. Santana could almost imagine that it was the middle of July despite the snow that lay like a soiled sheet over the landscape.

Santana typed Luis Garcia's name on the MDT keyboard in his Crown Vic. His name, last known address, and criminal history were in the computer system, as Santana had suspected, though there were no current wants and warrants. Garcia lived in a craftsman-style red brick bungalow with a gabled dormer on the corner of Kennard and Conway just west of White Bear Avenue.

Santana parked the Crown Vic at the curb and navigated his way across a sidewalk still icy with unshoveled snow. The street was deserted. Most kids were in school, and it was too early for the gangbangers to be out.

He walked up the steps and rang the bell. After a moment the door opened slightly and a heavy-set Hispanic woman peered out past the security chain.

"I'm Detective John Santana."

She stared at the ID he held up and then at him. Cautious. Unsure.

"I'm looking for Luis Garcia. Can I come in?"

Her dark eyes darted nervously back and forth. *"No comprendo, señor."*

"Es Luis Garcia su hijo?"

"Si," she said, surprise showing on her dark, Indian face. "He ees my son. What has he done?"

"I'd just like to ask him a few questions."

"He ees not home."

Santana could hear voices in the background. Then he realized that she had the television on.

"Perhaps I could talk to you, Mrs. Garcia."

She glanced inside like she was worried about something. She might have dealt with the police in Mexico and figured she had little choice but to let him in. If she were here illegally, dealing with the police would only add to her fears. She started to unlatch the chain and then hesitated a moment longer, weighing her options.

"Talking to me might help your son," Santana said, offering encouragement.

He saw concern register in her eyes.

Finally, she unlatched the safety chain, opened the door, and allowed him to step into the living room with its unpolished hardwood floors and faded white curtains on the windows. It was a small room that needed a fresh coat of paint, yet it was as expensively furnished as a showroom. A black curved leather sectional that was too large for the space sat against one wall opposite an oak armoire. The armoire held a brand new Sony flat screen twenty-seven inch color television with a built in VCR and DVD player.

Santana stood next to a black leather chair in front of four rectangular windows that looked out onto the street. A radiator ran along the wall beside him. Beyond the walnut archway that led into the dining room were a shiny oak table and four chairs. On one of the walls was a two-foot crucifix, and on another were three shelves filled with a collection of porcelain angels.

"I go to work soon," Mrs. Garcia said, standing in front of the leather sectional with the remote in her hand.

She wore white shoes and a plain gray maid's dress with CROWNE PLAZA printed on the nametag pinned just above her left breast. The nametag read: Ester Garcia.

Santana remembered a time when he and Rita Gamboni had enjoyed a dinner in the restaurant on the top floor of the hotel. The restaurant had booths that circulated like a slow-moving merry-go-round while you ate, offering a full view of the city through floor to ceiling windows. It was early in their relationship, a time when everything he said seemed interesting and significant to her, a time when her touch felt as if she had a constant fever.

"This won't take long," Santana said, giving Ester Garcia a smile.

She turned off the TV and lowered herself reluctantly to the couch, as though she were about to sit in something unpleasant.

He said, "You have a very nice home, *señora*."

She averted her eyes, obviously embarrassed by her expensive surroundings.

"Luis help out."

Santana took off his overcoat and folded it over the back of the cushioned chair. He took out his notebook and pen and sat down in the chair.

"Does Luis work?"

"When he can," she said softly.

"Where's that?"

"He no work in a long time. There are few jobs for …" her voice trailed off.

"Illegals," Santana said.

Ester Garcia's eyes grew large with panic and her mouth fell open. The radiator let out a hiss of steam like a cat alarmed by an intruder.

"Don't worry, Mrs. Garcia. I'm not here about your legal status. Everything you tell me will be between you and me, *comprende?"*

She looked at him for a long moment, still hesitant but less uneasy. *"De dónde es, señor?"*

"Colombia."

She gave a knowing nod. "How many years?"

"Twenty."

"It was hard for you, no?"

"Very. It's easier now."

She stared at him, motionless, still trying to make up her mind whether or not to trust him.

He said, *"Usted, señora? Cuantos años?"*

"Four years," she said.

"Viniste aquí con Luis?"

"With Luis and my husband, Jorge. He work in the meat packing plant in Worthington."

"Tienes otros hijos?"

"Only Luis."

Santana could tell by her body language that she was more relaxed now, more willing to talk. "Is your husband here in St. Paul, or is he still in Worthington, *señora?"*

She thought about it for a while before responding. "One day Jorge go to work and no come back. I wait for two months in the apartment where we live with another family in Worthington." She held up two fingers for emphasis and shook her head resignedly. "I think he get tired of the work and go back to Mexico."

"Why didn't you go back after him?"

Her lips formed a melancholy smile. "Jorge like the tequila more than work." She held the smile for a moment and then let out a sigh that carried with it something other than weariness.

"More than me, I think."

She gazed out the windows to her left, out into the cold, empty street where melting snow ran in dark, dirty streams along the curbs and down into the sewers.

"How did you end up in St. Paul?" Santana asked.

"One of the women in the apartment had a sister who live here and work at the hotel. She talk to Mr. Mendoza. He get me a job. Mr. Mendoza was a good man. When I hear on the TV that he die, I was very sad."

"Did Mendoza get Luis a job, too?"

"Si."

"Did he help you get the house?"

"I do not know. Luis brought me here one day a year ago. He say this is ours now. He say soon I no have to work anymore. We will have papers. We will be citizens. But I can always work. I don't mind."

Santana wondered how many Ester Garcias were working in the restaurants, fast food places and hotels throughout the city. All of them wanting to become citizens but many going about it the only the way they knew how — the wrong way.

"Do you know where Luis is now?"

"Sometimes he ees with his friends at Diáblos."

"I know where it is. Would you have a picture of Luis that I could borrow?"

She pushed herself up from the couch and went to drawer in the dining room where she took out a thick photo album and brought it back to the living room. She sat down on the couch again and set the album gently in her lap.

Santana watched her as she turned the pages, gazing at the distant memories captured in each of the photos.

Removing a photo from the album, she looked up at him. Her eyes were dark pools filled with concern and hope.

"Luis is a good boy, *señor.* Very smart. I try to get him to finish school here. But he no read so good. He has a lot of energy and a temper, too. Sometimes he get into trouble."

She held the picture of her son with both hands close to her heart, reluctant to give it up.

"I understand, *señora*."

Santana held out a hand.

She looked at him and then at the distance between his outstretched hand and hers.

"I'll return it safely to you," he said.

Her mouth began to tremble and she looked at Santana again, as if giving her son's photo to him in some way implied that she was turning her back on her only child.

"And my son too, *por favor*," she replied.

That was a promise Santana could not make.

Diáblos was located at the bottom of the bluff near Cesar Chávez and State. Traffic was usually heavy in the area and the sidewalks were busy with Hispanic shoppers, most of them without hats and gloves and heavy coats. Santana parked his car at the curb a half block down behind a customized, white and blue, low rider '64 Chevy Impala with fender skirts. It had been washed and waxed recently and the finish shone like a polished floor.

A bank of dark clouds had rolled in suddenly from the west, covering the sun and dropping the temperature ten degrees. Snow crystals blown by wind gusts pricked Santana's face and sliced across his skin like razors.

From the outside Diáblos looked like a pueblo with its white walls, red tiled roof and board-and-batten door. From the inside it looked and smelled the same as a thousand other bars, the stink of stale beer and cigarettes hanging like body odor in the air. On Santana's right was a long bar with red padded stools running the length of the room. Behind the bar was a Mexican flag and rows of multi-colored bottles, an alcoholic's wet dream. The bartender, an old Hispanic man with craggy features and white hair, looked up momentarily as Santana entered and then went back to washing glasses.

Sets of square tables and chairs were loosely organized in front of the bar. Ceiling fans sat motionless above him. In an alcove to the left were a pinball machine, pool table and a couple of high-topped tables.

Diáblos was nearly empty at this time of the day, so Luis Garcia was easy to spot. He was a muscular kid, about five feet seven inches, and dark like his mother with the same flat nose and Indian features. His jeans were baggy and low on his waist. He had a gold bandana tied over his head like a pirate. The tight black T-shirt he wore showed off a pair of large biceps. He was playing pool with another Hispanic kid the size of the Goodyear Blimp. The kid looked younger than Garcia, maybe nineteen, and wore his long, shiny, dark hair in a ponytail. A Vikings sweatshirt hung over his belt and expansive gut.

Santana walked over and stood near Garcia. He could see now that Garcia was trying to grow a mustache and goatee and having little success.

A young Hispanic girl with bleached blond hair, a leopard skin skirt and black turtleneck sweater sat on a stool at a round high-top table, smoking Lucky Strikes and drinking shots of tequila from a half-empty bottle.

Santana flipped open his badge wallet, revealing his shield.

Garcia gave it a cursory glance and said, "*Qué es lo que este pinché cabrón quiere?*"

The Hispanic girl giggled.

Santana had understood what the girl was laughing at. Garcia wondered what this fucking pig wanted. But rather than let on, he ignored the insult. Garcia was showing off for her, letting her see how tough he was. Santana had expected it.

"I'd like to ask you a few questions about Rafael Mendoza, Luis."

Garcia looked at him as though Santana had two heads. He had a thick, silver chain around his neck and a five-pointed crown tattooed on his right forearm, a symbol of the Latin King Nation.

"I don't know any Mendoza, man. Hey, Reínaldo," he said to the fat kid across the pool table. "I know any Mendoza?"

Reínaldo shook his head dutifully. "No, man."

Garcia turned around and looked at the blond girl sitting at the table behind him. "Liz, *mija*. Do I know any Mendoza?"

Liz smirked and took a drag on her cigarette. "No way."

Garcia turned and faced Santana again. His right foot was tapping against the tile floor, keeping a constant beat to some internal rhythm. He spread his hands and said, "See, man. I don't know anybody by that name. You're wastin' your time."

Mr. Honesty.

Santana decided to play along until he could catch Garcia in a lie. He figured it would be easy to do, despite Garcia's obvious practice.

"Mendoza was murdered at the Riverview Lofts, Luis."

By the puzzled look on Garcia's face, Mendoza's death could have been years ago instead of days.

"I heard the Latino who got whacked that night was named Córdova, man. I don't know nothing about any Mendoza." He was setting up to bank the six ball into a corner pocket. "I'm trying to play a game here, man." He leaned over the table, concentrating.

"We could talk downtown if you'd like, Luis."

Garcia took the shot and missed. "Shit, man." He looked at Reínaldo. "Can you believe that, *vatos*?" He stared at the big kid in frustration. "I'm gonna lose the game, homeboy."

Santana said, "You could lose more than the game, Luis, if you're not straight with me."

Garcia looked at Santana with wary eyes, like a hungry animal trying to decide whether it should go for the bait in a trap. "You threatening me, man?"

"Whatever way you want to play it, Luis."

"Hey," Garcia said with a big, phony smile, "no need to get *loco*."

He began gently tapping the tip of the pool cue on the table.

Reínaldo was moving around the table, acting as though he was ignoring the conversation, just looking to get the best angle for his next shot, but trying to get closer to Santana in case the shit hit the fan.

"How long have you worked for Mendoza, Luis?"

Garcia slowly lost his phony smile. His dark eyes were suddenly as hard and as lifeless as the eight ball on the table.

He looked at Reínaldo and said, *"Ponte detrás de el."*

Santana said, "Your fat friend isn't going to get behind me. And if he tries anything with that pool cue, I'll shove it up his ass and haul him downtown for assaulting a police officer."

"Hey," Garcia said. "You understand Spanish, man. You didn't tell me that when you came in." He wagged an index finger at Santana. "That's not fair, man."

"I'd guess most things in life aren't real fair for you, Luis."

"You got a sense of humor, too, man. I like that. But you are not Mexican."

"Colombian."

"Ah, *si*." He waved the pool cue at Reínaldo. "This is a good lesson for you, Reínaldo. You don't fuck around with a Colombian, unless you want your ass handed to you."

"That's the most intelligent thing you've said since I came in here, Luis."

"Yo no soy idiota."

"So why don't we sit down at a table near the bar and cut the bullshit."

Garcia gave Santana a long look, like he was the one in charge. "Okay, man. I got time. I was losing this fuckin' game anyway."

He formed a wide U with the first and last fingers of his right hand. Tapped his heart twice and flashed the gang sign to Reínaldo. Then he tossed the pool cue on the table, turned around and sauntered over to Liz and gave her a deep kiss on the lips, holding the back of her head with one hand and giving her plenty of tongue.

"I'll be right back, *míja*."

Garcia strutted toward an empty table near the bar with the same carefully practiced gait that belonged to every gangbanger who wanted to be cool. He slid into one of four wooden chairs at the table as Santana took off his overcoat and sat down in a chair directly across from him.

Garcia said, "I'd offer you a drink, *hombre*, but I don't think you can drink on duty, eh?"

"Looks to me like your two friends aren't old enough to be drinking."

"You gonna bust 'em?"

"That's not why I'm here. But maybe the girl," Santana said with a nod in her direction, "shouldn't be drinking. She's starting to show a little. That your kid she's carrying?"

"It better be, man, if the *Chicána* bitch knows what's good for her."

Garcia tipped his head toward Liz. She smiled at him as she sat alone at the high-topped table with her cigarettes and booze, waiting for her man to summon her.

Like a hundred other *Chicána* girls Santana had seen before, Liz wore her pregnancy like a badge of honor. She naïvely believed that having a child would somehow make her matter in a culture where pretty young girls were viewed by young men like Luis Garcia as nothing but chattel. Despite Luis' warning about faithfulness, he would soon grow tired of her, and Liz would be passed around and shared like the bottle of tequila she was drinking from. She would have three or four more children with a series of men and one day in the not too distant future she would wake up and look in the mirror and discover that her beauty and figure had deserted her along with all the young men who once found her so desirable, gone after still younger and prettier girls. Santana saw no way out of this cycle. Even if he took Luis Garcia off the street, there were ten more just like him waiting to take his place — and plenty more like Liz.

"Now that it's just the two of us sitting here quietly, Luis, and you don't have to impress your friends, why don't you tell me what you really know about Rafael Mendoza?"

"Hey, man, why don't you believe me?"

Garcia was looking for an Academy Award nomination; acting like Mendoza was a complete stranger.

"I've been to your house, Luis. I've talked with your mother."

Garcia's eyebrows lowered and his nostrils flared in anger. "You been to my house, man?"

"It's a very nice place for a mother who's busting her ass at a minimum wage job and a kid with no visible means of support."

"Hey, I help out."

"How's that?"

Garcia remained silent.

"How about I tell you," Santana said.

"You're so fuckin' smart, go ahead."

Santana said, "Rafael Mendoza got worker visas for your family. But when your old man took off for Mexico and left you and your mother alone, you overstayed your time. Now you're here illegally. You found out Mendoza was scamming the government, bringing illegals in for jobs that didn't exist and making a small fortune. You were helping him, Luis, for a cut of the profits. According to Mendoza's bank records, he made the same withdrawals twice a month. Those withdrawals were payouts to you. My guess is, he paid you in cash since you probably don't have a bank account."

Garcia laughed, but it was hollow. "You're really *loco,* man."

"What happened, Luis? You get too greedy? Have to kill Mendoza when he wouldn't agree to up your take?"

Garcia jumped up, the chair skidding across the floor away from him. "This is bullshit! I didn't kill Mendoza."

"Everything okay, Luis?" Reínaldo called from the pool table.

"You better come clean, Luis," Santana said.

"Or what?"

"Or I go to ICE. Let a couple of agents know about your mother."

"You fuckin' do that and I'll —"

"What, Luis? You're not threatening a police officer now, are you?"

Garcia glared at Santana. Contemplated his next move. Gave Santana a badass stare designed to keep his gangbanger buddies and his compliant girlfriend in line. Santana had no intention of turning in Garcia's mother, but he had to make sure Garcia absolutely believed that he would.

He said, "Chill out, Luis. You cooperate with me, I won't talk with ICE." With his left foot, Santana slowly pushed another chair out from the table. "Sit down before I put you down. And tell Reínaldo everything's all right."

"You think you're pretty tough, man."

"No, Luis. I know I'm pretty tough. That's one of the many differences between you and me. Now are you going to play this macho game all day, or are you going to tell me what you know. I'm losing my patience."

Garcia postured for another ten seconds before he said in a low voice, "Okay. But only because we're brothers, man."

"Get this straight, Luis. We're not brothers. We've got about as much in common as you do with the Pope."

Garcia sat down in the chair to Santana's left. "You always this hostile, *amigo*?"

"Murder investigations tend to bring out my irritable side."

"It's all right, *vatos*," Garcia called to Reínaldo. He gave his homeboy a reassuring smile. "The detective and me, we just had a disagreement. He understands now."

Garcia waved at the bartender. "Bring me a rum and Coke, Juan. And for my friend here, Detective …"

"Santana. A hot chocolate if he has one."

"Hot chocolate?" Garcia said. "What the fuck kind of drink is that?"

"A warm one."

"Yeah. It's fuckin' cold all right. Hey, Juan," Garcia said to the bartender, "go to the restaurant next door and get Detective Santana here a hot chocolate. But bring me my rum and Coke first."

Garcia leaned over and said quietly, "You don't really think I killed Mendoza, do you, Santana?"

"Tell me why I shouldn't?"

"Hey, I tell you what I know, man, I could go to jail."

"You'll go to jail if you don't tell me, Luis. But if you help me, I'll help you."

"Yeah, like I'm going to trust a cop."

"What choice do you have, Luis?"

He thought about that for a while.

The bartender arrived with the rum and Coke and then grabbed a coat from the rack near the door and went out for the hot chocolate.

Garcia said, "Look, Santana, it would be stupid to kill Mendoza. He was a lawyer. Without him, there's no way we keep things going."

"You and your gangbanger buddies were providing the muscle in case one of the illegals got picked up and started making noise."

"Hey, man, you never know what one of those leaf blowers are going to do."

Garcia was rolling a quarter between the fingers of his right hand like a magician.

"How often did you go to Mendoza's place?"

"Once a month."

"You sure it wasn't twice?"

"I'm sure, man. It was the fifteenth of every month."

"Was someone else working with you?"

"No, man. Why?"

"I'll ask the questions, Luis."

"Hey, no problem."

Santana noticed that Garcia had gradually lost his heavy Mexican accent. He suspected that Ester Garcia was right. Her son was a bright kid. Probably hyperactive. Not well educated, but street smart enough to be worried.

"How much you get from Mendoza, Luis?"

"Enough so it didn't make any sense to kill him."

"You know anything about the night Mendoza died?"

Garcia hesitated. The table jiggled as his knee jackhammered against the table leg, his foot in constant motion.

"You've got to trust me, Luis. If you're telling the truth and you had nothing to do with Mendoza's death, then I'll help you. If you lie to me …" Santana let the sentence hang in the air.

The bartender came back with a cup of hot chocolate and placed it on the table in front of Santana, a smile on his face.

Santana took a drink. It was warm and heavy with chocolate. *"Gracias, señor."*

The old man seemed pleased.

When he left, Garcia said, "I don't know anything about that night, man. I wasn't there. Mendoza was my meal ticket. I wouldn't kill him."

"You have any idea who would?"

He shook his head.

"Tell me how you collected your payments."

"Mendoza gave me a card for the underground garage, so I could avoid security. He had two spaces reserved. I usually parked in a space next to his Mercedes. But I got shit now." He gave a disgusted wave. "All the money was in Mendoza's accounts."

"You ever meet any of Mendoza's friends, Luis?"

"Like who, man?"

"Like Julio Pérez?"

"I never met him. Everyone in the community knew who he was, though."

"Mendoza ever talk about Pérez?"

Garcia shook his head.

"How about Rubén Córdova?"

"I didn't know Córdova either, man."

Santana drank some hot chocolate and watched Garcia carefully, looking for any "tells" that he was lying. In the background, he heard the familiar ping of a pinball machine.

"You and your mother lived in Worthington for a time. Your father worked in a meat packing plant."

"Yeah. So what?"

"Córdova was arrested for protesting in Worthington."

"Doesn't mean I knew him."

Garcia sat back in his chair as a crooked smile played across his face.

"What, Luis?"

Garcia quit playing with the quarter. He took the straw out of his rum and Coke and started tapping it against the edge of the glass like a drummer. "I do know something that might help you, man. But I gotta have your word you gonna leave me out of all this."

"I told you before, Luis, I'll do what I can for you. There are no guarantees. You know that."

Garcia's dark eyes gave nothing away except that they were old beyond his years. "Okay, man. I gonna trust you. You got *cojones*."

"I'll cherish the compliment. Now tell me what you know."

Garcia let out a cough of a laugh. "Mendoza was a *joto*, man."

"I know he was queer, Luis." Santana also knew that *joto* in Mexican was worse than anything in English.

Disappointment wrinkled Garcia's brow. "Really? How you know that?"

"I'm a detective, Luis. It's my job to know."

Garcia raised his hands in surrender. "Okay, man. So you're pretty smart."

"What gave you the idea that Mendoza was queer, Luis?"

"I met his boyfriend once," he said with a grin.

Santana leaned forward and put his elbows on the table, interested now. "Where?"

"At Mendoza's loft. When I showed up one day to collect, Mendoza wouldn't open the fuckin' door at first. There was a lot of noise, you know. Like maybe he doesn't want me to see what's going on. When he finally lets me in, he's acting all embarrassed. But I figure what's the big deal? Mendoza's got this reputation as a chick magnet, right? I start giving him a hard time, telling him I want to meet his *chiquita*. We get in an argument and I pushed him and he lets out a yell and falls over a table. All of a sudden this tall, black guy comes charging out of the bathroom with no shirt on. I couldn't believe it."

Garcia shook his head as if he had just seen a pig fly. "Mendoza made me promise I'd never tell. I said I wouldn't long as he upped my monthly check. And I never did tell, Santana. I'm a man of my word."

"I'm sure."

"Doesn't much matter now that Mendoza is dead." Garcia drank some of his rum and Coke.

"You know the black guy's name, Luis?"

"*Joto's* name is Donelle Walker. Used to play basketball at the University. Played some pro ball in New York for a while. Owns a jazz club downtown. The Sweet Spot."

Santana knew what Garcia was thinking now that Mendoza was dead. "Forget about, it, Luis. I hear anything about Walker having to pay hush money, and I'm going to come looking for you. *Comprende?*"

"Hey, man. What do you take me for?"

"A criminal."

Garcia feigned a shocked expression. "Man, that's harsh."

Santana finished his hot chocolate and removed a business card from his badge wallet. He wrote a phone number on the back of the card and set it on the table.

"You remember anything else about Mendoza or the night he died, you call me at the station or on my cell."

Garcia picked up the card. *"No hay problema."*

Santana stood up and put on his coat. Despite the shithole Garcia had dug for himself, Santana wanted to help him and his mother.

"That it?" Garcia asked tentatively.

"For now. You stay cool, Luis. I don't want to have to come back and bust your ass."

"Hey, Santana, don't worry. You know, I been doing some thinking. Maybe I'll get a job."

Santana believed that about as much as he believed Córdova had been responsible for Mendoza's murder. Still, he decided to make Garcia an offer.

"You want to get in touch with someone that can help, Luis, I wrote a number for *Latinos in Minnesota* on the back of my card. They have people who can get you a legitimate job."

"Hey, I've heard of it, man. You got a deal."

"And Luis?"

Garcia was lip reading Santana's card and looked up.

"Take good care of your girlfriend."

"You know me, *amigo.*"

"Yeah," Santana said. "I'm afraid I do."

Chapter 16

THE PHONE ON SANTANA'S DESK at the station rang as he was taking off his coat. Rita Gamboni wanted to see him right away in Carl Ashford's office. Gamboni cut off the conversation when he asked her why, which was never a good sign.

As he walked down the narrow corridor between cubicles, Santana saw Nick Baker sitting with his feet up on the corner of his desk, eating a bagel smothered with cream cheese.

Baker said, "Wait a minute, John."

Santana stopped and leaned against the cloth-lined divider.

Baker sat up and placed both feet on the floor. Nicorette gum wrappers littered his desk.

"Gamboni and Kehoe are meeting with Ashford in his office. Word is, something's goin' down with the Córdova case. You got anything that proves Córdova and Torres are innocent, John, you better give it to 'em."

"I just got a call from Rita. I'm on my way there now."

"Christ, I hope Ashford's not gonna give you the red carpet treatment."

Because the carpet in the assistant chief's office was red, it was a standing joke among detectives that if you were called to his office and reamed out, you were getting the red carpet treatment.

"I've got a lot of assumptions and hunches, Nick, but still *nada*."

Baker shook his head. Pointed with a nicotine-stained finger. "That's not good for you."

"Or for Córdova and Torres," Santana said.

He walked over to Ashford's office and knocked on his door.

The assistant chief's deep baritone voice said, "Come in."

As Santana shut the door behind him, he noted that the blinds to the main office were closed. Another bad sign.

"Have a seat, Detective," Ashford said. "The three of us were just discussing the Pérez-Mendoza case."

Rita Gamboni and James Kehoe were seated in front of Carl Ashford's desk. Santana sat down in the empty chair to Gamboni's left. Kehoe was seated to her right. Like the carpet, the chair cushions were red.

The walnut desk in the assistant chief's office was the size of a cathedral door. It had a quarter inch piece of glass on top, along with a phone, intercom and an eight by twelve inch frame with a picture of Ashford's wife, a former Vikings cheerleader, and their two teenage children, both boys. Their six year-old daughter had died of sickle-cell anemia seven years ago. Since then, Ashford had been a regular solicitor for the sickle-cell foundation. On the wall behind the desk was a picture of his deceased daughter, a picture of Ashford receiving an award from the president of the foundation, along with a series of framed pictures of Ashford in his college days as a football star with the Gophers and in his Army and patrol officer uniforms.

Ashford said, "We believe we've got enough ammunition to push Canfield to seek an indictment against Angelina Torres as an accomplice in both murders."

"What exactly do we have that leads to that conclusion?" Santana thought he might have put a little too much sarcasm on the 'we.'

Ashford's smile suddenly became a frown.

"Well, for starters, John," Gamboni said, jumping in quickly, "we've got the .22 that killed Pérez. Ballistics confirmed the bullet the ME removed from Pérez's brain came from the gun that belonged to Rúben Córdova. The same gun he gave her when she drove to Minnesota from California. The gun she returned to him prior to Pérez's murder."

Santana said, "The lab confirmed there was no GSR on Córdova's hands."

"You know damn well that doesn't mean he didn't fire the gun," Kehoe said. "It's easy to get rid of gunshot residue."

"There was no backspatter on his shirt either."

"Maybe he changed his clothes before he went to Mendoza's loft," Kehoe said with a shrug.

"There's also evidence that someone broke into Córdova's house recently," Santana said. "Someone could've broken in and stolen the gun, so they could set up Córdova for the murders."

"Did Córdova report it stolen?" Gamboni asked.

"No. But the gun was originally reported stolen in California. That's probably why Córdova didn't report it missing."

"How can you claim the gun was stolen from Córdova's house," Kehoe said, "when Córdova had it on him when he was killed?"

"Someone could have taken it, used it to kill Pérez, and then planted it in Mendoza's loft after he pushed him off the balcony. Córdova had an appointment with Mendoza about the time he died. I think Córdova came on the scene, recognized the gun, realized he was being framed, and took it with him."

"That's a real stretch," Kehoe said.

Santana paused a moment, maintaining his composure, looking at each one of them.

"So you all believe that Córdova killed Pérez and then Mendoza. Then he framed Mendoza for the Pérez murder and tried to make it look like Mendoza committed suicide."

"That's the way it's looking," Ashford said.

"And Angelina Torres?"

"She was part of it," Ashford said.

"Why would Córdova use his gun to kill Pérez?"

"You just pointed out the gun was stolen in California," Gamboni said. "If we didn't find Torres' print on it, they would've gotten away clean."

"Then why didn't Córdova just leave the gun in Mendoza's loft? Why take it with him?"

Kehoe said, "You and Anderson showed up unexpectedly right after Córdova pushed Mendoza off the balcony. Córdova probably panicked. It was his mistake. Most murderers make 'em. That's why they get caught."

"Like you would know," Santana said.

"Careful, Detective," Ashford said. "No need to get personal here."

"Okay," Santana said, "let's say for the sake of discussion that Córdova did kill Pérez and then pushed Mendoza off his balcony to make it look like a suicide. What's his motive?"

"Glad you asked that, Santana," Kehoe said. He looked at Ashford, as if waiting for permission to speak.

"Go ahead," Ashford said.

"It seems that before Mendoza began litigating on behalf of immigrants," Kehoe paused, letting the word immigrants hang in the air as if it was an epithet, "he made his money defending companies like Greatland Industries."

Santana looked at Gamboni for clarification.

"They're a global company based in Minneapolis, John, with their fingers in lots of pies. Fertilizer. Farm machinery. But their primary source of income comes from the manufacture of pesticides."

Despite Nick Baker's warning that something was up, Santana was unprepared for the feeling of dread that suddenly washed over him like a wave.

"Córdova made a name for himself writing stories about what companies like Greatland were doing to migrant workers in the grape fields of California," Kehoe continued, clearly enjoying Santana's obvious discomfort and the chance to show off in front of Ashford and Gamboni. "Córdova and Torres's parents worked in those same fields. They both believed their parents died of cancer from pesticide poisoning. It's clear that they held Greatland responsible for the death of their parents. Mendoza defended Greatland in the lawsuit. That's their motive."

"As for Pérez," Ashford said, "Detective Kehoe believes that Córdova killed Pérez so that he could take over *El Día*."

"It's perfect," Kehoe said. "Córdova gets revenge on Mendoza for defending the company responsible for the death of his parents, and he takes over operation of the largest Hispanic newspaper in the Midwest."

Kehoe looked at Ashford. "Good detective work, Chief, is just putting two and two together. And," he added smugly, "not getting sidetracked by another agenda."

"And what agenda is that?" Santana asked with an edge in his voice.

"I understand you were over at Angelina Torres's apartment the other night."

Santana felt the heat in his face. "What the hell are you suggesting, Kehoe?"

"Not a thing. Other than maybe you should've spent more time investigating Córdova than his girlfriend."

Santana came out of his seat, stepped past Gamboni, and grabbed Kehoe by his lapels, yanking him up so that their faces were inches apart.

"Don't you ever suggest any shit like that again, you hear me, Asshoe!"

"Detective Santana!" Ashford's voice boomed. "Let go of Detective Kehoe and sit down!"

Santana could see the smirk on Kehoe's face and it only angered him more. His heart thudded in his chest. Hot blood pumping throughout his body roared into his head and eardrums.

"Unless you're looking for an immediate suspension, Detective," Ashford said, "you better sit down right now!"

"John!" Gamboni said. "Listen to the chief!"

Santana leaned close to Kehoe's ear and whispered, "Your time will come, Asshoe."

He let go of Kehoe and backed away, accidentally stepping on Gamboni's right foot before he sat down again in the chair.

Ashford said, "I don't want to see another goddamn outburst like that, Detective Santana. Is that perfectly clear?"

Santana nodded, feeling embarrassed about stepping on Gamboni's foot and thankful that she had suppressed a yelp. It must have hurt like hell.

"And as for you," Ashford said, looking directly at Kehoe, "I don't want to hear any unsubstantiated allegations. We've had enough of those regarding this case. Is that understood?"

Kehoe adjusted his sport coat and gave a nod.

"Then sit down."

Kehoe sat, as if pulled down by an unseen hand.

"Now," Ashford said, obviously making an effort to remain calm, "do you have anything further to add to this discussion, Detective Kehoe?"

"I think I've made my case."

Ashford turned his attention to Santana.

"How about you, Detective? Do you have anything constructive you want to add to this investigation?"

Santana knew he had to regroup. He had let Kehoe bait him into an angry outburst. He took a deep breath and let it out, trying to focus his attention on the case. Ashford still knew nothing about the visa scam. Neither did Kehoe. Money was certainly a motive for someone other than Córdova to kill Mendoza. The obvious suspect was Luis Garcia. But Santana wanted to keep Garcia and his mother, as well as the Feds, out of the investigation if he could. Once it was known that Mendoza was running a visa scam with illegals, Kehoe would be all over Garcia, and Santana wanted to avoid more false accusations. He still believed there was connection between Pérez and Mendoza. Until he discovered what that connection was, he refused to let go of the thread that tied the two of them together.

Santana looked at Rita. Her right foot was shoeless and resting on her left thigh. She was gently rubbing her foot with both hands. He could tell by her expression that she knew he was tempted to tell Ashford about the visa scam. Telling Ashford would give Santana some momentary satisfaction for not pressing Torres earlier and for allowing Kehoe to make him look like a fool in front of the assistant chief. But Santana also realized Gamboni wanted to avoid telling Ashford that she had kept important information regarding the investigation from him. Kacie Hawkins and Nick Baker were the others who knew about the visa scam. Santana was certain neither of them would tell Kehoe. He was relying on instincts that told him Gamboni still trusted him enough to follow his lead. By not saying anything to Ashford, he was risking his job and Rita's career. He was willing to take the chance. He hoped she was as well.

"I do have a couple of questions for Kehoe." Santana refused to call him detective.

"Go ahead," Ashford said.

Santana looked at Kehoe. "How'd you figure out the connection between Córdova, Torres and Mendoza?"

"I looked into Mendoza's background and talked with Torres."

Santana felt as though an icicle had just pierced his heart. He had always felt that Angelina Torres had been keeping something from him. Now, her lack of full disclosure had come back to haunt both of them.

"During my questioning," Kehoe said, "Torres mentioned you'd had dinner with her at her apartment."

Santana saw Gamboni staring at him. He thought there was something more than mild interest in her blue eyes but maybe not.

"Is this true, Detective Santana?" Ashford asked.

"It's not what it seems, Chief. It was strictly business."

"You just have to know how to question someone," Kehoe said, unable to resist one final shot at Santana.

"Well, then," Ashford said, placing both palms flat on his desk, "I think it's time I talked with the county attorney again."

He stood, signaling that the meeting was over.

Santana started to get up.

"I'd like you to stay a minute, Detective," Ashford said.

Santana's eyes met Gamboni's for a moment. He gave a little shake of his head, trying to convey the message that she had nothing to worry about.

After Gamboni and Kehoe left the office, Ashford stood behind his desk with his arms crossed, looking like a huge Buddha, and said, "What the hell is going on with you and Kehoe?"

"Other than the fact that he doesn't know what he's doing, you mean?"

"Where do you get off with that?" Ashford said, spreading his hands. "Kehoe's the one who established an obvious motive for Córdova and Torres. We're damn lucky the mayor's office has stepped in to help with this investigation. You're my best detective. What the hell have you come up with?"

Santana started to answer, but Ashford cut him off.

"I'll tell you," Ashford said, settling his large frame in the chair behind his desk. "Diddly squat. That's what you've come up with. We got two very prominent members of the Hispanic community dead, and you've got diddly squat."

"Look, Chief, there's more here than you're seeing."

"Well, for crissakes, Detective, then let's have it."

Santana knew he had to give Ashford something. He felt like he was about to step into a minefield and one misstep could mean his job.

"I did find out that Pérez and Mendoza were born in the same city."

"And?"

"I believe they knew each other. These murders could have something to do with their past."

Ashford rubbed his face with his hands. "Have you got any evidence that corroborates that theory?"

Santana shook his head, realizing now how thin the link was, how weak his argument must seem.

"Mendoza's murder may have something to do with his lifestyle. He was gay. He had a lot to lose."

Ashford let out a heavy sigh. "So apparently one of the most eligible bachelors in the Twin Cities turns out to be gay. So what? Being gay isn't a big deal anymore."

"Not to you but maybe to Mendoza."

"What the hell does that mean?"

"That didn't come out right," Santana said.

"Not much that you've done with this investigation has, Detective," Ashford said, obviously impatient now. "Maybe it's time for you to take a vacation."

The urge to tell Ashford about the visa scam was strong, but Santana realized he had nothing except Luis Garcia to offer as a suspect and little else. Accusing Garcia instead of Córdova and Torres wouldn't solve the murders. And if the Feds were brought in now, they could trample the evidence and take over the investigation.

"Maybe I will take some time off," Santana said as he stood.

"One more thing before you go, Detective."

Santana waited a long moment before Ashford continued.

"The train is about to leave the station regarding this investigation. It's time for you to get on board. As much as I respect the work you've done in the past, I can't be responsible if your career runs off the tracks. Do you understand what I'm telling you?"

"Perfectly," Santana said.

"Good. Then I expect to have your full cooperation in indicting Angelina Torres as Rúben Córdova's accomplice in the murders of Julio Pérez and Rafael Mendoza."

Chapter 17

A PLUME OF WHITE VAPOR from a tall smokestack at the X-cel plant hung motionless in the cold blue sky as Santana crossed the Wabasha Bridge to the West Side.

He was angry with Kehoe and Ashford and Gamboni and Angelina Torres. He was angry with Rick Anderson. But most of all, he was angry with himself. Maybe Angelina Torres had been playing him. Maybe she had been an accomplice. Maybe she and Córdova had committed the murders. He needed to calm down before he lost all focus and perspective, before he lost sight of his objective.

Torres hadn't told him that Mendoza had represented Greatland Industries. She had withheld information and it could cost her. *And it cost me, too,* he thought. It was clearly a motive for Mendoza's murder. Her parents and Córdova's parents had both died of cancer from pesticide poisoning. Mendoza represented the company responsible for the pesticides. Córdova wrote articles condemning it. Still, the question remained. Why kill Mendoza now?

He parked the Crown Vic at the curb in front of Julio Pérez's house, walked up the sidewalk and rang the bell. He had expected the bell to be answered by Sandra Pérez and was surprised when the door opened and Gabriela Pérez stood facing him.

"What are you doing here?"

The tone of her voice, like the day's temperature, was just above freezing.

Santana said, "I'd like to speak to your mother."

Her eyes regarded him with cold speculation. "She's not home. She's staying with a friend."

It would be hard for Santana to say he was disappointed that Gabriela was here instead of her mother. After all, Gabriela was much more pleasing to look at. However, he knew he would need a very large blowtorch to thaw the wall of ice that seemed to separate the two of them.

"Perhaps you could help me?"

"Help you what?" she said. "I already know who killed my father."

"Look, Ms. Pérez, I know you think the case has been solved, but I've been doing this for a long time. I'm good at it. If I could come in, perhaps I could explain why I'm continuing the investigation."

While she thought about letting him in, Santana thought about her.

She was wearing a crimson cashmere sweater that matched her lipstick, black stretch pants and knee high black, suede boots. Her small, perfectly shaped earlobes held gold loop earrings and a gold chain with a heart-shaped pendant hung around her elegant neck. Her dark hair was parted in the middle and pulled back into what Santana called a *trenza* or a French braid. The sleeves of her sweater were pulled up to her elbows and tiny beads of sweat dotted her smooth forehead.

Finally, she said, "This better be good, Detective Santana. I'm very busy."

"I'll give it my best," he assured her, and stepped into the house and out of the cold.

He sat on the same cushioned chair he had sat on the day the investigation began. Gabriela Pérez sat on the tweed, striped couch where she had sat that same day consoling her distraught mother. Now Santana had to convince her that he knew exactly where the investigation was headed even though he felt it had nearly reached a dead end. Confessing that he was no closer to finding her father's killer than he had been when they had first met would keep a frown on her beautiful face. And it would probably guarantee he would get little, if any, help from her.

"I've been packing up my father's clothes," she said, glancing in the direction of her parent's bedroom. "My mother could not do it. She would prefer that things stayed the way they were."

Gabriela Pérez scanned the room, her gaze resting on each item, as though mentally recalling where it had come from.

"People need time before they can move on," Santana said.

She looked at him for a time before she said, "Please don't think I'm heartless. I loved my father very much. But I've never been much for sentimentality. As a woman … a Hispanic woman in this country, I've had to be very strong. Do you understand?"

"Yes, I do."

Her dark eyes remained focused on his, as though she wanted to be sure he wasn't just telling her what she wanted to hear.

"This is a very different culture than I knew as a child, Detective Santana. Women are more respected here but less …" she paused, searching for the right word, "protected."

Her dark eyes shifted away from his, and for the first time since he had met her, she appeared vulnerable. He was uncertain where she was heading, but he knew that if he gained her trust, she would help him.

"It's never easy coming to a new country," he said. "Trying to adapt to another culture."

When she looked at him again, some of the heat in her dark eyes had dissipated.

"Thank you for listening, Detective Santana."

"Listening is an important part of my job."

"Yes, I'm sure it is. But you are a good listener." She smiled a little. "For a man."

"Well, some of us do have a few positive qualities."

She hesitated a moment longer before she said with a sigh, "So, what is it that has you so convinced you need to continue the investigation."

"Your father called Mendoza at his loft in downtown St. Paul on the day he was murdered."

She started to protest, but Santana held up his hand in a stopping gesture. "Let me finish. Mendoza's number is in your father's Rolodex. We checked the phone records. He made the call at four-twenty p.m. The medical examiner puts the time of death around five p.m. It was the last call he made."

"But my father never talked about Mendoza."

"That doesn't mean he didn't know him. According to phone records, your father called Mendoza on three other occasions prior to his death. Ask yourself, Ms. Pérez, why didn't your father ever mention Rafael Mendoza to you or your mother? They were both prominent Hispanic men in St. Paul. Their paths must have crossed at some point. Coming from the same city in Mexico would create a bond between them. It would make sense that your father would talk about Mendoza. Unless …"

"Unless what?"

Santana paused; hesitant to go in the direction the conversation was taking him. It had crossed his mind that Julio Pérez could be gay like Mendoza, but there was no evidence indicating that he was. Still, he had to ask the question even though he felt he was about to step on a thin sheet of ice covering a very cold lake.

"Unless there was something in your father's past he didn't want to share."

"My father was a good man. He exposed the corruption and drug dealing in Mexico. It nearly cost him his life." There was a chill in her voice again. "I don't understand what you're getting at."

"It's not important."

"I don't believe that for a second," she said. Her dark eyes narrowed with suspicion. "Tell me, Detective Santana, when you came to my house earlier this week, you suspected I had something to do with my father's death. Why would you trust anything I had to say now?"

"Solving a crime means finding answers to lots of questions, Ms. Pérez. If I ask enough questions, sooner or later I usually get the answers I need. Because I ask you a question, doesn't mean I suspect you of anything."

She sat very still, looking at him. "Do you still have the photograph of my father I gave you?"

"Of course."

"When I picture my father in my mind, that is how I see him. Always with the white shirt and tie. Smelling like Brut." Her eyes welled up and she looked away.

"What I need from your mother is some idea of where your father lived in Valladolid. A *barrio*."

"And I can help you by telling you where my father lived in Valladolid?"

"I believe so."

She let out another sigh and looked at him again. She was beautiful, cautious and not nearly as tough as she pretended to be.

"Well, my father grew up in an area of Valladolid known as the *Sisal Barrio*. I only know that because my mother told me. My father rarely spoke about his childhood."

"Did you ever wonder why?"

"Sometimes. But I never questioned him. Besides, his family moved to the area around Cancún for the jobs when he was a young boy. I have never been to Valladolid."

Neither have I, Santana thought. But that's about to change.

Chapter 18

The Sweet Spot was the newest of three jazz clubs in St. Paul. Santana sat on a stool at the large, rectangular bar facing the stage in the nearly deserted club, drinking a Sam Adams and waiting for Donelle Walker to join him. It was 8:00 p.m., an hour before the first set.

The room was dusky and dimly lit and had a lingering smell of cigarette smoke. Heavy maroon-colored velvet drapes covered the windows, and candles on the tables provided most of the light. Small lamps on the brick walls illuminated pictures of famous jazz musicians. On the stage was a set of drums, piano, bass and saxophone, all bathed in soft white light.

"You Santana?"

Santana looked up, way up. Donelle Walker had to be six feet seven or eight.

"That's right."

"Bartender said you wanted to see me. What can I do for you?"

Santana opened his badge wallet and discreetly showed Walker his shield. "I understand you knew Rafael Mendoza."

Walker's demeanor changed quickly from friendly to wary. "Says who?"

Santana wanted to keep Luis Garcia out of it, so he ignored the question. "Look, Mr. Walker, what I have to ask you is just between you and me. I didn't tell the bartender I was a cop."

"Maybe I need to talk to my attorney."

"Far as I'm concerned we're just two guys having a conversation. But that's up to you."

Walker thought it over for a while before he said to Santana, "Let's sit down at a table." To the bartender he said, "Jack. Bring me a Bailey's and coffee. You want another beer, Detective?"

Santana said," No, thanks."

Donelle Walker was a light-skinned African-American with straight white teeth, neatly trimmed hair and Caucasian features. With the pinstriped, three button suit and white, silk, open-collared shirt, and the obvious fact that he kept himself in shape, he could have easily been on the cover of GQ.

"You like jazz?" Walker asked, as they sat down at a table in a corner away from the stage.

"Some. I like Latin music. Particularly *boleros*. My father used to listen to it."

"I heard it when I was in New York. Mostly Cuban musicians."

"Paquito D'Rivera once described *boleros* as a ballad with a little black beans on the side."

Walker smiled. "I like the African rhythms. Startin' to see more Latin music around town."

Santana wanted to keep the conversation low key and informal. Encourage Walker not to be too defensive.

"I was a pretty good salsa dancer as a teenager," he said. Talking about dancing reminded him now of how much he missed it.

"You take lessons?"

"Growing up in Colombia, it was in our blood."

"Colombian, huh? I used to eat at a good Colombian restaurant once in a while when I lived in New York. Seeing more Colombian restaurants around here, too."

"I don't get out much," Santana said. "Watch a Timberwolves' game on TV now and then. Saw you play a couple of times when you were with the Knicks. You could play."

"Made a living."

"How'd you end up owning a jazz club?"

"Had to find something to do at thirty-two. Too early to retire completely. Always enjoyed jazz. Like people. I thought, why the hell not? I got the money and the time."

"Nice to have," Santana said.

Walker gave Santana a long look. "I'm enjoying the conversation, Detective. But you didn't come here to talk about salsa, restaurants and basketball."

"No, I didn't." Santana waited as the bartender delivered Walker's drink and left. "How long did you know Rafael Mendoza?"

Walker picked the hazelnuts off the top of the whipped cream and held them in the palm of his huge hand. "About a year."

"You know anyone who would want to harm him?"

"The man was a lawyer. You've heard the jokes. Probably made some enemies along the way."

"You one of them?"

Walker bright teeth gleamed in the dimly lit room. "No, Detective."

"You're a big guy, Donelle. You keep yourself in shape. If Mendoza didn't jump off his balcony, then somebody helped him."

Walker shook his head slowly, as if trying to understand. "When the paper first reported Rafael's death as a possible suicide, I didn't believe it. I would've known if he was depressed. We were … good friends. I know he didn't jump. Somebody must've pushed him. But it wasn't me. I had no reason to harm him."

Walker paused. He popped the hazelnuts into his mouth, took a drink and set the cup down.

"Ever since Rafael died, I've been asking myself who could've done this." He wiped whipped cream off his lips with a napkin, thinking. After a long moment he said, "But why are you still looking for the murderer? I heard on the news that the suspect was killed in a shootout and an accomplice arrested."

"The case is still open," Santana said, knowing that could soon change.

"Rafael and I were close, Detective. I'd like to help. Really."

Santana reached into his inside pocket and pulled out the photo Gamboni had found in Mendoza's bathroom. He had signed it out of the evidence room before coming to the club. Handing it to Walker he said, "I'd like you to look at this. But it's hard to see in this light."

Walker held up his index finger indicating he needed a second. He took out a penlight and focused the small beam on the photo. "Where'd you get this?"

"I found it hidden in Mendoza's bathroom."

Walker stared at the photo.

Santana said, "Know who these two men are?"

Walker moved the beam closer. "No."

"So what was Mendoza doing with this photo?"

Walker looked at Santana. "He wasn't into porn if that's what you're thinking. You couldn't have found any other photos like this."

"No," Santana said. "We didn't." He sat back in his chair, drank some beer. "You have any idea why Mendoza had this photo?"

"None."

"Got to be some reason why he had this photo and why he kept it hidden."

"You're the detective," Walker said. "Isn't it your job to find out?"

It was 9:30 p.m. when Santana got home and disarmed the security system. He made a phone call to Nick Baker, another to

Continental Airlines, and a third to Ricardo Vasquez, a cop in Houston. Then he changed into a pair of trunks and a sweatshirt with the lettering GOLD'S GYM across the front and went to his exercise room.

He did three sets of bench, incline and overhead presses, bicep and tricep curls and squats. He finished off the workout with one hundred sit-ups. Then he took a long shower, hoping a steady stream of hot water would wash away the remaining fatigue that still clung to his body like a set of wet clothes.

Afterward, he slipped into a clean NIKE sweat suit and a pair of deck shoes. He went into the living room where he put a Marc Antoine CD in the stereo and then into the kitchen where he set the oven temperature to 375 degrees. He took out a box of *pandebono* mix, a large bowl, a baking pan, a cup of milk, an egg, and a package of shredded white cheese and placed everything on the counter top. He added three cups of cheese along with the egg and mix to the bowl, slowly pouring in the milk as he worked the ingredients first into dough and then into two-inch diameter balls. He placed the balls he made on an oiled pan six inches apart and pressed them into the shape of one-inch thick donuts. Then he put them in the oven and set the timer for eight minutes. While he waited, he drank a couple of shots of aguardiente Cristal. Fifteen minutes later he was sitting in the living room with his feet on the coffee table, eating warm *pandebonos* off of a dinner plate and drinking a cold bottle of Sam Adams.

He thought about what Donelle Walker had told him regarding the photograph of the two men engaged in fellatio Gamboni had found in Mendoza's loft. If Walker was right about Mendoza not taking pornographic pictures, then there had to be another reason why Mendoza had the photo. Was he blackmailing someone? Or was he holding onto the photo for protection? If Santana knew who the man with the appendectomy scar was, he might have some answers. The scar in the photo was reddish and not white like an older scar. It was a long shot, but he could have Nick Baker check hospital records in the Twin Cities. Find out the males who had their appendix out within the last year or two. Nick might come across a familiar name.

In his mind Santana tried to connect the dots between Julio Pérez, Rafael Mendoza and Rubén Córdova. Gabriela Pérez had insisted that her father hadn't known Rafael Mendoza. Her mother had agreed. Yet, the last call Julio Pérez had made before he died had been to Mendoza. A check of Pérez's phone records had revealed he had called Mendoza from his home three other times within a two-week span prior to his death. Why would Pérez call Mendoza? Córdova worked for Pérez and was interviewing Mendoza about his dealings with illegal immigrants. Still, Santana believed someone else must have known all three men. That someone wanted Pérez and Mendoza dead and Córdova framed for their murders.

He ate one more *pandebono* and washed it down with a swallow of Sam Adams. He remembered something he had once read in a Kurt Vonnegut novel. Something about staying close to the edge without going over because out on the edge was where you could see all kinds of things you had difficulty seeing from the center. That's where Santana knew he had to stay if he wanted to solve this case. Out on the edge.

Chapter 19

DAY 6

The Continental flight from Minneapolis to Houston took three hours. Santana had plenty of time to think as the plane flew just above a seemingly endless bank of white clouds like a ship across a churning sea.

He had met Ricardo Vasquez when he flew to Houston two years ago to pick up Joey Moore. Vasquez had worked Homicide in Mexico before taking a job in Houston after falling in love with a woman from the city.

Santana had a one-hour layover before he caught a flight to Cancún. He was sitting in an airport bar where he had agreed to meet Vasquez when the detective walked in.

Vasquez's steps were slow and careful as he threaded his way through the gauntlet of tables in the bar. There was no wasted movement. It was just the opposite of his wary cop eyes, which darted from person to person, never resting until they spotted Santana.

Two years ago when Santana met him, a very thin Vasquez had recently married. Since that time he had put on some weight.

Santana finished off his bottle of Sam Adams, stood up and shook Vasquez's hand.

"Married life must be treating you well."

Vasquez smiled. "My wife cooks like a chef in a fancy restaurant. What can I do but eat?"

He had a thick, dark mustache and spoke with a slight Mexican accent.

Santana motioned for him to sit down and Vasquez sat in the chair opposite Santana.

He ordered a Budweiser, Santana another Sam Adams.

"You married yet?" Vasquez asked.

"Not yet."

"Any time soon?"

"I don't get out much."

"Well, my advice is to date some before you propose."

"I'll keep that in mind. Homicide keeping you busy?"

"Me and funeral directors. How about you?"

"Rarely a dull moment."

"We've had a couple rounds of budget cuts. Things keep going in that direction, only high profile cases are going to get solved. Must be what you're working on since your department sent you down here."

"Nobody sent me. It's my dime."

Vasquez raised a thick eyebrow. "Doesn't surprise me. First time we met, you struck me as the bulldog type. Once you get your teeth into something, you aren't going to let it go."

"I don't see how you can be in Homicide and be anything else."

The beers arrived and Santana picked up the tab. While they drank, he reviewed the Pérez-Mendoza case with Vasquez, hoping that another perspective might shed some light on it.

"Well, if you think Córdova isn't good for it," Vasquez said when Santana had finished, "it stands to reason it has to be someone who knew him well enough to set him up."

He pulled a business card from his shirt pocket, slid it across the table and turned it over.

"Name on the back of the card is a cop in Valladolid. I don't know him personally, but a cop friend of mine in Mexico City knows him. Says he's good … and honest. I made a phone call this morning. He'll pick you up at the airport in Cancún."

"I owe you, Ricardo."

Vasquez waved as if he were brushing away a fly. "Don't worry about it, *amigo.* I just hope you find what you are looking for."

A hot wind hit Santana like a punch as he stepped off the plane and walked down the air stairs and toward the terminal in Cancún. He took off the spring jacket he had worn on the plane and put it in his carry on. Underneath he wore a light blue Polo shirt, stone colored chinos and a pair of white NIKE Airs with blue stripes.

The cop's name on the back of the business card Vasquez had given him in Houston was Carlos Montoya. Santana had trouble spotting him right away because Montoya looked young enough to be his son.

"I know what you are thinking, *señor,*" Montoya said as they shook hands. "But I am thirty-three years old."

He wore a white *Guayabera* shirt, *pantalones de mezclilla,* and *Huarache* sandals. He had a firm handshake and a police badge clipped to his right jean pocket.

"The badge helps," Santana said.

"It usually does."

A *Mestizo* or mix of Indian and Spanish, Montoya was lean and stood just under six feet with black hair cut close to his skull. His eyes were dark and intense, in marked contrast to his warm smile and baby face.

He badged Santana through customs and led him to a navy blue Volkswagen Jetta parked at the curb. "Been to the Yucatán before?"

"Haven't had the pleasure," Santana said.

"Since you are not here on vacation, *señor,* we will take the toll road to Valladolid. What you miss in scenery, you make up for in time. We will not have to deal with the *topes* that slow down the cars before every village. Every time I hit one of those speed bumps it upsets my stomach."

Montoya turned on the air conditioning and said, "Hard to believe Cancún was once a tiny fishing village of five hundred people. The name in Mayan means snake nest."

"How many people live here now?"

"Over eight hundred thousand. Tourism is good for the economy, but bad for those who prefer a quieter lifestyle."

"Like you?"

"Si, señor."

"Call me John."

"Okay. You call me Carlos."

They drove out of the airport and away from the turquoise water and high-rise hotels along the Cancún strip.

"We don't get so many tourists in Valladolid," Montoya said. "The region is mostly made up of poor *Campesinos* who still believe that Xtabay, goddess of the forest, lures travelers deep into the *la selva* with her song. But that is beginning to change. Valladolid is no longer a sleepy village in the jungle. There are more than sixty thousand people in the area. We are even building an airport near *Chichén Itzá*. I used to tell my friends from the States when they arrived in Valladolid that they needed to set their watches back several hundred years. Where we are going has always been known as a *ciudad de paso."*

"A place you pass through to get to someplace else," Santana said.

Montoya looked at Santana and smiled. "I'm glad you speak Spanish, John. It will make my job easier."

Billboards and piles of limestone boulders dumped in the center median and spray-painted in bright colors were the only scenery along the four-lane toll way at the edge of the jungle.

Santana turned away from the window and looked at Montoya. "You speak English very well."

"I graduated from the University of Texas. My accent is a mix of Mexican, Texan and English. People have a hard time figuring out where I'm from when I'm in the States."

"I can relate to that. I'm from Manizales, Colombia."

"So what the hell brings a Minnesota detective from Colombia to Valladolid?"

Santana outlined the details of the case as they drove, especially his belief that Pérez and Mendoza had known each other as children in Valladolid.

At Nuevo Xcan they crossed the border between the states of Quintana Roo and Yucatán. The average forest height had gradually risen as they neared Valladolid. Though it was the dry season, the forest appeared to lose much of its scrubby look. Tree limbs became more slender, the leaves broader and thinner, the color a softer yellow-green rather than a hard, silvery gray. Trumpet trees appeared, their large palmate leaves shaped like a hand with thick fingers arising all around the palm.

Good idea to stay away from the water," Montoya said. "You get *turista,* you will spend the whole day investigating *los baños* instead of the case."

"Thanks for the warning."

"The Catholic Church keeps sacramental records," Montoya said. "Primarily baptisms and marriages. If Julio Pérez and Rafael Mendoza were born in Vallalodid, then their names should be in the church register."

Looking out the passenger side window, Santana spotted a black vulture along the shoulder eating road kill. "Pérez grew up in the *Sisal Barrio* if that helps," he said.

"Then the *barrio* is where we will begin."

Santana got a room at the *El Mesón del Marqués,* a colonial style hotel on the plaza. The room had a high, beamed ceiling, heavy wooden furniture, air conditioning and a balcony overlooking the pool. He had promised Montoya he would meet him for dinner at the restaurant in the hotel, but not before he changed and cleaned up.

At 9:30 he was seated at a table with the Mexican detective in a courtyard with a bubbling fountain and a garden of hanging plants and bougainvilleas the color of blood.

Montoya ordered for both of them the *pollo pibil,* a regional specialty of chicken marinated in Seville orange and spices barbecued in banana leaves. They drank cold bottles of *Dos Equis* with dinner.

"You should try the *salsa habanera,*" Montoya said, pointing to a small bottle of ugly green sauce on the table. "It is made from the *chile habanero.*"

"Much hotter than *jalapeño*?"

"The Mayan name for it means 'crying tongue.'"

"I think I'll pass."

"You know, John, many Mexican men say *salsa habanera* is better than great sex."

"So why don't you have some."

Montoya smiled. "Nothing is better than great sex, *amigo.*"

"*Salud,*" Santana said, raising his beer in a toast.

"You want a *Cohíbas?*" Montoya asked, after they had finished their meals. "They are said to be hand rolled on the thighs of *Cubano* virgins."

He inhaled deeply as he held the unlit cigar under his nose.

"No thanks. But I'll take an after-dinner drink. Maybe a Kaluha."

Montoya called the waiter and ordered two Kaluhas.

"So," he said, lighting his cigar. "How is Colombia?"

"From what I read in the newspapers, not so good."

"You have not been home recently?"

"Not recently."

"And your family?"

Santana held Montoya's gaze and then shook his head slowly.

"I see," Montoya said, exhaling a cloud of smoke.

The visit to Mexico was Santana's one and only trip out of the States since he had arrived twenty years ago. He had dreamed many times of his country during his first few years in Minnesota, and he had continued to renew his passport, thinking he would return some day. But those dreams had come less frequently in the ensuing years until the memory of them had dimmed and finally faded away like a light from a distant shore.

"You know," Montoya said, "I remember what it was like living in the States. A society where everything has a price but nothing has value. One has to wonder about the long term consequences of this thinking."

"Ever been to Colombia?" Santana asked.

"No."

"There's your answer."

Montoya thought about it for a while. "It is true that corruption has no borders, *amigo*."

"What's the crime rate in Valladolid?"

"Nothing like Mexico City, or Texas for that matter. Although I think Texas operates under the same Napoleonic Code. Guilty until proven innocent." He smiled.

"Saves a lot of time," Santana said.

"So does a well-placed bullet."

Montoya took a long drag on his cigar and let the smoke out slowly. "I make no apologies for my country or myself. Unfortunately, when you combine a thirst for blood with poverty and corruption, it leads to many kidnappings. Especially of Americans."

"It is the same in Colombia."

"Ah, but Colombians are still more civilized. Your kidnappers do not send pieces of the victim to his family. Here it is common practice."

"Estamos cortados con la misma tijera," Santana said.

"Yes. We are all cut with the same scissors. I can see it in your eyes, *amigo*. Violence is like a shark swimming just below the surface."

The Kaluhas arrived and Montoya made a Mexican toast. *"Arriba, abajo, al centro, pa'dentro."* Up, down, in the middle, inside.

Montoya drank and then took a knife from the table and cut a narrow leaf from a nearby palm tree. In a few minutes, he had fashioned what looked like a green insect the length of his hand. He set it gently on the table directly in front of Santana.

"I'm reminded of the tale of the frog and the scorpion, John. Have you heard it?"

"No."

Montoya said, "The scorpion asks the frog to take him across the river because he cannot swim. The frog believes the scorpion will kill him and refuses. The scorpion explains that it would be foolish to kill him because then they would both die. The frog agrees. Halfway across the river, the scorpion stings the frog. The stunned frog asks the scorpion why he stung him, knowing that they both will die. The scorpion replies, 'It's my nature.' Violence is in our Spanish blood, John. It's our nature. But unlike the scum we deal with, we're able to control it."

"Most of the time," Santana said.

They drank in silence for a while until Santana said, "I remember a quote I read once that said in violence we forget who we are."

"Perhaps during the act itself."

"And after?"

He shook his head. "Afterward, if you forget who you are, you are lost."

Santana took a long drink of Kaluha, letting the thick coolness of it mask the alcohol that burned his insides. "My partner back in Minnesota killed a suspect in a murder," he said.

"Will your partner ever remember who he was before the shooting?"

"I don't think so."

"This is not a surprise, *amigo.* Most species will not kill their own kind. Killing causes a fever in the soul. But sometimes," Montoya said, jabbing the air with the cigar, "there is no choice. Men kill in war. Men kill to save their own life or to protect the life of another. You either learn to live with the knowledge you have killed or you die with it."

Santana knew Montoya was right. He knew it from the moment he first pulled the trigger and killed another human being. The shadow of death and violence had forever darkened his life and corrupted his soul. He lived with it because he had to. But living was never easy.

"You know," Montoya said, "humans have spent the last five million years being aggressive. It is hardwired into our brain."

"Survival of the fittest."

"Exactly. We are competitive and territorial. There are those who say they would never harm anyone. That killing is never justified. But you ask a mother what she would do to protect her child? If she is honest, she will admit that she would kill to protect the life of her child. Violence is in all of us. The only thing that changes is the justification."

"Violence is a much talked about subject in the States," Santana said. "But not death."

"*Si,*" Montoya said. "It is a society in search of the fountain of youth."

He drank from his glass of Kaluha, puffed on the cigar, contemplating, before he continued.

"Mexicans celebrate *La Muerte.* Even in the States, they celebrate the Day of the Dead. One of my favorite writers, Octavio Paz, said that death is our most lasting love. I believe Paz writes the truth."

Santana had not embraced death like Montoya, but he lived in its shadow whenever he carried his shield.

A trio of Mexican guitarists moved through the restaurant under the canopy of night. They were singing, *"Yo soy tú sangre mi viejo, soy tú silencio y tú tiempo,* I am your blood old man, I am your silence and your time." The music and the words triggered pleasant memories of Santana's past before violence cleaved his world in two.

"You like this music, John?"

"Yes." He was feeling the languid effects of the long trip, heavy meal and drinks. "It reminds me of Colombia and my father. He loved the old music."

When the trio finished playing, Santana thanked them and tipped them ten American dollars.

"It is good to be a tourist," Montoya said, "unless you are in trouble with the law. You can be kept in jail here for up to thirteen months without bail or a jury trial. It is a long time to be in jail in any country, but a very long time in a Mexican jail. The courts are very hard on drugs and firearms, John. I assume you are carrying neither."

"I'm looking for information, Carlos. Not trouble."

"Good. Then tomorrow we will talk to a priest. See if we can find Pérez and Mendoza's names in the church register. But for now, we will relax." Montoya sat back in his chair. "Have you ever been in a *casa de piedra*?"

"A stone house?"

"It is more than a stone house. The Mayans call it Temazcal. A secret bath."

"I've not had the pleasure."

"Then you must have one, *amigo*. It will cleanse your soul as well as your body."

The stone house was actually a small, stone hut with a palm-thatched roof and a blanket over the door located near the *Xkeken Cenote,* one of the cool, underground streams in Valladolid. Stones heated over a fire were placed in the center of the dirt floor and then doused with water creating a sauna-like effect.

Montoya said, "The Mayans are a very superstitious people, you know."

"Just like Hispanics," Santana said.

Montoya laughed. "What do you expect? Valladolid was the ritual and ceremonial center of their civilization. They called it Zaci. It means white hawk."

They both were sitting cross-legged on the floor, wearing only a towel wrapped around their waists. Beads of sweat ran down Santana's forehead and dripped into his eyes.

Before entering the hut, they had been asked by an old Mayan Indian to make an offering to the gods to help guide them on their paths in life. The Indian stood over them now, striking them lightly with leaves made of sage and tobacco. The scent of each leaf permeated the moist, thick heat.

Santana closed his eyes. The only sound was the gentle rustle of leaves as they brushed against his skin. Time gradually became as ephemeral as the steam rising off the stones. Soon, a kaleidoscope of strange images appeared before his eyes.

And then he was on the bridge again.

Flames from a burning river of oil below charred the crosses, which served as bridge supports, and melted the fog that seeped off the snow surrounding him. A woman's anguished voice called to him as she had called to him in a dream before. She was much closer to him now. Still, he could not move or feel. Yet, he could sense that there was someone else lurking in the shadows, someone with the woman. He knew he was neither awake nor asleep but floating just below the surface of consciousness. There were clues here in this netherworld if only he could see them. But as he concentrated harder, his eyes straining to see more than the shadows in the cold mist ahead of him, the delicate balance needed to remain in this state shifted suddenly, and his mind began the gentle ascent toward consciousness.

Chapter 20

DAY 7

SANTANA AWOKE WITH A START TO THE DIN of chirping birds. He was lying on his hotel bed, looking at the lasers of early morning sunlight that pierced the small spaces between the blinds.

He sat up and placed his feet firmly on the floor. The sudden movement caused a blood vessel just above his left eye to begin pounding in rhythm with his heart. He remembered leaving the *casa de piedra,* swimming briefly in the cool waters of the *cenote,* and then riding back in Montoya's Jetta to the hotel. He knew he had taken no drugs, yet his memory of last evening was like the lyric of an old, favorite song. Lost for the moment but not completely forgotten.

He showered, put on a fresh set of clothes and ate a breakfast of juice, fruit and eggs before meeting Montoya in the hotel lobby.

They were walking across the square near the hotel now, past flocks of flamingos, herons, cormorants and gray pelicans, and Mayan women selling handmade dresses, T-shirts, and silver and gold jewelry. The weathered, gray Cathedral of *San Gervasio* loomed like a mountain above the tree branches to the south. Like all Spanish colonial towns, Valladolid was built around a church and a square. The square was a large garden with cobblestone walkways and a fountain in the center. Narrow paths off the main walkways led to shady dead ends and white cast iron benches. Beneath large trees in the central square were chairs connected so that they faced each other. A young Hispanic couple was sitting in one, looking at one another, as if they were the last two people on earth.

"Did you sleep well?" Montoya asked.

"Like the dead," Santana said. "Though my memory of what happened after we left the *casa de piedra* is a little fuzzy."

"Yours is not an unusual experience the first time in the *Temazcal*. But perhaps you learned something that might be helpful."

Santana thought about the recurring dream of the bridge again. He felt frustrated that he could neither solve the meaning of it nor the case before him. Instinct told him that the solution to both was right in front of him. He just had to keep his eyes wide open and trust his intuition.

"There are seven churches in the eight *barrios* of Valladolid, counting *El Centro* or *Zocalo*," Montoya said. "Only the *Bacalar Barrio* has no church. The church in the *Sisal Barrio* is called *San Bernardino de Siena*. It is the oldest in the Yucatán. There is a convent, but it is no longer used. Asking questions and getting no answers is what I like least about the job. So I called the priest this morning. I told him what we were looking for and that we were coming early, before most of the tourists. He agreed to meet us. It is a short walk from the main square."

The sun was like a flame in the brilliant blue sky, the air already thick with humidity and smelling of fried beans and *tortillas* as they passed a restaurant where a young woman sat on the tile floor beside a small fire making *tortillas* out of corn meal for the tourists, compliments of the restaurant. Santana wondered how many *tortillas* she made sitting here all day like a one-person assembly line.

They walked along a narrow street, which Montoya called *Calzada de los Frailes*, or the street of the Franciscans. It had old-fashioned streetlamps and was paved with cobblestones and fronted by restored homes with pastel colors and colonial facades.

The huge arches and thick walls of the *San Bernardino de Sisal* convent were imposing and appeared unchanged since its founding in 1552. The façade was a checkerboard pattern devoid of any religious symbols or art. Above the arches were a choral window and a Franciscan shield.

Montoya explained that the convent and church were built to be self-sufficient and to withstand Indian attacks. The first word that came to Santana's mind was fortress.

"We are meeting Father Santos in the monastery garden," Montoya said. "Visitors need special permission from the priest to see that area of the convent, so it will be quiet and we can talk in peace."

The priest was waiting for them near an ancient mule-powered water wheel and a stone-domed gazebo that covered a *cenote* well. A young woman wearing a *sombrero* and a white cotton blouse and pants was on her knees, tending to the red and white flowers tucked among the large leaves of the elephant ear plants in the garden.

"I understand from what Detective Montoya told me, that you have come a long way for information, *señor*," the priest said in Spanish. His hair was white, his mouth a dry line, yet Santana saw a light in his eyes that suggested he was more youthful than he appeared.

"Two men are dead," Santana said. "Two men who grew up in Valladolid in the sixties."

"How do you think I can help you?"

"I'm looking for a motive for their murders."

The young woman tending the garden glanced in Santana's direction, and then looked away quickly when their eyes met.

"And you expect to find it here?" Father Santos said.

"I don't know. But I believe something ties these two men together. It could be something from their past."

The priest gave it some thought before responding. "The register shows that Julio Pérez and Rafael Mendoza were baptized in this church."

Santana's momentary excitement at hearing the news was tempered by the knowledge that it proved nothing.

"How long have you been a priest here?" he asked.

The light changed suddenly in the priest's eyes. "Not long enough to have known the families or anything about them."

"Is there someone else who could help us, Father Santos?" Montoya asked. "Perhaps someone you know who was born about the same time and who still attends the church?"

"I'm afraid not."

Santana saw the young woman's eyes flick in his direction again, but she went back to her gardening the moment he looked at her.

The priest turned and walked away, his body slightly stooped, as though he had carried the weight of the world and all its sins on his shoulders for too many years.

"You think he knows more than he is telling us?" Montoya said to Santana.

"Probably."

"We can ask around the *barrio*. Someone might remember Pérez and Mendoza."

"We could."

"What other choice do we have?"

Santana walked over to the young woman working in the garden. Montoya followed.

"You overheard our conversation."

She looked up at Santana, her brown eyes squinting in the bright sunlight. "No, *señor*."

"Maybe you can help us."

"I don't think so," she said. Tiny streams of sweat had formed tracks in the dirt smudges on her dark, pretty face.

Santana squatted down beside her. "All I need is a name. Someone who grew up here. No one needs to know who gave it to me."

"I cannot help you," she said.

"I'm trying to bring a murderer to justice, *señorita*."

She put down the digging trowel, pulled a few weeds out of the ground and looked at Santana. "There is a woman who lives in the *barrio*. I work in her garden. She has always been kind and helpful to me. Perhaps she will help you."

"What's her name?"

"Daniela de la Vega," the young woman said.

Montoya sucked in a breath, as if oxygen had suddenly gone out of the air.

"You know her?" Santana said.

"I don't know her. But I know who she is."

Ten minutes later they were standing outside the door of a large house a few blocks from the railroad station and the *Cine San Juan*, the only theater in town.

Santana was admiring the wrought iron grilles over the eight-foot high Moorish windows when a maid opened the door.

Montoya showed her his badge. She asked him to wait. Shortly, an elegant looking older woman appeared, her still-shapely figure framed in sunlight.

"Señora de la Vega. Buenas tardes."

Santana could tell by Montoya's deference that he was in awe of the woman.

"Señora. Soy Carlos Montoya. John Santana." Montoya held out his badge. As he did so, he looked at Santana and said in English, "Daniela de la Vega was a famous Mexican actress."

"Not was, Mr. Montoya," she said in perfect English. "I still am." Her voice had a sultry rasp that suggested confidence rather than anger.

She wore a simple cotton print dress, cut low over her large breasts and a plain beaded necklace around a throat that was just beginning to show a few wrinkles. Her black hair was straight and fell over her shoulders and down her back nearly to her waist.

Santana made her for fifty though she easily could have passed for forty.

Montoya said, "We hate to bother you, *señora,* but we are looking for someone who might have known a man named Julio Pérez. He lived in the *barrio* some forty years ago."

Her stunning indigo eyes looked Montoya over carefully and then, when they came to rest on Santana, he felt a sudden tingle along his spine, as if she had run her tongue down his back.

"I knew Julio," she said.

Santana's pulse quickened. He gave Montoya a glance and said, "I wonder if we could ask you a few questions about him? We won't take much of your time."

She paused a moment longer before gesturing gracefully toward the living room.

Santana noticed the few age spots that marred her delicate hand. He remembered his mother had called age spots *flores de cementerio* or cemetery flowers.

Daniela de la Vega led them into the living room, moving with a proud elegance Santana associated with good breeding or royalty.

The room had an eighteen-foot high-beamed ceiling and wrought iron chandeliers. Mosaic tile covered the floor. The double wooden shutters on the Moorish windows were open, and sunlight spilled into the room.

They sat on colonial furniture, two chairs and a couch, arranged in a circle around a large square coffee table.

"I was just about to have some tea," she said. "Would you gentleman like something?"

"We don't want to inconvenience you, *señora,*" Montoya said.

"There is no inconvenience, Mr. Montoya. What would you like?"

"Do you have beer?" he asked hesitantly, as if he were asking for monkey urine.

"Of course. And Mr. Santana?"

"Beer is fine."

She summoned a maid.

Santana had missed the slight tremor in her hand when they were introduced, and the way her head bobbed nearly imperceptibly. But now he saw it and knew at once that she was in the initial stages of Parkinson's disease.

"I rarely allow visitors," she said, focusing her attention on the two of them. "But I am wondering why you are looking for someone who knew Julio. I have not seen him since we were children."

Santana said, "I'm also a police officer, Ms. de la Vega, but in the States. Minnesota to be exact. I'm sorry to have to tell you that I'm investigating Mr. Pérez's murder."

She quickly raised a hand to her mouth. *"Es terrible."*

"Yes, it is. I believe that Mr. Pérez's murder might be connected to something that happened here, in Valladolid, when he was a child. I'm hoping you can tell me what that connection might be."

"I can't imagine," she said. "I left Valladolid and went to Mexico City when I was eighteen. I won a beauty contest."

"Not just a beauty contest," Montoya said. "She was Miss Mexico. And eventually, Miss Universe."

Santana half expected Montoya to ask her for an autograph.

"That was such a long time ago," she said with a mixture of embarrassment and nostalgia. "Much has happened since."

On the end table next to the couch were two 8 x 11 framed photos of Daniela de la Vega from the shoulders up. She was wearing a white terrycloth robe with a towel wrapped around her hair in both photos, as if she had recently emerged from a shower. She looked remarkably the same in each photo despite the fact that one had last year's date written in the frame's corner and the other frame a date twenty years earlier.

The maid returned with the beers and tea.

Santana poured a bottle of Corona in a clear glass and took a long drink.

Montoya said, "How well did you know Julio Pérez, *señora*?"

"We attended the same church."

"Did you know his family?"

"Not well. My family and Julio's ... well, let me say that we did not see each other outside of church."

She was being polite, but Santana understood the underlying message. Social class was just as important here as it was in Manizales where he grew up. The original families who settled the city at the turn of the 20th century came from the cities of Abejorral and Sonson near Medellin in the state of Antioquia. If you were descended from this group, as Santana's family had been, you had certain advantages. Heritage in Manizales's society was everything. And no amount of money, legally or illegally gained, could ever change that.

"Did you know Rafael Mendoza?" Santana asked.

"Why, yes."

Santana looked at her without saying anything.

"Was Rafael murdered, too?"

"I'm afraid so."

Her right hand shook more now as she held the teacup and saucer close to her mouth. Maybe it was the weight of it that caused her hand to shake more and maybe it was something else.

"Something happened here, *señora,*" Santana said. "What was it?"

He had seen a moment of recognition in her eyes. Mendoza's name had triggered a long forgotten memory.

Daniela de la Vega set the teacup and saucer on the coffee table in front of her. Her full lips twitched slightly and her face grew pensive. She appeared to be composing herself, as though she was about to audition for the role of a lifetime.

"It was such a long time ago," she began. "I did not remember what happened until you mentioned Rafael Mendoza. He and Julio were best friends."

She was looking at Santana now, but her eyes were focused in the past and seemed scarred by some inner turmoil.

"As I recall, their families were very close."

Santana glanced at Montoya. He wanted to make sure Daniela de la Vega's recounting of the events would continue without questions. But he could tell by Montoya's expression that he, too, understood the importance of what she was about to say and had no intention of disrupting the moment.

"Julio looked after him like they were brothers. The boys did everything together." She hesitated a moment and looked directly at Santana.

"Go on," he said.

She took a deep breath and let it out slowly. "I am very much a woman of the world, Detective. I have seen a great many things in my life. And I have done things I am not especially proud of."

She paused and forced a smile.

Daniela de la Vega was an actress used to playing different roles. Santana was certain that she could slip in and out of character as easily as she could a pair of shoes. But there was no character to play, no rehearsed dialogue to repeat now. There was only the past. And it was real and obviously painful.

"What you have to tell us could be very important, *señora*," Santana said.

"Yes. I understand. I am just surprised that even today, it is difficult for me to speak of these things."

A warm breeze blew in the open windows gently lifting the edges of the napkins and exposing the glass underneath. The breeze brought with it a hint of rain and perhaps a storm to come.

"I am a Catholic," she continued. "I was brought up to respect the church, as were Julio and Rafael. They were altar boys."

She took a moment more to compose herself.

Behind her, in an alcove next to a bedroom, a long, rectangular table was covered with a tablecloth of embroidered white lace. On the wall behind the table were framed pictures of the Virgin of Guadalupe and the Immaculate Conception. On the table was a blue wooden cross with the word *INRI* in gold lettering written at the apex. Along the vertical post underneath the word Jesus were gold symbols representing an angel, a chalice, a dove, the Eucharist and a tablet of the Ten Commandments. Leaning against the base of the cross was a picture of Jesus wearing a crown of thorns. Around the cross were the *constelacion de santos*, the constellation of saints, six lighted candles and two, small vases of flowers.

"There was a young missionary here at the time that everyone admired," she continued. "Especially the two boys. Nothing was ever proven, but there were … allegations."

Montoya sat forward in his chair and leaned his elbows on his knees.

"You're suggesting the boys were sexually abused," Santana said.

She gave him a long look and then a slight nod, as if repeating the words would damn her soul forever.

"Do you remember the priest's name?"

"There were only rumors," she said. "This might not have happened. You understand."

"The name," Santana said.

She looked at Montoya for support.

"Please, *señora*," he said. "Do you remember?"

She looked at Santana again, and he could see the cool resolve in her indigo eyes. "I will never forget his name. It was Scanlon. Richard Scanlon."

The shroud of sky outside the window of the 757 exploded with light every few seconds, like artillery shells fired in battle, as lightning zigzagged out of the black, anvil-shaped clouds looming high above the plane that carried Santana along the edge of a gathering storm.

He was thinking about his sister, Natalia, how he had left her when he fled Colombia twenty years ago, how he regretted never having said good-bye. In a recurring dream he would see her walking away from him along busy *Avenida 12 de Octubre* in Manizales, forever seven years old. He would call out, asking her to wait for him, running between and around people on the sidewalk, trying to catch her. But she would keep walking until the crowd swallowed her.

When he arrived at the place where he had last seen her, he would find nothing ahead of him but impenetrable darkness, darkness so cold and ominous that fear kept him from following. In his heart he believed that Natalia was alive and safe in a convent somewhere in Colombia, and that the darkness merely represented loneliness, the ache he felt whenever he thought of her. It was, for Santana, confirmation that a small part of him still lived, still believed that there was good in the world. He feared that if he ever lost this feeling, he would die completely inside. So he welcomed the ache and ignored the voice inside his head that warned him the dream could represent only one thing.

He peered down at the distant lights firing the landscape, as though he were God looking down on creation. He wondered how many husbands living in the houses below went to church on Sunday and then went home and abused their children or beat their wives? How many couples cheated on each other? How many were drug addicts or alcoholics? How many stole company profits, cooked the books and gutted pension plans? How many cared about nothing or no one but themselves? Most people would call him a cynic. Santana preferred to think of himself as a realist. No sane person could spend time in Homicide without coming to the conclusion that this was one very sick world.

It was easy to convince himself that he was above it all, that his job gave him carte blanche to do whatever he deemed necessary in the name of justice. But he was no hypocrite. He readily acknowledged that he had broken the laws of society and of the commandments, that he had murdered his own soul. He did this knowing that someday, if there truly was a God, he might have to pay for his sins, if not in this life, then in another.

It was nearly 8:00 p.m. on Monday evening when he entered his house and turned off the security system. The long flight and abrupt change in weather left him feeling vulnerable to a wind that was like cold steel pressing against exposed flesh.

He disregarded the blinking red light on his phone, left his luggage and clothes on the bed and took a hot, steaming bath. He lay in the tub with his eyes closed and let warm water massage away the chill that was a deep bruise embedded in his muscles. He imagined the hell that would break loose in the department and city if he were to accuse Archbishop Richard Scanlon of sexually abusing two boys years ago in Valladolid, Mexico. He saw the abuse as further justification for his loss of faith in a religion that had once had a profound influence on his life.

Once, he would never have questioned anything he heard inside a church or a confessional. He believed the words spoken there were more than those of a priest; they were the word of God. And God made no mistakes. But the strong cord that bound

Santana to his faith had loosened considerably when his father was killed by a drunken driver and had completely unraveled when his mother died a senseless death as well. Suddenly, it was hard to believe in the goodness of a god who would allow this to happen. Now, he trusted a priest no more than he did anyone else.

Julio Pérez and Rafael Mendoza had been trusting and vulnerable once, too. They had been taught to believe in the goodness of the church and of God. And each had been betrayed in the most intimate of fashions, sexually abused at the hands of a priest, forced to carry the shock and humiliation with them like a cancer all of their lives. Fate had brought them separately to St. Paul, literally within miles of one another, though indications were that the traumatic experience they shared as children had kept them light years apart.

On the surface it appeared that they had come to terms with the abuse. Both were successful, one as a journalist and publisher, the other as an attorney. Yet, Mendoza's life was much different from the one he projected in public. Mendoza had pocketed thousands by bringing illegal immigrants into the country on phony worker visas. He had maintained the image of an eligible heterosexual while leading a secret life as a homosexual. Was it Scanlon's appointment as archbishop that finally upset the delicate balance Mendoza had achieved in his life? Were both men finally forced to face the demons of the past?

Santana wanted very much to confront Scanlon, but even if the sexual abuse allegations were true, it didn't prove that the archbishop had murdered Pérez and Mendoza. And Santana knew that without solid evidence to substantiate the charges of abuse or murder, it would be career suicide to accuse Scanlon of the crimes. There had to be another way.

Before going to bed Santana unpacked his shaving kit. Inside it he found the scorpion Montoya had made for him out of a leaf. It reminded him of the story about the frog and the scorpion, and he wondered for a moment if he could ever change his nature.

He placed the scorpion on the fireplace mantel and went to his computer where he read a short biography of Richard Scanlon the *Pioneer Press* had recently run on its website. Scanlon, sixty-five, had grown up in St. Paul, where he graduated from Seton Academy. He had received a B.A. at St. John's University in Collegeville, Minnesota. After graduation he had entered the St. Paul Seminary where he was ordained. Later he had received a Doctorate in Divinity at the Catholic University in Washington where he had done some teaching. He had also studied at the North American College in Rome. Before his appointment as Archbishop of St. Paul and Minneapolis, Scanlon had been a priest at the Church of the Guardian Angels in St. Paul, had taught at Seton Academy, had served as a diocesan bishop in San Antonio and had been past president of the National Conference of Bishops. Speculation had it that Scanlon was offered the position of archbishop because of his midwestern roots and because the current three auxiliary bishops in charge of the three regional vicariates in St. Paul were less qualified. Consideration was given to Scanlon's "intellectual qualities, social sense, and spirit of cooperation," according to Pro Nuncio James O'Connor. Scanlon could serve as archbishop until he retired at seventy-five. According to the *Pioneer Press* reporter, the rapidly growing Hispanic population in the Twin Cities, and the fact that Scanlon spoke fluent Spanish and had spent time in Mexico as a young priest helped secure his appointment.

Then again, Santana thought, perhaps Scanlon's experience in Mexico might not help him one damn bit.

Chapter 21

DAY 8

TUESDAY MORNING'S WEATHER REPORT predicted snow flurries and falling barometric pressure. Winds were pushing a storm in a northeasterly direction out of Nebraska and toward the upper Midwest. Forecasters were on high alert, interrupting regularly scheduled programs and running dire warnings across television screens. If the storm stayed on its current path, the Twin Cities could receive up to a foot of snow. Then again, if it veered slightly east, there would likely be only an inch or two. It was hard to tell precisely which direction the storm would go because computer models were generating conflicting reports.

Driving the Crown Vic across the Wabasha Bridge and into the West Side of St. Paul, Santana wondered what it would be like if homicide detectives were afforded the same latitude as meteorologists. He pictured himself telling Ashford that information he had fed into a computer was predicting the murderer might be Archbishop Scanlon or it might not. No matter whether he was right or wrong, he expected to keep his job. He laughed to himself, but it was a laugh of anxiety as much as humor. In reality, Santana knew he could not afford to be wrong. Not this time. Not ever.

From a distance the tall steeple on the Church of the Guardian Angels appeared to impale the low, dark clouds that hung like a veil over it. Oak and maple trees lining the narrow neighborhood streets were stripped bare, their naked branches withered hands reaching toward heaven.

In his mind's eye Santana saw Richard Scanlon and Thomas Hidalgo at Calvary Cemetery right after the graveside service for Julio Pérez. There was a moment when Hidalgo introduced Scanlon. The way Hidalgo looked at Scanlon, the way he touched the older priest on the shoulder. It was a simple gesture that might have meant something and might have meant nothing at all. But Santana wanted to find out for sure.

He parked the Crown Vic in a parking lot and walked along the sidewalk behind the church to the rectory. It was a small stone Tudor with a tall chimney and a pair of steeply pitched gables. Thomas Hidalgo answered the doorbell.

"Yes," he said tentatively. He had a puzzled expression on his angular face and then a look of recognition. "Detective Santana. What brings you here?"

"I'd like to ask you a few questions."

Hidalgo's eyes looked past Santana at the church before shifting upward toward the darkening skies for a moment, apparently waiting for God to provide an appropriate response.

"I don't see how I can be of any help," he said at last, his eyes settling on Santana's face again.

Santana gave him a friendly smile. "How can you be sure when you don't know what I'm going to ask you?"

"I'm kind of busy."

"This won't take long."

"All right," he said with a reluctant shrug. "Come in."

Gray light bled into the small, dark living room with the walnut floors and French provincial furniture across from a brick fireplace that looked like it had never been touched by flames. Even though Santana had his coat on, he still felt the chill in the air, as if the thermostat had been turned down to fifty-five degrees. The whole atmosphere was gloomy, not unlike the world beyond the walls.

"Live here alone?"

"No," Hidalgo said. "With a seminary student."

He sat down on a couch and brushed an invisible piece of lint off the sleeve of a pale white shirt that nearly matched his chalky complexion.

Santana stood with his hands in his coat pockets near the fireplace. Above the mantel was a large, framed artist's sketch of the St. Paul Cathedral.

"Want to sit down, Detective?"

"No thanks. I was on a plane all day yesterday flying back from Mexico. Think I'll stand."

"Vacation?"

"Business."

Hidalgo crossed his legs and then uncrossed them again quickly, making sure he kept the perfectly straight crease pressed into his khaki pants.

Santana said, "How long have you been at the Church of Guardian Angels?"

"Nearly three years now."

"Grow up here?"

"On the West Side. My family was poor. I was lucky enough to attend Seton Academy on a scholarship."

"Always known you wanted to be a priest?"

"Since about twelve or thirteen. It was what my mother wanted for me. I was a good Hispanic boy." He offered a weak smile.

A framed photo on the mantel depicted a serious looking Hispanic woman Santana assumed was Hidalgo's mother.

"Not all good Hispanic boys become priests."

"True," Hidalgo said. "But you must've felt some of that same pressure."

"Not really. My mother always wanted me to be a doctor like her."

"So why aren't you?"

"My priorities changed."

"And was she disappointed when you became a police officer?"

"She died unexpectantly when I was sixteen."

"Oh. I'm sorry."

Hidalgo's white shirt was fastened tightly around his thin neck, and he unconsciously touched the top button now with an unsteady hand.

"Pardon me for asking, Detective, but are you ever troubled by your choice? I mean with all the violence and death you have to deal with."

"No," Santana said. "You?"

"Certainly not. I feel the priesthood is a special calling. I was very fortunate to be chosen to proclaim the gospel of salvation."

He spoke without conviction, like he had merely committed the words to memory.

"I think my being a detective is a calling of sorts, too," Santana said.

"Well, if I may disagree, being a detective is quite different than being a priest."

"Really?"

Hidalgo nodded his head vigorously.

"We both deal with death, Father. And people confess all sorts of terrible things to me. Just like they confess terrible things to you."

Hidalgo chewed on his bottom lip and gave it some thought before replying.

The air held a breath of ammonia. A grandfather clock on the opposite wall ticked another second off eternity.

"I was given unique powers at ordination to administer the sacraments and to reconcile a sinful people with their God, Detective Santana. I take that very seriously."

"I'm sure you do. And my badge and my gun give me unique powers. Even the power of life and death. Believe me, I take that very seriously as well."

Dark eyes focused inward, Hidalgo seemed at a loss for words.

"Tell me what you knew about Julio Pérez," Santana said.

Hidalgo gazed at Santana again and cleared his throat. "He was one of the founders of this parish. Served as an usher for more than twenty years. There is a story that the parish's first Mass was held in a renovated bingo parlor. The only people in attendance were Julio Pérez, his wife and young daughter and the priest. The collection that day amounted to seventy-five cents."

He smiled a little at the memory.

"How about Rubén Córdova?"

"He attended church infrequently, so I didn't know him well."

The scornful tone of Hidalgo's voice suggested that perhaps if Córdova had attended church regularly he might be alive now and not the prime suspect in a double murder.

"You believe Córdova killed Julio Pérez?"

"It is difficult to believe anyone could take the life of another."

Not exactly a ringing endorsement of Córdova's innocence, Santana thought.

"What can you tell me about Angelina Torres?"

"A caring person," Hidalgo said. "Willing to give of her time. She's helped many of the Mexican immigrants."

"Have a lot of Mexican immigrants in the church?"

"More all the time."

"Most of them illegal?"

Hidalgo hesitated. "Many are, yes."

"How about you?"

His complexion darkened. "My parents came here legally, Detective."

"Do you speak Spanish?"

"What I learned as a child, I've mostly forgotten."

"Might be helpful with all the immigrants in your congregation."

His posture appeared to stiffen. "There are those in the church who are bilingual. But English is the language of this country. The country Mexicans chose to come to. They should learn to speak it. I certainly did."

Hidalgo apparently thought his heritage was a disease from which he had fortunately recovered.

Santana took out his notebook and flipped a few pages until he found what he was looking for.

"When you and Angelina Torres came to my office the day after Rafael Mendoza's death, you told me you didn't know him very well. Yet, according to Angelina Torres, Mendoza got work visas for many of the Mexican immigrants your church helped support."

Hidalgo's white complexion burned red. His dark eyes darted back and forth, apparently searching for a response that could explain the discrepancy.

"Just because we worked with many of the same people, doesn't mean that I knew him well. You must've misunderstood what I said, Detective Santana."

"I don't think so. I have your exact words written here."

"Perhaps, then, you misunderstood what I meant."

"Perhaps," Santana said.

He flipped a few pages until he found a clean sheet in his notebook. Took out a pen. Looked at Hidalgo again. "How do you know the archbishop?"

Hidalgo's eyes brightened in the gray of the room. "After I graduated from the University of St. Thomas, I entered the St. Paul Seminary and was ordained. I then went to divinity school at the Catholic University of America. Father Scanlon was teaching there."

"Then you've known him for some time."

"Yes."

"Think he'll make a good archbishop?"

Hidalgo's lips tightened. "Of course."

Santana wandered over to an end table, picked up a framed 5 x 7 photo. Hidalgo was standing next to Scanlon in front of a log cabin. The color of the leaves and their heavy jackets indicated the picture had been taken sometime in late fall. Hidalgo's dark hair was longer than he wore it now, and it curled over his forehead in the same way Christopher Reeve's did in the Superman movies. He had his right arm around Scanlon's shoulder and a cast on his left arm. Santana could see that the cast had quite a few signatures written on it though he couldn't make out any of the names. Someone standing just out of the frame of focus cast a long shadow that fell on Scanlon, partially obscuring his face.

"How's your arm, Father?"

Hidalgo appeared surprised.

"I noticed you had a broken arm in this picture."

"Oh. Well, that was taken a while ago. I had fallen on some stairs and chipped a bone in my forearm. It healed fine."

"So you didn't need surgery?"

"No."

"Ever have any surgery?"

"Never. My health is fine. Why do you ask?"

"Guess it must be the unfulfilled doctor part of me coming out," Santana said with a smile.

"Yes, I suppose it could be."

Hidalgo sounded as convinced as he would be if Santana had claimed he was the Second Coming of Christ.

"So, Father, what else do you know about Archbishop Scanlon?"

"What do you mean?"

Hidalgo tried to match Santana's hard stare but gave it up after a few seconds and peered down at his Hush Puppies instead.

"I'm not sure why you've come here, Detective Santana. I thought we were going to talk about Julio Pérez or Rubén Córdova. Not the archbishop."

From where Santana was standing he could see into the small dining room. On one wall was a print of the Creation of Adam and on the opposite a copy of Da Vinci's, The Last Supper.

"You're very close to Father Scanlon."

Hidalgo looked up at Santana again. His left eye twitched. He glanced at the framed picture Santana was holding and then looked away. As he did so, his chest appeared to shrink inward, as if his ribcage had suddenly collapsed from a weight he was carrying.

"Once," he said, softly.

Santana set the frame down and came around the coffee table. "I want to show you another photo, Father."

He sat down on the couch close to Hidalgo, took the photo Gamboni had found in Mendoza's loft out of his coat pocket and offered it to the priest. Getting him to identify Scanlon as one of the men in the photo was a long shot, but Santana figured he had nothing to lose.

"Recognize anyone?" Santana asked calmly.

The priest took the photo reluctantly, not looking at it at first. When he did, he seemed to recoil from it. He let out a muted cry and dropped the photo on the floor as though he had touched a burning cross. Standing abruptly, he stumbled toward the fireplace and reached out to the mantel for support.

Santana looked down at the photo at his feet and then at Hidalgo.

The priest stood facing the fireplace, both hands gripping the mantel tightly. Peering down at the floor. Gagging like he was about to be sick.

Santana had hoped for a reaction, but this was more extreme than he had expected. He looked down at the photo once more, then at Hidalgo again. Suddenly, he felt as if he had jumped into an icy stream.

"That's you, isn't it?" Santana said. "The one on your knees."

Hidalgo was shaking his head and trying to speak, but the words were unintelligible.

"Is it Scanlon you're with?"

"Get out," Hidalgo said in a weak, hoarse voice.

"You can tell me."

"Go," Hidalgo said.

Santana picked up the photo and stood up. "If you need to talk, Father."

"Please. Go."

He spoke like a man without hope.

Santana pulled a business card out of his shirt pocket, set it on the coffee table. "Do the right thing. Give me a call, Father. I'll be waiting."

Hidalgo's shoulders shook as if he were crying, though there was no sound.

Santana turned and walked out the door.

Chapter 22

SANTANA DROVE DOWN A BLOCK from the Church of The Guardian Angels where he sat in the Crown Vic watching the rectory and listening to a female dispatcher calmly directing radio patrol cars in pursuit of a burglar running down an alley. It reminded him of his early years as a police officer; the nights he spent driving through the streets and alleys of St. Paul. Most of the chatter between RPCs and dispatch was like background music, something he tuned out unless it was in his patrol area or he heard his call number. While those on the wrong side of the law often found cover in darkness, Santana found solace, knowing that as the pimps, pushers, gangbangers and thieves moved along their predictably dark paths, he would be waiting — as he waited now for Thomas Hidalgo.

It was evident that the young priest was one of the two men in the photo. While Hidalgo had committed no crime, the act itself put him at odds with the teachings of the Catholic Church. If Scanlon was the other man in the photo, was Mendoza blackmailing him? Was Mendoza seeking revenge for the abuse he suffered as a child years ago in Valladolid? Santana had sensed that Hidalgo was torn between the desire to please his mother and the need to acknowledge his homosexuality. Could this fear of exposure have led him to commit murder? It had been Santana's experience that when confronted with damaging evidence against them, criminals often sought reassurance from their accomplices. Santana was hoping that Hidalgo would react in a similar manner and contact the other man in the photo. Then he would follow.

Gusts of whistling wind rocked the car and handfuls of snow blew off the tops of the hard snowbanks that lined the street like ocean spray bursting off the bow of a sailboat.

An hour passed. Then a green Toyota RAV pulled into the parish lot, and a young man in a purple St. Thomas letter jacket got out and went into the house.

Santana started the Crown Vic, let the heater cut the chill inside the car, and punched the Toyota's license number into the Mobile Data Terminal in the console between the front seats. In a moment the MDT computer listed the car's owner as Daniel McCutcheon. His address was the same as the rectory. He had no wants or warrants, but he had received a speeding ticket a year ago. No doubt McCutcheon was the seminary student who lived with Hidalgo.

A few minutes later, when the female dispatcher reported a Code 3, it took a moment for Santana to recognize the address and another to wonder why dispatch would be reporting an emergency at the rectory requiring squads to use their red lights and sirens. Then he shoved the Crown Vic in gear. Stepped on the gas and was in the church parking lot and out of the car, running toward the rectory as sirens wailed in the distance.

What Santana saw as he rushed through the doorway hit him like a blast of Arctic air. Thomas Hidalgo had tied one end of an electrical cord around the stair railing on the second floor landing and the other end around his neck and then jumped, fracturing his windpipe and severing his spinal cord. His body hung limply about three feet off the floor like a side of beef in cold storage.

Santana looked away, but it was too late. Memories of his mother's death had already been unleashed, and the demons of the past were free once again to prowl his mind and haunt his soul.

"I was sorry to hear about your mother's death," the Colombian official from *EL DAS* said. "I had the pleasure of meeting her on more than one occasion. There was not a better woman in the city of Manizales. She did much to help the poor."

Santana stared at the tiny hairs that sprouted from the official's large ears as the man loosened his red tie and unbuttoned his shirt collar. Smoke from the Cuban cigar in the ashtray on his desk curled upward, forming a thin cloud that hovered over the room.

The official's gaze shifted to the office window, then to the plaque on the wall with the Department Administration of Security lettering on it, and finally to the papers scattered on his desk. His eyes were the color of burnt almonds, and they had a hard time settling on Santana for any length of time.

"And my sister?"

"She is with the nuns now."

The official brushed at his thick, gray mustache with the back of his pudgy fingers. Tears of sweat forming at the edge of his sideburns slid down his haggard cheeks and into the stained shirt collar around his flabby neck.

"What are you going to do?" Santana asked.

"What can one do in the case of suicide but mourn?" He shrugged his heavy, round shoulders, as if that explained everything.

"Suicide!"

"I am afraid that is what it appears to be."

"My mother's hands were tied behind her back!"

In his mind's eye Santana saw his mother hanging naked from a beam in the ceiling in their home, her swollen tongue protruding from her mouth, her dark eyes bulging out of her head as though she were wearing a bloated, blue death mask.

"How old are you, Juan?"

"Sixteen."

"Well, you are too young to understand these matters. Let us handle the investigation. When it is complete, if we find that your mother's unfortunate death was not a suicide, we will arrest the perpetrator, of course. Once we find out who he is."

He gave Santana a thin smile.

"Of course you will," Santana said.

Through the French doors Santana could see the moon, a pale horse rising in the sky. A sheet of albescent light lay on the patio, and the leaves on the rubber trees hung motionless in the cool stillness of the night. He sat motionless on a chair inside the house that was as dark as his heart, letting a flame of anger burn what was left of life out of his soul.

"I spoke to the police earlier today," he said. "They will do nothing."

Ofir sat facing him in a rocker, her long white hair shimmering in the darkness like a beacon on a treacherous sea. "The police are afraid."

"But I am not."

"You would be if you knew who they were."

"Tell me."

"They are evil. This is not the first time they have taken a life."

"Why, Ofir? Why did they murder my mother?"

"Because your mother could not save theirs."

"I do not understand."

"A woman was brought to the emergency room after falling from her horse. Your mother was attending physician. She tried to save this woman's life, but there were complications. Her sons hold your mother responsible. Now they want you to suffer as they have."

It was pointless to ask Ofir how she knew of these men. In all the years Santana had known her, he had come to believe that it was more important to understand what she knew rather than how she knew it.

"If I had not gone to the *galeria* to find fresh fruit and vegetables," she said.

"It's all right, Ofir."

"You know, in the supermarket, the fruit and vegetables are so bad."

"You could not have done anything," he said. "Just tell me who these men are."

"So you can kill them?"

"Yes."

"Your mother would want me to protect you."

"There is nothing to protect me from."

"But yourself."

Santana sat forward in the chair. He could smell the scent of rose water lotion on her and see the faint outline of her wrinkled face. Outside *chicharras* buzzed in the night.

"You worked in this house for over thirty years, Ofir. You loved my mother. She loved you. These men raped her before they killed her. Help me to avenge her death. Please."

"Killing them will not be easy," she said. "And once you do this, you must leave the country and never return."

"You told me of my destiny a long time ago, Ofir."

"Sometimes," she said, and her voice broke, "you hope the dream is not true."

Dust motes floated like a swarm of insects in the afternoon rays of sunlight that shone through the stained glass windows and suffused the interior of the small chapel at the Gemelli School with gold light. The chapel was located inside a small, square brick building that served as guest quarters for visiting priests. It sat on a hill overlooking the metal and concrete barrack-like buildings of the school.

"I want you to promise me, Father Gallego, that you will look out for my sister," Santana said. "Always."

The Franciscan priest's kind, hazel eyes settled on Santana, searching for answers to the questions he dared not ask. The air was heavy with the smell of incense and candle wax.

"Remember, Juan, the end does not justify the means. Let God judge those who do harm to others."

"A drunk driver killed my father and my mother was murdered for trying to save a life," Santana said. "I will not wait until eternity for God's judgment — if there even is a God."

Father Gallego shifted his weight in the pew, obviously uncomfortable with what Santana had said. He wore his ash-brown hair long and the traditional simple brown robe with a rope around his waist. Because of his well-trimmed light beard, everyone in the school called him Father *Chivas,* short for *chivera.*

"Faith means believing without proof," he said. "Trusting without reservation. You must not lose your faith and let evil prevail. You must look to God for understanding."

"What is there to understand?"

The priest let out a deep sigh like a dying man exhaling his last breath. "Given the tragic deaths of your parents, Juan, I realize how difficult it must be to understand God's plan. Perhaps there is another way. One that involves mercy and forgiveness."

Santana knew there would be no mercy or forgiveness for the men who had murdered his mother. Not if he had anything to say about it. But he remained silent and let the priest continue.

"You have always been an intelligent, studious boy who wished to become a doctor like his mother, a person who saved lives. You can do so many wonderful things with your life, Juan. I am afraid that what you are seeking to do will only harden your heart and tarnish your soul forever."

They were alone in the small chapel, and in the silence, that was as still as a tomb, Santana could hear the beating of his heart.

"You are my favorite teacher, Father. I have learned much from you. I am not asking you for your blessing or even your understanding. All I am asking is that you promise me you will protect Natalia."

"I will make sure your sister is safe. But what about you?"

"It is better that you do not know."

The priest's reluctant nod indicated he knew that it was useless to debate the issue further.

"Your mother told me after your father's death that if anything happened to her, I should handle the estate. Your family was not rich, but there is a considerable amount of money put away for you. You will need it to continue your life. You will have to let me know where you go so I can get the money to you."

"These men who killed my mother are very dangerous. If they find out you know where I am, Father, they will make you tell them."

Father Gallego gave a reassuring smile. "There is only one other person besides me who will know where you are, Juan. And that is God."

"**T**his is *escopolamina,*" Ofir said. "On the streets it is known as *burundanga*." She held up a small vial containing a finely ground powder in her wrinkled hand. "You can put it in a drink or in food. It is odorless, colorless and tasteless. But you must be careful not to use too little or too much."

The kitchen was filled with the aroma of *mondongo* brewing on the stove, a stew made of potatoes and the stomach of a slaughtered pig. Out the window behind Ofir, the setting sun flamed the sky, left the horizon blood red.

Santana had heard stories about the drug that had been used by Colombian Indians since before the Spanish conquest. The *borrachero* or get-you-drunk tree grew wild in the countryside. Its orange and white flowers looked like long, thin bells hanging beneath the green leaves. His mother had once explained to him that the alkaloid from the tree was used in medicines to treat motion sickness and tremors from Parkinson's disease. But she had also warned him that eating the seeds could be deadly. In small doses men became so docile that they would help thieves empty their bank accounts. Women had been drugged and then gang-raped or rented out as prostitutes. And because *escopolamina* blocked the formation of memories, it was impossible for victims to identify the perpetrators. Still, Santana wondered if the stories were true.

"I have heard of it," he said. "But it might be difficult to put the drug in a drink or in food these men will take."

"There is another way," she said. Her round copper eyes were clear and brilliant, nearly orange in color, like those of a cat, and seemed to bore into his skin.

"What will these men do when I give it to them?"

"Whatever you want them to."

The *El Cerro de Oro* nightclub sat on the crest of the hill high above the eastern edge of the city. From here Santana could look across all of Manizales and see the water tower atop the hill in the *Chipre Barrio* where he lived and the city below, encircled by the towering Andes. The land was green and rolling and covered with rubber trees, wax palms and the red flowers of the *cambulo* trees. Houses for the four hundred thousand inhabitants were tightly packed together and spilled out across the valley floor all the way to the base of the mountains. The spire of the *Cathedral de Manizales* rose like a statue from the center of the city.

Santana would often go to the nightclub with his friends around 11:00 p.m. on weekends to dance and listen to American music. There was no drinking age limit in Colombia, and he and his friends often ordered *media de aguardiente* or *media de ron*, a half bottle of rum, to mix with the Cokes they drank while they danced. Afterward, at 4:00 a.m. when the dancing ended, they would buy hot dogs from the vendor outside the club before heading home.

Inside the club was a dimly lit lower level with a bar in the corner surrounded by stools. Across from the bar a large picture window looked out on the lights of the city far below. Walking into the club was like entering a movie theater after the feature had started, and it always took a moment for the eyes to adjust to the darkness. Tables encircled a small dance floor while a rotating disco ball in the ceiling dappled the faces of the crowd with lasers of light as a disk jockey played *salsa, merengue, paso doble* and American rock, usually in blocks of six songs. On the second floor was the *la Taverna Mexicana* where they played *Rancheras.*

Santana had waited in the parking lot of *El Cerro de Oro* on three consecutive weekends charting the times Enrique and Emilio Estrada arrived and left the club, looking for any consistent patterns of behavior. The Estradas were easy to spot in their new, black Ford Ranger pickup with the smoked-glass windows.

They were the twin sons of Alejandro Estrada, head of the Cali cartel. Estrada was known as *"la Piraña"* in the drug trade because of his practice of feeding those who opposed him to the piranhas he kept in a large water tank on his farm outside Cali. He had tried to keep his sons away from the drug business by sending them to exclusive private schools. But no amount of education could change the fact that his twenty-year-old sons were raging sociopaths.

At 12:20 a.m. the brothers drove through the archway into the lot in front of the club, angle-parked along the *guadua* fence and stepped out of the pickup. They were nearly identical in appearance, just under six feet, hard and lean, with dark, razor cut hair. Each of them wore a skin-tight black pullover and pants, thick gold chains and watches, and gold rings with large emeralds on their fingers.

One of them took a package of Derby's out of his breast pocket. Put a cigarette between his perfectly white teeth and lit it with a gold-plated lighter. Then they walked across the asphalt lot jammed with cars, past the two heavy-set bouncers at the entrance and in the door of the club.

Santana could see small groups of teenagers lingering near the front entrance and around the hot dog stand. The night pulsated with the rhythm of *salsa* music, the ground beneath his feet quivered with tremors, as if there was a quake. Car tires hummed along the asphalt and a full moon left a bright hole in the black curtain of sky.

Santana had learned from his previous weekend visits to the club that the Estradas were creatures of habit. They usually arrived after midnight and left by 3:00 a.m. Putting *escopolamina* in their drinks would be easy in the dimly lit club, but getting both of them outside and into a car without arousing suspicion would be difficult.

He had another plan.

At 3:10 a.m., the brothers exited the club. Strutting with rum-induced self-confidence toward their Ford Ranger.

Santana opened the jar of Vaseline he had carried with him and rubbed a thin layer of gel around his nostrils and over his lips and mouth, coating his breathing passages in order to catch any drifting particles. He placed the Vaseline back in the car. Put on a pair of his mother's surgical gloves. Checked to make sure he had his father's .38-caliber revolver in a jacket pocket. Removing the vial of *escopolamina* from another pocket, he poured half the powder in each hand. Then he followed the Estradas to their pickup.

"Do you have a light?" Santana asked as he approached them.

He could feel his heart thudding in his chest. Hear the sound of blood rushing in his ears.

The Estradas turned and glared at Santana as though he were a bloodstain on their shirts. Their dark eyes were flat and soulless and looked like they belonged in a corpse.

"Go to hell, *malparido,*" one of them said and they both laughed.

Santana imagined them laughing as they raped his mother and then looped the rope around her neck and pulled the chair out from under her feet. He saw himself wrapping his arms around his mother's bare legs as he tried to lift her up in a desperate attempt to ease the tension in the rope, thinking between sobs that if he could only get some slack in the rope she would breathe again and everything would be as it was the moment before he had entered the house, when hope and truth and beauty still existed in the world.

He flung handfuls of powdered *escopolamina* in their faces and stepped back, taking care not to inhale.

"Hey," one of them said, as they tried to brush away the light powder clinging to their dark shirts. Then both their heads tilted back, their mouths fell open and their jaws went slack.

Santana hesitated for a long moment, uncertain if the drug had actually taken effect, before he told them to follow him to his car. Despite what he had heard about the power of the drug, it surprised him when they complied without question.

He ordered one of the Estradas into the back of his mother's Suzuki jeep and the other into the passenger side. He stripped off the gloves, climbed into the driver's seat. Like most teenagers in Colombia, Santana had been driving legally since he was thirteen and was confident in his ability to handle the red jeep with a five-speed gearshift mounted on the floor.

He drove out of the lot, past the eucalyptus trees and the farmhouses and up into the mountains where the night air blowing through the open canopy of the jeep was ripe with the rich scent of coffee beans and ozone from an approaching storm. He kept looking nervously at each of the Estradas seated to his right and behind him, fearing that the drug would wear off before he could get them both safely away from the city. But the brothers sat quietly with arms down at their sides, faces staring straight ahead, as if in a trance.

Black clouds moved like shadows across the moon as Santana turned onto a dirt road, the jeep bouncing hard off the shoulder. He followed the beams from the headlights through thick stands of *guadua* for a half-mile until he swerved onto the grassy floor of the forest and into a small clearing near a wooden bridge that crossed a river. There, he shut off the engine but left the lights on.

He sat quietly in the jeep for a time, remembering this clearing in the forest as a special place where his parents would take him as a child to fly kites during *los vientos de agosto,* the winds of August. The air smelled of wet leaves, and clouds of mist hung like spider webs around the trees. He could hear the rumble of thunder from the approaching storm now, the river running over the rapids, the incessant buzzing of *chicharras,* and the sound of his breathing.

"Bajate del carro," he told the one sitting in the passenger seat.

The man obeyed and Santana walked him to a thick *guadua* tree. Directed him to stand with his back against it. Then he went back to the Suzuki and got the other one out of the back seat and walked him to a spot five feet in front of his brother, who was still standing passively against the tree, squinting into the glare of the headlights.

Santana removed the wallet from the second man's back pocket. The ID inside read Emilio Estrada. He tossed the wallet on the ground and took the British made .38-caliber revolver out his jacket pocket. He released the top catch so that the barrel and cylinder swung down, exposing the back of the cylinder. He removed five of the six cartridges, leaving a round to the left of the hammer. Then he closed the barrel and cocked it.

He placed the gun in Emilio Estrada's right hand and stood directly behind him. Told him to raise his arm and fire at the tree in front of him.

Sparks flew out of the barrel as the shot echoed through the forest. Enrique Estrada let out a grunt as the bullet slammed him back against the *guadua.* A dark circle of blood formed in the center of his chest as his legs gave out and he slid down the trunk until he was sitting on the ground. He sat there with his head resting against the base of the tree, his breath rattling in his chest and blood trickling out the corner of his mouth. Then he rolled on his side like a listing ship and lay still.

A long wisp of smoke drifted out of the muzzle of the gun and rose up and into the mist. A bank of dark clouds veiled the moon and a branch of lightening broke across the black sky. A sudden wind shook the leaves in the trees and rain began falling.

Santana took the gun from Emilio Estrada, the barrel hot in the palm of his hand. He walked over to Enrique Estrada and looked down, wondering if what he had heard about evil as a child was true, if, in fact, Estrada's soul would burn in hell for all eternity because of the crimes he had committed during his short but violent life.

As he watched blood flow out of Enrique Estrada's body and form a widening pool of darkness, Santana felt as though his innocence was draining out of him. He wondered about his own soul now, wondered about the warning Father Gallego had given him in the chapel of the Gemelli School. *El fin no justifica los medios,* the end does not justify the means. Sweat dampened his shirt and his body began to tremble in the cool night air. It would be hard to kill the twin, harder than he had ever imagined. He felt sick to his stomach.

"Enrique!"

The voice seemed as loud as the roar of the gun, and Santana's heart leapt into his throat as he spun quickly toward the sound.

Emilio Estrada stood in a low crouch, unsteady on his feet, his dead eyes staring into Santana's.

Santana fumbled for the bullets in his jacket pocket, but before he could reload the gun or react, Estrada jumped him, knocking the .38 from his hand, and sending them both to the ground. Santana felt his right hand slam against a *guadua*, and he cried out as the sharp *riendas* around the trunk of the young tree sliced open the back of his hand.

Fueled by anger and revenge, Estrada forced Santana on his back and sat on top of him, his knees straddling Santana's chest. Using his forearm as a wedge, he pressed it against Santana's throat.

Water soaked through Santana's jacket, and he could smell the mix of rum and cigarettes on Estrada's breath as the man leaned closer to his face. He punched Estrada hard in the side with one hand, tried to push the forearm off his neck with the other. Struggling to breathe, his consciousness beginning to slip away, he heard the distinct click of a switchblade, saw the glint of the blade in a flash of lightening as Estrada brought a knife out from behind his back and raised it over his head.

Santana reached out with his left hand and grabbed Estrada's wrist. He pushed with all his strength. Tried to hold the knife away from him. But Estrada was too strong.

In that moment before the blade ripped open his chest and he knew his life would end abruptly at sixteen, he smelled his father's cherry blend pipe tobacco, his mother's French perfume. He saw her watching a kite rising high above the forest floor in a gust of wind, its white rag tail looking like a vapor trail against a blue sky.

With his heart thudding against his ribs and pumping massive amounts of adrenaline into his blood stream, his will to survive overcame his deficiency in strength. His bloody right hand shot straight up, and he buried two fingers deep in Emilio Estrada's dead eyes.

Estrada let out a scream and sat up, instinctively reaching both hands toward his eyes for protection.

Santana felt the weight lessen on his chest as Estrada's balance shifted. He pushed Estrada off and scrambled to his feet.

In the glare of the jeep's headlights, Estrada stood up, eyelids blinking, face twisted in anger, wet hair matted against his skull. "Emilio's got something here for you *hijueputa!* Something from me and my brother! Why don't you come and get it you piece of shit!"

He rubbed his eyes with one hand and swung the knife wildly in front of him with the other, as if clearing a field of sugar cane with a machete.

Santana stood in the hard rain with his fists balled tightly at his sides, taking short, quick breaths of oxygen between his clenched teeth. Then he felt something cold and dark rising like a serpent inside him.

"Where are you, *hijueputa?*" Estrada yelled.

Santana picked up the gun lying on the ground and loaded a round into the chamber.

"I'm here *malparido.*"

Cocking the revolver, he stepped closer, aimed, and fired.

The bullet struck Emilio Estrada squarely in the face and blew out the back of his head.

Chapter 23

"RAISE THE BODY A LITTLE SO THE cord slackens," Reiko Tanabe said to a couple of uniformed officers. "And then cut the cord near the top. Leave the noose on the neck and be careful."

She was peering at Hidalgo's body hanging from the second floor landing like she would a slide under a microscope.

The officers did as they were told and then laid Hidalgo's body gently on the hardwood floor.

"Make sure you cordon off the area outside," Santana said to the two officers. "Nobody in or out unless they're with the department."

"You okay, John?" Tanabe asked, looking at Santana.

"I'm fine."

"First hanging?"

Santana shook his head. "Not my first."

Tanabe kept her eyes on Santana for a time. Then she crouched down next to the body.

The electrical cord had cut off drainage through Hidalgo's jugular and other veins, forcing deoxygenated blood back up into the tissues of his face. Small capillaries had ruptured from the pressure on his neck and formed tiny rivers of blood in the sclera of his eyes, which protruded like a frog's from his blue face.

"There's a half-knot in the electrical cord," Tanabe said. "You have anything that suggests this was a homicide?"

Santana's gaze was focused on a stain on the wall, though in his mind's eye he could see his mother hanging from a beam in his boyhood home in Manizales, her once beautiful face a contorted death mask exactly like the one now worn by Hidalgo.

"John. Did you hear me?"

Santana gazed down at Tanabe.

"You have any evidence that this was a homicide?"

"No," Santana said. "Hidalgo committed suicide."

"You sound awfully sure of yourself."

As Santana was about to explain, James Kehoe came in the front door behind a blast of cold air, stomping snow off the soles of his shoes as he stood in the entryway. His electric tan had turned red compliments of the falling temperatures and increasing wind chill.

Santana said, "I was here just before it happened, Reiko."

Tanabe rose to her feet and arched her back, as if easing a muscle cramp. "You were here?"

"Not in the house. I was outside in my car."

"Doing what?" Kehoe asked.

Seeing Kehoe standing on the opposite side of Hidalgo's body drew Santana's thoughts away from the past and back to the present.

"Counting the crystals in a snowflake," he said.

"Look, Santana, that smart ass attitude may play well around the water cooler, but it gets you shit upstairs where it counts. The Pérez-Mendoza investigation is history."

"What makes you think I was here about the Pérez-Mendoza investigation?"

Kehoe hesitated before responding, his eyes betraying his momentary confusion. "What else would you be doing here?"

"Maybe I just wanted to talk to a priest."

"Yeah. And maybe I'm Mother Theresa."

He glanced down at the young priest's body on the floor and crossed himself quickly.

Santana said, "I didn't know you were Catholic."

Kehoe gave him a dismissive look. "It's apparent you don't know a lot of things, Santana. Like you shouldn't have been talking to Hidalgo when this case is already closed. What did you say to him anyway?"

Santana kept silent.

"Well, since you're in the early stages of Alzheimer's disease, let me refresh your memory. Ashford put me in charge of this investigation. Not you."

Kehoe glared at Tanabe. "You let me know the results of the autopsy, Reiko, and no one else. ASAP."

The ME looked at Kehoe and then at Santana.

"You hear me, Tanabe?" Kehoe said.

She glared back. "I heard you."

Kehoe looked like he was about to say something else to her and then thought better of it. Instead, he turned back to Santana.

"I know you're counting on Gamboni to protect your ass because she made a mistake and let you inside her pants, but that ain't going to happen."

Santana could see his own reflection and his blue eyes in the mirror on the wall behind Kehoe. They were as cold and flat as a frozen lake. His eyes locked on Kehoe's. "How long has it been?"

Kehoe cocked his head, as if he had just heard a strange sound.

"John," Tanabe said, clearing her throat. "Why don't we wrap it up here?"

Santana ignored her. "Come on, Kehoe. You know what I'm talking about."

Kehoe gave a little shake of his head.

"How long has it been since you've been laid?"

Kehoe's complexion went from red to crimson. "All right, Santana," he said, pointing a thick index finger. "You don't want to talk to me about what you were doing here, fine. Let's see if Ashford can change your mind."

He turned and barged out of the room, letting the storm door slam shut behind him. The air that blew in the room felt like it had been chilled in a freezer.

"Kehoe always wound that tight?" Tanabe asked.

"Seems to be."

"He married?"

"Was."

She nodded, as if it all made sense. "You think Hidalgo's death has something to do with the Pérez-Mendoza murders, John?"

"I do."

"Want me to call you with the autopsy results?"

"I'd appreciate it."

"You got it," she said.

Daniel McCutcheon was seated on the living room couch across from the fireplace with his face in his hands where Thomas Hidalgo had sat just an hour ago. He still wore his purple St. Thomas letter jacket with the white sleeves.

Santana stood in front of the couch with McCutcheon's driver's license in his hand.

Twenty year-old Daniel McCutcheon had blond hair, hazel eyes, and the narrow shoulders and hips of a long distance runner.

Santana said, "You have another place you can go for a while?"

"Yes," McCutcheon said, without looking up.

"If you need someone to drive you somewhere, I can arrange that."

McCutcheon lifted his head out of his hands and gazed up at Santana with eyes that were dark with frustration and confusion. "I don't understand this," he said, gesturing toward the dining room. "I don't understand this at all."

He had an innocent face that Santana rarely saw in the young men he often had dealings with.

"Father Hidalgo must've been murdered," McCutcheon continued in a voice that was leaden with doubt. "He would never commit suicide. It's against the teachings of the church."

"I'll get an officer," Santana said.

"No. It's all right."

McCutcheon stood up slowly and shook his head, as if coming out of a trance. "I'll drive myself."

"You're sure?"

"I'm sure," he said, and took a step toward the front door.

Santana put a hand on the young man's shoulder and said, "Why don't you go out the back door."

McCutcheon hesitated.

"You'll need this." Santana held out the driver's license.

McCutcheon's glazed eyes focused on the license and then on Santana.

"Nothing you can do now," Santana said.

McCutcheon took the license and gave Santana a rueful, little smile. His hands shook as he put the license back in his wallet.

Santana handed him a business card. "Put this in your wallet, too. If you have any questions, call me. Also, let me know where you're staying in case I need to get in touch with you."

The young man slid the card in his wallet and walked away. His steps were short and tentative, like someone trying to cross a lake just after the ice formed.

Before he left the room, Santana took the photo of Scanlon and Hidalgo out of the frame on the end table. Slipped it in his pocket and put the frame in a drawer.

"It's not like you killed Hidalgo, John," Nick Baker said. "He took his own life."

"Maybe," Santana said. "But if Hidalgo was standing on the edge of a cliff, I was the one who suggested he jump."

Santana was sitting in a booth across the table from Baker in the non-smoking section of the St. Clair Broiler on Snelling Avenue near Macalester College, eating a cheeseburger with french-fries and washing it down with a large glass of Coke. Baker was eating a mid-day breakfast of eggs over easy, pancakes, bacon and heavy doses of black coffee.

A low hanging lamp on a chain nearly blocked Santana's view of Baker. Small, framed glass pictures of St. Paul at the turn of the 20th century dotted the walls. Through the windows that faced Snelling, Santana could see newspaper boxes along the sidewalk that held the *Wall Street Journal* and *New York Times* and hear the wind that hummed like a stiff wire suddenly pulled taut.

"Look," Baker said. "Hidalgo was a priest. He was also gay. Given what's happened in the Catholic Church, that scenario doesn't play real well with the traditional values crowd. He knew it was only a matter of time before someone found out. The internal conflict was probably driving him crazy. He was a tormented man."

Baker held an unlit cigarette between his fingers like a child unable to let go of a security blanket.

"Aren't we all tormented in one way or another, Nick? We just choose different paths leading to the same destination."

"Lots of ways of dealing with our demons," Baker said. "Sex, drugs ... suicide."

"And religion," Santana said.

Baker gave a knowing nod and glanced at the cigarette in his hand. "Seems to me if you want to survive, you've got to figure out your own opiate. Find something that lessens the pain and gets you through the day. Otherwise, you can drown in your own shit."

"Hard to be a homicide detective and an optimist."

"A real oxymoron," Baker said, chewing on his last strip of bacon.

Outside, clouds dark as body bags floated across the sky. Tiny ice crystals rattled against the windowpane.

"So, Nick, why the phone call to meet?"

"A couple of reasons," Baker said. "First, Ashford's not real happy you're still poking around in the garbage of this case. He's got Kacie and me looking at cold cases. See if we can close a couple. I'm guessing he's got the same thing planned for you."

"I imagine Kehoe's been giving Ashford an earful. He showed up at Hidalgo's place just after the Code 3 went out."

"You've got to give Ashford something, John. Tell him what we know about Mendoza. If he decides to bring the Feds in, at least you've covered your ass. Kehoe is looking out for himself. It's time you did the same."

"What about Córdova and Angelina Torres?"

"Córdova's dead. Nothing you do is gonna bring him back. And the case against Torres is weak. Vega will get her off if the Grand Jury indicts. Which I doubt they will, given the lack of evidence."

"I'm not so sure, Nick. And speaking of evidence, did you know Mendoza represented Greatland Industries, a company that makes pesticides?"

Baker shook his head slowly. "I didn't. Is it important?"

"It was. Some of the families of farm workers who died from pesticide poisoning while working in the grape fields in California brought a lawsuit against the company. Córdova and Angelina Torres were part of the lawsuit. Mendoza helped defend Greatland. Ashford believes that was their motive for murdering Mendoza. You should've caught that when you did the background check on Mendoza, Nick."

"Shit, John, I must be slipping in my old age."

"It's too late now. There's a murderer still out there. And I think I have an idea who it might be."

"So let's hear it."

While they ate, Santana told Baker what he had discovered about Julio Pérez and Rafael Mendoza in Valladolid, Mexico.

Baker gave a slow shake of his head when Santana had finished. "Well that's damn interesting, John. 'Cause that's the second reason I wanted to talk to you."

Baker wiped his fingers with a napkin, reached into the side pocket of his sport coat and took out a folded sheet of paper. "You asked me to check the hospitals in town for appendectomy operations within the last year." He opened the paper on the table and smoothed it out with his cigarette stained fingers.

Santana looked at the name Baker was pointing to on the paper and then at the skin wrinkling at the corner of Baker's bloodshot eyes.

"Makes you wonder what his opiate is, doesn't it, John?"

Tony Novak looked up from the microscope he was peering into as Santana entered the crime lab.

Santana said, "I need to look at Córdova's appointment book again. And any trace evidence you found on Mendoza."

"Well, I was beginning to wonder if anyone was interested. Kehoe sure as hell isn't. I heard Ashford put him in charge of the investigation."

"I'm still working the case."

Novak gave a knowing smile, as though he had expected Santana's response. He pushed himself off his stool, retrieved the evidence envelope containing Córdova's appointment book from a small locker, and Mendoza's file, containing the crime scene evidence inventory, from a metal cabinet.

Opening the file on the laminate counter next to Santana, Novak said, "We found strands of hair under Mendoza's fingernails. Microscopic examination of the hair root indicated the presence of sheath cells. Sheath cells are present only when hair is pulled out, not if it falls out naturally."

"So there was a struggle," Santana said.

"I'd bet on it. I can also tell the gender by the sheath cells. They came from a male. But we need exemplars from the suspect to make a positive ID."

"I've got a suspect," Santana said. "But I'll need a court order unless he gives them up voluntarily."

"Either way, make sure he pulls them out, John. Don't cut them. And get at least a dozen or more from the head and body."

"Anything else I should know?"

"I found something else under Mendoza's fingernails that I couldn't identify at first, so I ran it through the GC-mass-spec." Novak pulled a printed readout from the file. "The material was a combination of resin, which is a mixture of boswellic acid and alibanoresin, water-soluble gum, bassorin, some volatile oil and plant residue. In otherwords, your basic olibanum."

"Olibanum?" Santana said. "Never heard of it."

"Sure you have. The common name is Frankincense."

"You mean incense. Like you'd find in a Catholic Church."

"Exactly. If I'm not mistaken, it's the primary ingredient the church uses in their incense. Now, Mendoza could've been handling incense in his condo."

"Or it could've come from the hair samples or the perp's clothing," Santana said.

"More than likely. You find any incense in Mendoza's place?"

"Not that I recall. But we weren't really looking for it."

"Better if there wasn't any there. A good defense attorney could make a case that the incense didn't come from the perp."

"I'll check it out. Thanks, Tony."

Santana sat down on a stool, opened the evidence envelope and removed Córdova's appointment book. His first read of the book in the offices of *El Día* had been cursory. He had been looking for information that would connect Córdova to Mendoza and he had found it. Córdova had planned to meet Mendoza at 7:30 p.m., the same time Mendoza died. But there had been something else in the appointment book that Santana had copied in his own notebook, and he wanted to take another look at it now.

He turned to the last day of Córdova's life and looked at what the journalist had scribbled below his 7:30 p.m. appointment with Mendoza. His handwriting was nearly illegible, but it appeared that he had written *learn more about scandal.* Santana looked at the last word closely. *scandal.* Maybe it was scandal but maybe not. It was hard to tell.

Santana turned to the previous page and then the one before that, working backward through the last days of Córdova's life. He went back two weeks and three days and there it was. Córdova had an appointment with *scandal* on December 29th. Only it wasn't *scandal.* It was *scanlon.* The name had meant nothing to him when he began the investigation. But it meant everything to Santana now.

Chapter 24

SLEET HAD FALLEN IN THE LAST HOUR, coating everything with a thin layer of ice. The plastic scraper Santana used to try and clear the windshield was about as helpful as a match in a gale. He left the defrost switch on high for ten minutes before the blowing heat melted the sleet so he could see to drive.

The offices of the Archdiocese of St. Paul and Minneapolis were located on Summit Avenue next to the St. Paul Cathedral. The archbishop's secretary stood up behind her desk as Santana walked in the office. She wore a white blouse and dark skirt that hugged her narrow hips. Most people probably thought she was in her thirties, but her gray eyes were older and more experienced.

Santana showed her his badge and asked to see the archbishop.

"He's not in his office. He may be out walking, or he may have stopped at the Cathedral. If you'll leave me a number where you can be reached, I'll have him call you as soon as he returns."

"I'll see if I can catch him at the Cathedral. If I can't, have him call me on my cell. And one other thing." Santana opened his briefcase; picked up the photo he had taken from Córdova's house and showed it to her. "Recognize this man?"

In the photo Rubén Córdova was standing in front of the Church of the Guardian Angels with Julio Pérez and his family.

She took her time looking at it. "I believe I do."

"Can you check the archbishop's calendar for December twenty-ninth? I believe that's the day Córdova was here."

She turned a page of the appointment calendar on her desk. "Why, yes. He had an appointment with the archbishop at two o'clock that afternoon. Is there a problem concerning Mr. Córdova?"

"You read the papers or watch the local news?"

She shook her head forcefully, as if he had asked her if she watched pornography. "No, Detective. There's way too much crime, too much violence for my tastes. I prefer to read good literature. And the lives of the saints."

"Pretty much all you need, is it?"

"Yes," she said. "It's all anyone ever needs."

Entering the cathedral at one of the north side entrances, Santana was struck by the silence and the heavy aroma of incense in the air. Six elderly women knelt between the pews, their rosary beads wrapped around their hands. He walked past a chapel and a statue of St. Matthew where a food shelf had been set up for needy families, spotted the archbishop standing near a confessional.

"Detective John Santana. We met briefly at Julio Pérez's funeral." He didn't offer Scanlon his hand.

"Yes," Scanlon said with a comfortable smile. "How's the investigation proceeding?"

"Starting to come together. I wonder if I could ask you a few questions if you aren't too busy?"

"Questions?"

"About Father Hidalgo."

Scanlon still had the smile on his face, but it was lopsided now, as if Santana had just asked him to climb in the back of a hearse.

"I have an appointment in thirty minutes," he said, checking his watch.

"This won't take long."

"Yes, of course."

Scanlon said it without enthusiasm and sat down in a nearby pew, next to his overcoat and flat-top hat.

Santana sat down beside him. "You knew Father Hidalgo well?"

"Quite well, actually. He was my former student when I taught at the Catholic University in Washington. I was truly stunned when I first heard about his death."

Scanlon might have been stunned, but the way he leaned back and rested one arm along the top of the pew, as though he was commiserating about the weather, said otherwise.

"You have any idea why he would commit suicide?" Santana asked.

"None at all. I saw no indication that Father Hidalgo was depressed. Do you think his death might not be a suicide?"

"Not at this time."

Scanlon rubbed his gunmetal gray hair and said, "Well, I believe you're a homicide detective are you not?"

"We want to make certain his death wasn't something other than a suicide."

"I understand. So much of what happens today makes little sense. It helps to have a strong faith in times such as these, to know that God created the universe. That He has a plan for everything."

"You ever think that maybe we have it backward?" Santana said. "That maybe we created God?"

Scanlon looked at Santana like he had said two plus two equals six. "Are you Catholic, Detective?"

The question caught Santana off guard. "I was raised Catholic, yes."

"That wasn't my question."

"But that was my answer."

Santana could feel the weight of Scanlon's eyes on him, studying him as though he were trying to decipher a recently discovered Dead Sea Scroll.

"I've been a priest for many years, Detective Santana. Like you, I have worked with many souls in need of help and guidance. I may not be a trained investigator, but I can recognize someone who has lost his faith. So I hope you'll pardon me for being so forward, but when exactly did you lose yours?"

Santana had chosen never to disguise his distrust of religion with all its platitudes and false promises, so it came as no surprise that Scanlon had sensed his feelings. But he was surprised that the words still stung.

He said, "Hidalgo's the one you should be concerned about, not me."

"I'm concerned about all God's children."

Santana recognized the irony in that statement.

"In Colombia," he said, "there is a city called Tunja. It has more seminaries than any other city in the country. The people are very Catholic and very superstitious. For over a hundred years they have seen strange lights in certain buildings late at night. This haunted part of the city is known as Lighthouse Street. When workers began renovating the buildings, they found the remains of young pregnant girls buried within the walls. The girls were murdered because their families didn't want to face the condemnation of the Catholic Church."

"That's a tragic story, Detective Santana, but I fail to see your point."

"My point is that the church should concern itself with its own problems before it starts worrying about mine."

Santana opened his briefcase and removed the photo of Córdova standing in front of the Church of the Guardian Angels with Julio Pérez and his family and showed it to Scanlon. "You recognize this man?"

"He looks familiar."

"His name is Rubén Córdova."

"Ah, yes. Now I remember the young man. He was a reporter for *El Día*. He came to see me a few weeks ago. Shortly before his death."

"About what?"

Scanlon smiled as a parent would to a child who had asked for dessert just before dinner. "It was a private matter, Detective."

"My partner shot and killed Córdova at the Riverview Lofts."

Scanlon nodded solemnly. "I didn't realize that you and your partner were involved when I read about it in the paper. But I can assure you, Detective Santana, that nothing Mr. Córdova and I discussed is remotely connected to his death."

Santana said, "Let's get back to Hidalgo's death for a moment. You spend much time with him?"

"Well, as you may know, I've recently returned to the state. I hadn't seen Father Hidalgo in quite a few years until we met again at Julio Pérez's funeral."

"You know Pérez before?"

"Before?"

"Yes. Before you attended his funeral."

"No. I don't believe I ever met him."

Santana showed Scanlon the picture again. "Pérez is here in the picture. Standing next to Córdova."

"I'm sorry. I don't recognize him."

"Did you know Rafael Mendoza?"

"No."

The movement of Scanlon's facial muscles was nearly imperceptible, and had Santana not been watching carefully, he would have certainly missed it.

Santana reached into his briefcase and took out the photo of Hidalgo and Scanlon he had taken from its frame on an end table at the rectory. "The date on this photo is last fall."

He offered the photo to Scanlon who looked at it as though he had been offered steak on a Friday during Lent.

"I remember now," Scanlon said. "I did come back for a visit when my name first surfaced as a possible candidate for archbishop. I became quite ill. Turned out to be appendicitis. I had surgery here in town."

Had Baker not shown him Scanlon's name earlier at the St. Clair Broiler, Santana would have been surprised by Scanlon's disclosure that he had surgery. Still, he had difficulty keeping his excitement in check now that Scanlon had confirmed Baker's discovery.

He said, "That your cabin in the background?"

"Well, my brother actually owns it. He rents it out. Uses the money to make repairs." Scanlon's smile was thin as a wafer.

"Where's the cabin located?'

"Near Two Harbors. On Lake Superior."

"Who took the picture?"

Scanlon looked at Santana for a long moment. "A friend."

"Does your friend have a name?"

Scanlon paused before he said, "Father Wells."

"Does he live in the area?"

"I'm afraid Father Wells passed away just before Christmas."

"That's unfortunate," Santana said. *And convenient,* he thought.

"Look, Detective Santana," Scanlon said with a sigh, "I'm sorry I can't be of more help regarding Father Hidalgo's death, but I really have to be going."

He started to get up.

Santana put a hand lightly on Scanlon's forearm, nudged him gently back in his seat. "Just a few more questions, Father."

"All right," Scanlon said impatiently, checking his watch again.

"You said you've been out of the state for a number of years. I understand you spent some time in Valladolid, Mexico."

"Yes. Shortly after I became a priest."

"Still speak some Spanish?"

"Of course."

"Dios no esta exento de pecado. El hizo el mundo."

"I've heard the saying before, Detective, but I disagree with the idea that God is not without sin because he made the world. It is man who is the sinner, Detective Santana."

"True enough."

"So what is your point?"

"There were two young boys in your parish in Valladolid. Julio Pérez and Rafael Mendoza."

"My parish was quite large. I couldn't possibly remember everyone's name after all these years."

"But they remembered you."

Scanlon shook his head, as if there was a ringing in his ears. "I don't know what you're getting at. But I really have to go."

Santana's grip on Scanlon's forearm was firmer this time. "Sit down, Father. I want you to look at one more photo."

Scanlon's eyes blazed. He stared at the spot where Santana had grabbed him like it was on fire.

Santana put Córdova's photo back in his briefcase and took out the one Gamboni had found in Mendoza's loft and showed it to Scanlon.

"That's a disgusting photo, Detective," Scanlon said glancing at it.

But the momentary parting of his lips, the lowering of his brows, and the slight tenseness in his lower eyelids suggested surprise and controlled anger rather than disgust.

"Oh, it's more than that," Santana said. "It's the reason Hidalgo killed himself."

Scanlon looked at the photo again and then at Santana. "Father Hidalgo would never be involved in something so vile."

Santana knew he could push Scanlon only so far. But the priest's indifferent attitude was like a stick poking at the caged demon inside him.

"It's not Hidalgo I'm concerned about," he said.

Santana met Scanlon's cold stare with one of his own. "Do you know who you're talking to, Detective Santana?"

"Oh, yes. I know exactly whom I'm talking to. The man in this photo with Hidalgo has an appendectomy scar. The date on the photo is not long after your surgery."

Scanlon straightened up slowly and glared at Santana. The whites of his eyes were flooded with tiny rivers of broken capillaries.

"I'm a powerful man, Detective. Are you prepared to risk your job and your career with these unsubstantiated allegations? Because that's exactly what you're about to do."

Santana leaned forward so that he was close enough to Scanlon to feel his sour breath on his face.

"We have a saying in Colombia, Father. *Sepulcros blanqueados.* On the outside, people are white and pure, but inside, they are dark and decaying like a tomb. You're a pedophile, Scanlon," Santana said in a tone that was as hard as marble. "You killed Mendoza and probably Pérez to cover it up. And even though you didn't put the rope around Hidalgo's neck, if there's ever a judgment day, I'd say you're good for that one as well."

Scanlon kept his eyes locked on Santana's for a time. Then he rose slowly. Put on his overoat and hat. "I'm going back to my office now, Detective, and make a couple of well-placed phone calls. I don't expect we'll be having any more conversations. I wish you well. Hopefully, you'll be more successful in your next career than you were in this one."

He gave Santana a tight smile. "Oh, and may God forgive you."

He turned and made his way slowly out of the cathedral, acknowledging parishioners with a casual nod, as though the previous conversation with Santana had never taken place, as though he was Satan himself.

Santana viewed a murder investigation as putting together a large jigsaw puzzle, without the benefit of the picture on the box cover to guide him. The whole picture came together as he fit each small piece, each separate clue, in its proper place. His approach was often trial and error. Sometimes a clue fit and helped complete the puzzle and sometimes it didn't. It took patience and legwork. But as with any puzzle, there was a moment when Santana realized that he finally had the picture clearly in his mind. His instincts told him he was close to that point now. Adrenaline urged him to move quickly. But he had to make certain he had every piece, every shred of evidence, and that it all fit neatly together. One mistake and Scanlon could walk.

He left the cathedral and drove back to the station. It was nearly six in the evening and the Homicide Unit was quiet. Santana had one voice mail message from Angelina Torres. That she was distraught over the sudden death of Father Hidalgo was obvious by the tone of her voice. She wanted Santana to return her phone call, but he knew that it would be a mistake. Nothing he said would change the fact that Hidalgo was dead, and that he had been at least partially responsible for the priest's death.

Santana spent an hour on his computer typing up a report of the investigation since his return from Mexico. All the while, Scanlon's threats to make some well-placed phone calls lingered like a nightmare in his mind. Instinctively, he knew Scanlon was guilty. But if he were wrong about the archbishop, it would cost him his job. He figured someone besides Father Wells must have taken the picture of Scanlon and Hidalgo at the cabin in Two Harbors. Someone Scanlon preferred not to disclose. But there was no way Santana could prove it. Instincts and his own anger had driven him to confront Scanlon, though in hindsight it was probably a mistake. He needed solid evidence to support his allegations. Tomorrow he would recheck Mendoza's loft for incense. But it was the hair samples that he was relying on. Without a DNA match, the case against Scanlon was circumstantial at best.

He called Kacie Hawkins at home, gave her the phone number of the archdiocese, and asked her to check her copies of Julio Pérez's phone records for a match.

Four minutes later she said, "Pérez made two calls to the archdiocese, John. Both in December."

"Any other calls over the last year?"

He waited while she checked.

"Nothing I can find."

"Thanks, Kacie."

"What's up?"

"I'll let you know when I'm sure."

Santana hung up and poured a cup of hot chocolate. What had prompted Pérez to make those two phone calls?

He leaned back in his swivel chair and thought about how Scanlon could have killed both Pérez and Mendoza. Using his notes as a reference, he started with the discovery of Pérez's body and worked methodically forward. He created a mind map on a yellow legal pad by drawing circles and filling them in with his thoughts and ideas. Then he drew lines between the circles, making connections. Córdova could have told Scanlon he knew about the sexual abuse in Mexico thanks to Mendoza. That would give Scanlon a motive to frame Córdova for Pérez and Mendoza's murders. But how did Scanlon know Córdova had a gun? Would Córdova have told him? Did Scanlon break into Córdova's house and steal the gun?

Santana looked at his notebook. On the current page were the notes he had taken during his interview with Luis Garcia. He closed out the report he had been working with on the computer and logged into the department's criminal record database using his password. Then he typed in Luis Garcia's name and waited a moment while the program found Garcia's criminal history.

According to the file, Garcia had been busted for assault, burglary and possession of narcotics. Enough of the charges had either been dropped or plea-bargained down, so that Garcia had not done any time. But it was the name of the narcotic's detective who had busted Garcia, rather than his arrest record, that sent a jolt through Santana.

He shut down the computer, put his notes in his briefcase and hurried out the door.

Chapter 25

SANTANA PARKED THE CROWN VIC at the curb on Sherburne Avenue and navigated the slippery sidewalk like a soldier crossing a minefield. The predicted snowstorm had missed the city. The wind had died and tree branches heavy with sleet shone like glass in the glow of streetlights. He could hear the splash of tires as they rolled through the puddles of melted sleet and thumped over the potholes in the asphalt. He rang the doorbell a couple of times and waited for a good minute before the porch light came on and Rick Anderson opened the front door.

"John! What brings you out on a night like this?"

Anderson was wearing a MINNESOTA TWINS sweatshirt with the sleeves cut off at the biceps, blue jeans with paint stains on the thighs, and a pair of worn slippers. He had a two-day beard and smelled like he needed a shower.

"I want to talk to you, Rick."

"Hey. Sure. Come on in."

As Anderson held open the screen door, Santana got a whiff of booze on his breath.

"Sorry the place is a mess, John. I wasn't expecting company." He smiled, giving Santana a clear view of the food lodged between his teeth.

The living room was furnished in early American rental. On the coffee table were an empty Domino's pizza box, a half-empty bottle of Jack Daniels, a can of Budweiser, a few napkins and an empty shot glass. The walls in the living room were bare except for a framed photo of a much younger uniformed Rick Anderson receiving a commendation from a former mayor.

Anderson hung Santana's coat in the front hall closet and removed a *Sports Illustrated* magazine from the seat of a La-Z-Boy, revealing a wide strip of gray duct tape. A black electric cord running from underneath the lounger connected to a wall socket.

"Sit down, John," he said, and then, noticing some crumbs on the seat, used the magazine to sweep them onto the carpeted floor.

Santana sat down in the lounger and immediately felt something underneath him.

While Anderson was bent over, with his back to Santana, lifting up the cushions and newspaper pages scattered on the couch, Santana reached down between the seat and the side of the lounger and retrieved the remote.

"This what you're looking for?"

Anderson straightened up, turned and gave a sheepish smile. "Never can find that damn thing."

Santana handed him the remote and Anderson turned off the television. "Nothing worth watching anyway," he said with a nervous laugh. His eyes drifted to the bottle on the coffee table and then back to Santana. "Sorry I don't have any hot chocolate, John."

"Don't suppose it would do any good to ask you to fix yourself a cup of coffee."

"I don't need a cup of coffee."

Santana studied Anderson's face. "I guess not."

"Look, John. Things have been really slow. I'm still waiting to hear from IA. As soon as they clear me, we'll be back in business. Partners, just like before."

Santana held his gaze.

Outside, a branch scraped against the windowpane like an animal scratching to get in.

"Have one with me," Anderson said.

"That make it easier?"

Anderson licked his chapped lips. Then he stroked the stubble peppering his cheeks and chin with a hand. It sounded as if he were rubbing his face with sandpaper.

"It's never easy."

"Drinking yourself into a stupor isn't going to change anything, Rick."

"How would you know? You've never killed anyone before."

Santana looked at him but said nothing.

Anderson said, "You think I can't cut it anymore."

"Not if you're half in the bag all the time."

"I'm only pulling a desk assignment. Things will change when I'm back on the street."

Anderson tossed the remote on the couch, picked up the empty pizza box and went out to the kitchen.

Santana heard the crunch of cardboard as the pizza box was stuffed in a wastebasket, a cupboard door open, the rattle of glasses, and the opening and closing of a refrigerator door.

Anderson came back into the living room and sat down on the couch. He set a can of Budweiser and a clean shot glass next to the used one and poured Jack Daniels in each. He picked up the used shot glass with one hand and the clean glass with the other and held it over the table.

"To partners."

Santana hesitated a moment and then took it.

The liquid flamed his throat and esophagus as it went down. He picked up the fresh can of Budweiser, popped the tab and took a swallow of cold beer.

Anderson said, "So now that you've done the twelve-step bit, tell me why you're really here." He set his empty glass on the coffee table, chased the whiskey with beer and used a napkin to wipe his mouth.

"I need you to tell me what you know about James Kehoe."

"Kehoe? Why Kehoe?"

"You were his partner for three years in narcotics. What do you know about him?"

Anderson arched an eyebrow. "This isn't personal, is it, John?"

"What I think of Kehoe has got nothing to do with it."

"Then it's not because I gave him information."

"No."

"You going to let me in on why you want to know?"

"If there's anything to it."

Anderson reached for the Jack Daniels. He poured another shot and offered the bottle to Santana.

Santana shook his head and drank some beer.

"Kehoe and I used to stop at O'Leary's after work," Anderson said. "We went deer hunting together a couple of times. He was really into this militia crap. Always carried a combat knife with him that you can flip open with one hand. He belonged to a group that went out in the woods once a month and played paintball. Hunting each other like it was the real thing."

"Kehoe ever serve in the military?"

"No. I think it bothered him knowing that I did. He asked me to come with him a few times, but I wasn't into the paintball thing. He did help me get through my first divorce. But after his wife left him, everything went sour."

"You know why she left?"

"Well, it wasn't because of another woman if that's what you're thinking."

"How about her?"

"She could've been seeing someone. Only met her once or twice." He drank the whiskey and took another swallow of beer. "Based on first-hand experience, there's any number of reasons besides cheating that might cause a marriage to go south. Kehoe's wife struck me as someone who thought she could do a lot better than a cop."

"You have an address for her?"

"No. But last I heard she was living in White Bear Lake." Anderson set the shot glass on the table. His speech was a little slower now, a little less precise.

"You ever know a snitch by the name of Luis Garcia, Rick?"

Anderson considered the question and then shook his head. "Not that I recall."

"Never heard Kehoe talk about him when you two were working narcotics?"

Anderson's eyes were red and glassy as he looked at Santana. "Did Garcia have something to do with the murders?"

"Possibly. Or he might know who does."

Anderson gave a little nod. Went quiet for a time. His gaze was inward, as if he was thinking. Finally, he said, "Where are you going with this, John? What are you getting at?"

"I'm not sure yet."

"You think Kehoe had something to do with the Pérez-Mendoza murders?"

"I don't know."

Anderson held Santana's gaze for a time. Then he drank a long swallow of beer, wiped his mouth with the napkin. "Maybe you think Kehoe and I are working together, John?" Anderson paused and his eyes locked on Santana's again. "Maybe you think I took out Córdova deliberately."

Santana recalled losing sight of Córdova for an instant. Then seeing him take a round in the chest. He remembered Córdova lying on his back in fragments of broken glass with the .22 Smith and Wesson tucked in his waistband. He said nothing.

Anderson slammed the can down. Beer spilled on the table. "Hey, fuck you, John. We've been together for three years and if that's what you think of me, then go fuck yourself."

"I never said you deliberately took out Córdova."

"No. But you never said I didn't either."

"Why were you feeding Kehoe information about the case?"

"I already told you. He's got influence with IA through the mayor. I feed him some information about the ballistics on Córdova's gun and Kehoe gets me back on the street sooner. Quid pro quo. You know it works, John."

"I know how it's supposed to work. I know that Kehoe's got his fingers in all of this somehow. I know that you were his partner for three years and might be able to tell me something that's going to point me in the right direction."

"So you think Kehoe murdered Pérez and Mendoza? That he set up Córdova to take the fall?"

"I don't have all the pieces yet. I need some more information from you."

Anderson picked up the beer can.

"And I need for you to stay sober so you can think straight."

Santana could see the sudden flash of anger in Anderson's bloodshot eyes, and then recognition that maybe Santana had a point.

Anderson set the can down. "What do you need to know?"

"Where did Kehoe grow up?"

"Right here in St. Paul. Went to Seton Academy. Think he played some football."

Santana nearly dropped the can of beer as adrenaline shot through his body. "Seton?"

"That's what I said."

"What year did he graduate?"

"Damned if I know. But it'd be easy to find out."

Santana took another drink of beer, tried to slow the thoughts that were suddenly racing inside his head.

"What's up, John?"

"Something," Santana said. "Maybe something that's been right in front of me all the time."

Santana had changed into faded jeans, a black T-shirt with Cancún written in blue letters across the front, and a pair of deck shoes on his bare feet. He was sitting on the couch in his living room in front of the fireplace with the rheostat lights down low, drinking aguardiente Cristal, listening to a *Los Panchos* CD and field stripping his Glock. There were less than three dozen parts and Santana could do it quickly and in his sleep.

Glocks were the current issue weapon for the SPPD. Uniformed officers were issued the larger service-size G-22 that fired fifteen rounds plus one in the chamber. Investigators were issued the smaller G-23 with the shortened slide and grip that fired thirteen plus one.

Unlike some of the officers who were skeptical of the Glocks when they were first issued, Santana immediately saw the advantages. His G-23 was the same size in his hand as a compact 9mm, yet it produced about the same stopping power as a .45. The Glock's lightweight polymer frame absorbed most of the recoil, and the forged barrel increased the velocity of the jacketed bullets. He preferred the Luger-like grip and the Glock's fast trigger reset, which was far superior to the double-action models like the Smiths, Berettas and Sigs. With the Glock all he had to do was hold the trigger back as the gun fired and the slide recycled the action. By letting the trigger out just until the click, he could immediately fire again. There was no need to remember to drop the hammer for safety reasons.

Santana had just reassembled and reloaded his weapon when the floodlights attached to the motion detector on the garage switched on, bathing the driveway and back yard in bright light. Instinctively, he pulled back the slide and eased a round into the chamber.

A shadow slid past a window and a moment later the back doorbell chimed. He rarely had visitors, especially this late. It was one of the reasons he had chosen to live far out of the city.

He moved cautiously, the Glock held at chest level, and looked through the peephole in the thick oak door. Then he lowered the gun, unlocked the door and opened it.

Rita Gamboni stood on the back stoop, dressed in a white parka, a light blue fleece roll-brim hat and gloves, and a matching scarf tied at the neck. A few strands of her blond hair fell below the brim of the hat just above her left eye.

"What the hell's going on, John?" The glass panes in the storm door muffled her voice.

He unlatched the door and held it open. "I take it this isn't a social call."

She regarded him silently; her blue eyes shifting from his face to the Glock in his hand and back again. "You going to shoot me or invite me in?"

"It might depend on what you have to say."

She shook her head disgustedly and pushed past him, the scent of jasmine and orange blossom wafting like a spring breeze around him.

While he put her hat, gloves and scarf in the pockets of her coat and hung it up in a closet, she left a trail of melted snow on the hardwood floor leading into the living room.

"Rita. Do you mind?"

She turned around, hands on her hips, realized what she had done and came back and unzipped her black boots and left them on the throw rug by the back door.

He used a rag to wipe up the water on the floor and then brought in a couple of birch logs from the wood pile out back and laid them on the dying embers.

"Can I get you something to warm up?" he asked.

"I'll have whatever you're having."

She was standing in her white socks in front of the fire, rubbing her hands. Her cable turtleneck sweater was cardinal red, her fine wale cords were cream colored, and the Glock holstered on her slim hip was jet black.

Santana said, "You never liked aguardiente, remember?"

"Things change."

He poured her a shot glass.

She grimaced as she drank it down.

"Want another?"

"No, thanks." She set the glass on the coffee table and sat down on the base of the stone fireplace.

The sound of the trio's harmony on *Solamente Una Vez* moved like a fine wine through Santana's body.

"You want me to turn up the lights?" he asked.

"No. I think this setting is an apt metaphor." She used a hand to indicate the room. "You're keeping me in the dark on this case."

"That's not true."

"The hell it isn't, John." Her complexion had a red tinge to it and her teeth shone bright white behind her pink lips. "I want to know what you were doing at Hidalgo's house and where you've been for two days." She wasn't yelling, but her tone had the force of a strong wind.

He sat down on the couch across from her, set his Glock on the end table and put his feet on the coffee table between them. The combination of Jack Daniels, beer and aguardiente had left his head feeling like a helium balloon that was about to float away from his neck.

Logs crackled and hissed in the fireplace as the flames fed on the wood; the hot, sweet smell of burning bark drifted through the room. He rested his head against the soft leather cushion and gazed up at the long shadows on the beamed ceiling, and then at the painting above the fireplace of the *arriero* with his two mules carrying sacks of coffee down a dirt road in the mountains of Colombia. His childhood friend, Pablo Chávez, had done the painting. Santana had found it on a Colombian website. An artist friend had ordered it for him. He was happy to see Pablo was selling his paintings, but he was careful not to put his friend in danger by contacting him.

Santana told Rita about Mexico, Scanlon, Hidalgo, and Hidalgo's death. He skipped the part about what Hidalgo's death reminded him of, and about his wounds that had been opened again, like scabs ripped from his skin.

She listened silently, showing little emotion other than an occasional cloud of skepticism that moved across her blue eyes.

"It's weak, John," she said when he had finished. "Real weak."

He sat up and placed his feet on the floor and pushed the photo she had found in Mendoza's loft across the coffee table.

"The man on his knees in that photo is Thomas Hidalgo. The one standing with the appendectomy scar is Richard Scanlon."

"So Scanlon had his appendix out recently." She stared at the photo on the table for a time. Then she looked at Santana again. "You can't tell that it's Scanlon in the photo. It's all speculation."

"Hidalgo didn't kill himself because of speculation, Rita."

"Look, John. Ashford doesn't want shit on his hands if this investigation goes badly. Not when he's thinking of running for mayor."

"Ashford told you that?"

"He didn't tell me. But that's the current buzz. He's still pissed at the mayor for building the new LEC and forcing us to share operations with the sheriff's department."

"So maybe we use that to our advantage."

"How?"

"Let me think about it."

She used the tips of her fingers to push her blond hair behind her ears. "Even if I buy your argument, John — and I'm not saying I do — you're going to have a hard time selling it to Ashford. Especially since the murder weapon belonged to Córdova and Torres' fingerprint was on it."

"I'm still not convinced she was an accomplice."

"If it ever goes to trial, I hope her attorney's got a better defense than you're offering," Gamboni said with a curt laugh.

"Come on, Rita. Work with me on this. Tony Novak's got hair samples he found under Mendoza's nails. He also found traces of incense. I'm betting the hair samples are Scanlon's."

She considered the idea for a few seconds and then gave a slow shake of her head. "Jesus, John. You've got to be careful where you're going with this. You start screwing with the wrong people and Ashford will pull your shield."

She poured herself another shot of aguardiente and sipped it.

"I don't think Scanlon is in it alone, Rita."

Her eyes never left his as she held the glass against her chin. Her face was smooth and soft in the firelight, and there was a pink stain around the edge of the glass where it had touched her lips.

Santana said, "I think Kehoe killed Pérez."

She swallowed the rest of her aguardiente and coughed.

"You okay?" he asked, leaning forward.

She waved him away. Took a deep breath and let it out slowly. "For God's sake, John! You're not serious!"

"Give me some time and I can prove it."

"Time? You don't have any more time. If Ashford finds out you're trying to pin this on Kehoe and the archbishop, you can kiss your career good-bye."

"Ashford has got to trust me on this, Rita."

"Trust! You can't expect him to trust you regardless of what you do."

"Is that Ashford talking or you, Rita?"

"You think I don't trust you?"

"No. I just don't know how far you're willing to go to nail the guy who killed Pérez and Mendoza. Especially if it involves a cop."

Her nostrils flared and she set the glass down hard on the coffee table. "I've covered your ass this whole damn case. Risked my career by not telling Ashford about Mendoza's visa scam. What more do you want?"

"Two days. Just give me two more days to see what I can come up with."

She got up and stood with her back to the fire, arms crossed. "I don't like it," she said.

"Why?"

"Because you're willing to risk everything on a hunch."

"And you're not."

"Damn right. I worked hard to get where I am." She spread her hands. "Do you think it's easy for a woman to be in a position of authority in an occupation that's nearly always defined by the size of your balls?"

"You're still part of the club."

"It's different."

"How?"

"This job is who you are. Detective John Santana," she said sarcastically.

"And who are you, Rita?"

She looked at him without responding. There was something in her eyes that he remembered from when they were lovers, and then it was gone.

Finally she said, "I'm your boss. And I'm telling you, I want you to drop this investigation. Now. Before you bring us both down."

She strode toward the back door and he followed.

"And if I don't stop, Rita. What then?"

She yanked on her boots as if they were three sizes too small, grabbed her parka out of the closet and put it on. "You're dangerous, John. Dangerous to yourself and to others."

"That's not all of it," he said.

"No, you're right."

She zipped up her coat and put her hat crookedly on her head. Her eyes shifted in the direction of the fire, as if seeking an answer. Then she blew out a breath, releasing the anger that had flamed inside her.

He could almost feel her mood shift.

She took his right hand in both of hers and with an index finger she gently touched the long, jagged scar on the back of his hand.

"You live out here alone, John, with all this security, waiting for someone to kill you."

"They haven't succeeded yet."

Raising her face to his, she said, "They will. Someday, they will."

She let go of his hand and turned away from him. Unlocked the latch on the door and opened it.

He put a hand on her forearm. "And?" he said.

Her eyes regarded him silently. They glistened in the dim light.

"And," she said, "you won't even tell me why."

She walked out and closed the door behind her.

Chapter 26

DAY 9

Seton Academy was less expensive than some of the other Catholic high schools in town, but it had the best reputation, primarily because it produced more professional athletes than any other school, public or private, in the Twin Cities. The tuition at the 9–12 all-boys school was out of reach for most young athletes unless a coach wanted you. Then tuition was usually free.

Santana leaned on a counter in the main office and introduced himself to the headmaster's secretary, a heavy-set, fifty-something woman who had probably settled for her second choice after considering a nunnery. The nameplate on her neatly arranged desk said: Ms. Daggett. She wore no make-up and a plain white blouse with a cameo brooch over the top button. Her short dark hair was going gray and her pale skin had loosened and begun the slow, inexorable slide down the side of her face. Direct and to the point, she was a no-nonsense type, good with the computer and helpful — once Santana showed her his badge.

He told her he was looking for a former student's graduation date. The name was James Kehoe.

Her stubby fingers raced over the keys and in a moment she said, "James Kehoe graduated from Seton in June of 1989."

"Do you have a yearbook from that time?"

She got up and went over to a long shelf behind her desk, swaying like a penguin as she walked. She ran an index finger along the spines of the books, pulled one out, and brought it over to him and set it on the counter. 1989 SPARTANS was stenciled in large red letters on the white cover.

Santana opened the cover and began turning the pages that listed the Seton Academy faculty along with their pictures.

"Would you also have a copy of James Kehoe's transcript?"

"I'm sure we do," she said, sitting down at her computer. A few minutes later a printer spit out a copy. She brought it over to Santana and set it on the counter.

It took him another minute to find what he was looking for.

Santana took Interstate 94 to 694, which led north and east of the city, to White Bear Lake. The morning was cold and partly sunny, and he flipped the rearview to night vision to cut the sun's glare that glinted like a knife in the mirror.

The White Bear Lake business district, only a few blocks long and wide, with its numerous restaurants and shops, maintained a small town image, especially in summer when the lake became dotted with weekend boaters. In an earlier time, when an amusement park stood on the western shore of the lake, White Bear had been the resort home for the wealthy of St. Paul and the Midwest. Guests such as Scott and Zelda Fitzgerald, Sinclair Lewis, and Mark Twain had vacationed there.

James Kehoe's former wife, Janet, had remarried and lived in a house just up the road from the White Bear Lake Yacht Club in the wealthier community of Dellwood. It was a large colonial set well back from the road, with a long winding driveway lined with bare hedges. Santana parked the Crown Vic in the circular drive. He walked up the steps between the gleaming white pillars and rang the chimes.

Janet Mitchell, as she was now known, ushered Santana in and led him across the parquet floor and into a spacious living room furnished in French provincial. A tall, attractive woman with dark brown hair and chocolate brown eyes, she was conservatively dressed in gray wool pleated slacks and a red blouse.

Santana sat down on an uncomfortable love seat opposite a pair of French doors that opened onto a patio overlooking the lake and took out his notebook and pen.

Photographs of Janet Mitchell and her new husband, a distinguished older man with silver hair, were strategically placed around the room along with pictures of a younger man with his wife and two small children. The younger man was probably in his mid-to-late twenties and looked very much like his father might have looked thirty years ago.

"Can I get you some coffee, Detective Santana?"

"Thanks, but I'm fine."

On the coffee table was a morning edition of the *Pioneer Press*. The headline read: ST. PAUL PRIEST COMMITS SUICIDE.

"As I said on the phone, Mrs. Mitchell, I don't want to take up much of your time. I just wanted to ask you a few questions about your former husband."

"Are you with Internal Affairs?"

"No."

She nodded hesitantly, as if she didn't quite believe it, and sat down on the couch opposite him. "Is Jim in some kind of trouble?"

Santana was unaccustomed to hearing Kehoe addressed as Jim. The name had an uncomfortable sound to it, like fingernails scraped across a chalkboard. "Not at this point."

She lit a cigarette with a silver table lighter and looked at him a moment, thoughtfully, smoke misting around her face.

On the third finger of her left hand, she wore a gold band with a large pear-shaped diamond Santana guessed was at least a carat and a half.

"That's not a very definitive statement of innocence, Detective." She gave him a little smile and sucked hard on her cigarette, blowing the smoke through her nostrils.

Santana had contemplated how he should approach Janet Mitchell, how much he should tell her. He didn't want Kehoe to find out his former wife was being questioned regarding his possible involvement in the Pérez-Mendoza murders. He was unsure if she was on good terms with her ex-husband or if she even spoke to him. Their past and current relationship would dictate the conversation's direction and its eventual destination.

"What does your current husband do?"

"Roger's in real estate. Commercial property mostly. That's how we met. I got my real estate license after Jim and I divorced."

"How long were you two married?"

"Four years."

"Still on speaking terms?"

"I've only talked to my ex-husband a few times since the divorce."

"Was the divorce amicable?"

"That's not a term I'd use. Jim took it harder than I did. I guess that's to be expected since I was the one who wanted out of the marriage."

"Why did you want out?"

She gave him a thin smile and took another hit of nicotine. "You're rather direct, Detective."

"Sometimes I have to be."

She crushed out her cigarette in a glass ashtray on the coffee table, stood up and walked across the room to the patio window. Standing framed against it, she stared out at the thin sheet of gray that shaded the sun and seemed to merge with the lake on the far horizon.

"I came from a large Irish Catholic family. My father worked at the Ford plant most of his life. All my relatives drank, so I never realized my father was an alcoholic and an abuser until I was in my teens. He was very strict when it came to dating. In retrospect, I believe I rebelled once I got out of high school. I was quite wild. I was twenty when I met Jim. He was older, a police officer, very controlling. They say women always marry their fathers. I didn't think about it at the time. Jim was exciting. It wasn't until later that I realized how much the shift work and the hours bothered me. I really didn't like being alone. He didn't want me to work. But living on a policeman's salary doesn't get you very far."

"Is that why you divorced him?"

She crossed her arms, turned and looked at him.

Santana could hear the distant roar of a snowmobile as it skimmed across the frozen surface. See it weaving between the icehouses out on the lake.

"There were other problems," she said finally in a voice that was flat.

He could tell she wanted to avoid talking about the past. Most people he came across felt the same.

"Can you be more specific, Mrs. Mitchell?"

Her cheeks turned red. "I don't see what our marital problems have to do with anything you could possibly be investigating, Detective Santana." Her tone was more anxious than angry.

She stared at him without speaking for a long while. Then she came back to the couch, sat down and lit another cigarette. Inhaling deeply, she raised her chin and blew the smoke upward, but her eyes never left his.

It was apparent to Santana that a little education and a lot of money had managed to smooth out some, but not all, of Janet Mitchell's rough edges.

"Tell me, did Kehoe … Jim ever mention to you that he knew Richard Scanlon?"

She thought for a moment before responding. "Not that I recall. But the name does sound familiar."

"Richard Scanlon was recently appointed Archbishop of the Twin Cities."

"Oh, yes," she said, nodding.

"According to your former husband's transcript, Scanlon was one of his teachers at Seton Academy years ago."

"Really?"

"How about Thomas Hidalgo?"

Her gaze drifted down to the newspaper on the coffee table and then back to Santana. "No. But I recognize the name. His death was reported in the paper this morning."

"Did your ex-husband own property up north near a lake?"

"We never owned any property when we were married. But when we were dating he used to go up north once in a while. Someone he knew owned a cabin on Lake Superior."

"Do you remember where exactly?"

"I believe it was near Two Harbors."

"Did your ex-husband have any hobbies?"

She blushed slightly and bit her lower lip. "He liked to take pictures."

"Pictures of what?"

She took a long drag on her cigarette and let the smoke out slowly. "Things he shouldn't."

The chill in her voice and the hardness of her stare told Santana that going down this road would only lead to a dead end. He changed direction.

"Did you ever collect alimony?"

"For a couple of years. Neither of us had much at the time. Jim always thought he could get me back if he got a promotion or made more money. But I just wanted out of the marriage.

I suppose I could have asked for more, but I wasn't terribly vindictive."

"Should you have been?"

She removed a grain of tobacco from the tip of her tongue with her index finger and thumb and gave Santana a long look. "What exactly is it that you want to know, Detective Santana?"

"I want to know exactly why you divorced him."

She reacted as if he had slapped her. "I don't have to answer any more of your questions. In fact, I could ask you to leave."

"You could. But you won't."

"And why's that?"

"Because your ex-husband is a bully, Mrs. Mitchell. You said women often marry their fathers. That's what you did. And like your father, Kehoe controlled and abused you. You put up with it until you found out he was also bi-sexual. You finally decided to get out. Make a new life for yourself. But you haven't forgotten or forgiven him. Now you've got an opportunity you thought you'd never have. Don't let it go by."

She gave a quick, uncertain smile and sat back on the couch. "You think I'm looking for revenge?"

"No need to look for it when it's right here in front of you."

"I take it revenge is something you're familiar with, Detective Santana."

"Oh, yes," Santana said. "Very."

Chapter 27

Luis Garcia's shiny low rider Chevy Impala was in the driveway as Santana parked at the curb in front of Garcia's house and walked up the steps to the door. Garcia answered on the fourth ring. His face was puffy, and he had a thin groove embedded in his right cheek from sleeping on a wrinkled pillowcase. He had removed his do-rag, and Santana saw that his hair was shaved close to his head.

"You alone, Luis?"

"Yeah."

Santana stepped forward quickly and shoved open the door with enough force that Garcia was propelled backward.

"Hey, man. What's the problem?"

Santana slammed the door behind him and grabbed Garcia by the front of the shirt, pulling his face close. "You lied to me, Luis. I'm not very happy."

"What'd you mean, man?"

Santana shoved him. Garcia's heels hit the front of the couch and he sat down hard.

Santana said, "You didn't tell me Kehoe had busted you for narcotics. But I checked the criminal database. It's on your record, Luis. You were Kehoe's snitch, weren't you?"

"What're you talking about?"

"I'm talking about you going down for murder one, Luis."

"I didn't kill no one."

"Last chance, Luis."

"You are *pinché loco,* man."

"Have it your way." Santana made a move to leave.

"Wait a minute," Garcia said.

Santana paused. "Only if you come clean, Luis. You bullshit me, you're going down."

"Look," Garcia said, spreading his hands. "Kehoe, he bust me a couple of times for drugs. The last time I have enough on me to do a long stretch. So we cut a deal. I tell him Mendoza was making money bringing in illegals. He made the drugs disappear. I don't do any time."

"You told him you were working for Mendoza?"

"Yeah. Mendoza was pissed when he found out, but what can he do? Go to the police?"

Santana pulled off his coat and sat down in a cushioned chair across from Garcia. "So the two of you were collecting from Mendoza every month."

"I don't know about Kehoe. But he wasn't keeping quiet for nothing."

Santana took out his notebook and pen.

"Has Kehoe contacted you since Mendoza's murder?"

Garcia shook his head slowly.

"You have to agree to testify that Kehoe was involved in the visa scam, Luis. That's your only hope of avoiding significant jail time and a one way ticket back to Mexico."

"Testifying against a cop. *Estás loco pinché cabrón.*"

"It's not as crazy as you going down for murder one."

Garcia looked at Santana and for the first time, Santana saw a hint of fear in his eyes.

"I keep telling you, man. I didn't do Mendoza."

"Maybe you didn't, Luis."

"Then why you keep asking me about it?"

"Because you're the last loose end."

"There are no loose ends, man. Everything's history now that Mendoza is dead." Garcia reached into a front jean pocket and pulled out the card Santana had given him at Diablo's. "Besides, Santana. I'm changing my life. Going straight. I'm going to call the number you wrote on the back of your card."

"I'm not talking about the visa scam, Luis."

The reply stopped Garcia for a moment. He cocked his head and said, "If you don't think I killed Mendoza, then you think someone else did. You keep asking me about Kehoe. But why would he kill Mendoza? Without Mendoza, he don't get paid."

"Kehoe didn't kill Mendoza, Luis. But he knows who did and why. And he knows that you're a major liability." Santana leaned forward, rested his elbows on his knees. "Kehoe had you break into Córdova's house and steal his gun, didn't he?"

"Hey, Santana, I didn't know why Kehoe wanted the gun. And I didn't know it was Córdova's house, man. I didn't even know the guy. All Kehoe gave me was the address."

"How did Kehoe know Córdova had a gun?"

"Maybe Mendoza told him."

Santana thought about it. Córdova was working on an article about Scanlon's sexual abuse based on what Mendoza had told him. Córdova had told Angelina Torres he was afraid and had asked her to give him the gun. Maybe Córdova told Mendoza who mentioned it to Kehoe, not knowing what Kehoe and Scanlon were planning.

Santana said, "You have a cell phone where I can reach you, Luis?"

"Sure."

"You better find another place to stay until I can talk to the department and the county attorney. Until I can bring you in and you can tell your story."

"I ain't afraid, man."

"Take my word for it, Luis. You'd better be."

Chapter 28

LIKE A RUNNER IN A MARATHON getting a second wind as he neared the finish line, Santana was moving faster now, feeling an adrenaline rush as he drove over to the Riverview Lofts.

The security guard's brown eyes lit up with recognition as Santana walked into the lobby and came toward the director's chair where he was seated behind a computer monitor in his gray security uniform.

He pushed himself out of the chair and stuck out his hand as Santana approached. The name written on the ID clipped to the shirt pocket over his heart was Reggie Williams. He was about six feet, heavy-set, with surprisingly smooth black skin for a man who was probably in his mid-sixties. He had a white trimmed mustache and a full head of curly white hair, which he wore short.

Santana showed him his badge.

"I remember you, Detective." His dentures were a little too white and large for his mouth, but his handshake was warm and firm.

"You've got a pretty good memory, have you?"

Williams touched his temple with the tip of his left index finger. "All cylinders still functioning."

"I need to check something out in Mendoza's loft. Then I'd like to ask you a few questions about the night Mendoza went off the balcony?"

"Be my guest," he said, giving Santana a key.

Santana took the elevator up to the eighth floor. He wanted to verify that there was no incense in Mendoza's loft. He did a thorough search and came up empty. This reinforced his belief that Scanlon had been in the loft the night Mendoza was killed.

Santana went back to the lobby to return the key. Williams had pulled up a second director's chair opposite where he was seated. He gestured for Santana to sit down.

"Have you been working here long, Mr. Williams?"

"Call me Reggie. And yes. Been here since it opened two years ago. Before that, I worked security for the North Star bank. And before that, I spent twenty-five years with SPPD. Mostly worked out of the southwest station around Highland Park. Retired in 2002."

"I don't remember seeing you around."

"I never was able to get in plainclothes. More opportunities for minorities now." He tilted his head and looked at Santana. "You got a little accent. Where you from, anyway?"

"Colombia."

"No shit."

Santana often got that response, yet never quite knew how to respond.

"Well, it's good the department's recruiting more minorities. Even if they have to go all the way to Colombia to get 'em." Williams smiled, hoping Santana got the joke. "I liked working the street. Spent a lot of years ridin' shotgun. Didn't agree with the decision to go with single officers in squads. Don't like that they're closing the old station downtown either. But, what the hell," he said with a shrug. "Don't matter much to me anymore."

Williams smelled of talcum powder and Old Spice. His nails were clean, and his neatly pressed uniform was stretched tight over his substantial middle. It was obvious that he took his current job seriously.

Santana said, "Tell me what you remember about that night, Reggie."

"I remember it was colder than a well-digger's ass," he said with a deep chuckle. "Seems the older you get, the colder you get. Winter gets inside your bones like a disease." He shook his head as if his analogy was as confusing as rocket science. "The missus and me are moving down to Arizona next fall. No more winters for me." He let out a sigh and folded his thick hands over his stomach.

"About that night, Reggie."

"Oh, yeah. Well, I get off at eleven. Security company has a college kid come in for the eleven to seven shift. I try and keep busy in the evening. I tend to fall asleep if I watch too much TV, so I move around. Know what I mean?"

Santana let him talk.

"Didn't notice anything unusual that night. People pretty much kept to their regular schedule."

"You know most of the tenants?"

"Most of 'em, sure. Building this size, you can't know everyone real well."

"But the building is pretty secure."

"Absolutely."

"What about the emergency exit at the bottom of the stairs on the main level?"

"The door automatically locks when it closes. No one gets upstairs without a key or without being checked in."

"Unless they come in through the underground garage," Santana said.

"Well, they have to have an ID card to open the garage door."

"What about visitors coming up here from the main lobby?"

"Anyone who comes to see someone in the building has to sign in and out."

"Does that include the time they arrive and leave?"

"Damn right. Residents have to be safe."

Santana opened his briefcase and removed the photo of Rubén Córdova standing in front of the Church of Guardian Angels and showed it to Williams.

"Recognize him?" he asked, pointing to Córdova.

Williams reached into his jacket pocket and pulled out a case with his reading glasses and opened the snap. He took the photo from Santana and held it gently between his thick fingers. Put his glasses on the end of his nose and stared at it for a time.

"He looks familiar."

"That's the guy who was killed in the atrium. Rubén Córdova."

He nodded uncertainly. "Oh, yeah."

"So how did Córdova get up to Mendoza's that night, Reggie?"

William's eyes danced back and forth and his cheek twitched. "He signed in."

"Did you make the call to Mendoza telling him he had a guest or did Córdova make the call?"

"I always make the call."

"You sure it was Mendoza who answered the phone?"

"It sounded like him." Williams bit his lower lip. He looked down at Córdova's picture in his hands and then at Santana again. "I wish I would've known what he was planning to do that night."

"Why don't you show me the guest book," Santana said. "Specifically the time Córdova signed in."

Williams got up and went behind the counter where he picked up the guest sign-in book, brought it back and sat down. He opened the book and flipped the pages until he came to January fourteenth. "Córdova signed in at seven twenty-eight p.m."

"Is that accurate?"

He gestured at the clock on the wall behind the counter. "Accurate as that clock there."

Santana looked at his watch and then the clock on the wall. "So Córdova signs in at seven twenty-eight p.m. and takes the elevator up to the eighth floor?"

"That's what I told the detective."

"What detective? Do you remember the name?'

"Can't say as I do. But you must've read my statement."

Santana had not read it because Kehoe had taken charge of the murder book before all the witness statements were included and after Santana had made copies. But he could guess who had taken William's statement.

"Was the name Kehoe?"

"Sounds familiar."

"Muscular. Electric tan."

"That's him."

"You say Córdova signed in at seven twenty-eight and took the elevator upstairs."

Williams pointed to the guest book in his lap. "Says that right here."

"I've got a little problem with the timing, Reggie. My watch has the same time as that clock on the wall. Detective Anderson and I got to the lobby that night at seven thirty just as Mendoza was going off his balcony. So how could Córdova sign in, get into the elevator and up to the eighth floor in time to push Mendoza off his balcony?"

Williams took off his glasses and looked at Santana. "I had a problem with the timing, too. But I didn't say anything to the detective that night."

"Detective Kehoe."

"Yeah. I mean, I'm just a security guard, you know, though I was a police officer. But he's the detective." Williams rubbed his palms on his pant's legs and cleared his throat. "I don't know. It's like I told you. I called up to Mendoza's loft and … well, I figured Mendoza was home. I mean I wouldn't know for sure 'cause he usually uses the garage and takes the elevator up to eight." Tiny beads of sweat had formed on his brow, and he rubbed them away with a shirtsleeve. "But I keep thinkin' that maybe the papers are wrong. Maybe Mendoza wasn't murdered. Maybe he did commit suicide. I'd hate to see an innocent man get the blame." He handed Córdova's picture back to Santana, as if it contained the answers to all his questions.

Santana put it back in his briefcase.

"I suppose it's possible somebody else could've come in through the garage," Williams said, thinking out loud. "We always warn tenants to make sure two cars don't enter at the same time, but you know how that goes. Some don't pay any attention to the rules." He paused for a moment and blew out a breath for emphasis. "But you already got the tape from the garage for that night. You should know if there was anything suspicious on it."

"There's a tape from the garage?"

"Course there is. I gave it to the detective that night."

"Detective Kehoe."

"That's right."

Santana began to put it all together now. How it had gone down the night Rafael Mendoza was murdered.

He said, "You tell anyone else there was a security tape for the garage?"

"No one asked except for Detective Kehoe."

That's because everyone else figured Córdova was good for Mendoza's murder, Santana thought. Only Kehoe knew for certain that Córdova was innocent. That whoever killed Mendoza came in through the garage and not the main lobby door.

Williams licked his lips, let out another sigh. "Look, Detective Santana. I don't want any trouble. Six months and I'm out of here. I got a good pension. You understand."

"I do."

"But I think I could get you a copy if it'd help. You see we're using two systems now. Just got the new digital one up and running a couple of days before Mendoza was killed. The video is recorded directly on a computer hard-drive. Detective Kehoe just took the VCR tape. Don't think he knew we had a new digital system."

"Could I get a CD copy off the computer hard-drive?"

"I believe you can. You'd have to talk to the security company about that. But it's kinda curious you haven't seen that tape, Detective Santana. Maybe a little department politics going on," Williams said with a smile. "It wouldn't be the first time. You know how it is. Can't help but feel sorry for Mendoza's family though."

"I don't believe he had one."

"Oh, that's too bad. Man all alone like that. Everyone should have family."

Santana didn't reply.

"Seems like nowadays there's more bad than good in the world. Man my age, well, I'm not gonna be around much longer, so I guess it don't really matter a whole lot. But for you, workin' Homicide, it must be kinda depressing. I mean, you put 'em away one day, and there's two more the next takin' their place."

"We have a saying in Colombia, Reggie. *Mala yerba no muere.* Bad weeds never die."

"Man, ain't that the truth."

Santana sat behind the steering wheel of the Crown Vic and stared out the driver's side window at the cold, dark face of night. He was thinking that there was one remaining piece to the puzzle of this case, and it might be found in the Ranch style house where James Kehoe lived.

The house was dark behind the windows and sat on a corner lot near Lake Phalen on St. Paul's East Side. Santana was counting on the fact that Kehoe would be attending the five hundred dollar a plate dinner tonight at the University Club where the mayor was scheduled to announce his bid for a second term. Still, he had parked a half block down from the house where he waited and watched the neighborhood for twenty minutes before deciding it was safe.

He took a miniature flashlight from the glove box of the car, stepped out and closed the car door quietly behind him. The night air was sharp with the scent of wet pine and spruce. Ice smothered the bare branches of the oaks, glistened like a steel blade under the harsh glare of the streetlights.

He moved quickly down the driveway to the garage where he cleared the moisture from a side window with a sleeve. Turned on the flashlight and aimed the beam through the glass.

Kehoe's car was gone.

Santana clicked off the light. Staying in the shadows, he jumped over the three-foot high chain-link fence that enclosed the yard and crept along the back of the house until he came to a door. He paused a moment and shined the light over the back windows, searching for any evidence of a security alarm. Then he pointed the beam toward the backyard, looking for dog droppings or a doghouse.

When he was satisfied Kehoe had not installed a security system and that there was no dog to contend with, he retrieved a pair of latex gloves from one coat pocket and slipped them on. In another pocket he found the leather pouch containing his picks. He turned on the flashlight again and held it in his mouth as he worked the picks in the lock. In less than a minute he was able to push the pins and open the back door.

He stepped into a small kitchen that smelled like something had recently been burned on the stove. He closed the door and locked it behind him. Paused a moment until his eyes adjusted to the darkness.

He had little time. The mayor's dinner was over at 9:00 p.m. and, according to the clock on the microwave, it was 8:50 now.

Following the narrow beam of light, he went through the house quickly until he located a bedroom at the end of a hallway. It appeared that a wall had been removed between two smaller bedrooms, creating one expansive master suit. A king-size, four-poster bed sat in the center of the room. A wrinkled white shirt and black trousers were tossed on the unmade bed. Leather straps were tied around each of the posts. A 35 mm Nikon camera and tripod were set up about five feet from the foot of the bed.

Santana probed the darkness once more with the flashlight beam, watching as it flared off the mirror behind the dresser near the bed where there were three framed pictures of Kehoe dressed in hunting gear standing proudly over dead deer.

Santana walked to the nightstand and sat on the edge of the bed. On top of it was an A.G. Russell catalogue on knives. The headline across the front cover read: KNIVES SUPPORT U.S. TROOPS IN WAR ON TERROR. Underneath the catalogue was a newsletter on photo developing entitled Formulating.

Inside the nightstand drawer Santana found a box of Trojan condoms, a prescription vial of Viagra, an address book, and a 5 x 7 colored photo. The woman was younger and her hair darker, but there was no mistaking Janet Mitchell. Apparently, the divorce decree had not severed the matrimonial bonds that still held Kehoe to his ex-wife.

Santana took the address book out of the drawer. Alphabetical tabs divided the book into sections by last names. On a hunch, Santana flipped open the "S" tab. Halfway down the page, he found the name he was looking for. Richard Scanlon. Feeling lucky, he flipped open the "M" tab and quickly found Mendoza's name. When he tried "P" for Pérez, however, his luck ran out. He put the address book back and closed the drawer and went to the closet. Behind the louvered doors were Kehoe's dress and casual clothes and shoes along with a one-piece King of the Mountain wool suit and a two-piece Bug Tamer suit, both in 3D camo, a fluorescent orange cap and vest, a Springfield 30.06 rifle with a telescopic sight, and a box of 150-grain cartridges.

He went to the dresser and opened drawers. The top two drawers contained underwear, socks and T-shirts. The bottom drawer held a rectangular cardboard box. Santana removed the cover. The beam of light revealed a stack of magazines. Santana pulled out two of them. The magazines were titled UNZIPPED and FRESHMAN and featured muscular, naked men in various sexual poses.

Underneath the magazines Santana found a videocassette with a label on which was written in large block letters: RIVERVIEW LOFTS. Adrenaline shot through his veins as he held it in his hand. He was certain that this was the tape Reggie Williams had given Kehoe the night Rafael Mendoza was murdered. It was evidence that could possibly link Kehoe and Scanlon to Mendoza's murder. Still, he had no search warrant and no excuse for being in Kehoe's house. If he took the tape with him, he couldn't prove that it came from Kehoe's house. Worse yet, if Kehoe caught him here, he could claim Santana was attempting to plant the tape in order to frame him for Mendoza's murder.

Santana checked his watch. It was 9:12. He was pushing his luck. He set the magazines and videocassette back in the box and left the bedroom.

Halfway down the hallway he found a door that led to a basement. He went down the creaking wooden stairs slowly, the narrow stream of light from his flashlight cutting through the darkness like a laser.

He stopped on the bottom step and scanned the skeleton of two-by-fours and conduit with the flashlight. At one end of the basement were two barbells of free weights and a bench for presses. At the other end nearest the stairs was an unfinished room with plasterboard walls.

He walked across the concrete floor into the unfinished room and pulled the cord on the overhead light, which revealed a counter with a sink and trays for developing photos, a photo enlarger, timer and safe light. Shelves full of chemical containers of amidol, glycin, silver nitrate and ferric oxalate lined the wall behind the counter. Behind him was an 11 x 14 print easel. There were four color prints on the easel. The prints were taken in sequence and showed a bare-chested man wearing a dark head mask and holding a whip. The masked man stood near the head of a four-poster bed Santana recognized as the one upstairs in Kehoe's bedroom. In the first print, he was bending over a second man who was naked and lying spread-eagled on the bed. Leather straps attached to the posts bound the second man's wrists and ankles. In each of the next three prints the masked man was bending farther over until in the final print he was clearly kissing the man tied to the bed. Santana could not see the face of the second man because his head was tilted back on the pillow, away from the camera, but based on his muscular physique; he guessed that it was Kehoe. The first man was easier to identify. The mask concealed his face, but not the appendectomy scar on Scanlon's abdomen. It appeared that Kehoe, like Julio Pérez and Rafael Mendoza, was another one of Richard Scanlon's victims.

Inside a counter drawer, Santana found strips of negatives. He wondered if one of the strips contained the negative of Scanlon and Hidalgo taken at the archbishop's cabin near Two Harbors. It was difficult to decipher the black and white images even as he held a strip up to the light bulb hanging from the ceiling. He would need to enlarge the images, but time was his enemy now. He glanced at his watch. It was 9:23. He had to go.

He turned off the light and went up the stairs. As he reached the top step and opened the door, headlights swept across the living room indicating a car had pulled into the driveway.

Santana stepped into the hallway and then into the darkened living room, moving carefully around the shadowed furniture, keeping the narrow beam of light low to the ground so that it could not be seen through the slits between the drapes and blind. He moved quickly to a window to his left that faced the driveway. Peered between the blinds. The garage door was open and the light on. If he went out the back door he would run straight into Kehoe.

He waited until he saw Kehoe come out of the garage and through the gate along the fence. Then Santana went to the front door and slipped out of the house. He went across the front lawn and down a sloping hill to the sidewalk and headed toward his car. The urge to run was strong, but he suppressed it, knowing that running might draw suspicious looks from prying neighbors.

The clandestine visit had been worth the risk. In Santana's mind he had established a definitive link between Kehoe and Scanlon. He needed to convince Ashford to issue a search warrant before Kehoe destroyed any evidence that connected him to Scanlon and to the murders. Yet, he was still troubled. He had been unable to lock the front door from the outside without a key. He hoped that Kehoe would think he had forgotten to lock it when he left for work this morning.

Chapter 29

DAY 10

SANTANA WAS SITTING ON A STOOL next to Tony Novak in the crime lab. On the counter in front of them was a PC with a seventeen-inch monitor.

"Most everyone is switching to digital systems now that the price has come down," Novak said. "Plus, you get better resolution with digital."

"Then why keep using tapes?"

"Because computer hard drives have been known to crash. If that happens, all the data is lost. So most security outfits that install a digital system also install an analog videotape system as a backup because it's still more reliable."

Novak turned on the computer and pushed the CD Santana had gotten from the security company into the CD-ROM drive on the computer.

"You're looking at another reason why digital is used more today, John. We'd have to fast forward a tape until we found the right time. With a CD I just type in the date and time we want. Sort of like you do with a remote for a track on a music CD."

On the monitor, the security camera appeared to be mounted above the garage door and showed a full view of the large rectangular parking area under the building. At 15:02 the camera focused and panned toward a late model Lexus sedan as it entered the garage and parked in an empty space near the elevator. A blond woman got out carrying a bag of groceries. She pointed a remote entry transmitter at the car and the lights flashed on and off indicating that the automatic door locks were activated. As she headed for the elevator, the camera followed her.

"Looks like an automatic focusing and tracking system," Novak said. "That's good news. Tough to recognize anyone who parked at the far end of the garage without it."

Santana said, "Type in nineteen hundred hours."

Novak complied and seconds later they were looking at a motionless garage.

"Keep your eyes on those two empty parking spaces on the left of the screen, Tony, about half way between the elevator and the garage door. Mendoza owned both spaces."

At 19:02 a couple came out of the elevator and walked to a Lincoln Town Car and drove out of the garage.

Three minutes later Santana said, "I recognize Mendoza's Mercedes. I checked it out after I talked to the security guard."

"There's a car right behind it, John," Novak said. "It's pulling into the space next to the Mercedes."

Santana noted the time was 19:05.

"Looks like a light-colored Honda," Novak said.

Mendoza got out of the Mercedes, closed the door, bent down and looked in the Honda's passenger side window. Then he straightened up and headed briskly toward the elevator.

The Honda's driver's side door swung open and a man in a flat-top hat and overcoat got out, shut the door and hurried after Mendoza.

"He's got his back to the camera," Novak said. "I can't get a look at his face."

The man in the hat caught up to Mendoza at the elevators and grabbed him by the arm.

Mendoza shook free and pressed the up button. The man spread his hands and seemed to be pleading his case.

"Looks like they're having a disagreement of some sort," Novak said.

The elevator doors opened, the men stepped inside and the doors closed.

"Stop it right there," Santana said. He noted the time was 19:08. "We've got twenty-two minutes until Mendoza goes off the balcony."

"You get the license plate number on the Honda, John?"

"No. Go back a few minutes and let's see if we can get a better look."

Novak keyed in a new time and in a moment the scene they had viewed before was repeated as Mendoza's Mercedes entered the garage followed closely by the Honda.

"Pause it," Santana said.

Novak froze the frame just before the Honda pulled into the parking space and while its back end was still visible to the security camera. "The damn plate is covered with mud, John."

"He knew there were security cameras."

"Who knew?"

"Zoom in on the dashboard and the rearview mirror."

Novak leaned forward, clicked on the zoom and enlarged the picture. "Looks like rosary beads hanging from the mirror and a religious statue on the dash."

Novak kept staring at the computer as if he couldn't quite believe what he was seeing. Then he looked at Santana and said, "Mendoza had incense under his fingernails. Now this. You telling me a you think a priest had something to do with Mendoza's murder?"

"Not just a priest."

Novak swallowed hard. "Holy shit!"

"Exactly," Santana said.

From where Santana was seated in Carl Ashford's office, he could see sunlight between the slats in the blinds on the windows. See it burning through a thin layer of clouds, bathing the downtown landscape in a glow, as if a light switch had suddenly been turned on. The brightness outside was in contrast to the gloom that pervaded the room.

Pete Canfield was seated in the chair next to Santana, examining his manicured nails.

Rita Gamboni stood in a corner with her arms crossed and her back against a wall, listening as Santana told Ashford what he knew about the Pérez-Mendoza murders and what he suspected.

"So let me see if I've got this straight," Ashford said. "You're telling us you believe Pérez and Mendoza were sexually abused by Richard Scanlon when they were children in Valladolid, Mexico. And when Scanlon became archbishop, Pérez and Mendoza decided they were going public with their allegations unless Scanlon withdrew."

"That's right," Santana said. "According to Pérez's wife and daughter, he had never talked to Mendoza. Then, right after Scanlon was named as archbishop, Pérez had four telephone conversations with Mendoza over a three-week period. In fact, the last phone call Pérez made on the day of his murder was to Mendoza. Both Pérez and Mendoza also made calls to Scanlon's office. What do you suppose they were discussing, Chief? The weather?"

Gamboni cleared her throat and peered up at the ceiling, as though saying a silent prayer.

Ashford's eyes narrowed. "They could've been discussing any number of things, Detective Santana. Unless you have a tape recording of their conversations, it's purely speculation. And, I believe Pete would agree, it's certainly not enough to indict Scanlon as an accessory to murder."

Ashford waited a moment until Canfield looked at him. Taking his silence as a tacit acceptance, Ashford said, "Let's hear the rest."

"James Kehoe was a student at Seton Academy when Scanlon taught there. His name is on a copy of Kehoe's transcript, so they knew each other. Scanlon has a cabin near Two Harbors. I talked to Kehoe's ex-wife. She confirmed Kehoe used to go up to Two Harbors when they were married. The first photo I gave you, Chief, is of Hidalgo and Scanlon taken at Scanlon's cabin. Hidalgo had it in a frame at his house. The date on the photo confirms it was taken just before Scanlon had his appendix removed. I believe Kehoe took that picture."

Ashford glanced at the photo and then at Santana. "It's supposition, Detective."

"The other photo on your desk is also of Hidalgo and Scanlon."

"How the hell do you know that?"

"Because the man standing in the photo has an appendectomy scar. Scanlon had his appendix out last fall the same month the photo was taken. I think Mendoza told Scanlon he had the photo and would give it to the press if Scanlon didn't withdraw as a candidate for archbishop. Scanlon was looking for the photo the night he killed Mendoza."

"Any idea where Mendoza got the photo?"

"My guess would be Kehoe, but we'll never know. What we do know is that the man on his knees performing fellatio is Hidalgo. Shortly after I showed Hidalgo this photograph, he committed suicide."

Ashford shook his head slowly and examined the notes he had written on the yellow legal pad on his desk. "I don't believe this," he said, but without a whole lot of conviction. He peered again at the photos Santana had given him and then handed both to Canfield.

"So tell us how you think all of this went down, John," Gamboni said.

Santana had kept her out of it. He hoped she would back him, despite her misgivings. He continued.

"Kehoe found out about Mendoza's visa scam through his snitch, Luis Garcia, who he'd busted a couple of times when he was working narcotics. Kehoe decided to blackmail Mendoza into giving him a share of the take. Mendoza paid Garcia for muscle to keep the illegals quiet, and he paid Kehoe to keep the cops off his back."

"You think Kehoe's accounts are going to show the monthly deposits?" Canfield said.

"I doubt it. I'd say he took the payoffs in cash to avoid any trace."

"Got any idea what he did with the money?"

"We should look into that."

"Go on," Gamboni said.

"Everything went smoothly between Mendoza, Garcia and Kehoe until Scanlon was chosen to be the next archbishop. Mendoza told Kehoe what Scanlon had done to him and Pérez when they were children in Mexico, not realizing what Kehoe's relationship was with Scanlon. Pérez had already convinced Mendoza to give Córdova the story on Scanlon, which was going to be published in *El Día*, Pérez's newspaper. I figure Mendoza told Kehoe that Córdova was squeezing him about the visa scam. Kehoe decided that if Mendoza was willing to tell the press about Scanlon, maybe he was willing to talk to Córdova about the visa scam as well. Kehoe and Scanlon decided to kill Pérez and Mendoza and set up Córdova to take the fall. Kehoe had Garcia break into Córdova's house and steal the gun he could use to frame him for the murders."

"You have evidence Garcia broke into Córdova's house?" Gamboni said.

"I found fresh scratches on the bolt. And Garcia will testify that he broke in."

"How'd Córdova know about the visa scam?"

"He got a tip from an illegal named José López."

"You think Córdova suspected he was in danger?"

"That's what he told Angelina Torres when he asked for the gun back. The same gun Kehoe used to kill Pérez and gave to Scanlon."

"How the hell do you convince a priest to commit murder?" Ashford asked.

"The archbishop was either a willing participant or Kehoe blackmailed him. I'm guessing blackmail because of the sexually explicit photos Kehoe has of Scanlon in his house."

"How do you know Kehoe has these photos in his house?"

"I was there last night while Kehoe was at the mayor's fundraiser."

Ashford gave Canfield an incredulous look.

Canfield shrugged.

"I didn't take anything, Chief, or leave any prints."

"I hope like hell you didn't." Ashford closed his eyes tightly and rubbed his forehead as though he had suddenly developed a severe headache.

"Go on, John," Gamboni said.

"Scanlon went to the Riverview Lofts with the intention of murdering Mendoza and planting Córdova's gun in a place where Kehoe or someone else from the department would conveniently find it. The idea was to make it look like Mendoza killed Pérez and then committed suicide by jumping off his balcony. The security camera tape from the garage placed Scanlon there approximately thirty minutes before Mendoza was murdered. Córdova signed in at seven twenty-eight. When Scanlon realized Córdova's was coming up, he panicked. There was a struggle and Mendoza went off his balcony." Santana looked at Canfield. "If we get hair samples from Scanlon, they'll match the ones Novak found under Mendoza's nails. There was also incense under Mendoza's nails and on his clothing. Tony Novak identified it as the same type used in the Catholic Church."

"Do you know what you're suggesting?" Ashford said.

"I know exactly. Scanlon is a pedophile, Chief, and a murderer. I think he was still in Mendoza's condo when Córdova arrived. Córdova recognized the gun and realized someone was setting him up. He grabbed it and took off. I heard Córdova opening the stairwell door and went after him. Kehoe and Scanlon caught a break when Anderson killed Córdova. There were no witnesses, no one to tie them to the murders. Pérez, Mendoza and Córdova were all dead."

"Why kill Pérez?" Canfield asked.

"Because Pérez knew about Scanlon, too. And because Córdova worked for Pérez. The reason we couldn't find any evidence of forced entry at Pérez's house is because he let Kehoe in after seeing his badge. They went into the study where Kehoe killed him. It was easy for Kehoe to make it look like Córdova had the means and the motive. When Angelina Torres' print was found on the murder weapon, Kehoe tried to implicate her as an accessory before the fact."

"If what you're saying is true, John, the case against Torres won't hold up. I'll have to kick her loose. But I need more to nail Scanlon and Kehoe."

"Like a confession," Gamboni said.

"There's still one loose thread," Santana said.

"Garcia," Gamboni said. "He's the only one who can tie Kehoe to the visa scam."

"I'll offer Garcia a deal if he gives up Kehoe," Canfield said.

"What about this?" Ashford asked, holding up the CD from the security cameras.

Santana could tell by Ashford's tone of voice that he was becoming a believer.

"Kehoe knew there were security cameras in the garage as well as the main entrance because he'd been to Mendoza's before. So he took what he thought was the only copy of the garage tape to cover Scanlon's tracks. The tape is in a box in a dresser in Kehoe's bedroom. But Kehoe made a mistake. There's a digital copy and Scanlon's on it. He borrowed a car and covered the plates with mud went he drove to Mendoza's. But the digital copy clearly shows a statue of St. Jude on the dashboard and rosary beads hanging from the rearview. It's his secretary's Honda. I checked."

Ashford drummed the pencil he held in his hand on the legal pad and said, "I know you've had your disagreements with Detective Kehoe before, but this is …" He made a sweeping gesture toward Santana's open briefcase on the corner of his desk, appeared to be struggling for the right word. "Well, I don't know what the hell to say."

How about, Thanks, Santana thought, but he figured that might be pushing it.

Instead he said, "I could never figure out why Kehoe was always one step ahead of me, Chief. But he knew how everything went down. Once he was put in charge of the investigation, he could direct it any way he wanted."

Ashford shifted his eyes from Santana, studied the tip of his pencil.

Not wanting to embarrass Ashford further, Santana tossed him a bone.

"Look, Chief, Kehoe is one of the mayor's special investigators. Politically, it's going to be a disaster for the mayor when Kehoe goes down for this. Especially when he's running for re-election."

Santana could see the wheels turning behind Ashford's eyes as the assistant chief imagined the mayor trying to quell the political fallout after one of his chief investigators was implicated in a double homicide. It would be great theater and a golden political opportunity for Ashford, especially if he could take credit for solving the murders and quieting the outrage in the Hispanic community. Santana saw the slight smile on Gamboni's face.

Ashford said, "Let's get a subpoena for a sample of Scanlon's hair. We've got to convince Garcia to roll over on Kehoe. We still don't have enough evidence linking Kehoe to the murders. And no reason yet to issue a search warrant for his house."

He looked at Santana. "Pick up Garcia. I want to hear what he has to say. And for God's sake everyone, let's keep this out of the press until we have all our ducks in a row."

Santana went to Rick Anderson's cubicle. He thought he saw tears in Anderson's eyes, but maybe it was just the light.

"They cleared me on the shooting," Anderson said. "But not the breath test."

"What are you going to do?"

"Wait until the chief makes a decision," he said. "What else can I do?"

Santana pulled up a chair and sat down next to him. "I need you to do something for me."

A glimmer suddenly shone in Anderson's eyes. "Name it, partner."

"I want you to tell Kehoe that I'm investigating him for the murder of Julio Pérez."

"What?"

"You heard me. I want you to tell him I believe he's responsible for Pérez's murder and that he tried to frame Córdova for it."

"You're serious."

"Dead serious. I told you before I might want you to give Kehoe information. Tell him I've been to Seton Academy and looked at his school records. Tell him I know he's been up to Scanlon's cabin near Two Harbors. I want you to act like you don't believe he's involved. Like you think I'm crazy."

"That won't be hard. Are you?"

"I'll recap the case and let you decide."

Santana spent the next thirty minutes going through his case notes and the evidence, explaining to Anderson why he thought Kehoe and Scanlon were good for the Pérez-Mendoza murders.

When he finished Anderson said, "Maybe if you play hardball, you can get Scanlon to drop a dime on Kehoe."

"Maybe I could, if he had a conscience."

"So now what?"

"I'm worried Kehoe could walk if Garcia can't or won't testify. I want to make sure that doesn't happen."

"Does Ashford know what you're planning to do?"

"No. And we're not telling him."

A flicker of a smile wrinkled the corner of Anderson's mouth. "Okay, John. You want Kehoe to come for you."

"I'm counting on it. This isn't paintball with some of his militia buddies. This is the real thing. I don't think Kehoe can resist the opportunity to prove how good he thinks he is."

"You're gonna need backup."

"No. I'll take him myself. Besides, if the plan goes south, you could jeopardize your last opportunity to stay with the department."

"Yeah, but it could work the other way, John. If we take down Kehoe, that will play well with Ashford and the chief. Particularly when Kehoe is the mayor's chief ass kisser. Besides, what else have I got?"

"I don't know."

"I'm off the sauce. I can handle it."

Santana gave Anderson a long look before he said, "All right."

Chapter 30

INSIDE HIS HOUSE, SANTANA DISARMED the security system and changed into a black turtleneck pull-over, jeans and Nikes. He put his Kevlar vest on the counter and made hot chocolate in a large pan on the stove. The kitchen phone rang as he was drinking a cup of chocolate and loading a clip with .40 caliber cartridges.

He picked the phone up on the third ring and said, "Hello."

Whoever was on the line immediately hung up.

Santana tried star 69, but the line was blocked.

He called Rick Anderson's cell phone. "Where are you?"

"Just coming up your driveway," Anderson said, sounding like he was breathing hard.

"Are you all right?"

"Fine. Just a little out of shape. I parked my car in your neighbor's driveway. You sure they're out of town?"

"I'm sure. Come around back."

A minute later Anderson knocked on the back door and Santana let him in.

Anderson wore a navy blue down jacket with a hood, jeans, leather gloves and ankle-length snow boots.

"I'm fuckin' roastin' to death," he said, slipping off his hood, gloves and unzipping his jacket.

"You won't be once you're sitting on your ass for a while and not moving. I made us some hot chocolate." Santana handed Anderson a cup. "You have your two-way?"

Anderson patted his coat pocket and drank from the cup.

"What about Kehoe?"

"He met me for a drink at O'Leary's."

Santana gave Anderson a look.

"Don't worry, John. I had a Coke."

"You told Kehoe everything?"

"Just like you said."

"What happened?"

"At first, nothin'. Then Kehoe got this weird look. It took me awhile to remember where I'd seen it before, but then it came to me as I was driving out here. Joey Moore."

Santana recalled Moore's unfeeling eyes; the lips pressed together, the barely noticeable lifting of the upper lip on one side of his face. Not disgust or contempt, rather a scorn for everything and everyone.

Anderson looked as though he wanted to say something else.

"What is it?" Santana asked.

"Kehoe asked me if you'd said anything about Luis Garcia."

"You didn't mention Garcia's name."

"Hell, no. But I think Kehoe could tell I knew something."

"Shit," Santana said. He picked up his phone and dialed the cell number Luis Garcia had given him.

"Hola?" Garcia said.

"Where are you Luis?"

"Hey, Santana. How you doin', man?"

"Tell me where you are, Luis."

"I'm at *Latinos in Minnesota*."

"It's after seven. What are you doing there?"

"Talking to a social worker, man. Trying to get my life together. Like you tell me to."

"I told you to find yourself a safe place until I talked to the county attorney."

"I feel safe here."

"Did Kehoe contact you?"

"Not yet."

"The county attorney's willing to deal, Luis."

"Why should I trust him?"

"Because when he tells you something he means it."

"Like you, huh, Santana?"

"Like me, Luis. I want you to get lost for a while."

Santana could tell that Garcia had placed his hand over the receiver and was talking with someone.

"Hey," Garcia said, coming back on the line. "The social worker wants to talk to you. Name is Angelina Torres."

"Detective Santana," she said. "How are you?"

"Fine, Angelina."

"You heard the charges against me were dropped this afternoon?"

"I did."

"Thank you for believing in me."

"You don't need to thank me. Just do me one favor?"

"Whatever you want."

"I want you and Luis to get out of there. Find him a safe place. He has some information that could help me solve the Pérez-Mendoza murders, and he's agreed to cooperate. But his life may be in danger. And yours, too, if you're with him."

"What's happening?" she asked.

Santana could hear the fear in her voice. "Just do what I tell you, Angelina. Now."

"All right," she said. "Here's Luis."

"Hey, Santana," Garcia said, coming back on the line. "Everything is cool."

"It will be, Luis, if you find a safe place."

"Where is it safe anymore, man?"

"Use your head."

"Maybe I come out and stay with you, huh?"

"Tonight's not a good night to do that, Luis."

"I was kidding. I find some place."

"You do that, Luis. Keep your cell phone close. I'll pick you up tomorrow."

"*Hasta luego*, man."

"*Hasta luego*," Santana said, and hung up the phone.

Anderson said, "He going to be all right?"

"If he does what I told him to do."

"There's no guarantee on that."

"That's what worries me."

"How long you think we have to wait?"

"Not long. Kehoe called just before you arrived."

Anderson looked as if a rat were crawling up his leg. "What'd he say?"

"Nothing."

"Then how'd you know it was him?"

"I know." Santana finished loading the clip and slammed it into the butt end of the Glock. "You ready?"

Anderson reached into a coat pocket, removed his Glock and jacked a round into the chamber. "I'm ready now."

Santana picked up his Kevlar vest and put it on. "You have your vest?"

Anderson nodded. He looked a little pale.

Santana said, "Find a place out front where you can keep an eye on the road but can't be seen. I'll watch the back of the house. If Kehoe comes your way, give me a call on your two-way. Don't try and take him yourself."

"The same goes for you."

"Remember," Santana said, "Kehoe doesn't have anything to lose."

"Don't worry, John. I've got your back. Like always."

Santana leaned against a birch tree next to the garage where he could see the back of his house and the near end of the driveway. In the distance, he could hear the rush of cars on the freeway bridge over the river and smell the moist scent of moss and birch bark, wet with melting snow. With the temperature climbing and the wind calm, fog hung over the snow-covered marshes and lowlands along the riverbanks like smoke over a wet fire.

A lunar eclipse had turned the full moon into a drop of blood lying on a dark sheet. Astrologers were calling the eclipse "The Harmonic Concordance," an alignment of planets that could have positive or negative consequences. The astrologer's description reminded Santana of the night Mendoza was killed; how an alignment of circumstances brought Córdova and Mendoza together and caused the deaths of two innocent men. Santana promised himself that Kehoe and Scanlon, the two men responsible, would pay for the consequences of their actions.

Fifty-seven minutes after they had walked out of the house, Anderson's voice came over the two-way. "There's a car coming up the road, John. I can hear it."

"Where are you, Rick?"

"North of the driveway behind the stone wall."

Could Kehoe be that stupid? Santana thought.

Headlights raked the driveway.

Anderson said, "I can't make out who it is, but it looks like an older model Ford Escort."

The light on the motion detector above the garage door flicked on as the Escort pulled up to the garage and stopped.

Santana moved behind the birch tree where he could remain out of sight, yet have a clear view of the area in front of the garage door.

The driver's side door swung open and Angelina Torres got out.

"Can you tell who it is, John?"

"It's Angelina Torres."

"What the fuck is she doin' here?"

"Stay put," Santana said. He walked out from behind the tree and toward the car. "I'll take care of it. And stay off the two-way. Kehoe could hear you."

She said, "Detective Santana," as he approached her with the Glock along his leg. She wore gloves and a bulky hooded parka that looked a little big for her.

Her gaze slid downward to the gun in his hand and then rose to his face. "What's going on?" She closed the car door and looked around her as if the answer to her question could be found somewhere in the darkness.

"I might ask you the same thing."

"It's about Luis. After your call he told me about the trouble he was in. Then he got a call on his cell from a detective who wanted to meet him, but Luis told him no."

"Was it Detective Kehoe?"

"Yes. Luis argued with him. I got on the phone." Her cadence had suddenly shifted into overdrive. "The detective asked me who I was and I told him. I must have said where we were because after Luis hung up, he came to my office. He said he was arresting Luis for the Pérez-Mendoza murders. He put Luis in handcuffs. Before he took him away, he told me I better let you know right away what was happening. When you didn't answer your phone, I drove out here, hoping you were home."

"How did you know where I lived?"

"When you were at my apartment, you told me you lived in St. Croix Beach along the river in a house that is secluded and private. It is not hard to find when you are determined."

"I can see that."

"What are you going to do?"

"The first thing is to send you back home."

"But what about Luis?"

"Don't worry about Luis," Santana said, suppressing the worry in his own mind. He took her arm and gently directed her to her car.

"You know," she said, "when Detective Kehoe told me I should contact you right away, he had this smile on his face. It was very strange."

"Strange?"

"Yes. Like he wanted you to know what he was doing."

Santana halted and called Anderson on the two-way. "Rick."

There was no answer.

"Rick, can you hear me?"

Still, no answer.

"Change of plans," Santana said, taking Angelina Torres by the hand. "You need to get inside the house and stay there."

A shadow moved out from behind an oak tree twenty yards away, and he knew instinctively they could not make it safely across the open space between the driveway and the back of the house. He pulled Angelina to the ground just as a shot rang out and a bullet thudded into the side of the Escort where they had been standing.

Santana's Glock boomed as he fired four quick rounds in the direction of the muzzle flash, each shot exploding like small cannons in the still night. Then he aimed the Glock at the motion detector light above and behind him and took it out with one shot, severing the cord of light around the garage door.

Angelina had her hands cupped over her ears. She did not scream, but appeared to be expending great effort to hold herself together.

Santana fired three more rounds at where he thought the shooter might still be and yanked her to her feet. "Follow me."

They scrambled to the front of the Escort where he squatted and she crouched down close to him. He could feel the heat radiating from the engine block.

"Are you all right?"

"Yes," she said.

Santana's ears were ringing from the gunshots, and he could barely hear her voice.

"Who are you shooting at?" she asked.

"It's Kehoe."

The bright light from the motion detector had dilated his pupils, and he had trouble seeing much beyond the car until his eyes adjusted to the darkness again.

"What are we going to do?"

"We're not going to panic, Angelina. I'll get you out of this. I promise." His tone was firm but calm.

With another full clip, plus the seven rounds remaining in the Glock, Santana was more concerned about his partner than his ammunition. Unless Anderson was severely wounded or dead, he would have opened up with his Glock the moment Santana did, trapping Kehoe in a crossfire. Santana had been reluctant to use Anderson as backup, and now the decision to do so may have cost his partner his life.

Squinting into the darkness beyond the car, he looked for movement but could see nothing except shadows. He hoped that one of his rounds had found its target, but he couldn't count on it. He had to assume Kehoe was still out there behind the oak tree, waiting to finish what he had started.

"Rick," Santana said quietly into his two-way. "Rick, can you hear me?"

Maybe it was the wind and maybe it was just the echo from the gunshots still ringing in his ears, but Santana thought he heard Anderson's voice. He tried again, but this time he was certain Anderson had not responded.

The pine trees that grew along the southern edge of his property were twenty-five yards to his left. It was a long way to run in the open if Kehoe had a night scope, a distinct possibly given his penchant for hunting.

Santana slipped out of his jacket and then his Kevlar vest.

"Put the vest on," he said, handing it to Angelina Torres.

"What about you?"

"I need to move quickly. Just do as I tell you, *por favor.* And put your coat on over it."

She did as she was instructed.

"I'm going to try and get behind him. If you hear shots, stay low and run to the house. The back door's open. Get inside, lock the door and call 911."

"I will."

He detected no fear in her voice, no trace of doubt. He wondered if this was the courage she had displayed as a young girl years ago, crossing the border.

"Be careful, *señor.*"

"You, too," he said, giving her a smile for reassurance.

Santana stayed in a crouch as he ran across the flat, lifeless ground with its patchwork of snow and multi-layered shadows toward the tree line at the southern edge of his property. He was thankful that the eclipse had deadened the light from the hunter's moon, left it looking as if it were bleeding from a wound. Still, he kept waiting for a bullet to rip into him as he moved low and fast, holding the Glock firmly, hoping he could surprise Kehoe by coming up behind him.

He made it safely to the trees and turned west, running hard to the stone wall and the shadow-draped evergreens that were silhouetted against it. A sudden gust blew through the branches giving him cover as he crossed the driveway and squatted behind a thick evergreen to catch his breath. White plumes of exhaled carbon dioxide condensed in the air, and the wind whispered in the tall trees.

He parted the branches and stared into the blackness looking for Kehoe. Though his vision had adapted to the dark, he knew shadows could play tricks with his sight. Still, he saw no furtive movement in the ebony pool beneath the oak about fifteen yards in front of him, only what his eyes perceived as a dark shape.

He raised the Glock to chest level. Gripped the barrel with both hands and moved quickly in a crouch away from the evergreen and toward the oak dead ahead.

It took him less than three seconds to cover the distance between the evergreen and the oak and even less time to realize that the dark shape he had seen beneath the tree was Anderson, not Kehoe.

His partner lay on his stomach, one hand underneath him, the fingers of his other outstretched hand still wrapped around the butt of his Glock.

"Rick," Santana whispered, kneeling beside him. "You all right?"

Santana rolled him on his back and knew immediately by the low moan that Anderson gave that he was badly hurt. He took a small flashlight from a coat pocket and flicked on the switch.

Anderson's pale hand was pressed against his abdomen just below the vest, like a leaking damn trying to contain dark streams of blood oozing between his fingers.

"Fuck," Santana said softly.

He moved the beam of light up to his partner's face.

"It hurts like hell, John." Anderson tried to make a smile behind gritted teeth. "He caught me by surprise. Used his knife."

"Hang on, partner."

"I will. You get the bastard, yet?"

"Soon."

"Listen, John, if I don't make it, I want you to promise me you won't blame yourself."

"You're going to make it."

"It was my idea to cover your back. Not yours. Promise me, John."

"All right."

"What about the girl?" Anderson asked.

As if in reply, Santana heard Angelina cry out his name.

He looked to his right down the long driveway at the dark outline of the Escort where she waited.

In the light from the Escort's open driver's side door, he could see that Kehoe was directly behind her. He wore camouflage fatigues and had a gun pressed against her temple. A dark patch appeared to be expanding just below his right collarbone.

"Don't try anything stupid, Santana, or I'll kill the girl." Kehoe's voice was loud and racked with pain.

"Give it up, Kehoe. It's over."

"Fuck you!" he yelled.

Kehoe forced Angelina into the front seat, climbed in and started the car.

Santana looked down at Anderson.

"Get the asshole, John."

"You're sure?"

"Hell, yes."

By the time Santana got the Crown Vic out of the garage and onto the road, Kehoe had a thirty second head start.

Santana held the steering wheel with one hand and with the other he buckled his seatbelt. He jammed his Glock into a pocket in his ski jacket and zipped it shut. Then he grabbed the portable bubble flasher. Swung it out the driver's side window onto the roof and switched on the light. He reported an officer down at his address and that he was in pursuit of a felony wanted, armed and dangerous, driving a light blue Escort.

The small car had to be doing at least sixty, but it was no match for the Crown Vic, which rapidly closed the gap between them as they raced down County Road 18.

Kehoe made a wide right turn onto the freeway entrance ramp, and the Escort's back tires careened off the curb. In the glare of the Crown Vic's headlights, Santana could see him fighting to regain control as he sped up the ramp toward the bridge over the St. Croix River.

Santana radioed dispatch that the suspect's car was heading east on Interstate 94 toward the Wisconsin border.

Orange and black signs at the ramp entrance warned that the westbound lanes over the river were closed due to bridge construction. Traffic was down to one lane in each direction and drivers should slow down and use caution.

A highway patrol car with its siren screaming and red lights flashing streaked by as Santana came off the entrance ramp and onto the bridge. Invisible hands from the wash of turbulence grabbed the Crown Vic's steering wheel and nudged the car toward the curb along the pedestrian walk.

Santana let up momentarily on the gas until he was able to regain control.

Up ahead, he saw the patrol car veer into the westbound lane as it overtook the Escort and tried to force the smaller car against the curb.

Kehoe suddenly slammed on the brakes sending the Escort into a skid.

The patrol car darted ahead of the Escort as though hurled from a slingshot. The officer braked and his car began fishtailing. The rear end slid right. When the officer overcorrected, his car went into an uncontrollable spin, skidding into oncoming traffic where it was broadsided by a semi truck going in the opposite direction. The impact sliced the patrol car in half and sent its rear end whirling back across the eastbound lane, gasoline spewing from its shattered tank, directly into the path of the slowing Escort.

Kehoe swerved sharply, trying to avoid the wreckage, but he was too close to the pedestrian walk. Sparks flew as hubcaps ground against cement. The sparks ignited the gasoline just as the Escort rammed the remains of the patrol car. The collision lifted the wreckage over the pedestrian walk and sent it hurtling through the guardrail. For a moment the rear half of the patrol car appeared to hang in the air, as if suspended by a chain, before it exploded in flames and plummeted into the fog-shrouded blackness and river below.

Santana had hit his brakes at almost the same instant as Kehoe, but the Crown Vic's momentum still carried him forward, straight toward the Escort. He knew that hitting it at his current speed would most certainly send the small car through the gaping hole in the guardrail.

He pulled the steering wheel hard to the left, trying to avoid the Escort, only to realize in one horrifying moment that he had turned the Crown Vic directly into the path of the semi's jackknifed trailer, which had swung across the two open lanes of the freeway like a huge metal gate. Tires screaming, hands gripping the wheel, he stood on brake pedal. Knew immediately he couldn't stop the Crown Vic in time.

He released his seat belt and shoulder harness and in one quick motion opened the driver's side door and leapt out. His feet hit first and catapulted him forward. He heard a loud crunch of metal and glass, the whine of the Crown Vic's engine, and then silence as he hugged his chest and tucked his chin and let momentum carry him forward. He hit the concrete hard. Felt the air rush out of him as he rolled, once, twice, three times before he landed on his back and stopped.

The sky dimmed above him, and a momentary flash of panic overcame him as he struggled to breathe. Then his diaphragm relaxed and his lungs began filling with air again. He moved his feet, his hands. Lifted his legs and arms. Hoped that his heavy jacket and jeans had cushioned the impact, kept him from breaking anything. He got up slowly.

Debris from the patrol car lay scattered on the freeway amidst serpentine ribbons of burning gasoline and black smoke. The Crown Vic was halfway under the semitrailer. Its roof had been ripped back like the lid on an aluminum can. Somewhere in the fog that blurred the light from the street lamps and swept over the bridge like a fast-moving glacier, distant sirens wailed.

Santana took a step. Wobbled for a moment. Saw spots in front of his eyes. He stopped again and got both feet planted firmly under him. He took a deep breath, cleared his head. Then he drew his Glock from a pocket in his ski jacket and moved cautiously between the flames toward the Escort.

The driver's side door fell open. Kehoe staggered out, a gun in his right hand. Blood soaked his camouflage shirt, and a deep gash ran across the bridge of his nose.

When he saw Santana coming, he reached into the front seat with his free hand and dragged Angelina Torres out as he would a body bag. Clamping one arm around her chest from behind, he held her in front of him.

"She's still breathing, Santana." He pressed the muzzle of the gun to her temple, and Angelina moaned as if in reply. "But she won't be if you come any closer."

Santana was within ten yards of Kehoe and Angelina. He held the Glock with both hands, the barrel pointed at the two of them, as a cloak of thick fog suddenly dissolved their features into shadows. The milky vapor misted on his face and eye lashes.

The fog, the bridge, the flaming river, and the two shadows before him were oddly familiar. As heat from the small fires along the freeway burned away the haze like the parting of a curtain, Santana suddenly remembered his recurring dream. Now he understood why he felt he had known Angelina before, and whom it was he had felt lurking in the shadows.

Kehoe said, "Drop the gun, Santana."

It was Angelina who had been on the bridge in his dream, not his sister, Natalia. Ofir could have helped him see that it was a premonition of the future and not a dream of the past.

"Drop it, Santana, or I swear I'll kill the fuckin' spic."

"Let me," Santana said, and fired a round into Angelina's chest.

Kehoe's jaw dropped. "What the fuck?" Letting Angelina Torres go, he watched in stunned silence as she slid down his body and lay still on the ground. Eyes wide with astonishment, Kehoe stepped back from her as though she was suddenly lethal.

"Drop your weapon, Kehoe, and get down on the ground. Now!"

Kehoe shifted his gaze from Santana to Angelina, and then to Santana again. The expression on his face slowly changed from shock to understanding.

"Don't do it," Santana said.

Kehoe's face split into a crooked grin. The barrel of his gun moved in Angelina's direction.

Santana shot him.

The impact dropped Kehoe to his knees. His gun clattered to the pavement as he pressed both hands against his stomach in a futile attempt to stop the blood loss before he toppled over and lay curled in a fetal position.

Santana walked over and stood beside him.

Kehoe's breathing was quick and shallow as he slipped into shock. He gave a sideways glance and coughed up blood. "You gut shot me you prick."

Santana said, *"Solo se capa al marrano una vez.* You only cut the balls of a pig once, Asshoe."

"I need a paramedic," he rasped.

Santana waited. The sirens he had heard earlier were louder now and much nearer.

Kehoe opened his mouth to speak, but then his body convulsed, his eyes rolled back in his head, and he released a final breath.

Santana holstered his Glock and went to Angelina Torres. She lay on the cold pavement with her eyes closed, still as a corpse. He knelt down beside her.

The night suddenly came alive with the sound of doors slamming, men shouting and feet slapping on concrete. Then two paramedics appeared and dropped to their knees, one next to Kehoe, and the other opposite Santana.

"I'll need you to move back, sir."

"I'm a cop," Santana said.

"Hey!" the paramedic kneeling beside Kehoe said, "this guy's been shot."

The paramedic kneeling next to Angelina Torres appeared to be about twenty-five. He peered at Santana through a pair of dark framed glasses and pointed to the bullet hole in her parka. "This one's been shot, too."

Santana unzipped Angelina's parka and looked at where his .40 caliber slug had lodged. "Give her a moment."

"She's wearin' Kevlar," the paramedic said to Santana, with a questioning look.

"Angelina," Santana said.

When she remained motionless, Santana feared something had gone terribly wrong. But then her eyelids fluttered and opened, and her honey-colored eyes gazed up at him, as if she had awakened from a long, deep sleep.

"What happened?" she asked.

"There was an accident."

She placed a hand on her chest, palm down. "It hurts here."

"You'll have a bruise for a while, but then the pain will go away."

"And you?" she said, grasping his scarred hand in both of hers.

Santana could see the sky and stars clearly now that the fog had lifted, but not the hunter's moon. A cloud had slipped across it, and shadows fell like dark spirits around him.

Epilogue

WINTER LINGERED LIKE AN ILLNESS until mid-May when the temperature finally started climbing, the spring rains came, and the grass changed from dull brown to bright green.

Construction was progressing on the new Ramsey County Law Enforcement Center on the lower east side after the city council became convinced that the SPPD would not have to merge with the Ramsey County Sheriff's Department and would have as much space as they had now.

Santana spent his free time working out and walking in the woods along the riverbank with *Gitana*, the golden retriever he had left at the pound after finding it in Rubén Córdova's house. While *Gitana* clearly enjoyed the walks, she stayed close to him, whether they were in the woods or the house. Often, Santana caught her looking at him with her big doe eyes, wondering, perhaps, if he intended to leave her again.

In the evenings he would sit on his balcony with the dog and a cup of hot chocolate, watching the bald eagle that perched in the tall, dead oak along the shore. He would think about Colombia and his sister, Natalia, and the choices he had made that launched him on his mission and led him to this moment in time. He would wonder why justice was only a temporary salve for the wound infecting his heart, and why the peace that he sought was always as fleeting as the twilight and as elusive as a bird.

Rick Anderson had died on the way to the hospital from the injuries suffered as a result of the stabbing. Santana was one of the six pallbearers at his funeral attended by hundreds of police officers from around the state.

Luis Garcia was found handcuffed but alive in the trunk of Kehoe's car. Garcia's attorney, Alvarado Vega, eventually cut a deal with Pete Canfield and the Feds in which Garcia got a reduced sentence and a guarantee he would not be sent back to Mexico in return for his cooperation regarding Kehoe's involvement in the visa scam. Santana promised he would keep an eye on Garcia's mother while Luis served his time.

The highway patrol officer involved in the accident on the bridge had miraculously survived the crash with the semitrailer with only a few bruises and was already back at work.

Richard Scanlon had been arrested; a grand jury returned an indictment, and the archbishop was arraigned and released on $250,000 bail. One of Scanlon's former students came forward and agreed to testify that Scanlon had sexually abused him while he was teaching at Seton Hall. Pete Canfield was confident the student's testimony along with the video tape from the Riverview Lofts and DNA evidence would be enough to convict Scanlon for Rafael Mendoza's murder, despite Scanlon's not guilty plea. After nearly two months of deliberation, the Catholic Church had appointed a new archbishop. Scanlon's trial was expected to begin in July.

Gabriela Pérez had called Santana to thank him for bringing her father's killer to justice and to offer an apology for not trusting him. She had decided to become managing editor of *El Día*, her father's newspaper. A free dinner was waiting for Santana at *Casa Blanca,* the restaurant she formerly managed, whenever he wanted. She hoped he would accept her offer, soon.

James Kehoe's involvement in the Pérez-Mendoza murder case had generated a lot of heat at city hall, and the mayor's standing in the pre-election polls plummeted. The current Chief of Police resigned and mounted a law and order campaign against the mayor. The Chief was expected to win in a landslide. Deputy Assistant Chief of Operations, Carl Ashford, was appointed Chief of the SPPD after taking much of the credit for solving the Pérez-Mendoza murders. The appointment momentarily assuaged the disappointment Ashford felt about his lost political opportunity.

Santana spent a week in Sante Fe with Philip and Dorothy O'Toole, visiting, relaxing and eating home-cooked meals. Talking through a homicide investigation with Phil, an ex-homicide detective, always helped Santana bring closure to a case.

After returning to St. Paul, he took Rita Gamboni for dinner at W.A. Frost's. At a quiet candle-lit table, they ate steak and drank an excellent bottle of Cabernet.

She thanked him for keeping his promise he would not tell Ashford that she had known about the visa scam. Then she said, "Tell me something honestly, John. You baited Kehoe, didn't you?"

Santana drank some wine and looked at her without answering.

"I suppose it really doesn't matter now," she said.

"Anderson's death matters."

"You shouldn't blame yourself for that."

"I didn't need a backup."

"He was your partner."

"He was more than that, Rita."

It would have been easy for her to say that he should have followed procedures and eventually Canfield would have made his case and Kehoe would have been charged with murder one like Scanlon. But she kept quiet. Maybe it was because she still loved him, or maybe it was because she had once been his partner and knew what he was feeling. He chose to think that maybe it was a little of both.

She said, "You would've gone with Anderson if the roles were reversed."

Santana knew that what she said was true, but also knew that Anderson would never have put him in that situation. Anderson would have played it by the book. If anything had gone wrong, it would have been a procedural mistake rather than a fatal one. But Santana had never let procedures get in his way.

They talked about a cold case she wanted Santana to look into, and then, over snifters of brandy, she gazed into his eyes and said, "You want to tell me now, John?"

"It's not easy."

"You promised."

"I remember."

"You can trust me to keep your secret."

He had trusted her with his life when she was his partner. He knew he could trust her now to keep the secret of his past. Yet talking about his mother's death and how he had killed the Estrada brothers when he was sixteen made it seem as if it had all happened yesterday.

He took a long time telling it.

When he finished he gave her a smile to lighten the mood, but it felt tight and forced.

"I'm so sorry, John."

Her eyes were warm and gentle, and as she leaned forward, closing the distance between them, she gazed at him with a tenderness that caused a lump in his throat.

"It explains a lot about you," she said.

"Like what?"

"Like why we ..." she paused, and he sensed her sudden reluctance to continue.

"Why we're not together?" he said.

"Yes."

"You're beautiful and smart, Rita. Smart enough to know that I'm too much of a risk."

"Physically or emotionally?"

"Both."

"Maybe I'm willing to take that chance."

"Tonight maybe, but not tomorrow."

She sat back in her chair and let out a sigh of frustration. "You think I'll let my rank get in the way of our relationship?"

"Maybe you won't, Rita. But someone else will."

"You're always so damn sure of yourself, John Santana. Never any doubts."

"Doubts can get you killed."

"Maybe that kind of thinking makes you feel safer," she said, "but it can also leave you isolated and alone. Is that the way you want to spend the rest of your life?"

That was a question for which he still had no answer.

An Invitation to Book Clubs

I would like to extend an invitation to book club members across the country. Invite me to your book club and I'll be happy to participate in your discussion. I'm available to join your book club discussion either in person or via the telephone. (Book clubs should have a speakerphone.) You can arrange a date and time by contacting me through my website: *www.christophervalen.com*. I look forward to hearing from you.